Adolf Hausrath, Mary Joanna Safford

Antinous

a romance of ancient Rome

Adolf Hausrath, Mary Joanna Safford

Antinous
a romance of ancient Rome

ISBN/EAN: 9783337383398

Printed in Europe, USA, Canada, Australia, Japan

Cover: Foto ©Andreas Hilbeck / pixelio.de

More available books at **www.hansebooks.com**

ANTINOUS

A ROMANCE

OF

Ancient Rome

BY

GEORGE TAYLOR

FROM THE GERMAN BY MARY J. SAFFORD

NEW YORK
WILLIAM S. GOTTSBERGER, PUBLISHER
11 MURRAY STREET
1882

PREFACE.

In walking through the Roman Museums, we see no head so frequently as that of the Emperor Hadrian. Usually the bust of his favorite, Antinous, stands near, and a greater contrast than the one presented by these two faces could scarcely be found on earth. The emperor's countenance is a veiled secret—the brow deeply shaded by the hair hanging over it; the neglected beard seems to proclaim indifference to the opinion of the world, and yet is said to be intended merely to hide an ugly mark; the glance is restless, at once complacent and distrustful; a stern expression, blended with one of merry sarcasm, hovers around the pinched lips; the wrinkled face reveals a shade of kindness, yet flashes with a look that reminds us of the storm of passions which furrowed the countenance. It is only an illustration of this portrait, when Hadrian's biographer says that he was both sensual and temperate, a hardy soldier and effeminate courtier, at once grave and merry, condescending and dignified, hasty and irresolute, artful and frank, cruel and gentle, always inconsistent. Poet and scientist, artist and sculptor, architect and astronomer, he understood just enough of all these things to be thoroughly dissatisfied with the imperfection of his own performances. Tortured by ambitious jealousy of his predecessor Trajan, he had yet been unable to retain the former's most brilliant conquests, and while his æsthetic nature deeply scorned Trajan's sturdy roughness, Rome held the opinion that the simple soldier had offered the world greater artists and through them more sublime works, against which Hadrian, in his arrogance as a connoisseur, had sinned heavily. Continually goaded by the consciousness of having failed to execute his highest plans, he became doubly irritable in old age. The traits of malice and caprice in his character constantly became more conspicuous, and the Roman world, which owed him so much and whose life he had enriched and beautified more than any Caesar before him, often anxiously remembered Tiberius, who up to old age had been the very symbol of self-control and moderation, and then first revealed the tiger-nature in his breast. He lived separated from his wife, the sullen Sabina, and had appointed as his heir the consumptive Aelius Verus, because, the Romans declared, he foresaw that he would survive him. Bitter hatred existed between him and his brother-in-law Servianus and his grandson, who had expected to inherit the throne. So he walked wearily along his lonely way to the end, oppressed at last by Servianus's curse, who condemned by Hadrian, in his dying hour besought the gods to refuse Hadrian death, when he desired it.

With those explanations of the ancient author in hand, it is not difficult to unveil the sorrowful secret of the busts of Hadrian. It is the unquiet spirit of the prince, tortured by restless ambition, goaded by the consciousness of failure, that speaks in these interlaced wrinkles. The features are the image of a ruler, whose intelligence was stronger than his will, who knew everything but could accomplish little, who was too cultivated to have a harmonious nature and be happy, and at last, exhausted and wearied by a thousand excesses of mind and body, fell into deep melancholy and desired only one thing—death.

This lonely man, who remained incomprehensible even to friends and favorites, and whose mortal enemies, as Spartianus expresses himself, had first been his bosom friends, was devoted for a long time to a Bithynian youth, whom he loved as Socrates loved Alcibiades, and Caesar Brutus. This was *Antinous*, with whose busts and statues Hadrian has filled the world. What a totally different impression the lad's thoughtful beauty produces upon us from the passion-seamed visage of the master, to whom he was the dearest thing in life. Innocence and resignation, melancholy and aimless longing have found imperishable expression in these features. A head bowed mournfully, with waving locks falling low over the forehead, deep-set, mysterious eyes, brows gently curved, cheeks rounded like a girl's, which form a singular contrast to the sorrowful expression about the lips and the delicately-moulded chin: this is Antinous. The thoughtful, earnest, spiritual head rests upon a strong neck and unusually broad breast, which reveals the athlete, while the body, with its daintily-formed limbs, is as perfect an ideal of beauty as artist ever dreamed in honor of Apollo or Hermes.

Yet this statue also offers us an enigma, which occupies our minds. The melancholy expression, that bows the young head and attracts the eyes to earth, forms a singular contradiction to the exuberant youthful vigor of the form. The mystery excites us all the more, after we have seen several statues of Antinous, in which he still beams with the unclouded joy of youth and can be distinguished from the smiling Apollino only by his broad breast and narrow forehead. But all the other statues strengthen the impression of melancholy, whether because art surpasses its type, or gives us here the history of a soul-life concerning which historians are silent. History tells the tale of Hadrian's weather-beaten face, but only imagination can guess the cause of this touching sorrow, for the ancient author's account is brief and contradictory. It is certain that Antinous was oppressed by his relation to Hadrian, yet religious motives, as well as personal ones, had an influence on this relation. For such a motive Antinous voluntarily sacrificed his life for his Caesar, and Hadrian, after the youth's death, commanded that he should be honored as a god, to make amends for the wrong he had done him. What was his guilt? Whoever looks at the two statues will be answered: How a healthy nature was ruined by companionship with a diseased one—is the history of Antinous and his Caesar.

ANTINOUS.

CHAPTER I.

" SLEEP, thou whimsical god, that lulls the nursling in
its mother's lap till it nods while still at the breast—that
rocks the boy to slumber with his toys yet in his hands,
and chains the impetuous youth with pleasant dreams,
why dost thou flee from the old, the sick, who doubly
need thee ?   Never did the lad's parched lips press the
foaming cup more eagerly, or the dusty athlete yearn
for the dewy beaker, than I sigh, hour after hour, for
thee !"

The man, who tossing restlessly to and fro amid his
coverlets and pillows, uttered these lamentations and
entreaties, was the Emperor Hadrian, who after an
impetuous career, now, on the threshold of old age, was
forced to learn that nature measured Caesars and ordinary mortals by the same standard, if in work, passion or
pleasure-seeking they exacted more than she could give.
He had come to Tibur to hasten the building of his villa,
and meantime occupied the gardens of the Quirinus
above the waterfalls of the Anio.   The throng of workmen brought with him quickly gratified every whim.
One thing alone they could not arrange to his satisfaction
—a sleeping-room. The rush of the waterfalls drove him
from one, another seemed damp and musty; voices, not
human ones that could be hushed, but those of birds

and cicadas compelled him to leave a third. So he had once more been tossing for weary hours amid cushions, pillows and coverlids, reproaching the god that denied the Cæsar what he granted the beggar by the wayside. Starting from his disordered couch and clenching his gouty hands, he shouted into the dark stillness, where only the light of a lamp standing in a hidden niche cast a feeble ray:

"Morpheus, I am a god as well as thou, I have more temples, thou rulest only by night, while I also reign by day; where would thy. kingdom be if I should drive sleep from all my subjects? What a pity Phlegon isn't here; wouldn't it be a subject for the finest epic poem: 'Hadrian's war against Morpheus?' But my imagination has gone on leave of absence with him, I can neither reign nor compose alone. My verses are a foot too short, and my enemy is a head too long, or Servianus's would have been lying in the sand beside his grandson's long ago. Yet why? My dear kinsmen only want to give me that for which I yearn, sleep, sleep, eternal sleep!"

Again he gazed wearily at the motes dancing in the slanting ray of light cast obliquely across the chamber by the lamp standing in the niche. He tried to think of nothing, imagined cornfields swayed by the wind, the rising, swelling and breaking of ocean waves, a perfectly empty space, passed instantly from every idea that strove to present itself to another, counted up to a thousand to weary his mind, until at last, renouncing farther attempts, he snatched the shade from the lamp, exclaiming with sudden fury:

"Oh! if they only knew how the purple galls! I would rather their swords struck me to-day than to-morrow, but they shall not say I kept body-guards like Nero, or spies like Domitian."

This outburst of wrath seemed to soothe the invalid's excitement. His head sank wearily on his pillow, and sleep began to descend upon his lids. Suddenly a noise, that sounded to his tired brain like the sharpening of a dagger, roused the exhausted man again. The sound of a file or chisel grating on some hard substance, was distinctly audible in the darkened room, a tapping and boring, which at this hour was incomprehensible, and therefore uncanny to the lonely emperor.

" Phlegon is absent, and Antinous in one of his death-like slumbers," muttered the Caesar.

He had already seized a silver wand to strike the metal basin, but laid it down again.

"The scoundrels will run before the slaves come, and to-morrow I shall be told the usual lies. I'll see for my-self who is sharpening daggers here, or paying a visit to the gems in the tablinum."

The tall figure, weakened by disease, rose slowly, and the old soldier gradually gained the mastery over his gouty limbs. Casting a glance behind the hangings of the adjoining room, he saw with surprise that Antinous's couch was empty and he was left without attendants. Mechanically his hand groped for the place on the wall where his sword usually hung, but an angry hiss, like an enraged serpent's, escaped his lips. The sheath hung in its place, the weapon had been removed.

" So this is why Phlegon could no longer control his longing to see his wife, this is why Antinous sat so silent yesterday in the corner, casting troubled glances around him."

With feverish haste Hadrian glided back to his couch

to seek his dagger.　This too was missing, yet Antinous
alone knew where he kept the weapon.

"Thou too, my son, thou too, Brutus!" quoted the
emperor, still a rhetorician, even in the mortal agony
that thrilled him.　"What did they offer thee, my boy,
to betray me?　Is not man naturally a viper, since even
against his own advantage he must sting the breast that
warmed him?　But they are mistaken, if they suppose
I shall die of fright like Domitian.　They shall feel the
arm to which their adored Trajan owes his best laurels."

Glancing around in search of a weapon, he saw a
large candelabra which he took in his hand for a club,
exclaiming with an angry laugh:

"The Corinthian acanthus leaves and serpent eggs
shall make elegant impressions on your skulls."

Then, following the noise, which sounded louder, as
if a saw were cutting iron rods, Hadrian went through
the adjoining atrium, where the night breeze entering
from above made him shiver with cold.

From the tablinum, streaming from the adjacent hall
of gems, a ray of light fell through the half-parted curtain and played over the red ornaments on the wall,
whose reflection trembled in the basin of the fountain
like a pool of blood.

"Will Antinous's blood or mine flow with such a
crimson hue?" asked Hadrian sadly as he softly approached, then held his breath in amazement.　On the
floor before him crouched the graceful figure of his
favorite, absorbed in a task which made the perspiration
stream from his brow, while his cheeks glowed with
eagerness.　Antinous held on one knee the emperor's
sword, on which, with the help of some corrosive liquid
and several sharp files, he was engraving a hieroglyphic;

the same task seemed to be completed on the dagger that lay beside him. Hadrian struck the candelabra loudly on the floor, the youth started, gazed imploringly into the emperor's angry face, and then laid his finger beseechingly on his lips.

"What are you doing, boy?" asked the Caesar imperiously.

"Oh! now it was all in vain," replied Antinous mournfully, then casting the sword on the floor he added:

"The spell is broken."

"Who permits you to rob me of my weapons at night?"

The youth looked timidly at Hadrian.

"Don't be angry, Caesar," he answered in his deep, musical voice. "Hermas taught me the cipher that makes the sword invincible, and such sacred signs, as Menephta once told me, must be engraved before cock-crow, when the moon is full, without one word being spoken. Now you have destroyed the charm. You must not use this sword again, Caesar," he added sobbing. "Half-finished characters bring a curse."

"Do you know, foolish lad, that I came within a hair of crushing your head with this candelabra, that I thought Phlegon and you traitors?"

A convulsive tremor ran through the youth's pliant limbs, and fixing his large, expressive eyes on Hadrian with a look of deep sorrow, he asked:

"You could believe Antinous sought your life? I wished to make you invincible, guard you from the danger you are to meet."

Again a suspicious look rested upon the emperor's

withered, wrinkled countenance, as he darted a keen glance at the youth.

"What do you know of the conspiracy? When will Servianus remove me? Speak!"

"I know nothing," sighed Antinous, "except what has been daily on your lips for a year. Remember, it was about this time that we stood in spring on the downs at Pelusium, where you had Pompey's half-destroyed grave restored. You then uttered the line which accompanied us throughout the Egyptian journey and echoed in our hearts longer than the voice of Memnon, as you bewailed Pompey's fate.

 ' He, so rich in temples, like a beggar, lacks a grave.'

"What moved me still more deeply was your remark, that you too were destined to fall under Pompey's statue, like the adored Julius. Often, in my dreams, I saw assassins pressing upon you with their daggers, and when after our return, you allotted Pompey's theatre to the senate, I asked why you challenged fate. If he seeks to die, why in the theatre? Phlegon strove to soothe me; the gods, he said, did not perform the same play twice. While pondering how I might save you, Hermas the Christian whispered that the cipher of his God made every sword invincible. He sketched the monogram of the Christian's god and explained it. But I am not permitted to utter it, because I don't belong to the initiated. Menephta too, formerly showed me the protecting characters of his gods, and I wanted to engrave all on your sword. This is the conspiracy between Hermas and me. We said nothing to Phlegon, because he would only have scoffed at us. Whom will you still trust, Caesar, if you believe us murderers?"

"Whom shall I trust?" answered Hadrian gloomily, "after kindred and friends have betrayed me?"

"Oh!" said the youth beseechingly, advancing a little nearer Hadrian, "see if this conspiracy was not also merely an outgrowth of your own suspicion, Caesar. You wronged Servianus and his grandson by appointing Aelius Verus your heir, and yet did not win the weakling's heart, because he doubtless knows he will die before you, and only owes his elevation to his delicate lungs. Since you deceived them all, you lack confidence in them, and now even believe those who love you to be conspirators and murderers."

"Who loves me?" asked the emperor scornfully.

The lad threw himself passionately on the floor, clinging convulsively to the emperor's knees.

"Oh! Hadrian, if you could only trust, if there was but one tiny spark of confidence sleeping in your soul, that I might fan with my breath! But it is all in vain," he continued, bursting into tears. "After devoting myself for a lustrum to your service, body and soul, knowing nothing, thinking of nothing save you, you have imagined it possible that I wished to kill you!" A thrill of passionate emotion shook the youth's beautiful limbs.

The emperor passed his hand caressingly over his favorite's wet cheek.

"Don't rage so, my child, you know I have no love for tears. We will consider the matter by daylight to-morrow. Now let us go to rest," he continued, shivering. "We both need it." The lad helped the sovereign back to his couch, and stroking the sick man's head and cheek like a child, succeeded, as he had often done, in lulling the restless, tortured spirit to sleep. Thus, a thousand years before, a Jewish shepherd boy had sung his king, robbed of slumber by a similar demon, to repose.

The first sunbeam that stole into the emperor's room, illumined the old man's slumbering form and the sleep-fettered limbs of the beautiful youth, extended on the skin of a lion slain in Libya by his own hand. It was a remembrance of a happier time, when Hadrian, himself a mighty hunter, slept in the forests with Antinous, and the excitement of the chase drove away the evil spirits which now assailed him in the sick-room.

When Hadrian was roused by the brighter light that entered the chamber, an unusual sense of vigor pervaded his diseased limbs. The paintings on the walls assumed more vivid hues. His eye rested with satisfaction on the artistic objects, whose beauty was rendered more conspicuous by the sunbeams stealing through the curtain, to linger at last on the most exquisite thing in the apartment, Antinous's faultless face and figure, as he lay beside him in the happy slumber of youth. The emperor's eye gazed with loving admiration at the rise and fall of the arched chest, the quivering of the half-parted lips. What was the spell that bound him so mysteriously to this lad? First of all, probably, his personal beauty, which blended with the noblest Hellenic forms the pliancy of the Asiatic, the melancholy dignity of the Oriental, but also the deep sympathy he felt for this simple, boyish soul, into which no discord had yet entered and which therefore, even in the most insignificant remark, always rang with the pure tone of an unspoiled nature. How often he had passed his hand over the youth's waving locks and narrow forehead as he stood gazing into vacancy, and asked him of what he was thinking.

When Antinous replied: "Nothing at all, Caesar," this confession of a dreamer, just waking from the happy stupidity of boyhood, moved him more than the cleverest answer; for he felt that there was more real happiness in the lad's dreaming, than in the restless doubts in which his own ever active mind wore itself away. He himself loved the lad first for his beauty, but he also knew that his quiet temperament exerted a beneficial influence upon him, and the mild gentleness of this harmonious nature made him better and more cheerful than intercourse with those who were only an echo of his own anger and suspicion, thereby increasing his evil moods, instead of dispelling them. As the emperor moved his hand lovingly towards his favorite, it unexpectedly touched the cold hilt of the sword that still lay beside him, and recalled to memory the events of the past night. He angrily seized the weapon and perceived the characters Antinous had marked on the shining blade, but which were now surrounded by a dull stain of rust. He was not ignorant of the meaning of the letters I. N. R. I. The fish drawn beneath, probably copied by Antinous from some gem, was more mysterious.

"I knew Hermas's god had an ass's head," he muttered, "but I don't understand the meaning of the fish, whether sea-fish or river-fish, though this one looks like a well-fed carp. Did Hermas suppose he could pay his debt of gratitude for the life I spared, by leading the boy to do this?" Suddenly a vision rose before his memory of a narrow street in Ephesus, where a shouting, raging mob surrounded the tall, muscular figure of a grey-bearded workman, already bleeding from a dozen wounds inflicted by stones, sticks and clods, until the emperor himself silenced the throng by reproofs and blows.

"He is a Christian," shouted the rabble, "the divine Trajan's edict must be fulfilled."

But Hadrian had not only been impressed by the stoical calmness with which the Christian bore ill-usage, but irritated by the reference to his much-praised predecessor. So he placed Hermas under the protection of his train, and when opportunity favored sent him to one of his estates in Italy. Was it an emotion of gratitude, that had induced Hermas to seek to harden the Caesar's sword by the cipher of his god? When he recalled the old man's anxious, yet kindly face Antinous's explanation seemed credible. How often he had rejected accusations against the Nazarenes. "They set the city on fire," said his brother-in-law Servianus, "you ought not to endure them near you!" "Hermas helped put it out," the emperor replied, "see if he looks like an incendiary." Thus Hermas's residence at the court was rendered legitimate. "He helped put it out," said the slaves, who all liked the Nazarene, though he often made himself troublesome by warning them that people ought to be more industrious when their master was not looking on than under his eyes.

The emperor remembered all this, "and yet," he concluded, "the Nazarene's claws appear here—he seeks to force his crucified god upon the master of the empire. Intrusive brood!" he wrathfully exclaimed, as he let the sword fall. But he beheld Antinous's big brown eyes fixed timidly upon him, and instantly heard the boy plead in his deep, musical tones.

"Punish me, Caesar, I did wrong, but surely Hermas meant well."

" Let me not think the Christian has infected you
with his forbidden superstition," said Hadrian sternly.

" How does it happen," asked Antinous thoughtfully,
"that you hate this god, when on the Euphrates and the
Nile you exacted the hardest marches from us for days
together, to discover some ancient, forgotten sanctuary ?
If we found a few palm-trees with an engraved stone,
as at Skythopolis, or a marshy pond with a few lazy
crocodiles and a statue of the mother of the gods, as at
Mareotis, you became indignant at the desolation and
said :

   ' Oh ! foul disgrace ! The spider's web now veils the sacred temple,
   And o'er the deserted god within foul weeds their tendrils twine.'

" You wished to rear sanctuaries to all the gods, near
and distant, honored and temple-less, that all might
guard the repose of your villa. What has Hermas's god
done, that you forbid your Tibur to him alone ?"

" He has committed the crime of not tolerating other
gods, who are older than he. This presumptuous god
of the Jews, who first set Rome on fire, then Jerusalem,
the incendiary, shall not dwell under my roof."

Antinous was silent for a time, then with a boy's
sense of justice, said :

" If he won't tolerate the other gods, it probably
serves him right to have us, their servants, show him the
door ; but Caesar, do you know the thought often
occurs to me, that you will rouse evil deities against
you by searching their secrets too closely. When lately
I marked suitable oracles in Virgil for you, I felt so
sorrowful, as if we were sinning against the gods to
whom you zealously build costly temples, and your
conversations with Phlegon and Menephta about altering

the ritual, aroused the same thrill of horror I experienced at your last sacrifice, when the haruspex tore the entrails asunder before our eyes, to investigate the future of which you think too much, and a wise divinity has veiled from us."

"You don't understand, boy," replied Hadrian. "You pray for yourself, I must see that the nations do not forget to honor their gods."

"Oh! I am happy," said Antinous. "When I go up in the morning to the altar of the great Jupiter, I cover my face and raise my hands to him, but only until I feel he hears me, knows even me, the young, foolish lad, and when I experience the touch of his goodness I remove the veil, and the world lies before me so bright, so blue, so dewy in its morning freshness, that I can only sing and exult over this beautiful universe, and know not whether I would rather go east or west, through the streets that stretch before me. This is because I pray to the gods, but you want to help them, work miracles for them, utter oracles through their lips, and this offends them, so that they punish you with melancholy and anxious nights."

"The gods do not punish me for upholding their honor; another burden oppresses me—that I must represent them on earth. Yet how should you understand it? Even the youthful Hercules could not comprehend why Atlas groaned, until he had taken the globe from him for a time."

"Well, then let Aelius Verus, whom you have made your heir bear it, and we will ride away, as we used to do when you spent weeks with me in hunting. Oh! how I long for it!"

"Beware, my son! Everything for which I have

most ardently longed in my life, afterwards proved a misfortune," said the emperor gloomily.

"Oh! shake off this cloud, Caesar! Come, we will wander hand in hand out into the beautiful blue morning, towards the gleaming Volscian mountains, the Albanian chain, or jagged Soracte."

"Foolish child! Mountains lie, as well as men, they are not blue and misty, they don't rise near Heaven, they yield no happiness. Thistles, lime, serpents, bleeding feet, thirst and fever, would be the sole Elysium to which you wandered."

"Nay, Caesar, the mountains do not deceive, neither do men, if only you would not repel them from you. See, when I go out, all greet me kindly, every one speaks a friendly word. The peasant woman, who gathers peaches, bids me take the best, the young men challenge me to hurl the disk, the old wish me goodday, and the women warn me not to go up the mountain too fast. Why shouldn't I trust people who are always kind to me?"

"Kind," replied Hadrian, "because you are the Caesar's favorite. Were I to send you to the quarries to-morrow, they would persecute you, set a brand upon your brow, throw lime into your eyes, that they might be red like theirs, offer you no peaches, but snatch your bread from your hand, because a lad so well-fed needed no more food."

"That isn't true, Caesar," cried Antinous, starting up indignantly, "why do you seek to destroy all confidence in men? I'll put it to the test. Send me to the quarries in Sardinia, and if in a year I think of men as you do, you will have won. But if I have had different experiences from those you predict, you must believe me and shake off this sad, gloomy distrust, which is a misfortune to you and all the world."

"No, my friend," replied the emperor tenderly, throwing his arm around the youth's neck, "I would as willingly mutilate the merry face of the red Centaur in the anteroom, who daily smiles a morning greeting, as destroy this masterpiece of nature, which has no peer in Eastern or Western lands."

"Then send me to Rome in beggar's garb!" exclaimed Antinous, shaking off his master's caress, "and when you think I have gathered experiences enough, summon me; I swear you shall find me no misanthrope, and no experience shall be too painful, if I succeed in driving away the harpies and spectres that night and day poison your every pleasure."

"You need not take the journey to Rome, my boy, to obtain the experiences for which you long. I will expect you at the villa at the sixth hour, ere then the bandage will have been removed from your eyes."

The emperor seized a silver wand, and struck the large metal basin that summoned his body servant, indeed each tone indicated a different person among the household officials in the anteroom. The loud sound of the vessel, struck on its edge, now brought Hermas into the chamber. The figure that appeared in the doorway looked simple and rustic, despite the shining white robe. A rough beard framed a dark, sunburnt face, whose bright intelligent eyes and pleasant smile seemed to contradict the meaning of the low forehead and deep, harsh wrinkles. This countenance, which appeared somewhat hastily through the curtain of the door, would not have been specially attractive in itself, but the sickly impression produced by the Christian ascetic was contradicted by a look of great cheerfulness and good humor, that spite of the weary expression inspired confidence, while a line around the mouth, and the repellent carriage of the head and hands seemed to say :

"I will do everything for love of you, I am the gentlest, most peaceable man in the world, but I can't act against my conviction, though you all consider me a coward."

"You want to conquer the world for your god, and haven't yet got the better of your wife and sons," Hadrian once said to him jeeringly. Hermas could not deny it. He only sighed, "the Lord's ways are wonderful." In accordance with his character, Hermas felt somewhat anxious at the Caesar's unexpected summons. His heroic courage did not rise until he knew what the Lord desired of him. When Hadrian took the sword in his hand and pointed to the design Antinous had clumsily executed during the night, Hermas's face assumed a droll expression of perplexity.

"Who allowed you," said Hadrian, "to incite this lad to practise magic arts against me?"

"The first person, my lord," said Hermas, "that hammered iron and bronze was a murderer's grandson, Tubal-Cain, whom you, in your blindness, adore as Vulcan. But when his father Lamech swung the first sword, he said to his wives: 'I have slain a man to my wounding and a young man to my hurt.' Since that time people murder each other on earth, and there will be no change until all swords are marked with the sign of the Son of Man. I began with yours, for if yours remains in its sheath, all will rest; if yours is bare, all flash for the sin of fratricide. If I have done wrong,

here is my head.   I will die willingly for the name of
Christ."

Amused by these communications from a world
unknown to him, Hadrian said:

"It is fortunate for you, that you did not suggest to
me, as to this boy, your pretended anxiety for my welfare, but have so cheerfully confessed your boldness.
Yet, if it should ever occur to you again to mark my
knife, shoes, or shears with the cipher of your god, useless slave, you shall make acquaintance with this sword
or hang a few hours on the cross, that you may be able
to describe your god's passion to your brothers more
faithfully.   I have devised a different punishment for
your companion here.   Go to the goatherds' stables
yonder, choose the meanest, dirtiest, and most tattered
of all the hats, cloaks and blankets hanging on the rack,
and bring them here; the worst, I tell you, or you shall
hang on the cross."   Hermas bowed and hastily retired.

"There, my boy, now go to yonder coal pan, and
stain yourself black with dust from head to foot; then
without revealing who you are, visit all your friends in
the dress I shall give you, and you can spare yourself
the journey to Rome and Sardinia.   The temple in the
Canopus is to be roofed to-day, and I wish first to
thoroughly examine the rooms by daylight, you will
find me there before dinner.   If I judge your friends
correctly, you'll have more to tell than will be agreeable
to you."

On his way to the stables, Hermas's expression of
anxiety and fear quickly vanished.   His sense of justice
gained the mastery, as soon as he escaped the influence
of the emperor's imperious eyes.   The lean old man
gesticulated passionately, muttering:

"I'm no slave, I serve him voluntarily; what right has he to threaten me with a slave's death ?   I'll leave Tibur, I won't go back, I'll leave Tibur instantly—But if I don't take the clothes, he'll send some one after me and they'll bring me to him a prisoner.   Better let him go to his temples and gods at the villa, then I can get to Rome before he remembers me, or I'll wait till evening and go at night by the Appian Way."

On reaching the stable, he chose the meanest of all the peasant costumes, and another somewhat less soiled. "I can profit by the imperial idea and escape as a goat-herd too."

Laden with a huge pack, which did not smell exactly like ambergris, he again entered Hadrian's room.   The latter was still giving his young friend ironical instructions and advice how he might most speedily lose his good opinion of gods and men.   When the lad's beautiful form was blackened and his face disfigured almost beyond recognition, by streaks of dirt, Hermas was again startled.   "If he sends his favorite out so," he said, "the cross will soon come in good earnest.   No matter, if it is the Lord's will!   I've borne worse buffets.   But who would have thought he'd treat the poor lad so for such an offence!   What folly, what gloom!   Yet it's better for Antinous to be soiled in body than in soul; now he'll be saved, and the angel of darkness doesn't see that the angel of light is again wiser than he.   My lord," he said, turning to Hadrian with a touch of gayety, "even dirt is a matter of taste, so I've brought two suits, that your own choice might save me from the cross."

Hadrian tossed over the repulsive rags with his staff, handing garment after garment to the already

-disfigured youth. When the latter had drawn the felt-hat over his eyes, no one would have recognized the handsome Antinous.

"Do as I ordered you!" said Hadrian harshly to the lad, who left the room more cheerfully than Hermas could understand. The Christian thought his turn would now come, but Hadrian flung the second suit to him with his staff, exclaiming:

"Begone, and take this stench with you!"

CHAPTER II.

THE morning mist was still brooding over the plain, and a fresher breeze swept across the heights of Tibur, as Antinous entered the street. His disguise pleased him—he meant to amuse the emperor on his return with comical experiences and laugh at him heartily for the wager he had won. As on every other morning, he approached the circular pillared temple of Hercules, to pray to the god of youth, athletic sports and travellers. But scarcely had his foot pressed the first step, when he was thrust back by a rude hand.

"By Hercules, young chap, do you suppose I've swept the temple-stairs, to have every goatherd carry his dirt to the god? Can't you pray outside—and what is Hercules to you? Sacrifice to the fauns, that your kids may thrive. Begone from here!"

Was this the obsequious temple-servant, who usually greeted him every morning with a "Hail, Antinous!" bade his daughter strew roses on the steps before him, and not unfrequently dismissed him with tears in his

eyes and a benediction for his piety?   The youth's
gayety had suddenly vanished.   No jest, by which he
could have given the matter a jovial turn, entered his
mind.   The surprise was too great.   He withdrew, not
wishing to allow the hypocrite time to unmask more
plainly.   Hadrian must not be permitted to win his
wager.   As he turned the corner, his face brightened,
for he saw in the distance the fruit-dealer, who every
morning offered him her finest peaches.   The gift was
profitable, for Antinous from time to time gave her
Titius, a little curly-headed fellow of seven, a silver
coin.

"I must offer myself to her," said Antinous; "that
will raise a laugh.   But that detestable priest has put
me entirely out of tune."

"See if Antinous isn't coming yet," said the sturdy
young woman to her boy.   "Now Caesar lives here, I
needn't send my fruit to the city, where the dealer
scarcely paid me half the profits, and yet it wasn't worth
while to go myself.   The workmen, to be sure, pay
poorly, and if it wasn't for the noblemen in the Villa
Quirinus, I should do better, by Jupiter, to feast on my
figs and peaches myself, for I wouldn't keep them to sell
to fellows like these."   She pointed to the approaching
goatherd.   "Why, the peasant is really coming towards
me.   Keep three paces off!" she shouted; "your odor
is enough to spoil all the fragrance of my wares."

"Surely," replied Antinous gently, "you have some
cast-off fruit you can't sell, or a worm-eaten pear.   My
long night-walk has made me hungry, and I've no
money to buy a breakfast."

"You're mistaken in supposing I would lure such
fellows by gifts," scolded the angry little woman.   "No,

dirtiest of goatherds, the custom would be too large, if I entered that business."

But this time Antinous would not give up his wager for lost so quickly, and as he really was still fasting and felt hungry, said:

"Just give me one of the figs you have thrown into yonder basket on the ground, to feed the swine."

"Begone, shameless beggar," cried the woman, livid with anger, "or my broom shall sweep your face, which you've forgotten to wash!"

Antinous turned sadly away. Little Titius sprang to the basket, seized one of the fruits that had just been refused, and threw it so skilfully after the youth's retreating figure, that it squashed on his ear. The latter angrily raised his gnarled stick against the child, who only yesterday had been his pet, but the fruit-dealer screamed shrilly:

"Febronius, Marcus, here! A thief, a robber! Give the impudent goatherd a good drubbing."

The youth, who did not wish to be robbed of his mask already, hastily ran down the hill-side, while little Titius, to the detriment of his mother's pigs, skilfully pelted him with rotten figs and pears.

Tender-hearted Antinous's eyes filled with tears, as he remembered how only yesterday he had believed in the woman's unselfish kindness, and the child's good disposition. Walking mournfully down the hill, towards the building where Hadrian had appointed to meet him, he failed to hear the rustling of the dense foliage of the pine trees, which usually told him wonders of a higher world. Perhaps they too lied, as Hadrian asserted. He did not enjoy the shifting rays of light that glided through the laurel bushes, perhaps they too were also false serpents of glittering light. He reached a half-ruined fountain, where a moss-grown Triton spouted water into a crumbling basin. Lydia, the little flower-girl, with whom he daily chatted, was sitting there. She seemed pleased to be released from her loneliness, and he was agreeably surprised that she addressed him first, saying:

"Good-day, shepherd."

"Good-day to you also, maiden," he replied, seating himself on the other side of the fountain.

"Have your goats run away," asked the girl, "and do you expect a beating from your master, such as I get, when I don't bring home money enough? You slink along like our dog, when he's caught eating something."

"You're not far from the truth," he replied, "but give me a cup of water, I am thirsty."

"Just see the proud goatherd!" answered Lydia pertly. "Drink from the Triton's puffed cheeks, if he doesn't find you too dirty to kiss; you look as if you had slept among the ashes. Wait, I'll wash you," she added, and pressing her hand on the Triton's mouth, skilfully directed the jet of water straight into the youth's face. He hastily sprang aside, and fearing for his dark mask, tried to blacken his face again with the coal-dust that still clung to his hair. This did not escape the young girl's notice.

"See," she cried, "he has reasons for being so black. I said so at once, he's been eating something. Well, I won't betray you. Who of us would get anything, if he waited till it was given to him."

"So you don't earn much?" said Antinous evasively.

"Oh! I'm richer than you suppose," replied the

young girl, producing a purse with some pieces of money Antinous knew only too well.

"How did you get the purse?" he cried, horrified to the depths of his soul. Lydia hastily concealed it again, looking at him suspiciously. "Of course you found it?" asked Antinous, who had lost the purse several days before.

"No, a young man who sometimes comes here gave it to me, he took me in his lap, petted me and then handed me the purse. You shake your head. Oh! he has more. It was Antinous, Caesar's friend. If my mother knew it, she would have taken the money long ago; I shall keep it till I go to Rome."

"What do you want in Rome, girl?" asked Antinous harshly.

"Why, in two years, mother says, I shall be old enough to earn money in the city, like my sisters."

"And how is that?"

"How? Why, as they do, as flower-girls, dancers, flute-players."

"Why do you want to go to Rome, since you have so profitable a friend here?" replied Antinous. "And yet you said we should have to wait a long time, if we only took what was given us."

"Well then, he didn't really give me the money; as he was caressing me, I saw the purse in the folds of his robe and snatched it."

"You shall restore it to me!" cried Antinous, angrily tearing off his hat. The young girl stared at him with a pallid, startled face, but the same instant sprang down the slope at a single bound and vanished behind the gnarled trunks of the olive-trees amid the clumps of box and juniper bushes.

"That is enough," said the youth, "the time Hadrian appointed has not half expired, yet I could appear before him now and say: 'You are right, Caesar, they all lie.'"

When the emperor reached the Canopus about the sixth hour, his attendants saw a goatherd sitting on one of the blocks of building material scattered about, with his eyes fixed thoughtfully and earnestly on the ground. "I must speak to this Adonis," said the Caesar, dismissing his train, and seating himself on a marble column beside Antinous, who nodded sadly.

"Well, my boy," Hadrian began, "did your friends greet you as usual, share their property with you, accompany you with their good wishes?"

"Oh! Caesar," replied the youth, "why have you done this? Now I shall no longer believe in anyone, not even you or myself."

"Gently, my friend," replied Hadrian, "we must be able to bear the truth, without making wry faces. Now tell me your experiences."

When Antinous had finished, Hadrian said:

"This dose won't suffice for your cure. You would be the same to-morrow as you were yesterday, we must strengthen it."

He beckoned to one of the servants, who carried the architects' plans, and said:

"Order the temple-servant at the altar of Hercules, the fruit-dealer Tryphaena, with her son Titius, and the little flower-girl, Lydia, to appear here at once."

Antinous felt little curiosity about what might still happen, he was perfectly satisfied with the experience already obtained, and the Caesar's sport was repulsive to him. He angrily dug up the earth with his staff, while Hadrian spent the time in examining his plans.

When the voices of the temple-servant and fruit-dealer were heard in the distance, the emperor pushed his friend's hat lower over his brow and told him to muffle himself carefully again. He himself paced up and down before the youth with long strides, apparently in an angry mood.

The temple-servant and fruit-dealer—the messenger had been unable to find Lydia—on seeing the goat-herd, instantly supposed that the summons, which had greatly startled them, referred to him. Indeed, the Caesar began:

"This fellow here has stolen near me under suspicious circumstances; he is not what he desires to appear. The clothes he wears, it was discovered, were stolen from my stables. He was seen to-day talking with you; I am told he spent the night in the temple of Hercules, and you gave him a breakfast of fruit."

"By Hercules!" said the temple-servant with deep indignation, "I found this fellow sneaking around the sanctuary, evidently intending to find his way to the treasure-rooms in the rear, while I attended to the cleaning of the temple in front. He seemed to be hiding articles already stolen under his cloak, but I think he still feels the arm by which I shook him, before throwing him roughly down the steps."

"And you, Tryphaena, what have you to say in your justification?"

"Oh! my lord," replied the huckster, "my lodgers are witnesses that I called for help, when this wretch made an attack upon my property. My shrieks and my little Titius's bold pelting put the thief to flight, or it would have gone ill with me and my baskets."

"And where is little Lydia?" asked the emperor.

"Oh! my lord," sobbed the huckster, "we fear the wicked rascal has murdered her.   Her virtuous mother, who is supported entirely by the young girl's earnings, says that she did not return at the usual hour; but the rush-basket with her flowers is still standing by the wall, many are scattered and crushed, and stones are torn from the path down the hill-side.   Who knows what crime the horrible fellow yonder has committed?"

" And do you know nothing else about the matter?" asked the emperor.

" I believe he was sneaking about the palace yesterday evening," said the temple-servant, "for when I was closing the doors of the sanctuary I saw a figure that looked exactly like him, just turning the corner of the wall."

"And I haven't yet told," cried the huckster, "that he had a dagger under his cloak this morning, when he tried to force me to give up my property, and would have killed little Titius with his club, if the poor child hadn't jumped aside."

"Well, Antinous, what have you to say to these accusations?" asked the emperor laughing, as he raised the felt-hat from the shepherd's head.

If a thunder-bolt had struck the temple of Hercules, or a well-aimed kick scattered the contents of the fruit-dealer's baskets over the ground, the terror of the pair would scarcely have been greater than now, as they stood gazing at Antinous and Hadrian.   They had no other expectation, than that they should be instantly dragged to the newly-erected Tartarus, where people said the emperor intended to have criminals undergo all the tortures the poets related of Prometheus, Ixion, Sisyphus, Tantalus and the Danaids. Yet it was only half a deliverance to them, when Hadrian now said scornfully, while a sarcastic smile stirred the thousand wrinkles in his face:

"Go, my friends, you have performed your work admirably, I was not mistaken in you."

The pair set out on their return to Tibur, followed by little Titius, who had been greatly troubled that he too was not allowed to open his sack of lies, while a suspicion now dawned on his childish mind, that he would receive no more silver coins from Antinous. But the Bithynian gazed after them long and mournfully, until tears dimmed his eyes. Then he went to the Nymphaeum, where he washed and wrapped himself in a cloak an obliging architect willingly offered Caesar's friend.

CHAPTER III.

A second shepherd had left the Villa Quirinus about an hour after Antinous. This was Hermas, who had determined to leave the emperor's service. Neither slave, nor officer of Hadrian, he had lived as a client in the Caesar's house, and there found safety from religious persecution, yet without enjoying entire security from the sovereign's capriciousness. The suspicion directed against him the day before on account of his bold game with the sword, might still bear evil fruit, for it was Hadrian's way to overlook offences at first, only

to return to them with two-fold wrath in hours of anger,
after thinking them over during sleepless nights, endow-
ing them with motives and purposes, and swelling the
trifle into a crime.   Even the daily outbursts of his irrita-
bility were growing more unendurable.   Not long ago,
in his blind rage he had thrust a stylus into the eyes of a
slave, who spilled sherbet upon him.   When he saw the
man again for the first time after his recovery, he bade
him ask a favor.

But the slave answered proudly:

"Give me back my eyes, Caesar!"

Hermas had entered the emperor's house as a client,
not a slave, and it angered him deeply that Hadrian
had called him a servant.   A Roman citizen with a
small landed property not far from the Flaminian Way,
brother of the Roman bishop Pius, he was not without
a certain consciousness of his own dignity.   Endowed
with a talent for poetry, he had been conspicuous
among the prophets of the Roman parish, until his
wife's jealousy and the frivolous lives of his sons disgusted him with his home.   He therefore willingly
allowed himself to be sent abroad as a messenger from
the Church; in this way he had come to Ephesus, and
by injudicious propaganda excited in the community a
tumult, whose victim he would have become, had not
Hadrian rescued him.   He returned to Italy with the
emperor, and had consented to be employed in all kinds
of business, of which, with the restless Hadrian, there
was never any lack.   Regarded by the emperor, who
had collected around him priests of all the various
deities, as a person who knew the secrets of the
Christians, Hermas enjoyed his position, and as the
Roman Church set great value upon possessing the

emperor's ear through him, at first even hoped that
Hadrian in his restless tossing to and fro amid the different forms of worship, would finally throw himself into
the arms of the Christian faith. But he was soon forced
to perceive, how far removed from the Caesar's nature
was the genius of the Jews.

Strips of parchment, inscribed with the most beautiful passages of scripture, which Hermas thrust between
the rolls of MS. or laid on the table, Hadrian either
did not notice or made the subjects of offensive jests.
The attempt to mark the monogram of Christ on the
imperial sword had hopelessly failed. Hermas knew
the emperor well enough to be aware, that he would not
escape punishment for this trick, so he preferred to
remember his freedom, and return to his scolding wife
and dissolute sons, in order as he said, to maintain his
rights in his own house.

So, disguised as a goatherd, he had gone down
from the temple of Hercules, past the foaming cascades
of the Anio, to the bridge leading to the broad Roman
road. But on reaching there, he said to himself that
by daylight he might easily be recognized on the
crowded military highway. Besides, the heat of the
shadeless thoroughfare extending between lines of monuments on the right and left, seemed by no means inviting. Moreover, he considered it his duty to inform
the emperor of the reasons for his departure by Antinous, and cast a germ of the gospel into the youth's
heart before bidding him farewell. So he determined
to wait under the dense shadow of a group of pines for
Antinous, who must pass the spot in returning from the
villa.

The overflow from the fountain, by which Lydia had

sat, rippled merrily by and farther down fed the lime-pits of the workmen, who were building Hadrian's villa. Hermas seated himself in this leafy nook, then lying on his back gazed through the thick foliage of the pines into the dark-blue sky, and thought of the cedars of the old covenant, the green trees planted by living waters, the birds that dwell in the branches of the huge tree which grew from the tiny seed.

While the prophet was devoting himself to this occupation, three other persons who, coming from the Canopus, were slowly ascending the hot slope in the fierce glow of the sun, felt much less cheerful. The Caesar had dismissed the worthy temple-servant and fruit-dealer unpunished for their insolent lies; but though Hadrian played with them as a cat plays with a mouse, it was evident to both that their days at Tibur were numbered. It seemed plain to the temple-servant, that Antinous could no longer tolerate his presence in the sanctuary, where he daily performed his morning devotions, and Tryphaena could not conceal from herself that her tenure of the imperial flower-beds would be over, as . soon as the head-gardener heard how she had treated the emperor's favorite. Specially incredible did it appear to both, that Antinous would not seek to avenge himself, since their Italian blood had no conception of the young Bithynian's goodness.

"Let us wait here," said Tryphaena mournfully; "we'll throw ourselves at his feet and beg his forgiveness."

"That will do no good," replied the servant of Hercules. "So long as he lives, his mere presence will remind Hadrian of us."

This "so long as he lives," made Tryphaena thought-

ful. The Sabine's harsh features assumed a resolute expression, and she darted from under her tangled black
hair an enquiring glance at her companion, who was
looking aside, as if he had said nothing.

"One of us must go, he or we, that's certain," Tryphaena at last remarked. "If Antinous should suddenly
disappear, the emperor would forget to-day's farce in
seeking for his favorite; at any rate we should be safe
from the Bithynian's vengeance."

"Come, I have a plan," answered the temple-servant hoarsely. "You see yonder, behind the second
lime-pit, the old masonry which appeared yesterday
after the landslip, and you know Antinous seeks for
old stones and potsherds almost more eagerly than
Hadrian. We'll strew sand over the lime-pit till it looks
like the earth around it, then your Titius can show him
the grotto, and ere he reaches it he'll sink in the lime
and become an unrecognizable lump, before anybody
finds out where he is. At the worst people will suppose
it was an accident. Many persons have died in lime-
pits. Stop, I'll go to the temple and get some old coins,
they'll be the bacon with which we'll catch the Greek
rat."

Hermas had already lain some time on the warm
ground, rejoicing in the beauty of all his Creator's
creatures, when the movements of a man and woman
below, and the running to and fro of a little boy
attracted his attention. Through a gap in the laurel
bushes he could watch the three persons closely, unperceived by them in the gloom of his retreat. The work
going on among the trio seemed to him very strange.
While the boy brought sand from a high heap in one of
the workmen's baskets, the man and woman were

busily employed with shovels in covering the lime-pit lying close beside the slope, so that it was soon entirely indistinguishable from the sand around it.   If the enterprise had not shown itself to be a malicious one, dangerous to the ·community, the spiteful faces of the laborers, especially the jeering exclamations of the loquacious woman, would have left no doubt of their design.

"What work of darkness are they preparing?" Hermas anxiously asked himself.   "Tryphaena seems to be afraid."

"If the workmen find him," said the temple-servant to cheer the woman, who was glancing anxiously around her, "they'll keep silence to save themselves from suspicion.   Even an innocent man doesn't wish to be questioned on the rack.   But if we remove the sand from the lime directly after it happens, he may be burnt to ashes before the pit is examined at all."

Hermas had heard the last words distinctly, and no longer doubted that a crime was to be committed. . Soon the little boy came nearer.

"Lead him to this place," said his mother, "then move aside here and let him go the last steps alone."

"Wait," said the temple-servant, "we can make it still surer," and seizing a pole one of the masons had left, he tied his sandals to it, weighted them with stones, and thus imprinted footsteps on the loose sand, which extended close to the grotto.   "There," he continued, "now some steps turned backward, that he may not think of the lion's den."

"He has really concealed his work of darkness so skilfully," Hermas said to himself, "that unless angels accompany the victim, he must surely fall into the snare. The Lord did not guide me here in vain. I am plainly summoned to baffle this design of Satan." He looked about for a club and some stones, while the joyous smile that illumined his face showed that he had formed his plan.

Antinous had left Hadrian, in order to remove as speedily as possible the remainder of the soiled clothing, which had cost him so much confidence and peace of mind. The thought of getting rid of this Nessus shirt winged his steps. As he passed Lydia's fountain, he gloomily averted his eyes. A few paces farther on little Titius came to meet him, holding out gifts in both hands and whimpering:

"Forgive me, Antinous! I didn't know it was you I pelted."

"So you are allowed to throw things at poor people?" replied the youth.

"My mother told me you wanted to rob her. While you were sending her for the pears on one side, you meant to pocket the figs on the other, so I must take care. I pelted you, because I thought you were a wicked thief."

"Poor child," said Antinous compassionately, "you'll be a bad man yourself, if your own mother teaches you to distrust people. What have you in your hand?"

"I wanted to give it to you, so that you might be kind to me again." While speaking, he offered the youth a fragment of an ancient vase and the rusty coins.

"By Jupiter, they are rare pieces, Etruscan fragments and denares, such as I have only seen in the treasury of Hercules. Where did you find them, Titius?"

"The slaves uncovered some old ruins down below
here where they are building; when I was playing there,
I found a hole that extends deep into the mountain.
I picked up the coins yonder."

"You must show me," said Antinous eagerly; "it
will be something to amuse and occupy Caesar many
days. Guide me, Titius."

The boy ran on before, but a keener observer would
have noticed how he sometimes lingered. He turned
slowly towards the spot where the buildings were being
erected and walked silently forward, answering Antinous's questions in monosyllables or not at all. He
paused near the open lime-pit, but as if he had received
a threatening sign from the bushes, walked forward,
turned a few steps aside, and pointing to a break in the
sand before them, said: "The grotto is yonder."

"Why do you linger?" asked Antinous, noticing the
boy's timid manner. "You've probably been telling
lies again? Well, we shall see directly."

Turning hastily aside, he had just raised his foot
over the dangerous spot, when a heavy stone unexpectedly fell before him, splashing the liquid lime in every
direction.

"Beware, Antinous!" a well-known voice shouted
from the laurel-bushes at the same moment, "they are
luring you into a snare."

But at the first glimpse of the lime the youth had
already perceived the terrible danger, and as he turned
indignantly towards Titius, the sturdy fruit-dealer rushed
upon him like a furious Megara, to hurl him backward
into the pit. Antinous, steeled by practice in the gym-
nasium, was perfectly able to cope with a woman's
strength. He still carried the gnarled staff belonging to

his shepherd costume, and as it fell upon her shoulder the Maenad retreated with a loud howl.

"Hold out, Tryphaena," a third voice suddenly shouted from the bushes, "we'll soon get rid of the little fellow."

It was the cowardly temple-servant, who attacked Antinous with a long lever. The youth, in springing aside, came close to the edge of the pit, whose boundaries he could not distinguish, while Tryphaena prepared for another assault. But just at that moment, the temple-servant received so heavy a blow with a stone, that he staggered back, and as at the same time Hermas, swinging a huge club, emerged from the bushes, the abominable pair took to flight, leaving little Titius behind as prisoner. The child could not endure the fiery glance Antinous fixed upon him. Bounding aside, he tried to escape, but sank over his knees in the lime-pit. True, Antinous instantly seized him and pulled him out on dry ground, but the child's screams showed how badly he had burned his feet. Antinous instantly threw off his cloak and wiped the young rascal's legs, saying:

"See, you wanted to make a person who had never wronged you, suffer all this pain. Did you never hear the warning, that whoever digs snares for others, falls into them himself?" After carefully wiping the lime from the legs of the half-senseless child, he carried him to the spring, and tearing a piece from his ragged shepherd's dress, wrapped cool wet bandages around the inflamed spots. While engaged in this task, he suddenly heard Hermas's voice saying:

"In truth, you are not far from the kingdom of God, whose Master hath said: 'Love your enemies, do good to them that hate you.'"

"I owe you my life, my faithful Hermas!" said Antinous, raising his beautiful brown eyes with an expression of gratitude and love.

"Not to me," replied Hermas, "but to the Nazarene whom you despise, and who commanded me to be on the watch, that Satan might not finish his work."

Antinous was silent for a time, and slowly shook his beautiful head. Then he said kindly:

"I would willingly revere your god, but two things separate me from you. You ask me to revile all my gods as demons; Jupiter, in whose temple I so often and so distinctly feel the presence of the deity, Mercury and Hercules, who have faithfully protected me on a hundred journeys, Minerva and Diana, who have guided my spear, whenever I earnestly called upon them before throwing it. Were I to revile them as evil demons, it would be far worse than if I abused you, who have just saved me. But you require still another act of ingratitude. You say I ought not to be a man's favorite. But should I desert Hadrian, who believes in no one except me? Would he not go to ruin, if I too betrayed him?"

"The Lord, who saved you to-day, will lead you into His flock at the fitting time," replied Hermas quietly. "But if they tell you again He is no god, remember what He has done for you this day." Then, lifting Antinous's little patient on his shoulder, he walked silently beside the latter, who, still more excited by indignation than fear of the danger he had passed, told the Christian the story of the morning.

"You see, my good friend, to what the first deception leads," replied Hermas. "With the falsehood that you were not Antinous, not the emperor's favorite, you opened the door to the Evil One, and the Father of Lies

surprised unguarded hearts. Now atone for your guilt by
forgiving your enemies, and if any one asks who taught
you this, say: a Christian."

"It doesn't need your god," answered Antinous
smiling. "Hadrian's fatal advice, which I followed, lies
heavily enough upon my soul. They shan't be troubled
by me, do you hear, Titius? But, Hermas, if I see
aright, you too have concealed your rank, and are
walking about, as I did this morning, in a goatherd's
dress."

"I am now what I was and intend to be," replied
Hermas solemnly. "If you should need me, seek me
on the banks of the Anio at the sulphur baths of the
Albula, where my brother tends his flocks. I can no
longer endure life at the court, and the erring ways of
my family keep me aloof from my home. I shall go into
the wilderness, and see if God will speak to Hermas as
He did to John, for the time has drawn near!"

"You must not go without Hadrian's permission,"
said Antinous resolutely. "He would instantly believe
you a conspirator or criminal, if you escaped in secret."

Hermas hesitated. "If you are afraid, I'll ask
him for you," said Antinous good-naturedly, "but you
mustn't run away."

"I fear no man," said Hermas, "but I also need no
Caesar's permission when the Lord's call comes to me;
yet, that I may not lead Hadrian to sin, I will inform
him of my decision."

When the slaves had summoned Hermas to the
emperor's presence, they overheard a long, excited conversation in the room where the two remained.

"Hermas is bearing witness for the Lord," whispered the Christians among them.

It was even so. Hermas had unfolded the sacred books he had once given Hadrian in his brother's name. He pressed upon the emperor's notice the predictions of the prophets, repeated the most beautiful sayings of the gospel. But the Caesar, instead of the reported miracles, required one of Hermas's own experience. The latter could no longer restrain himself, and replied:

"The Lord has worked a miracle to-day, Caesar. By a falsehood you gave what is dearest to you to the devil, who is the Father of Lies, but Christ woke me to save Antinous for you."

Then, in the form of a lecture against Hadrian, who had drawn Antinous into deception, sought to destroy the youth's faith in mankind, set snares for the weak, and led them into temptation, Hermas now related the continuation of Antinous's history of disillusions. Hadrian listened with a wrathful smile.

"I am greatly indebted to your god," he said, "for having saved my dearest possession, and out of gratitude remit the punishment destined for you for contaminating my sword. My Tartarus has many divisions, and to you was allotted the *labor improbus* of opening to the dwellers in Hades, by your magic cipher, the way to the upper world. You are free. The coat you stole from my goat-stalls, holy man, I will give you."

When, on the following morning, Antinous came into the atrium of the palace and glanced towards the temple of Hercules, a gloomy shadow rested on his brow, because he would now always be reminded by the temple-servant's repulsive features, of the saddest day of his life. But he determined to conquer the feeling. He would speak frankly to his enemy, represent his wickedness to him, compel him to cleanse his hands, which had yearned for murder, ere they again performed any service for the god, and at the same time promise him forgiveness and secrecy. But when he reached the temple, another servant stood at the gate, who respectfully retired. Tryphaena's place was also empty. The hut behind it was closed.

"They have fled," said Antinous. "May little Titius's injuries heal as quickly as my wrath, and the wounds of their consciences remain open, that my unlucky masquerade may at least produce some good result." His conscience was calm, but to-day he pursued his way to the site of the villa without the sense of joy and exaltation, with which he usually descended from the beautiful circular temple and the view of the roaring falls of the Anio.

CHAPTER IV.

TOWARDS the evening of the day, which had been so exciting to Phlegon's friends, the latter, heated and weary, was ascending a narrow flight of steps leading between gardens and vineyard-walls from the temple of Roma and Venus, opposite the Palatine, to the *via lata*.

"Everything is attended to now," he sighed, " the message to the Senate and the large paper for the plans, the extracts from the Sybilline books and the flower-bulbs, a fresh throng of architects and secret decrees of exile. It's worth while to be private secretary to this restless brain, when he casts everything, from consular business to the offices of slaves upon the unfortunates, whose presence he still tolerates, and whom a foolish world calls his favorites. I pity Antinous while I'm away. The Caesar will employ the time in destroying every quality which has charmed him in the worthy youth. But the visit to the villa *ad pinum* could no longer be deferred. I must know what Ennia's ominous allusions to the state of the household really mean. Besides, my heart has fasted long since she left me at Aquae with the children, to return to Italy. How many years of happiness Hadrian has filched from me since I first clasped my Ennia in my arms, under the famous pines of the villa." An expression of joyous recollection flitted over the Greek's fine, expressive countenance. Before his memory rose the tall figure of the maiden of his love, whose reddish fair hair framed a blooming face with a pair of faithful, radiant eyes. There was a touch of sensuality about the full, soft outlines of her figure, yet it was active and energetic, while the face was both shrewd and gentle. Even as a girl she showed a trace of maternal tenderness, ever solicitous for the welfare of those around her. The freedman made powerful by Hadrian's favor, but who nevertheless stood an alien among the Roman nobility, attached himself to her. It was not that she had shown special reverence for his intellectual aspirations; she was a practical Roman maiden, and had inherited more traits of character from her father, the energetic Plautius, than from her mother Graecina, who walked through her own house as if in a dream —like a hen deprived of its brains, said her angry husband, who treated his timid, superstitious wife with soldierly harshness. Little, fair-haired Ennia was the only child of this strange marriage, and her auburn head was a guarantee to the father, that the race of Plautius, several of whom had borne the surname Rufus, would

be perpetuated in her, and not the degenerate type of
her mother's family, of whom Hadrian had said that
the last Pomponii all looked as if they were descended
from an ape and a goat, so closely were mischievous
restlessness and inquisitive stupidity blended in their ugly
features.

Amid her father's blustering and her mother's quiet,
ever-smiling weak-mindedness, Ennia had grown up
with the stability of a harmoniously-endowed nature.
She had inherited her father's practical, active temperament, and also resembled him in person, except for the
swollen vein on his brow betokening anger, while she
possessed her mother's inexhaustible patience and never-
failing kindness. Thus she blended her father's shrewd
vivacity with her mother's placid content, as if nature
had undertaken to create from two insufferable people a
character which possessed the utmost degree of amia-
bility. Hadrian, when seeing her pass between the
prematurely aged Plautius and the tottering Graecina,
had often quoted her as an example of the indestructible
vital energy of the Roman nobility, whose vigor even
triumphed over such a deformity as Graecina. If Plautius had lived, the Greek freedman would never have
been allowed to raise his eyes to the Roman patrician's
daughter. But he died, and the young nobles who sued
for the hand of the wealthy heiress, encountered more
obstinate opposition from her weak-minded mother than
they had anticipated. With the instinct of the feeble,
she perceived that each of them would install himself as
master at the villa *ad pinum*, and shut her up in some
room on plea of her weak mind. This consideration
was also a decisive one to Ennia, who clung to her
mother with the fidelity of a nature formed for loyalty

and gratitude. At the time of her father's death Phlegon had shown himself a faithful counsellor, and in the presence of Hadrian's official all the unjust pretensions raised by the Pomponian and Plautian relatives to the rich Graecina's property, were timidly withdrawn.

Graecina in return had pressed his hand, muttering unintelligible words about a germ of truth, that had fallen into his heart also. When Ennia showed her regard for the family friend more plainly, Phlegon ventured to try Graecina. Instead of the opposition he feared, Graecina, at the first suggestion, clasped his hands warmly, saying with a cordial glance :

" There is no distinction between us, we are all made free."

To obtain the consent of the family seemed a more difficult task, and not without embarrassment did Phlegon appear before its head to inform him that he, the son of a slave, who would never obtain the purple stripe and the fasces, wooed the daughter of a race so noble. But the man, to whom he spoke, well knew that Hadrian's freedman, without purple and fasces, possessed more real power than all the nobility of Rome, and with a slight touch of sarcasm, said that people were accustomed to extraordinary occurrences in Graecina's house and no opposition would be made to his design. Then began a series of blissful evenings, when after wearisome duties at the court, Phlegon sat on the terrace of the villa with Ennia, while the full moon sailed above the pine-trees in the garden, and the lovers gazed over the silent city at their feet towards the lighted windows of the palace, as the Greek told the listening girl of the strange doings in the emperor's house, where he played so important a part that people compared him to the great freedman

Narcissus, who ruled the empire under Claudius. Or, when the noontide heat brooded over Rome, and Hadrian was sleeping to make up the rest lost at night, Phlegon wandered over, sat with Ennia under the broad shadow of the pines, and read aloud to her the emperor's biography, which he was writing, or the odes he had composed, while she gazed quietly at her work; and the humming of the bees, the fluttering of birds and butterflies, the dreamy rustling of the tree-tops made the lovers forget that they were surrounded by the capital of the world and its bustle. Not even the Caesars, who had transformed the Palatine into a vast garden, could have made a quieter oasis amid the roaring wilderness of Rome. True, if the lovers emerged from the shadow of the trees and approached the wall, adorned with vases and statues, which divided the villa from the *via lata*, they were instantly thrown into the great world. To the left towered the mighty arches of the Coliseum, beneath which they beheld the long row of temples bordering the *via sacra* and the Forum; opposite, above the flowery sea of the Palatine garden, rose the magnificent buildings of the Caesar's palace. Everything here spoke of splendor, power, rank, and only lovers like this pair, the grave statesman, matured by heavy cares, and the vivacious daughter of a patrician race, could feel the contrast between their idyllic asylum and this theatre of the world, without a consciousness of want of harmony.

All these pleasant memories were passing through Phlegon's mind, as he reached the entrance of the *via lata*. He had not entered the villa for fifteen years, had not seen Ennia for two, and had been separated from the older children a still longer time. So he gazed with delight at the familiar rows of houses, whose front walls were adorned with magnificent statues, while over them hung luxuriant grape-vines, and clematis tendrils, starred with blue flowers, swaying gently in the evening breeze.

Phlegon walked on in a happy dream, until a broken place in the road roused him from his reverie. A gutter flowing from a neglected gate had transformed the highway into a marsh, which could be passed only by stepping from stone to stone.

"Nice neighborhood!" said Phlegon. "A Caligula is needed here! A Caligula who emptied into the aedile's toga the filth the latter had tolerated in similar streets." So saying, Phlegon passed the bad spot and suddenly paused in amazement. Surely these were the houses adjoining the villa *ad pinum*. Had he, absorbed in happy reverie, passed the proud structure? He turned.

"By all the gods of Agrippa, this is the rear of the house," he cried, "but where is the high wall, where are the statues, the marble battlements, the wealth of roses, and—great Zeus! Where are the pine-trees, from which this estate has derived its name since the days of the Scipios?" He closed his eyes, and after muttering a secret formula, lest some fiend had mocked him, opened them again—but the spectre remained. The splendor of the ancient trees had departed! Gone were the lofty battlements from which formerly looked down the merry Faun, Psyche, Flora, Hebe, and other pensive and joyous forms, in harmonious interchange with broad-handled vases. The wall, half-levelled, stood in ruins; behind it, bare and gloomy, rose Graecina's house, once the pride of the *via lata*.

"Righteous Zeus, hadst thou no thunderbolts to

prevent this crime?" exclaimed Phlegon. "Walls can be rebuilt, statues can be purchased, though none so beautiful; but the trees, the old pines that are unequalled in Rome!" It seemed as if all the fatigue of the journey was now felt for the first time, and his limbs had been suddenly paralyzed. Slowly approaching the gate and standing in the marsh formed by the gutter, he raised the well-known knocker to strike the metal plate.

"Well, who's in such a hurry? called an unctuous voice, that betrayed a eunuch or drunkard, from within the area between the vestibulum and highway.

"Open!" cried Phlegon impatiently.

"If you are a Brother," replied the voice, "you know the way; if you're a stranger, tell your business, that I may announce it to the mistress of the house."

"Open, slave, if you value your bones!" shouted the enraged secretary, trembling with fury.

"Graecina is at her devotions, and wants no visits," answered the disagreeable voice, while the shuffling steps retired until the sound died away behind the house.

"I'll burst the mouldering gate, worthless slave!" cried Phlegon, throwing himself with all his strength against it; but he instantly fell forward, striking his forehead violently upon the brazen bosses. The gate itself had not yielded, but part of the wainscoting he touched had instantly given way, having been sawed out and fastened with thongs. So this was the way known to the Brothers, and which was evidently intended to save the idle porter the walk from the slave's cell to the gate.

"So I must creep like a cat into the house, where I

hope some day to rule," muttered Phlegon, grinding i. teeth.

The sight of the area, usually so carefully kept, which extended in front of the steps of the house, sent a fresh pang to Phlegon's heart. The bearded Triton that had emptied the water into the round basin of the marble fountain had been removed, and as the outlet was stopped up, the water had trickled into the court-yard and undermined the wall. The open space in front of the stately house was overgrown with moss and weeds, while the walls threatened to fall. Only the door of the vestibulum separated Phlegon from his children, whose merry voices he heard within, but he could not bring himself to appear among them under the influence of the feeling that controlled him. He was robbed of the hour he had anticipated for years. Turning to the right, he passed the house, and went towards the gardens and woods. He would first learn the full extent of the destruction, and then appear as a judge before the grey-headed fool, and ask what she had made of the villa *ad pinum*. Already it aroused no surprise to see that the marble gods had vanished from the marble steps leading from the orchard to the first terrace. The stairs were sunken, almost dangerous, the climbing roses that covered the balustrades drooped half choked by wild grape-vines, here and there beseech-ingly thrusting a twig into the light, from beneath the luxuriant growth that stifled them. The forest had been laid waste till almost beyond recognition, but Phlegon's faithful memory for his friends instantly perceived that it was the useful timber a greedy hand had felled, while here and there a few camelia, tamarind, and other ornamental trees, looked down upon the surrounding

...olation. Their blossoms, gleaming amid the stumps and weeds, shone like silver chandeliers in the den of poverty. Through the hemlock and cypress-spurge, which had grown up in the path, Phlegon at last reached the vineyards. A few old trees still remained on the edge.

"The rascal, who rules here, has saved some firewood for next winter. They've felled from below upward, in order not to carry the wood far, instead of at least sparing the beautiful trees near the house and beginning with the last ones, that shade the vineyard."

As Phlegon spoke, a figure that unperceived had been stooping over a hoe, appeared among the vines.

"Eumaeus!" exclaimed Phlegon.

"It is I, my lord," replied the old man. "Thanks for remembering me."

"By Jupiter!" cried Phlegon, "there are many things here I don't recognize. Am I at the villa *ad pinum*, or is some fiend mocking me?"

"This *was* the villa *ad pinum*; it is now called *ad palmam*."

"Not for the stunted, sickly shrub, that stands in the place of the venerable pines? Who in the world destroyed the trees, the emblem of the estate? Did he not fear the Genius of the place, doesn't he still daily hear the sighing of the dryads?"

The old man shook his head mournfully.

"The Christians want the gods to sigh. Brother Nereus—you must know, my lord, that they're all brothers here—told the noble Graecina that the old slaves poured libations to the goddess of the grove, as usual, and therefore the anger of the Christians' god had fallen on the house. Everything lofty must be

brought low. The pine was the tree of the mother of
the gods, the palm the tree of Christ, and how beautiful it
would be to have a palm as tall as that in Nero's garden
to shade her house; when the wind whistled through a
palm-tree, its fans sent messages of peace to the spirits
of the dead—in short, he talked until the foolish old
woman said yes, and the very same hour he began to saw
and fell the timber, which the fat rascal hadn't tried to
do before."

"But, by Hercules, what harm had the old trees
done him ?"

"Oh, the neighbors wanted timber. I believe Nereus
made at least ten thousand sesterces out of all those
splendid logs."

"I suppose Graecina is crazy ? Speak."

"Not more so than she used to be, but it belongs
to her last superstition. They teach her so. You must
know that I went to the meetings for awhile too, because
they said the slaves would be as good as their masters,
as in the days of the Saturnalia. There I heard them
teach Graecina, that we must become childlike or we
shall not enter into the domain of their king, and a rich
man must be as stupid as a camel or he won't go through
the eye of the needle."

"Nonsense!" replied Phlegon.

"You can believe me, my lord," protested Eumaeus,
"I heard it with my own ears. They have perplexed
Graecina in this way, otherwise she's just the same as
before. They would have driven me away long ago,
and Tertius too, because we despise their mysteries, but
they need some hands to work; so I must attend to the
wine the Brothers drink, and Tertius to the vegetables
and orchard. It is seemly, Nereus says, that the wicked

should work for the righteous. So they leave me in peace about their god, lest I should demand the same rights as they."

Meantime, the two companions had reached the vegetable garden.

" Ho, Tertius !" Eumaeus shouted to another grey-beard, who was occupied among the beds: " Come here ! This is the man to help us. He'll smoke out the Naza-renes," he whispered.

" The gods be praised that you are here, my lord," replied the grey-haired Tertius, respectfully saluting Phlegon. " A master has long been sorely needed at the villa *ad pinum.*"

" I am glad," said Phlegon, " to still find two servants who work, though your field seems to be queerly arranged, my good friend."

" Oh ! my lord, is it my fault that cabbages and tur-nips are separated here as if in a nursery garden, and beans take the sun from the kitchen vegetables ? Graecina divided this acre into twelve fields, according to the tribes of the people of her god, she said, and that I might keep the barbarous names, wrote them with her own hand on white staves—see here, and here ! She even expects one of these staves will take root and grow green again the year the Messiah comes, about whom they talk so much in their meetings, when Brother Nereus sits on the throne, and Graecina takes her place beside Persis and Chloe. She doesn't know herself whether it is the staff of Benjamin or the staff of Judah, that is to grow green again, but comes and looks at the dry stakes every morning. If I'm ty-ing up the beans, she calls out that snails have attacked the land of Benjamin and destroyed the whole plantation of her god. Then I'm obliged to waste the whole morning turning over the cabbage-leaves and picking off the snails. Or if it's time to shell peas, she discovers that the land of Ephraim is too full of weeds, and I must thin them out. Or did you ever see strawberries planted in the shade of raspberries ? But the tribes must succeed each other here exactly as they are numbered in the sacred book, and when I begged her to alter the names of the vegetables she grew as grave as if the matter concerned the consular fasts. The little radishes must be called Benjamin and the big cabbages Ephraim, and the raspberries Reuben, because he was a thorny fellow. That has nothing to do with my business, and I wish she'd sell me, for I would rather bear the whip than this nonsense."

"But what put this abominable folly into her head ?" asked Phlegon.

"A Christian, who is really not a bad sort of man, sometimes comes here," replied Tertius. "His name is Hermas."

"Hermas !" exclaimed Phlegon in astonishment.

"You know him, my lord," said Tertius, "he was at the emperor's court, and boasted of having won you all. He explained the holy book, as the Sophists explain Homer, and when he came to the names of the twelve tribes, as they call them, compared each to a plant, adding all sorts of reasons well worth hearing. Graecina was perfectly bewitched by them, and the very next day I was obliged to dig over the whole vegetable garden ; then she divided it into twelve large and small beds, and set out the plants to which Hermas had compared the twelve tribes."

Phlegon burst into an angry laugh, and the two slaves grinned in unison.

"Please buy me, my lord!" said Tertius.   "True, I want for nothing here, and might· be as idle as the rest, but when I work it amounts to something."

"Never mind," replied Phlegon, "things shall be different now."

The slave shook his head.

"Your wife, the noble Ennia, said so too, my lord, and I believed, her.   But there was no change, and when at the end of six months I once found her alone and asked what had altered, she replied: 'Do you want me to deliver my mother over to the praetor and let him try her for being a Christian?'   'No,' said I, 'not Graecina, but Nereus, Chloe, Persis and the neighbors who use these wretches to rob her, to turn the water from the villa, and to steal our best grapes and fruits?'   'Isn't the praetor himself one of our neighbors?' she replied. 'How long do you suppose Celsus would hesitate to expose us all to trial as Christians?'

"'Then compel your mother to give different orders!' I replied.   But she only sighed, saying: 'You don't understand, my good Tertius; little can be done with people who defend themselves by their weakness.'   No doubt she's right, my lord," the old man added confidentially; "Graecina isn't so foolish as she seems. She's forgetful, owing to her years, but she only forgets what she chooses.   She's hard of hearing, like all old people, especially when she doesn't understand. Her eyes have grown dim, especially to the thefts of Brother Nereus, whose ribs I'll stick on the day the mistress dies, till he squeals to his god with his eunuch voice, like a sucking-pig that's being slaughtered."

"Oh! I know Brother Nereus already.   It was probably he who cut the door in the gate, so the cats

can find the hole open when they want to catch
mice ?"

" The very man, my lord I" replied Tertius.

" But how do the Galileans venture to strut so here?
Celsus, the praetor, is Graecina's nearest neighbor."

" The neighbors are to blame for all the mischief."

" The neighbors ? Are Celsus and Salvianus Christians too ?"

" No, but by constantly threatening to accuse Graecina, they do whatever they choose with her. Celsus,
the praetor, gets money from her; if she should refuse,
he'd send a lictor to drag her to trial as a Christian.
Salvianus turns her water away and fells her trees. The
ancient pines were hewn down, because they kept the
sun from his vineyard. ' He has moved the boundary
too, and takes the wood for his posts from her forest."

A longer stroll convinced Phlegon that the old man
had not said too much. The removal of the trees from
the borders of the estate had evidently been done in
the interests of Salvianus, whose land had also undergone a remarkable transformation. Where formerly a
scanty number of cisterns collected the water needed for
watering the plants, fountains and cascades, fed from the
villa *ad pinum*, now gushed everywhere. The worthy
man had left Graecina only sufficient water for necessary use, that she might not be forced to make complaints or weary him with entreaties. The boundary
was altered wherever it seemed to him desirable that a
tiny temple, arbor, or grotto should turn its ugly rear
wall to Graecina.

On the borders of Celsus's estate the changes were
less visible. He had an abundance of water himself;
wherever one of Graecina's trees stood in his way his

gardener had felled it, but compared with the brutal devastation on the eastern side, this was of little importance. Concerning the patrician's moneyed transactions with Graecina, the slaves could give no accurate information. The praetor, they said, wrapped himself in official ignorance, but Graecina always sighed deeply, when she received a visit from his wife, who was so very aristocratic that she was always conveyed in a litter over the twenty paces separating one door from another. She had been seen to re-enter the litter with a rare necklace, an heirloom of the Pomponian family, around her throat; Eumaeus had carried over heavy loads of gold, on one of which occasions Ennia, in the slaves' presence, had called the worthy neighbor a scoundrel.

Phlegon had now seen and heard enough. "The house is firmly built," he said to himself. "She may have destroyed the interior, but a building erected by Rabirius isn't to be ruined. The water can be conducted back, and perhaps Celsus, who must consider his position in the Senate, and fears Hadrian, can be compelled to make repayment. But no god can restore the old trees that have been sacrificed to this woman's folly, each of which was worth more than a hundred such creatures as she."

The sun was now setting west of the Palatine, gilding the battlements of the palace. The buildings of the city appeared steeped in a golden sea. The dome of the Pantheon, the lofty edifices of Trajan, seemed fairly transformed in the evening light. Like the Platonic ideal world, where pure forms dwell, was the relation this Rome bore to the coarse earthly one, displayed with all the defects and dirt of reality by the broad light

of day. But Phlegon was absorbed in his own thoughts,
striving to recover from the blow, which spite of all
Ennia's hints, had found him totally unprepared.

" Vengeance on the Christians and their abettors!"
This thought roused him, and he now went down the
hill with hasty steps. At the bridge, which led from a
lower terrace to a flat roof of the villa, he saw a fat
figure, singing a strange song, and at intervals eagerly
devoting himself to a round ampulla.

" I ought to know the unctuous eunuch-voice of that
happy songster," muttered Phlegon.

" It is Nereus," replied the slaves gloomily, as they
lingered behind the laurel-grove. Phlegon, on the contrary, approached the singer, who did not move from
the spot.

" What are you singing ?" he burst forth angrily.

" A song you didn't teach me," replied the fat man.
Then raising his swimming eyes towards heaven, he
added : " The Song of the Lamb!"

" Show me what you are drinking, fellow!" exclaimed Phlegon, snatching the flask from his hand.
" In the year of Pollio and Asinius, is the inscription on
the label. Do you suppose this has been kept thirty
years for your slave's throat, you dog!" At the same
instant he brought the bottle down with all his strength
on the skull of the fat monster, who covered with red
wine and crimson blood, instantly offered a spectacle
that perfectly harmonized with his howl of woe. " Tertius ! Eumaeus!" he shouted, " help, he is murdering
me! What, you laugh, you fiends!" he cried furiously.
" Graecina, Chloe! come, they're killing me!"

The shrieking lips had just been silenced by a blow
Phlegon added to the first one, when in the doorway of

the upper building appeared the tall figure of an old woman, whose white hair hung in disorder around her head, while her white robes fluttered about her tall, thin body as if it were a clothes-pole.

"Phlegon, you are killing my Brother!" she cried indignantly, and panting for breath, beating the air with her hands, advanced to meet the new-comer.

"Are these your Brothers?" shouted Phlegon, bringing down the last remnants of the flask he still held in his hand on the head of the slave, who fell apparently lifeless. "To-morrow he'll go to the praetor, and you too, destroyer of the world!" cried the irritated Greek.

The old woman stood before him with mouth wide open, while her face grew livid. She remained in this attitude, as if trying to catch the meaning of his words, then her vacant eyes became fixed and rolled upward till only the whites were visible, a convulsive tremor ran through the tall figure, and she fell backward into the arms of her daughter, who emerged from the gloom.

"It is my mother, Phlegon!" said a gentle voice. Phlegon's upraised arm fell by his side, as he exclaimed:

"Oh! Ennia, what a meeting!"

"Help, Persis! Chloe! Help carry your mistress in," said Ennia in terror. Graecina was writhing in convulsions, the women took her by the arms and feet and vanished within the house. Phlegon remained alone, it seemed as if he had raised his hand against a woman, and when he glanced behind him to see if any one had noticed his disgrace, the lifeless Nereus had also disappeared. This calmed him.

"If corpses come to life among the Christians, surely the demon that has entered into Graecina will depart." He went back across the bridge to the garden and sat down by a fountain, surrounded by a semi-circle of ruined masonry. From the iron pipe a few drops of water trickled into the huge granite basin, as if worthy neighbor Salvianus had counted them. So Phlegon sat in the twilight, absently drawing figures in the sand with a garden-tool carelessly left lying near, uncertain who was really wrong, he with his wrath in a stranger's house, or Graecina with her timely fainting-fit. Then he heard the sand creak lightly under a woman's foot. He well knew who moved with such an elastic tread, his heart leaped to meet his beloved wife, yet the deep wrath in his soul kept him in his place.

"Don't you want to see the children, Phlegon?" said a soft voice behind him, and he clasped the blooming figure of his wife, who stood before him, slender and rounded as Aphrodite. Drawing her gently towards him, a glowing kiss told her that even in these ruins of a baffled hope he still loved her. When his head had rested for a time on her soft, warm bosom his wrath melted, and he rose, saying:

"The villa *ad pinum* is a thing of the past, but its best pearl is safe and my own."

So the wedded pair, reconciled, went to their apartments, and when Phlegon, in passing Graecina's sleeping-room, heard a familiar voice muttering prayers, by which Brother Nereus was striving to keep away the demon of disease, he closed his ears and tried to hear nothing but the gay voices of his children, who now joyously surrounded him, and as he sat by his wife in the pleasant room, cheerily lighted by pine-knots, hugged by his little girls and cradling the youngest child on his knee, he would have seemed to himself an enviable man, had not the constrained, silent manner of the older children showed him that they knew of his first meeting with their grandmother. Besides, there was something else in their appearance that did not please him ; the way of cutting their hair and the simple style of their garments brought to his lips a question which he suppressed, that he might not instantly encounter fresh surprises. But when the little ones had been given to the nurse and the older children silently and formally held out their hands to wish him a good night's rest, he felt even more distinctly than at the first meeting, that the old pine-trees were not the only things he must mourn in his house, and gazed long and anxiously after his two boys and the slender figures of his daughters, as they disappeared behind the curtain draping the door on their way to their bedrooms.

"Ennia!" he said, fixing a firm, inquiring glance upon his wife; but instead of a reply, her blooming lips met his, her soft, round arms clasped his neck.

"To-morrow!" she said gently.

CHAPTER V.

WHILE Phlegon's tragical grief was finding an idyllic end in Ennia's soft arms, Graecina was lying in her own room, supported by pillows, listening with but partial attention to the reading and prayers of her faithful slave. Across her pendant under-lip came words like these: "Not the old tyranny again, not the old slave-yoke, I will remain mistress of my house!" Then another convulsive tremor ran through her limbs, the pupils of her eyes rolled upward till they seemed white

and vacant. Whoever watched the old woman's shadow
thrown sharply on the wall by the lamp-light, could not
fail to be reminded of Hadrian's malicious comparison
to the goat. The want of a chin made her mouth seem
large and ridiculous, the line of the nose across the
low brow to the hair was not straight like a Greek
profile, nor curved like a Roman one, but turned obliquely towards the ears. Her eyes wandered timidly
and restlessly from one wall to another, as she recalled
the many sorrowful hours, spent from youth up to her
fiftieth year within this room. When this late-comer
was brought to old Pomponius, who already had a fine
family of children growing up in his house, he cast a
gloomy glance at the feeble little creature's misshapen
head and said:

"Carry the sickly spider back. The days are past
when such children were exposed and left to die, but don't
let her cross my path again till she looks like a human
being." Even to the mother, whose health had been
impaired by the child's birth, the little creature was only
a cause for tears, as it lay in the cradle with distorted
limbs, gazing vacantly into the world with watery eyes,
and only showing by convulsive starts that it was still
alive. Little Graecina was committed to the care of an
old female slave, and left to grow up hap-hazard. As
her ugliness would have only impaired the family splendor,
it was almost pleasant to the parents to find in her feeble
mind a pretext for pushing her aside. The child never
appeared at the table, was never seen in company. She
was fed like an idiot, and people were the less disposed
to waste time on her education, as an early death was
expected, nay even desired. Graecina suffered less from
this state of affairs, than would be supposed. Her mind

was too weak to notice the neglect. She lived undisturbed amid her plays, dreams, and sickly fancies, in the most out-of-the-way corners of the house. No one opposed her wishes, and the slaves, the only persons to whom she clung, remembered that after all Graecina would finally inherit a small portion of the great estates, and it would be wise to win the grateful, kindly heart. To this feeling was added a strong sense of the injustice evident in the parents' conduct, so they prepared all sorts of amusements for the feeble little girl, who crept from one corner of the house to another. Her whole life was one long game. Even when all the other children of her age began to study, she still sat in her corners, where she had collected colored pebbles, flower-seeds, plants and tame animals. Here she could remain day after day, unweariedly arranging her treasures in childish combinations. The young girl had now grown old enough to repay the slaves for their love. She asked her mother for this and that favor, which the latter granted all the more readily, because she had so little else to give the poor creature. It now became Graecina's delight to share her presents with the slaves. Her pale eyes sparkled with a brighter light, and her large mouth, with its drooping under-lip, curved in pleasant lines. Soon she was told by the slaves, that some day she too would be a mistress and have property herself. The young girl was greatly pleased, because she could then do so much good.

In her thirteenth year an event occurred, which caused a great change in her family and especially her own destiny. All Pomponius's blooming children sickened in a single day, just as preparations were being made for the oldest daughter's marriage and the oldest son's entrance into the army. A mysterious disease attacked them, which varied in duration, but terminated fatally in every case. It was rumored that poison had been at work—but why had it spared Graecina? She had not been present at the family meals, said most persons. Some sudden illness might have assisted. The heads of the Roman aristocracy were again falling so numerously, that the murderer might have received his reward ere he had removed Pomponius's last heir. The nobility of Rome guessed at this and that author of the murder, but in the slaves' quarters conjecture took a very different course. "There has been no accident at work," was whispered here; "the sick child's favorites have helped her to the great inheritance." From the moment that their children became ashes, whose names looked mournfully down from the urns in the monument on the Appian Way, the parents vowed to the *dii Manes* of the dead, to atone for the wrong formerly done Graecina, for the aged pair looked upon the visitation as a punishment. Graecina, so far as she was capable of it, should be educated, that a suitable marriage might thwart the plans of the poisoner, who was perhaps still lurking somewhere in the background. But when an attempt was made to cultivate the intellect of the girl of thirteen, they first perceived how much had been neglected. Her mind was not only backward, but interested solely in the most trivial, childish things, and it was almost incredible in what ridiculous channels it preferred to go. On the other hand, her will was developed all the more strongly, because no one had thought it worth while to oppose it. In her secluded corners she had tolerated nothing, that did not proceed from her own wish. Besides the cowardice and love of concealment, fostered by being always excluded from the public rooms of the house, there was in her nature an immense amount of obstinacy and self-will, in all matters where nothing could be done by force. This obstinacy was all the greater, because not counterbalanced by reason. She persisted and persisted in a whim, without really knowing why, except that it was unendurable to her to do anything which did not emanate from her own will. She opposed an obstinate, though perfectly amiable resistance to the pedagogue, who was to instruct her in reading, writing, music and the Greek language.

"How do you find my daughter?" asked old Pomponius at the end of several months.

"Stupid and obstinate," was the philosopher's angry reply.

They were obliged to give up the attempt. The young girl again retreated with her slaves to her secluded nooks. At last one day the mother found in a corner of the attic innumerable wax tablets, on which exercises in writing were scrawled. Old Pomponius met his daughter in the woods, reading aloud with such eagerness, that she failed to hear her father's dreaded step. The old people, in a roundabout way, discovered the slave from whom the girl obtained her knowledge, and encouraged him to pursue his task. He was bribed to make Graecina take pleasure in gaining information in other departments of knowledge. By these strange paths they at last approached nearer to the goal, than was at first deemed possible. Graecina was now little inferior in elementary education to many normally gifted, but idle daughters of other families; but her negligent bearing, awkward movements, and manner of eating could no

longer be eradicated. She still remained an unlovely
object. In time her parents' interest in her future again
became paralyzed. The first emotion aroused by the
loss of their children was over, no one could recall
their dust to life. The attempt to make Graecina a
worthy representative of the family seemed hopeless.
Only for a short time did she seem able to gratify her
parents' ambition, when Julia, Drusus's daughter, felt a
compassionate interest in the poor creature. But the
strange friendship was scarcely formed, when Messalina's
poison snatched Julia away.

Then the parents invented the legend, which flattered
their vanity, that grief for Julia's death had clouded
Graecina's intellect. As a matter of fact, she was again
pushed aside, harshly treated when she ventured upon
any of her follies, and allowed to do what she chose in
her corners, if only the guests of the house saw as little
of her as possible. Here she soon relapsed into her old
childish follies. If she had no will in the great world,
things should go all the more to her mind in her own
little kingdom. Articles must lie exactly where she
ordered, and as her arrangements had no secret motive
or connection, she tormented her slave-women all day
long, though the most good-natured creature in the
world. No plant was permitted to grow as it desired.
If it had four branches on one side and three on the
other, she broke off the fourth, that the stronger side
might not feel proud. If a flower-stalk shot towards
the sun, she instantly turned it to the corner, that
the other side might also enjoy the pleasure of the light.
Once her finch laid four eggs, her parrot none, so she
took two of the finch's eggs and gave them to the
latter, and then was very angry because both birds

deserted their nests. Soon, to the haughty father's great vexation, society was full of tales of the eccentricities of the future heiress of his race. It was said she hatched the eggs of the birds in the aviary herself, and blew upon the branches of her flowering plants for hours, to balance the influence of the west wind.

In spite of this chronicle of follies, the wealthy heiress did not lack suitors. So long as the old man felt possessed of his full vigor, he would not permit his feeble daughter to marry. He remembered the fate of his murdered family, and avoided giving himself an heir. The young nobles, who pressed forward to woo this Helena, inspired him with little confidence. Moreover, he felt small interest in grandchildren, who might descend from Graecina's union with a stranger. It had been his object to see his ancient race worthily represented. Now he was forced to perceive that human arrogance has no power over Nature. Late in life, he had formed a friendship with a brave soldier, a distant cousin of the aristocratic Plautian family, who after a glorious military career wished to settle at Tibur, where stood the tomb of his ancestors. But idleness did not long suit the sturdy soldier, and he willingly aided his old comrade, Pomponius, in the management of his estates. Thus the latter felt a desire that even after his death, the property might remain under his friend's charge. Although Plautius might easily have been Graecina's father, Pomponius proposed that he should marry her and thus secure the inheritance. After some hesitation, Plautius consented. Thus the marriage was arranged like the sale of an estate, and was so intended by Plautius. Graecina's obstinacy was conquered in the usual way—by winning the slaves to the plan.

She herself was better pleased with the stately soldier
than with the young dandies, who had pursued her
with flattery, whose sarcasm she probably felt. The old
people died soon after their daughter's marriage, and
Plautius moved into the villa *ad pinum*. His wife
bestowed upon him a little daughter, who completely
denied her descent from so ugly a mother. From the
first day of her birth a charming little creature with
bright, merry eyes, little Ennia was to her father a sunbeam in his otherwise dreary house, to her mother an
object of worship, by which she was elevated herself.
Graecina, however, soon became as subservient to
her husband as she had been to her father. At first
Plautius had thought it an easy matter to rule so weak
a wife, thirty years his junior, who never ventured upon
open opposition, but soon perceived that she was by no
means so easy to guide as he supposed. She never
objected to his arrangements, except by an indistinct
murmur, but evaded them with an inventive cunning he
had never expected. The falsehood and cowardice of
this conduct exasperated his frank, resolute nature. At
every question Graecina watched his face, to shape her
answer accordingly; if the vein on his forehead swelled
larger, a contrary reply instantly followed, and if he
then asked what he was now to believe, might receive
a third and fourth into the bargain, all contradicting each
other, after which the discussion usually ended in a
burst of tears, while the husband angrily left the room.
Then he returned to the treatment to which Graecina
had been accustomed from her youth, and apparently
liked best. All the more important matters were settled
without consulting her, her foolish objections ignored as
mere useless noise; but she was permitted to rummage

among her secret drawers, rooms and corners, and as during her father's lifetime, again confined to intercourse with the slaves, whose views of the world, sympathies and antipathies more closely resembled her own. Her opposition to everything that surrounded her, was increased by the harshness with which her husband treated the slaves, clients, and poor people, and as no one noticed or troubled himself about her, the neglected wife, where a sterner spirit would have brooded over thoughts of vengeance, dreamed all the more frequently of a time when, by great kindness, she would win the love of all men.

Thus stunted and solitary, she first became acquainted with Christianity, and, like everything else that entered into her useless existence, began to play with it. Accustomed to secrecy, and fond of every form of concealment, she was pleased with these hours of secret whispering amid her own and other slaves. When Plautius was once absent for a longer time than usual, on some business for the emperor in Britain, she ventured to have Christian meetings herself at the villa *ad pinum.* The old enemies of the family took advantage of the circumstance, to accuse Graecina before the praetor of practising secret rites. The praetor saw through the informers' design, and, according to an ancient Roman law, referred the accused to the jurisdiction of her husband. Plautius returned to Rome, held a family council, and absolved Graecina from the charge. Yet there must have been some truth in the report. Some of the slaves were sold, Graecina was more strictly watched, Ennia removed from her care. Her existence was more slavish than ever, when her husband's death burst her chains. After his ashes had been placed in the ancient tomb of his race by the Anio bridge at Tibur, her own life first began. The attempt to wrest Pomponius's fortune from her and her child, was baffled with Hadrian's help, by Phlegon, Plautius's friend. He then went to distant lands with Ennia, while Graecina now lived happily in her villa amid her familiar rooms, and determined to make thorough use of the freedom obtained. The villa was completely transformed, with what results we already know. Christianity had little responsibility in the ruinous revolution. Yet it became important, because it soon gave a certain color and still greater familiarity to the intercourse between the slaves and their mistress.

Graecina had always been kept from the public exercises of religion, as well as all other public places. She had learned her superstitions from her slaves; everything that laid claim to objective value, she thought odd and foolish, like all that did not arise from her own mind. When still a young girl, the dogma of an expected Messiah among the Jews had been whispered to her as a profound secret, holy books were entrusted to her with the entreaty that she would guard them carefully. Her pleasure in concealment and mystery was aroused, but as yet she took no deeper interest in the contents of the volumes. Afterwards, when the unexpected trial under Nero came, she denied all her secrets in her usual way. The horrible persecution of the year 64 and the hatred of everything Jewish that succeeded the Jewish war, only made her think with a shudder of the perils with which she had played. The persecutions of Domitian and Trajan prevented her from again meddling with these dangerous matters, but under Hadrian's humane rule she heard more of the old secrets. The sacred MSS. entrusted to her had been buried under hundreds of toys for many, many years; only in stolen hours had she drawn them out, looked at them, and so far as her knowledge of Greek permitted, deciphered separate passages. Now that she was mistress, her slaves ventured to be more open with their mysteries. Chloe read and explained the Scriptures, and soon it became a necessity to her to be told about the Christians' Saviour, hear his mild, merciful words. To be baptized, was attractive to her from the secrecy that surrounded the act, and she eagerly seized upon the proposal to again permit the Brothers to hold meetings in her house. Her superb peristyle, with the adjoining triclinium,* was transformed into an assembly-hall, she herself rose to the rank of deaconess, and now sat daily before the benches of the common people, who never reproached her for her ugliness and folly, but on the contrary kissed and idolized her. Never had she been so happy. For the first time she experienced the pleasure of being popular in a certain circle, and if, here and there, a grave Brother or sensible Sister attempted to remonstrate with her about her domestic affairs, which were rapidly approaching total confusion, she had been accustomed to much harsher reproaches from her earliest childhood, and merely closed her ears, thought of something else, and in a few minutes it was all over.

How sincere Graecina's Christianity really was, would be a question difficult to answer. She heartily loved the Saviour, of whom the Gospels spoke,

---

* Triclinium, the dining-room of a Roman house. It was of an oblong shape and according to Vitruvius ought to be twice as long as it was broad.—*Smith's Dicty. of Greek and Roman Antiq.*

but the idea that he would return as a terrible judge
was really very unpleasant and alarming to her. If
Sister Chloe had not inspired her with such awe of this
day, she would have preferred not to believe in it at all.
So she tried to forget, and if a Brother preached about
it, shivered in every limb. The doctrine that all men
were brothers, that the poor must be helped, and all
property should be held in common by all God's children, received her cordial assent. What should she do
with her wealth? Her own capacity for enjoyment was
extremely limited. Pleasure in the mere possession of
property was foreign to her nature. She had been
scolded all her life on account of these estates, upbraided with being incapable of managing them, everything that was annoying and tiresome and disturbed her
in her usual follies referred to them; the sole use she
understood how to make of them was to give when she
was asked, and thus afford pleasure to others. One
shadow alone troubled many hours. Month after month
a roll of manuscript, bearing the seal of Phlegon or
Ennia, came from Germany, and her son-in-law's letters
always contained an injunction to take care of something she had long since lost or allowed to go to ruin, to
improve something that had long since dropped to pieces
or been given away. These exhortations excited her so
much, that she determined not to read them, but confine
herself to Ennia's affectionate messages. Thus ten
years elapsed. Ennia was surrounded by a family of children, and consideration for the education of the older
ones compelled Phlegon to send them to Rome.
Hadrian remained absent from the capital, and thus
kept his secretary away; even when the Caesar himself
could not avoid spending some time in Rome, he in-

variably left Phlegon behind in the province, to continue the administration of affairs according to his wishes. The husband and wife were therefore compelled to part. Phlegon was detained at Aquae in the Agri Decumates* country, where he was superintending Hadrian's superb buildings, his wife, after an absence of thirteen years, returned to her ancestral home.

Ennia's indignation at the state of affairs she found at the villa *ad pinum* was scarcely less than Phlegon's, although she had feared something of the kind, from her knowledge of Graecina. But to spoil the present by grieving over what could not be undone, was alien to her cheerful nature. She determined not to trouble Phlegon by informing him of these discoveries, and consoled herself by thinking that, after her mother's death, everything could easily be restored to its former condition. Her earnest endeavor was to keep Graecina from committing as many follies as possible, but she too had fought a useless battle. Her mother's love of secrecy and skill in dissimulation had greatly increased; she promised everything, always did the reverse, and then appealed to her forgetfulness, her deafness, her age, and declared that Ennia was injuring her health by so much agitation.

So Ennia was forced to let things remain as they were, but when she thought of the day her husband

* Agri Decumates or Decumani (from *decuma*, tithe), tithe lands, a name given by the Romans to the country E. of the Rhine and N. of the Danube, which they took possession of on the withdrawal of the Germans to the E., and which they gave to the immigrating Gauls and subject Germans, and subsequently to their own veterans, on the payment of a tenth of the produce. Towards the end of the first or the beginning of the second century after Christ, the country became part of the adjoining Roman province of Rhaetia, and was thus incorporated with the empire.—*Smith's Dicty. of Greek and Roman Geog.*

would return to this slave-governed household, the blood
left her cheeks, and she asked herself where all this
would end? Soon another cause of anxiety was added.
Ennia herself felt perfectly satisfied with the religious
rites of her youth, and honored the gods without thinking much about the matter—to ponder over unfathom-
able things was foreign to her practical mind. But her
boys were just at the age, when the human intellect
begins to think of the mysteries of existence. Phlegon
himself had fostered this philosophical inclination on the
part of his sons, by placing in their hands the writings
of Seneca and the equally famous passages from Plutarch and Epictetus. His own sophistical objections
had destroyed his faith in the gods of the people. Before the lads had reached any clearness of thought,
they returned to the capital. The formal instruction in
grammar and jurisprudence received in the lecture
rooms they visited, did not satisfy the spirit of investigation developing in the talented youths. Natalis,
the elder, tried to commence a correspondence on
religious subjects with his father, but the much occupied
man referred him to his tutor. Vitalis, the younger,
rummaged the house for books, and thus found Graecina's sacred MSS. The words of the Gospel and
Paul's thoughtful epistles fell like fructifying rain upon a
receptive soil. Assisted by the travelling Christian
teachers, among whom they made the acquaintance of
many admirable men, they read more and more of the
new faith. One day Ennia found them kneeling before
Graecina, who was embracing them, and to her horror
learned from their conversation, that they too had been
baptized. Wise and intelligent as the mother was in all
the ordinary affairs of life, she found herself helpless

where theoretical questions were concerned, and the lads' firm, positive answers utterly disconcerted her. It seemed very indiscreet and presumptuous, that her sons wished to announce a new god and profess a different form of worship from that of their ancestors, but she could make no answer to the objection, that their father himself derided the pagan gods. If she had not had her little children, she would have been utterly alone amid her mother's follies, the slaves' idleness, and the independent paths her older children had entered. She had inherited a touch of Graecina's secrecy, and concealed this important event also from her husband. Not until Natalis and Vitalis began to turn their backs upon the grammarians' schools and no longer heed her husband's positive orders, did she resolve to write to Phlegon and frankly tell him the condition of affairs; but at the same time an unexpected message announced his departure for Egypt and speedy arrival in the capital. What he found on reaching Rome, we already know. But Graecina now consulted with her faithful followers about the best means of maintaining her independence, that she might not be degraded by her daughter's husband to the position of prisoner in her own house, as she had formerly been by her own husband and father. Brother Nereus and Sister Chloe were even more terrified at the thought of an investigation of domestic affairs, and therefore took care to make the most exaggerated representations of the fate Phlegon would allot her, if she allowed him to have any influence in her home.

CHAPTER VI.

'The morning light streamed brightly upon Phlegon's couch; the sleeper opened his eyes and was gazing . with a dull, heavy look at the door through which it entered, when he heard footsteps· passing along the corridor towards the triclinium   Graccina could not possibly have so many servants.   Besides, he now clearly perceived that the majority entered through the garden gate opening on the *via lata*, and crossed the area one after another.   The murmur of voices, echoing from the triclinium and adjoining rooms, made him almost anxious.   His glance wandered around the chamber in search of a weapon, and he had already seized his dagger, when a sudden stillness ensued, and then a monotonous chant sung by about fifty men and women fell upon his ear.   He had heard such music once before, when on some business for the emperor he visited Hermas in his house at the *porta Salaria* — long-drawn notes, which with a sudden rise assumed an almost elastic character, then fell back into the former drawling, monotonous tone.   At last the singers paused. A powerful masculine voice seemed to repeat a prayer, or read something aloud.

Phlegon could endure his couch no longer, but went into the adjoining room, through whose opening in the roof the morning breeze blew cool and fresh.   For want of a slave, he washed the sleep from his eyes himself in the impluvium, threw on his toga, and walked lightly towards the gloomy room next the peristyle, through whose curtained door-way, unseen, he could overlook the whole row of apartments. It was difficult to find his way. Graecina had destroyed the garden in the centre of the peristyle, removed the fountains, filled up the basins, and covered the ground with a hard stone floor, on which stood two rows of benches. By adding the triclinium to this space, she had obtained a basilica with an open central nave, flanked on the right and left by two covered side naves, while the triclinium served as a choir. The place was capable of accommodating more than a hundred people, but at this early hour was only sparsely filled. Phlegon found himself face to face with about fifty Roman citizens of the lower class and slaves, who occupied benches in the triclinium. On one side sat the girls and women, among whom Phlegon, even had he not been their father, would have instantly singled out his own daughters, conspicuous by their blooming beauty, among those of the slaves and plebeians.

"Ennia isn't here," he said to himself in a tone of satisfaction. "But where can Graecina be?"

An angry smile flitted over his face, as turning his head he discovered the old woman's lean figure on the raised space in the triclinium at the right of the pulpit, where she sat in a separate chair, beside a maid-servant and a fat, good-natured looking plebeian woman, scanning with a slightly consequential air the behavior of the women opposite, while the chairs on the left, reserved for the oldest members of the parish, stood empty, with the single exception of the one intended for Nereus, who seemed to be continuing his morning nap. There were only a dozen men, principally slaves. Among these, as Phlegon now discovered with a frowning brow, sat his two boys. He was by no means in a mood to listen to the words of the preacher, who with a somewhat foreign, Oriental pronunciation of Latin, yet eagerly and warmly, addressed the congregation, some of whom evidently did not yield assent to his words. Suddenly it seemed to Phlegon as if he himself was mentioned. The little Jew spoke of a master, who returning unexpectedly from a journey, required an account from his slaves. He read a tale of a steward, who beat the slaves, became intoxicated, squandered his lord's property and was faithless to his trust, and the fearful sentence the master would pronounce upon him.

Phlegon involuntarily felt captivated by the Christian's · words, although distrust suggested the question whether his return had not put this subject into the preacher's mouth? Glancing at Graecina, he noticed that her lips were moving angrily, and a nervous quiver rippled over her usually expressionless face. One of the Brothers also seemed to perceive or share the feeling of the mistress of the house, for a long-drawn sigh, coming from the last benches, disturbed the speaker. Passages from the Scripture, in open contradiction of the explanation that the slave should honestly manage his master's property, were audible. " Where your treasure is, there will your heart be also," he heard a sighing voice say close beside him, a voice he instantly recognized as belonging to Nereus. But the preacher did not allow himself to be confused.

" I too," he cried, " have returned for the first time after a long absence to the church in Graecina's house, but as I passed through the outer-court and crossed the garden behind the mansion, I remembered a passage of

Scripture that runs as follows:" and the little man unfolded a roll of MS. and read:

"I went by the field of the slothful and by the vineyard of the man void of understanding.

"And lo, it was all grown over with thorns, and nettles had covered the face thereof, and the stone wall thereof was broken down.

"Then I saw and considered it well: I looked upon it and received instruction.

"Yet a little sleep, a little slumber, a little folding of the hands to sleep:

"So shall thy poverty come as one that travelleth; and thy want as an armed man."

"Take no thought for your life," sighed Nereus from his chair.

Others applauded the preacher; they too had already asked what would happen, if Graecina utterly ruined herself? To this thought was added fear of Phlegon, and a natural feeling of shame.

But Nereus now rose, saying:

"We have a different law here from that of providing for earthly estates. What says the Scripture: 'Go to now, ye rich men, weep and howl for your miseries, that shall come upon you!'"

"Sell that thou hast and give it to the poor!" cried Chloe's voice from the bench occupied by the deaconesses.

But the preacher raised his voice louder.

"The lord of that servant shall come in a day when he looketh not for him, and appoint him his portion with the hypocrites."

These words, however, were instantly drowned by the exultant shout of many voices, exclaiming: "The

Lord is coming! Go to now, ye rich men, weep and howl for your miseries, that shall come upon you.

" Your riches are corrupted, and your garments are moth-eaten. Your gold and silver is cankered;"

" And the rust of them shall be a witness against you, and shall eat your flesh as if it were fire," Brother Nereus's unctuous voice was heard exclaiming.

Graecina had sunk back in her chair, her eyes stared fixedly upward, then she rose and waved her long thin arms to command silence.

When all was still, she said:

" The spirit prompts me to obey the word of the Lord: sell that thou hast and give to the poor! Many Brothers and Sisters are still languishing in great poverty. True, the men and maid-servants are cared for by their masters, and each person is commanded to remain in the station in which he is called. But there are many poor people among the freedmen, and I have determined to give each a talent, that he may live upon it until the coming of the Lord."

A joyous cry of: "There speaks the Holy Spirit!" rang from the benches occupied by the plebeians. "Thanks, Graecina!" said others. The slaves remained silent, except Nereus, who muttered to himself like a drunken man: "Take no thought for your life."

" To obtain the means to do this," continued Graecina, I will sell what I have, the vineyards first."

" Not the vineyards!" exclaimed Nereus, suddenly sobered. " How will you strengthen the sick, to whom I daily carry an amphora, how shall we supply the Lord's table? Sell the woods, the vegetable garden, sell the water to Salvianus, who offered you large sums for it long ago."

"I warn you," said the preacher, "that the elders forbid these transactions. It is not seemly that God's assembly should be turned into a place of traffic."

"He speaks the truth," cried the slaves.

"Graecina must keep her promise," replied a dirty little freedman, whom Phlegon recognized at the first glance as the most obstinate beggar at Hadrian's court, where he always invoked the emperor's last favorite god. Besides, to his great satisfaction, it did not escape his notice that his sons exchanged glances of evident indignation. This discovery induced the watching Greek to interfere, and demolish at a single blow the spectre which had haunted him ever since he crossed the boundaries of this enchanted estate. Drawing aside the curtain, unnoticed in the throng except by those nearest, he walked to the pulpit, which the foreign Christian had now left, and rapping on the desk with the handle of his dagger, shouted at the top of his voice: "Silence!" The hall instantly became so still, that one could have heard a grain of sand fall.

A woman's shrill voice had shrieked: "Phlegon!" and the name of Graecina's son-in-law, whose sudden arrival had been the topic of the whispered conversation at the beginning of the meeting, was enough to diffuse an anxious hush over the assembly — Phlegon also noticed that some of the better-dressed people hastily withdrew and disappeared in the direction of the atrium.

This sight gave the secretary, who had himself risen from a low rank and grown up in an extremely humble position at court, courage to coldly inform the assembly, that the master of whom the preacher had just spoken, had really come, and would demand an account of the money, wine, trees and statues belonging to the house.

He would banish the stranger guests, and inform them that they had met here for the last time. While uttering these words, he saw Nereus force his way through the crowd to Graecina, and whisper eagerly in her ear. Just as he was on the point of ordering him to leave the room, Graecina rose, saying: "I invite the Brothers to meet here on the next Lord's day as usual. No one is master here except myself, and I shall yield my rights to nobody."

"Very well!" replied the Greek. "Whoever feels inclined to go straight from here to the stone quarries in Sardinia, or fight with the lions in the Flavian amphitheatre, is invited to meet here on the 'next Lord's day.' I will then make you acquainted with a master, who though not crucified himself, has already crucified many. His name is Hadrian, and his prime minister stands before you."

"Phlegon!" shrieked Graecina.

"Father!" cried his two young daughters, who had approached and were now gazing anxiously at him with their pleading blue eyes.

A portion of those present had again vanished through the side-doors, and when Phlegon came down he found only the slaves belonging to the villa, who were crowding timidly together, to hear whether Graecina would protect them, and his children, who pressed closely around their grandmother.

The eloquence of the Sophists seized upon Phlegon, and in a voice trembling with indignation, he related all the abominable things he had seen the day before in a walk around the villa, and after having, as he supposed, sufficiently crushed the aged woman, concluded by saying:

"I am bound, before the gods and men, to save my

children's inheritance. You have shown that you cannot rule your household, and must resign its government to firmer hands."

Graecina gazed around her as if in bewilderment; she had sunk back in her chair, and her long, thin neck seemed to be strangling a reply she did not utter. Her granddaughters lovingly embraced her.

"We have a better inheritance reserved for us in Heaven," they whispered. "We want no other."

But the repulsive voice of Nereus, who had crept behind the pulpit to the protection of the old woman's chair, was also heard:

"Deny not the Lord before men, remember the judgment."

"You here, dog!" cried Phlegon, turning pale with anger. Nereus, who still bore on his face the wounds inflicted by the bottle the day before, crouched silently on the ground without uttering a word in reply; but when Phlegon gave him a kick in his fat paunch, he met a glance from the half-shut eyes of the old tippler, that warned him to have the wine he drank in the villa *ad pinum* tasted ere he swallowed it. Graecina rose at the slave's cry of pain.

"Enough, Phlegon! I will not suffer you to abuse my servants before my eyes for the second time. If my house doesn't please you, seek another; but if you wish to remain here, interfere with nothing. I have been happy for twenty years, and hope to save my soul, we don't need your blows and reproaches."

"Perhaps the praetor will teach you another way," replied Phlegon coldly.

"I have long been prepared to appear before my judge."

"So are we all," added the eldest son. "Graecina will not go alone."

"Yes, father," said the daughters, "we will all go with her."

A murmur of applause from the slaves spared Phlegon the answer he was at a loss to make. He advanced towards them, saying sharply:

"Begone to your work, or you shall learn to know me."

When left alone with his family, he said to his children, gravely:

"Do you too go to your daily tasks; I will consult with your mother about what is to be done with you. Graecina may ruin her estates, but not my children's future!"

A harsh "go!" stifled the remonstrance which found expression in the children's eyes, and leaning on her granddaughters Graecina left the triclinium, while Phlegon stood confronting the empty benches, without having exactly the feeling of a conqueror. The odor from the slaves, which filled the wide hall, formerly so stately, the barbarous or grotesque figures that had been daubed along the whole peristyle beneath the Pompeian frieze, the vulgarity of all the arrangements oppressed him. He determined to go out into the garden, to form clear and firm resolutions in the open air.

As he approached the door, he saw beside a pillar the short figure of the Jewish preacher, who had just delivered so powerful an address to the congregation. He was about to pass coldly by the foreign Christian, but the Jew's large eyes, fixed so steadily on Phlegon's face, attracted him.

"You don't seem to find much pleasure yourself in

the state of affairs you have created here," he said to
the stranger indignantly.

"Do not lay to our charge the result of an old
woman's folly and the wickedness of a few slaves,"
replied the Jew. "Those who sit here call themselves
Christians to obtain Graecina's presents, just as in the
Egyptian temples they say they are servants of Anubis
to receive the sweet cakes offered as sacrifices, and as
they scatter incense before the emperor's busts, when
the Caesar dispenses his gifts."

"Nevertheless you are responsible for what a member of your community does in the name of your god."

"I came here, to be able to report to the bishop
what terrible progress the evil has made in Graecina's
household. Only have patience a little while, until the
bishop has set matters to rights here."

"I care nothing about the bishop, I shall go to the
praetor."

"Shed no blood, my lord!" said the Jew. "You
believe it will cool your thirst for vengeance, but it will
cry out against you night and day to the Most High.
For your own sake, my lord, have patience. You can
open the lion's cage, but when you have let him loose
upon your fellow-men, you will hear his roars in your
dying hour."

"I'll venture it," replied Phlegon harshly, and
passed through the door into the garden, over which
his gaze wandered towards the glittering pinnacles of
Hadrian's palace. The emperor was the firm and last
rock of his confidence, in case Graecina should not
yield. Looking for Ennia, to consult with her, he
heard his children's voices echoing from the playground, where he also caught the gleam of his wife's

white dress. As she leaned back in the low chair, directing the sports of the little ones, her rounded yet slender figure displaying its noble contour, while the small hand and white arm hung negligently over the back of the chair, and the sunlight flickered across her golden tresses, her careless, aristocratic bearing reminded him of the seated statue of Agrippina, the marvel of the emperor's palace. The children surrounded her, bringing her flowers, playing with pebbles, or making nets for their own hair.

"Is it so beautiful, mother!"

"Very beautiful."

"Mother, Tullius is taking my flowers away from me."

"Tullius must be good."

"My hands are dirty, mother."

"Then go and wash them."

"Tullius is naughty again."

"Tullius must wash himself too."

Such was the innocent prattle Phlegon heard, as passing behind the bushes he went down to the children's playground.

"Father!" shouted the little ones, vying with each other in bounding to meet him, clinging impetuously around him, and dragging him down to receive their caresses. Deeply engrossed by his own thoughts, he could only respond absently and mechanically to the endearments for which he had so long yearned. Then he sent them to the vineyard, that he might talk with Ennia alone.

"You know what happened this morning?" he began.

"I know."

" And what is your opinion ?"

" I had hoped things would be different."

" Tell me rather how the villa *ad pinum* has come to such a pass," he replied, pointing to the devastated estate.

" The worst had happened," replied Ennia sighing, " when I was at last permitted to return here from Germany. Nothing could be retrieved, and you know how hard it is to prevent Graecina from doing anything she has taken into her head. She listens to reasons without hearing them. She assents or remains silent, and the next day what she promises not to do is done, and if reproached for it she says that Brother Nereus or Sister Chloe has taught her a better way, and she must live up to her faith."

" But you see things can't go on in this way."

" What will you do ?" said Ennia, fixing her faithful blue eyes enquiringly upon him.

" I'll have her placed under guardianship."

" And do you believe a family council will uphold you ? Dear Cousin Fabius, who uses her purse to portion all his relatives; Frigidius, whose wife carries everything away from here that isn't chained; the Plautians, who were always opposed to my marriage with you ? Name *one* vote, on which you can rely."

" I'll appeal to the praetor and Senate."

" Phlegon, consider, you know as well as I, that the Roman aristocracy would never uphold the freedman against one of the Pomponii. They will cry out against your avarice, your desire to rule, the arrogance of the freedman, who wishes to lord it over a stranger's estate. No one will support you. Consider what an opportunity for heroism it will afford the nobles, if they can ill-treat

Hadrian's friend, without the Caesar's being able to harm a hair of their heads for it."

" All this is perfectly true, my wise Juno; but if you see so clearly what can't be done, tell me what might be."

" You can seek out the individuals, who prey upon Graecina. They will fear in you the friend of Caesar, much as they may despise the Greek. You can explain to them in a private interview, that they will no longer be permitted to take advantage of an old woman's weakness unpunished, that through you the whole city, Caesar himself, shall learn what sycophants are playing the Catos of the republic in the forum—they will not threaten to accuse you of being a Christian, and in any case the worst would be avoided for the future."

" This plan may serve for Salvianus and Celsus, but how am I to conquer the vermin that have built their nests in the house itself?"

" You must endure them, my friend. Graecina will part neither from Nereus nor Chloe. But they can do little mischief, if the trade of the principal sycophants is only stopped. The trees they have felled you cannot restore, the works of art they have thrown away are lost. Let it content you that the estate and the walls, which Rabirius, the gods be thanked, put together too solidly for even Graecina's folly, still remain, and Graecina is more than eighty years old. In ten years you must be master here, and I will obey you, as I am now obliged to obey my mother."

" If meantime another scourge is not growing up in the children, Ennia! By Zeus! how could you allow my sons, my daughters to become infected with the terrible superstition? Do you want to see the children dragged before the praetor, at the next hunt for the Christians ?"

"My friend, ask yourself that, not me."

"What, did I make them Christians ?"

"Yes, Phlegon ! Who was it that ridiculed the gods before the children, recited satirical Greek verses about the Olympians, laughed at Hadrian's superstition, and pitilessly assailed with biting witticisms every devout aspiration of their young hearts?   Thus prepared, your children returned to their grandmother's house.   But a young heart wants gods.   When it looks up to the sky, your wise explanation that it is air does not satisfy it, it seeks a mind for its wishes, an ear for its complaints. When the disk of the moon floats across the dark heavens, or the sun sinks like a fiery ball, it speaks to the lights you call stars.   I had told them that they were gods, you told them they were burning lights ; Graecina now came and said their parents were both right—they were lights which the kind God of the Christians moved to and fro, that the men He had created might not strike their feet against a stone.   She laughed at your wicked speeches about the gods, saying that their father was a clever man, but did not have the right faith, and then brought one roll of MS. after an· other from her sacred shrine. They contain many noble words, which I too liked to hear.   But there are also many other things, such as that people ought to give all their property away, that all rich men were sinners, and wild sayings that their God would come on the clouds of Heaven to battle with the emperor, that they must set Rome on fire, as they did in the reign of Nero, nay that their God would burn even the sky and the sea."

"The rabble must always be burning something,"

said Phlegon, grinding his teeth. "But could my clever boys believe such horrible nonsense?"

" 'They believed it at once. The books were Greek, which I did not thoroughly understand. But they were always searching them, and when I represented the absurdity of these expectations, they replied: ' They are mysteries,' or said the same things were in the Sybilline books, and then recited numerous hexameters the Sibyl had uttered, which sounded to my ears even wilder than Graecina's holy book."

Phlegon sank into a mournful silence. "I may have acted foolishly," he said at last. "Hadrian's mania for gods had irritated me to mockery. I am in a different mood now, I should give you no offence. The mischief is done, and will be hard to cure. The boys at any rate must be removed to a different atmosphere, I will take them to Bassus's house, their whims will vanish there. Do you consent?" .

"You are their master."

"Cannot Nereus be removed by the praetor?"

"No, Phlegon, and if you love me, say no more of tribunals. Do you suppose the scoundrel would quietly allow himself to be punished, without denouncing my mother, your children, as Christians? And would Celsus let such an opportunity of effacing the remembrance of how he has himself misused Graecina, escape? You will do nothing violent, that must plunge us into misfortune. If you wish to try to make the parasite and his adherents harmless, apply to their bishop. They call him Pius. He is a well-to-do tradesman, opposite the Theatre of Marcellus, a brother of Hermas, with whom you are acquainted. I know they boast of having converted Phlegon's whole household, and expect soon to win Hadrian himself. If you tell him of his followers' acts, he will probably interfere. Much cannot be accomplished with a man so thoroughly corrupt as Nereus, but perhaps something may be done."

" We'll try, Ennia, and now kiss me, my dear wife."

" Gladly, Phlegon, if you will promise one thing."

" And that is ?"

" Spare Graecina ! She is my mother, and an aged woman."

" I hope she will make it possible for me to do so."

" It will be possible, if you love me better than gold or land."

This was the conversation Phlegon had held with his charming, clever wife on the morning of the first day after his return, and it really seemed as if everything was to be made easier than the Greek had supposed at the first sight of the devastation; Graecina retired to her own apartments, where fat, whining Chloe read pious books aloud and talked to her about the signs of the Messiah's speedy coming. The rest of the day she spent in listening and giving alms to beggars, or sending her slaves to and fro with money and other presents, the gift often bearing no proportion to the long distance it was carried, or the money to the apparent need.

" We can't do everything at once," Phlegon said to himself consolingly. " Let us first get rid of the wolves, and then we'll drive away the moths."

So for a time he allowed his mother-in-law to do as she chose, especially as she avoided meeting him and always glided into her own apartments, whenever she perceived him in the distance. The slaves, from the first, had been inspired with a wholesome terror, when Brother Simeon's unexpected address had received so practical an illustration, by the startling appearance of Ennia's husband. They had all returned to their long neglected work, which they performed under Phlegon's eyes and with visible unction. The Greek had the satisfaction of having all noisy labor done outside his own door. In the garden, amid hosannas and halleluiahs, the slaves dug the fallow beds, which ought to have been sown long before, and the maid-servants beat the carpets while singing the Song of the Lamb. Even Nereus had fastened up the hole for the Brothers, and did nothing all day long, while apparently filling the office of porter. Phlegon looked on quietly at this also.

" First the wolves and then the rats," he said to himself, as he walked up the *via lata* towards the house of worthy neighbor Salvianus.

CHAPTER VII.

GREATLY in contrast to Graecina's dwelling, before her neighbor's gleamed a neat mosaic pavement, across which Phlegon walked to Salvianus's door. A touching motto, executed in bright colored pebbles, sparkled on the threshold. The courteous porter drew aside a Babylonian carpet, and in the atrium* Phlegon found his man, standing lost in pleasant thought before the impluvium,*

* Atrium or Cavum Aedium, as it is written by Varro and Vitruvius; Pliny writes it *Cavaedium*. Hirt, Müller (*Etrusker*, vol. i. p. 255), Marini, and most modern writers, consider the Atrium and Cavum Aedium to be the same; but Newton, Stratico, and more re-

transformed by the diversion of Graecina's water into a basin filled with leaping waves, amid which a bronze Triton spouted glittering spray.

" How can I serve you, noble Greek ?" said the corpulent man of business, who with a patronizing smile resting on his fat face, strongly reminded Phlegon of Petron's Trimalchio.

" First of all, with this Triton," replied Phlegon, quietly unscrewing the bronze statue, which he had recognized at the first glance as his mother-in-law's property. The fat man turned livid with rage and fear, and was on the point of shouting to his porter, when a glance at Phlegon, of whose return his clients had told him as the latest piece of news, sealed his lips. There was no doubt that the capricious emperor's all-powerful favorite stood before him, and he repressed his anger. Laying his hand on the Triton, which Phlegon had placed on the marble table behind the impluvium, he asked :

"Who are you, and what do you want? I didn't know the statue needed any repairs."

" Then it will be the more valuable to the owner. I am Phlegon, and come to reclaim certain things you

cently Becker (*Gallus*, vol. i. p. 77, &c.), maintain that they were distinct rooms.' It is impossible to give a decisive opinion on the subject ; but from the statements of Varro (*De Ling. Lat.* v. 161, Müller) and Vitruvius (vi. 3, 4, Biponi), taken in connection with the fact that no houses in Pompeii have been yet discovered which contain both an Atrium and Cavum Aedium, it is most probable that they were the same. The Atrium or Cavum Aedium was a large apartment roofed over with the exception of an opening in the centre, called *compluvium*, towards which the roof sloped so as to throw the rain-water into a cistern in the floor, termed *impluvium* (Varro, *l. c.*; Festus, *s. v. Impluvium*), which was frequently ornamented with statues, columns, and other works of art. (Cic. *c. Verr.* ii. 23, 56.)—*Smith's Dict. of Greek and Roman Antiq.*

have had the kindness to keep some time for the noble Graecina."

"I regret extremely," replied Salvianus, with a somewhat unsuccessful attempt to maintain his dignity, "that such a misunderstanding should have procured me the pleasure of an acquaintance, I have long and vainly desired to make. My noble neighbor sent me this statue as a gift at the last Saturnalia, or perhaps the one before the last."

"How much did you pay the slave, who brought you this masterpiece of Polyeuctus?"

"You don't expect that a slave, who brings a gift, would be permitted to leave the house of Titus Flavius Salvianus without a present," replied the other; "but as you seem to value the statue, and it is far from my desire to wish to keep an aged lady's gifts if the children disapprove, I will cheerfully return it. Caesar's friend may thus learn how loyal I am in my dealings."

"I am here for the very purpose of talking with Titus Flavius Salvianus about his honesty," said Phlegon drily. "Besides this Triton, which adorned the area before the house, stood, if my memory is correct, seven or eight huge pine-trees that shaded the whole *via lata*, beneath which men and beasts rested, and from which, if I am not mistaken, our estate for a century has been called the villa *ad pinum*. I hear that you have used these trees for a new building, and our people say you induced the old woman to thus despoil her house and the whole neighborhood."

The fat man's breath grew shorter as he listened to these passionate words. He changed color, then answered, panting:

"Follow me into the tablinum!* I'm not obliged to take an insult quietly, even from the emperor's secretary. Look at the account for the trees, and you'll see how honestly Titus Flavius Salvianus has acted in every-thing." Waddling with short steps before Phlegon, the fat man, panting for breath, bent over a chest of money at the entrance of the tablinum, raised the lid, and after some rummaging drew out a wax tablet, on which the slave Nereus testified to the receipt of a considerable sum of money for the delivery of eight large pine logs. True, Phlegon secretly doubted whether Nereus had really received the whole amount for which he receipted, as in that case he would hardly still remain at the villa, luxurious as his life there might be; but at sight of this document he could only ask, how Salvianus could have prevailed upon himself to aid a foolish woman in the execution of so mad an enterprise.

"You compel me to enter upon subjects concerning which I would rather keep silence," replied Salvianus angrily. "It is not my habit to touch my fellow-citi-zens' wounds. Graecina's sending me this work of art is connected with her horrible and criminal superstition, which I will not name, because some one might be listening to my words, and I should not like to be summoned as a witness in the terrible trial, which sooner or later will burst upon your household, noble Phlegon. She wished to get rid of the statue of the god, and I wanted to save Polyeuctus's masterpiece from destruction by reckless hands, so I took it. How generously Titus

* Tablinum was in all probability a recess or room at the further end of the atrium opposite the door leading into the hall, and was re-garded as part of the atrium. It contained the family records and archives. (Vitruv. vi. 4; Festus, *s. v.*; Plin. *H. N.* xxxv. 2.)—*Smith's Dict. of Greek and Roman Antiq.*

Flavius Salvianus restored it to the rightful owner, though for many reasons, no one could compel him to do so, you will bear witness."

" How about the trees?" said Phlegon impatiently.

" Well, it was the same thing with the trees," replied the fat man, smiling benignly. " Her porter came and told me his mistress had determined to fell the trees, because they were sacred to the mother of the gods and induced the slaves to worship her. I wanted to save them, because, as you said, they were an ornament to the whole neighborhood. By the righteous Zeus! I paid Nereus this large sum, for which I might easily have obtained timber more suitable for building purposes, so that she might not apply to anyone else. But instead of letting the trees stand until I sent for them — which, by Jupiter! would never have been done — the slaves felled them that very night and threw the logs before my door. I intended to separate the trees from the villa by a hedge, which would have soothed Graecina's conscience by preventing her slaves from sacrificing to the goddess, while the *via lata* would have kept its fairest ornament. I little thought my sacrifice in money would expose me to injurious suspicions."

" Then give me the receipt, that I may investigate the matter," said Phlegon harshly.

Fat Salvianus hesitated, but at last delivered up the tablet, adding:

" I don't like such complications, but you will consider that a trial would bring worse misfortunes on Graecina and your family than on me."

" Your noble views can certainly only yield you fresh civic crowns. But explain what generous care induced you to conduct Graecina's water to your villa."

"I needed the water," said the fat man more tartly. "What Graecina has retained is enough to convert the ground before your house into a marsh and flood the street. Graecina agreed to allow me to divert as much water as she can spare; she had her own reasons for doing so, and I advise you, as a friend and neighbor, not to disturb the arrangement. If I am constantly suspected, I shall be compelled to bring these matters before a court of justice, and on your head be all the consequences. I have served you as far as I could. Here my compliance ends. If you wish to ruin your family, I have warned you; for I'm a kind-hearted man and don't want to be the cause of having an old woman and blooming children die in the stone-quarries."

"You are an honorable man from tip to toe," replied Phlegon coldly. "But who tells you, that Graecina's safety lies nearer my heart than my children's inheritance? Perhaps I will take the risk, perhaps I desire a trial for Graecina and have means of rendering it harmless to my own family. What part Titus Flavius Salvianus, the man of ancient Roman virtue, will play in such a law-suit, you are best able to judge. You know I haven't yet finished my list," he added, as if at random.

Salvianus changed color and looked uneasily at Phlegon. "I can't do without the water," he said at last. "We'll see who has most to lose in a law-suit."

"Very well," replied Phlegon; "before we stake our heads, I'll offer you another agreement. You shall be allowed to guide all the overflow of water to your villa, from the height of our area to your lower garden. A pump, a hydraulic tower, or your slaves' pails can then convey it wherever you choose."

"And shall I then be left in peace?" asked the fat man craftily.

"You will restore the *boundary* as it was, and place in *my* hands, not Graecina's, a document, in which you promise to enter into no bargain of exchange, sale or donation with Graecina, without my knowledge."

"I must first consider the matter," replied Salvianus.

"You will place the document in my hands before noon, by the same slave who brings the Triton to my apartments," said Phlegon, with imperious curtness. "You will have the work of restoring the water to the old aqueduct above the villa *ad pinum* commenced by your people within an hour, and as soon as possible turn it into its former channel. When you have arranged your pond below, I'll see that you receive the overflow."

With these words Phlegon turned his back upon the fat merchant, walked through the atrium and vestibulum,[*] and descended the steps to the *via lata*. He had just finished telling the story to Ennia, when a slave who brought back the old bronze friend, placed in his hands a carefully-sealed manuscript.

"By all the divinities!" cried Ennia. "Hide the good sea-god! Graecina will fear every evil spell for her household, if she hears that he is again beneath her roof."

"So the gods of the empire must conceal themselves from the Nazarenes!" said Phlegon.

---

[*] The vestibulum did not properly form part of the house, but was a vacant space before the door, forming a court, which was surrounded on three sides by the house, and was open on the fourth to the street. The two sides of the house joined the street, but the middle part of it, where the door was placed, was at some little distance from the street. (Gell. xvi. 5; Macrob, *Sat*. vi. 8.) Hence Plautus (*Mostell*. iii a. 132) says, "Viden' vestibulum ante aedes hoc et ambulacrum quoiusmodi?"—*Smith's Dict. of Greek and Roman Antiq.*

"As you don't believe in these gods, respect Grae-cina's household rights."

"We will see."

The second visit Phlegon had to pay was to the neighbor on the left, and of a more difficult nature. Celsus was an aristocratic patrician, very influential in the Senate, and held the office of praetor, while his wife was one of the leaders in the highest circles of society. If there were persons who accused both of the basest avarice, the multitude accepted their conceited arrogance for genuine aristocracy, and the fewer the number with whom they condescended to associate, the more elevated in their haughty reserve did they appear to the people at large. Phlegon therefore enquired, with all due ceremony, whether it would be agreeable to the most noble Celsus to receive him. On being conducted into the atrium by a slave, he found a little, stiff nobleman, who even in the house did not lay aside his toga. The latter, with great dignity, conducted him past the portraits of his ancestors, which filled the tablinum, to the peristyle, amid whose beds of flowers he invited his guest to sit down, and instantly enquired about the health of the divine Hadrian. Phlegon praised Hadrian's excellent constitution, then passed to the praetor's public business, and skilfully turned the conversation to the remarks concerning the evil of an uproar about the Christians, which the emperor had casually made at the time of Hermas's release. He related to the praetor, who listened watchfully, several sharp remarks of Hadrian against the sycophants who took advantage of the Christians' dread of a trial, and then continued:

"You will perceive, Celsus, how little it would

accord with your dignity, to be numbered among these sycophants."

Celsus turned as yellow as parchment, while his eyes darted lightning flashes of anger.

"Why am I annoyed by that remark?" he asked.

"I entreat you," said Phlegon rising, "to repay the sums you have, directly and indirectly, extorted from Graecina by threats of dragging her to trial as a Christian. If your office demanded interference with the Christians, you might do this; but to profit by your official power to rob Graecina, renders you liable to banishment, if I should be compelled to appeal to the emperor. So I beseech you to restore her property."

"Has Graecina requested you to warn me?" asked Celsus.

"You will repay to my wife, her daughter, within twenty-four hours, the money owed by you and your illustrious wife, or I shall accuse you before Hadrian."

Celsus turned pale. Loss of office, expulsion from the Senate, exile to an island would at least be the result, he thought.

"I don't know what debts my wife has made," he answered coldly. "My business doesn't allow me to attend to every trifle. If I find your statements correct, you shall be satisfied this very day. I beg you not to trouble the Caesar with such follies. Will an order on my steward Quintus content you?"

"Perfectly."

"And what sum shall I write?"

Phlegon drew out his tablet, then thrust it into his pocket again, saying:

"You will want to speak to your wife. Perhaps her

items are not all included in my account, which relates principally to you. But I must beg you to settle the matter, before I make my next report to Hadrian."

So saying, he turned away and without any word of farewell left the peristyle, whose master stared at the ancestral portraits in his tablinum with a face, that seemed to ask if ever, since the battle of Cannae, a Celsus had played so contemptible a part as he did in this hour.

" He'll tell Caesar the affair after all," he muttered; "but I must remove this weapon from the scoundrel's hand," and going angrily to the treasure-chest in the atrium, tossed about the documents it contained. At the end of two hours, Ennia handed her husband a roll of manuscript, for which one of Celsus's freedmen requested a receipt.

After thus obtaining results, surprising even to himself, Phlegon thought the moment for arranging a reconciliation with Graecina had arrived, and begged his wife to take him to her.   Ennia had listened to his stories in her own way, without offering any objections, but Phlegon could not help perceiving that she did not set sufficient value on money or estates to express any special pleasure over the sums he had recovered from their wicked neighbors. The first nod of assent her husband won, was when he said that whether all the stolen property was really restored or not, one thing was certain—that for the future she was released from her nearest oppressors.

" I hope so too," said she, " but don't expect too much from my mother. The difficulties are in her, not in the neighbors, the servants, nor her relatives, who are neither better nor worse than people elsewhere."

With these words she rose and accompanied her husband to the upper story, where Graecina lived. The old woman started when she heard Phlegon enter, and hastily pushed aside a number of little heaps of money and wax tablets spread out before her. She listened silently to the Greek's report, her eyes wandering restlessly from one corner of the ceiling to another, and when he paused after relating what he had obtained from Salvianus, apologized for the disorder of her room. Phlegon, somewhat out of humor, then told her the agreement made with Celsus, at whose name she started violently. He interrupted himself to ask whether she had had any other disagreeable experiences with the praetor, and she hastily replied :

"Oh ! no, he is said to be a distinguished man, but lacks the humility I hope he may yet obtain."

After this reply, Phlegon quickly ended his story. But when he handed her Celsus's order on his steward, she thrust it carelessly into the folds of her robe, as one would put away a handkerchief. Phlegon asked if he should invest the large sum for her.

"Oh ! no," she answered, "Brother Nereus"—then correcting herself, "Nereus is unusually clever at such business."

"I hear he has received the sums you obtained from Salvianus for the eight pine-trees. Are your steward's books so arranged, that you can tell me how much you obtained for them ?"

"Oh !" said Graecina eagerly, "we keep an exact account, that all may go well, not only before God's eyes, but those of men."

She hastily stooped over an open chest, in which were a number of partitions, yellow, green, blue, decorated with all sorts of colors, and supplied with neat white labels, which instantly reminded Phlegon of the twelve tribes of Israel, whose acquaintance he had made in the garden the day before. At last she drew out a box, on which was inscribed: " For those who are in deep waters, yet not without hope."

Out of this appeared a small tablet, on which Nereus certified that he had used the amount received from the pines as follows: " For Titius three sesterces, for Ione four sesterces," then came a long row of trifling sums, and Phlegon was obliged to turn away and reckon the amount. At last he said:

" This isn't the two-hundredth part of what Nereus received, according to Salvianus's receipt."

" Oh! you've made a mistake in reckoning," said the old woman hastily, as she quickly seized her tablet again, and with trembling hands thrust it into her box and the box into a drawer.

" Not at all, reckon it up again."

" I can't, it tires me too much. Nereus had other expenditures. Besides, I don't want to be perpetually hearing about these money-matters. Everything is all right, don't disturb yourself. But I must dress now; visitors might come."

With these words she left Phlegon and her daughter, and vanished into another room.

" Accursed fool!" muttered the Greek, grinding his teeth, as he stamped angrily on the floor.

" You have no right to speak so of my mother," said Ennia reproachfully.

" And you neglect all your duties, when you allow this mischief."

" Change it if you can."

" By Jupiter! I will change it, and Nereus shall be crucified, so sure as my name is Phlegon !"

The husband and wife, much disturbed, returned to their rooms. Ennia sat silently at her work all the evening. The children read and spun, Phlegon paced restlessly up and down, reflecting upon the problem of how he might bring Nereus to the cross, without sending his own children to the stone-quarries.

The next morning also Phlegon was roused by the already familiar hymns, which, this time sung only by a few voices, echoed from the triclinium to his sleeping-room, adjoining the atrium. It seemed to be Graecina's usual religious service, at which the servants assembled. He rose indignantly. Ennia had provided for his wants, but this time also there were no slaves in attendance. The bath-room had no water, and to the spoiled Greek, this rendered the villa uninhabitable. He had seen the day before that Salvianus's slaves, according to his promise, had begun to dig the aqueduct; so he resolved, before the servants below had finished their worship, to ascertain how far the work had progressed, in order with the assistance of the old grey-beards, Tertius and Eumaeus, to put the lower one to rights again. While preparing for this task, his glance fell upon the droll features of the bronze Triton, and he could not resist the temptation of going out into the area and restoring the water-god, so long idle, to his former duties. But it seemed as if the Christian's demon had informed the mistress of the house of the danger that threatened him. When Phlegon went into the front garden, he saw that he had been anticipated. On the base where the Triton had been throned, was fastened a roughly-hewn lamb, from whose mouth and a wound in the side dripped the scanty supply of water that reached this last basin after supplying the house. A superstitious fear attacked the Greek, who involuntarily turned in his thumbs.

"Nonsense!" he muttered. "No, my water-god, we won't allow ourselves to be cut off so." With one stride he stepped across the outer basin to unfasten the animal, but could not succeed in loosening the screws. While still angrily shaking and pounding the statue, he suddenly heard Ennia's voice behind him:

"By all the gods! Phlegon, what are you doing? Anything but that. Graecina will pardon anything rather than such a deed of violence. Do you suppose the faith that induced her to sell the proud pines to plant yonder palm, will allow itself to be robbed of its symbol to set up our gods again?"

"Just to punish her for felling the pines, I'll destroy this absurd monster. Shall we become a laughing-stock to everybody who enters the house?"

"You will honor this god as little as that lamb," replied Ennia gently. "You are not master here, so no one will jeer at you. Don't let everything be wrecked for a matter, which, after all, is of no importance in your eyes. Keep your Triton until better times, he will be safer anywhere than here."

Phlegon sullenly returned with his bronze statue to his room, where he concealed it in his chest. After a gloomy hour spent with his family, he went to the vineyard to see what arrangement Tertius and Eumaeus had made with Salvianus's people. From below he saw the flutter of Graecina's dress, and soon distinguished her hurried, panting words scolding the slaves. She evidently heard him approach, and to-day her courage had increased so far, that, with her back turned as if she did not see him, she said to her servants:

" You have to obey me, not Phlegon — I am ruler here, not Phlegon ! I want everything to remain as I arranged it. If Phlegon wants a villa with unnecessary water, let Caesar give him one."

" So you prefer one that suffers from drought, like . this, Graecina ?" interrupted Phlegon.

" I want things to remain as I arranged them; I have my reasons," replied the old woman with trembling lips.

" Can't you tell these reasons ?"

" I want no quarrel with my neighbor, who may injure me."

" I have made him harmless. He has given me a written promise, as I told you yesterday, when you did not listen, to leave you unmolested for the future, on pain of having to deal with Caesar."

" But I don't want the constant trouble of so much water, the aqueduct was always broken, a pipe stopped up, a basin or pond overflowing."

" The slaves will henceforth work and attend to the matter, so the aqueduct won't be stopped."

" But I can't use the water at all. I've had another statue made for the lower fountain — the Lamb's wounds must drip, it mustn't spout a whole jet of water from its mouth, how would that look ? It would be absurd to degrade the Lamb into a water-spouting animal."

" I have obtained the Triton —" Phlegon began, but Graecina raised her hand:

"Away with your Pagan abominations. I forbid you to again introduce here the impurities of the heathen world. Leave my roof, if it doesn't please you;

who gives you the right to rule as master? Eumaeus and Tertius, you useless slaves, go down and attend to your fields and vineyards; whoever touches the aqueduct, I will send to Nereus for chastisement. This is the villa *ad palmam*, and your owner's name is Graecina!" After uttering these energetic words, the old woman turned and glided down the hill, now swaying to the right and now to the left, like a will-o'-the-wisp, but even from behind they could see how she was rejoicing over having so victoriously routed the enemy.

"She has at least the courage of cowardice," said Phlegon, looking after her. "It really seems as if I had undervalued her strength."

"You see, my lord," old Eumaeus began, "it's just as I predicted; Minerva herself would succumb in a battle with Graecina."

"Did ever any god witness such perversity as these Christians display?" sighed Phlegon.

"Ah! my lord," said the old man, "I've known Graecina from childhood, long before she became a Christian, and even at three years old she was exactly the same as she is to-day. She always seemed gentleness itself, and yet could see and tolerate nothing she had not ordered. She wanted to arrange and control everything, and thereby destroyed all she possessed. I gave her a little lemon-tree, and she instantly broke two or three lemons from every bough, because she wanted each branch to bear the same number, that it might be fairly treated, and as she transplanted it every week, it withered in a month. I gave her a bird that was setting on some eggs, but the third week she drove it from its nest, because her Pliny said if the young birds were not hatched the third week, the eggs were bad, and she didn't want the bird to trouble itself for nothing. But the little thing grieved itself to death. Sometimes she thought she must help Jupiter rain and Boreas blow, or matters wouldn't go right. As she now compels Tertius to plant the beans and cresses in twelve rows, I was then obliged to put her bowl of pap in the middle of a certain square of the table, her bread in another, her plate in the centre of a third, otherwise no blows would have induced her to eat a mouthful. So in her garden she turned and twisted, dug up and transplanted, till almost everything was destroyed, even before she became a Christian. Then, to be sure, matters grew still worse. First she aimed at the ornamental trees. They must be cut down, because she wanted nothing but wood that bore fruit. So we planted plum and apple-trees in the pleasure-garden."

"But when the fruit is ripe," added Tertius, "she lets it rot."

"Yes, why don't you gather the fruit when it ripens?" said Phlegon angrily.

"Oh! my lord, do not believe that she would allow any one to do work she has not ordered. If she sees a ladder carried by, if she hears the blows of a pole, she instantly appears on the roof, screaming in her feeble voice, which nevertheless can be heard for half a mile. 'Tertius, I have some money to send a poor man in the Transtiberian district,' and then starts me with half an as* to the end of the city; before I can get back,

---

* As, the earliest denomination of money, and the constant unit of value, in the Roman and old Italian coinages, was made of the mixed metal Aes. Like other denominations of money, it no doubt originally signified a pound weight of copper uncoined: this is expressly stated by Timaeus, who ascribes the first coinage of *aes* to Servius Tullius.—*Smith's Dicty. of Greek and Roman Antiq.*

Nereus and the neighbors' slaves have stolen the fruit — so I'd rather let it rot. If any work is suggested to her, you may be perfectly sure she will instantly order the opposite."

"There will be queer doings to-day," Eumaeus added with a disagreeable laugh. "She has sent Chloe through the whole community, to say that yesterday, before sunset, her God restored property of which she had been robbed, but she wished to give it before another sunset to the poor who suffered for righteousness' sake, that the sun might not go down upon her wrath. See, the procession is already beginning."

In fact Phlegon saw from the terrace, to which he had descended with his two companions, an old beggar woman totter with edifying slowness across the area and enter the vestibulum. After a time she returned with a small packet, which on reaching the front garden she instantly tore open, hastily counted some pieces of money, thrust them into her pocket and vanished with winged feet.

"That's old Philaenis, who trains young maid-servants for service," said Tertius spitefully. "Look! there's her neighbor, the worthy Messia. She plies the same trade. But who's that coming, leading a boy by the hand? She was never here before."

"I know her," said Phlegon. "It's the fruit-seller from the villa Quirinus at Tibur, with her son Titius. Could I have eaten my mother-in-law's fruit with Antinous at Tibur? I certainly didn't dream of that." Soon after Tryphaena appeared, weighing a little packet in her hand, while little Titius joyously waved a similar one in the air.

"A disgusting sight!" said Phlegon angrily, turning

away in order not to see the new groups of persons, who now arrived in increasing numbers.

"Yes, my dear lord," said Eumaeus, "how could you put the money in her hands? We've long been used to seeing unexpected sums, which Graecina considers gifts from her god, find their way to the Brothers, or the so-called poor."

"So this was my first success, of which I was so proud," muttered Phlegon. The day was completely poisoned, even the familiarity of the old slaves, who treated him as a sort of ally, annoyed him. He hastily turned his back upon them, and went into the house.

" He wanted to bring Graecina to reason, and frets himself green and yellow the very first day he makes the attempt. He won't stand it long," said Eumaeus.

"Well," replied the other, " Nereus at least got the hole in his head and the scars on his cheeks, which he scratches open every morning, to remind Graecina that he's not only a confessor, but a martyr. Come, we'll gather the peaches and carry them into the kitchen, before the martyr devours them."

" He won't need to scratch open the hole I'll make in him some day. It will not heal in a hurry!" said Tertius, ending the edifying conversation by spitting into his hands and making a gesture, which at least came from his heart.

CHAPTER VIII.

THE first battles had shown Phlegon, that Graecina was not so easily managed as he supposed. Discouraged and disheartened, he sat on the roof of the villa, gazing down at the bare, neglected terraces, which had once been so brilliantly adorned, when he heard a light step behind him. He thought it was Ennia, but irritated and vexed, averted his head. A girl's soft hand slipped a roll of parchment into his lap.

"Is it you, Paula! What have you brought your father?" he asked, looking up affectionately at the pure, fresh face of his fifteen-year-old daughter.

"You think our faith is evil, father, and after what you have seen and heard, that doesn't surprise me; but it has not always been so here, and the gospel did not teach Nereus and Chloe their laziness and wickedness."

"Did not your prophet say yesterday: 'By their fruits ye shall know them.' Why am I not to say the same of your religion?"

"I cannot argue with you, father," said the young girl gently. "But I entreat you, read this book and learn whether it teaches us any one of the things, for which you reproach us. You are so good and noble, you will not be able to help loving the Lord too."

While his daughter spoke, Phlegon had mechanically opened the roll of MS. and as he folded it back, said:

"See, here are the words Nereus was continually groaning yesterday: 'And why take ye thought for raiment ?   Consider the lilies of the field, how they grow; they toil not, neither do they spin—'"

"But father," interrupted Paula, "only come into our room and see how much we have spun this winter. See if everything doesn't go on in a more orderly way than with Nereus and Chloe."

"Then you don't act according to the directions of your sacred book," replied Phlegon. "It certainly says here that people must not spin or work."

"Oh, it doesn't mean that. Only we ought not to worry about it, but procure our food and raiment as quietly and trustingly as the flowers, which surely obtain food and clothing without making much ado about it."

"But how are people to be satisfied in winter, if nobody gathers into barns?"

"Please, father, come into our store-rooms and the kitchen and pantry, and see how mother keeps everything in order. It looks very different from idle Chloe's rule."

"That's because your mother is no Christian."

"Then I'll take you to other members of the community, that you may see how their homes look."

"I saw enough yesterday," replied Phlegon angrily.

"Then at least please read the whole of this book, and not merely single sentences."

"For your sake, my child," he replied, pressing a kiss upon her pure brow.

The young girl glided joyously away, and Phlegon turned the MS. in his hands. At last, as he had promised the child, he began to read a little. But his mind was too much embittered for him to find anything in the book except a confirmation of his reproaches. "What more shall I read here than I have always asserted?" he exclaimed. "We must allow ourselves to be beaten and trampled under foot like that cowardly Nereus, we must squander our property on beggars like that wise Graecina, we must neither sew nor spin, like idle Chloe, so it stands written here, and so have they done. The book is like the people, and the people are like the book,"—and he flung it into a corner, where poor Paula in the evening sorrowfully picked it up.

The calmness and gentleness, which emanating from Ennia, pervaded her whole family, did not fail to exert its influence on her husband also. He determined to avoid any discussion, nay, even controlled his indignation so far, that he again approached Graecina and endeavored to move her by friendly discussions and reasoning. But this method also proved fruitless.

"Ennia is perfectly right," he said to himself at last. "People who defend themselves by their weakness are the most difficult to manage. To interfere officially, is to deliver the poor old woman to justice; to reproach her, brings on an attack of convulsions; to secretly take things out of her hands, is to rob a weak-minded person." So as he had obtained a longer leave of absence, he resolved to wait for a time, hoping that some lucky accident might furnish an expedient. But this quiet looking-on was far harder than he had expected. True, the slaves had gone to work again, as Ennia noticed with pleasure. They feared in Phlegon the coming master. But Graecina seemed to perceive the change with annoyance rather than pleasure, and Phlegon soon had an opportunity to convince himself of the truth of old Tertius's assertion concerning the restless Graecina's inventive genius in disturbing, under all possible pretexts, the slaves at their work, calling them away, or ordering them to restore the confusion which, with the best intentions, they had endeavored to remove. After a few days the zeal of the servants, so uselessly sent to and fro, subsided, and not until the former sweet old indolence had again settled upon the villa *ad pinum*, did its mistress seem again at ease.

Phlegon had occasionally attempted to call her attention to some great evil, but she never had seen, nor would see what lay directly before her eyes. Any understanding between them was impossible. The motives from which she acted had no existence for him, and those from which he acted none for her. She ordered things to be done because they were touching, symbolical, full of meaning, or recalled some beautiful saying, or holy event. He wanted order, economy, thrift, and strict justice made the rule of the household. If he gazed at her like an idiot, when she told him that her principal reason for not liking Tertius was because he always struck his spade so furiously into the ground, as if he really wanted to hurt the earth, she could only pity him for seeing in Brother Nereus's swimming eyes nothing but the consequences of drink, and not the secret emotion of a regenerate heart. If on his return from the city, he found the door of the villa standing open to thieves and beggars, he probably uttered an angry oath, exclaiming: "What fiend has kept a hole open here?" Graecina in a similar case would raise her eyes to Heaven with deep emotion, saying: "He has sent His little angel before me, that I need not knock! Knocking always makes a disagreeable noise, which is by no means so edifying as hearing the voice of Nereus singing the Song of the Lamb in the distance."

If Phlegon called her attention to the fact, that the steps of the vestibulum were so covered with dirt as to be almost impassable, she answered with secret self-satisfaction :

" I daily thank the Lord, that I no longer receive such unpleasant impressions. I merely glance aside, and the next instant it is over."

He could not reprove the slaves themselves for such things. They made him feel that he was not their master. Punishments, even if Ennia ordered them, were not inflicted ; for when the time came Graecina had always " forgiven" everything, and was only angry with Phlegon for perpetually tormenting her about such trifles. When he once led Graecina to a hidden chest, belonging to her estimable Chloe, where a sum of money no slave could save was concealed, together with many valuable articles that had long been missed, and the old woman believed the lying wench's statement that she had only been keeping these things for Graecina, in case it should be necessary to sell the villa, his patience gave way. He desired Ennia to go with him to Tibur and leave her mother to her fate.

" She can't be helped," was the conclusion of his angry speech. " She can neither command nor obey. Servants who come to her industrious and willing, in a year's time are drunkards, thieves and rascals. Wherever I look, I see superstition and evil. I want you to put an end to this state of affairs. Let her go to destruction with her estate ! I won't have my children grow up in such a fool's household, and become fools themselves."

But Ennia positively refused to accompany him, reminding him of all his former promises, and firmly declaring that she would never desert her invalid mother.

She had only become his wife on condition that he would bear with Graecina's follies, since but for these weaknesses she would never have permitted her to marry a freedman. Besides, it could not be a matter of indifference to him whether or not the beautifully-situated estate was irretrievably lost, and he could not say that the atmosphere of Hadrian's court would be more healthful for his daughters, than that of their grandmother's roof; for Ennia had her own separate household with the very purpose of preventing the children from becoming accustomed to disorder and negligence. So the days dragged gloomily away, and as each pursued his or her path in sorrowful loneliness, Phlegon was at last forced to secretly acknowledge that his presence in the house diminished the happiness of his family, and it would be better to depart. He himself still seemed like a stranger among his children. It was not that they omitted any token of respect or dutiful obedience, but there was something alien between them, and when they became animated and began to talk about the stories with which the slaves amused them, the poor people, or repeat their proverbs and verses, a lump always came in his throat. If he then quoted some powerful passage from Phocylides or Archilochus, they did not think it beautiful, and if he repeated portions of Homer or Virgil, they replied that Graecina said all those things were untrue. At last he was forced to come to some decision.

Among Ennia's relatives was one named Bassus, with whom he lived on pleasant terms, and who had for his sons' pedagogue a learned Greek. With Ennia's consent, Phlegon one day took Natalis and Vitalis to him, with the statement that they would remain a year. The lads, pleased with novelty, willingly assented.

Graecina did not hear of the matter until it was settled, and when she perceived that her "ifs" and "buts" would not be of the least avail, consoled herself by thinking that she would now have a fresh opportunity to write edifying letters, a habit to which she was as eagerly addicted, as Brother Nereus was to his Falernian. The very same day a large roll of MS. that Phlegon beheld with indignation, was sent off to the boys.

At last the time for his return to Tibur arrived, and he took a cold farewell of the aged mistress of the house. Next morning, while ordering his luggage to be conveyed to the litter, which was to bear him outside of the city, where an imperial carriage would meet him, Ennia gayly approached, saying :

" My mother is going to give you a present too."

" Well, will she make over to me the sums I collected for her ?"

" You know little of her, if you think so."

" What then ?"

" The Triton ! And you must take a basket of figs to Hermas, a basket of peaches to the fruit-dealer Tryphaena, and a bag of nuts to little Titius."

" And a wagon load of cabbages for the street-beggars ?"

" Please, Phlegon—"

" Well then, in the name of Erebus, pack them up. Where is the water-god ? There—take this kiss, and now I'm off to the *via Tiburtina*, where the carriage is waiting."

Tears filled the beautiful woman's eyes as she gazed after the litter ; then with bowed head she returned to the house, from which rose the slaves' morning hymn.

Phlegon sat a long time in his litter, lost in sullen

anger, brooding over the thought of how much poorer in beautiful dreams of the future he was leaving the villa *ad pinum*, which he had approached so joyously a week ago. Doubtless a new structure could be erected on its site, in case Ennia succeeded in at least preventing the sale, but Phlegon would then be obliged to accumulate means for the purpose, and he was so unwilling to meddle with matters of economy; his position at Hadrian's court depended in no small degree, upon the emperor's faith in his unselfishness.

"It is possible," he said to himself, "that all the injuries may be repaired; but when the old fool is buried in the Pomponians' tomb, a fresh source of anxiety, thanks to her, will grow up in my sons. When the battle with the old woman's obstinacy is over, the conflict with her descendants' perversity will begin. Great Jupiter! It is a bad charge thou hast given the human race. If one isn't a demi-god, he had far better be an animal or an unconscious rock. To live and feel is to suffer! There are few notes of joy between the first cry of life and the last death-rattle in the throat."

He gazed enviously to the right and left at the gardens and villas, whose owners, with incomparably smaller means, had understood how to make their property an ornament to the city, while Graecina had so admirably managed to destroy an estate, which for a century had been the pride of the *via lata*.

Still engrossed by these sorrowful thoughts, Phlegon reached the *via Tiburtina*, where one of the carriages, which daily passed to and fro between Hadrian's villa and Rome, awaited him. But to his great vexation, his colleague Suetonius, the *magister-epistolarum*, one of the most garrulous of the household officials, who certainly did not bear with justice his surname of Tranquillus, was already seated in it. Banished for a time from the court on account of his intrusiveness and the liberties, which, showing great want of tact, he had taken with the Empress Sabina, he had been recalled by Hadrian, since the separation of the imperial pair.

The emperor's jealous nature found pleasure in the chronicle of crimes, with which Suetonius pursued the memory of former rulers. This man, a dealer in anecdotes of the most ordinary kind, who had been brought into prominence by Pliny, thoroughly despised Phlegon as a Greek and a freedman, yet forced himself upon him to-day, in order to be able to talk till he was satisfied during the three hours drive, and at the same time win the good-will of his companion, who was considered very influential.

"Whoever polishes Caesar's verses is an important person," said the old babbler. "I must be on good terms with Phlegon. Who knows how useful I may make him!"

The latter listened absently to the court chronicle of the last week. Only when he heard of the attempt on Antinous's life did he show an eager interest, although he could not understand much from the confused and exaggerated account given by his companion. The noisy officiousness, with which the latter strove to render him some new service every moment, was ill-suited to his present mood; it oppressed his breathing, like the sweet, sulphurous odor, which reached him from the sulphur baths of the *aquae Albulae*. They stopped at the magnificent bath-house at the sulphurated springs, and as his companion, while the horses were resting, sought fresh customers for his news among the guests at the baths, Phlegon availed himself of the opportunity to tell the driver that he would walk the rest of the way, and charged him to take care of his baggage, whose strange nature, a last undesirable remembrance of Graecina, made it unpleasant to drive into Tibur with it in person. Striking into a side-path leading to the quarries from which, fifty years before, Vespasian had taken the colossal blocks of stone for his amphitheatre, he escaped the glances of the court officials, whose carriages were collected here, climbed the heights above the moors and gazed with .delight at the blue Sabine mountains outspread before him, followed the silver thread of the Anio, inhaled the morning breeze blowing from the east, which swept the sulphurous odors in the opposite direction, and thus, with a certain sense of comfort, pursued his way, listening to the chirping of the cicadas, which disturbed his thoughts less than the courtier's ceaseless prattle. Like the bees buzzing on the right and left, his own mind dreamed on in a sort of pleasant stupor, until the notes of a reed-pipe, echoing from a valley, disturbed his reverie.

"Do the voices from Graecina's house pursue me even here, or is my mind already wandering?" said Phlegon. "There is no doubt that some one is playing the Song of the Lamb, which Brother Nereus understands how to whine in such an edifying way."

The backs of several sheep appeared on the next height, and Phlegon climbed it to see the Christian, who had chosen for his profession the contemplative occupation of sheep tending. He found a tall figure, wrapped in the cloak usually worn by the goatherds of the Sabine mountains, the face being shaded by a broadbrimmed hat.

"See, Phlegon," said a voice that seemed familiar,

" the sacred notes have lured you from your comfortable carriage and drawn you hither into the wilderness. Confess that my God works miracles, even at the present day."

" By Hercules, who guards the citadel of Tibur," said Phlegon, " it is you, Hermas! What means this masquerading ? Since when have you joined the goat-herds ?"

" I tend sheep, Phlegon, idly and happily. Here too there are saints and sinners, but the service is not so hard as your Caesar's, and until the end comes, I would rather be the keeper of these innocent creatures, than of the wickedness of men."

" I heard from Suetonius that you parted from Hadrian in anger, although you had saved his favorite's life. But Tranquillus thought you had returned to your family and were going to help your brother Pius build a tower, from which you could be the first to see your god's arrival from Heaven."

" When the Lord comes, Suetonius will give an account of every idle word he has uttered."

" That will be bad for him !" laughed Phlegon.

" True, I went back to my family in Rome, but as their conduct did not please me, I told Pius I would watch his sheep here in the wilderness ; here the Lord visits me ; here the Spirit speaks to me, and as I watched the movements in the stone-quarries, I wrote a prophecy about the building of the world, which like every tower, must finally be finished, and showed how each man must be a stone in this tower. Suetonius heard this through the Brothers, who daily bring me food from the villa, and to whom I read my book aloud, and in his way made blasphemy of it."

" I see you know how to pass your time in solitude."

" I am not lonely," said Hermas mysteriously. " A woman visits me—the church; a shepherd talks with me, my angel; the Spirit comes to me, and every creature seems a symbol of His kingdom. When the herds of buffalo from the country estates raise the dust on the highway, I think of the calamities which will precede the coming of the great dragon, the Behemoth, that will stare at us with glowing red eyes, like the buffaloes, till our hearts grow chill. When I see how some boughs in the forest become green, while others remain bare, so that we can instantly tell which were frozen and which retain their sap, I remember that in the present day the hypocrite cannot be distinguished from the true believer, but when the Lord's spring comes, it will be manifest which really has the sap of life. Or when I behold the summits of the seven hills, each one different, some wooded, some inhabited, the Spirit tells me that here below also each individual dwells on his special hill. The willow-boughs you see here I planted, that they might remind me how man grows in grace or withers. Those gnawed by the caterpillars are the sceptics, whom the devil found soft; those whose branches droop are not rooted deep enough in good soil—"

" What a pity," interrupted Phlegon fiercely, " that your pupil Graecina isn't here! She might learn from you another new plan of laying out a garden, to make the villa *ad pinum* a perfect mad-house."

Hermas flushed. " Your mother-in-law's house," he replied, "is ruled by two spirits; love, which is good, and self-will, which is evil. I have often told Graecina that a believer ought to have more reverence for the creature, and not fell trees that praise the Creator by their beauty; but Graecina took from my words only what suited her; the rest, it seems, she did not hear."

Phlegon looked sharply at Hermas, but unable to discover any deception in his clear, honest eyes, told the prophet, who listened sorrowfully, what the villa *ad pinum* had formerly been, what it was now, and what mischief had been done the slaves in the house under the name of the new doctrine.

" I'll see if I can help you," replied Hermas. " I knew that there were many false Brothers in your house, and Graecina has neither the gift of distinguishing persons, nor the desire to keep the best, if it imposes any constraint upon her obstinacy. But, my brother, if I subdue the evil spirits of others," he added, glancing kindly at Phlegon, "might I not increase yours? Don't you perceive that Mammon is your tormentor, who gives you no peace day and night? Look at the blooming plain, which sought to greet you with a hundred voices, but you passed unheeding, because your demon whispered: ' Now Graecina has given Celsus money again,' and rattled the denares in your ear till you heard them. The mountains saluted you from their blue summits, but the demon said: ' Now Salvianus is certainly taking the last drop of water from Graecina.' God sent his angel to meet you in the first breath of morning, to inspire cheerful thoughts, but your demon asked: ' How many bottles of old Falernian do you suppose Nereus has left?' When God sends the angel of sleep to you, the demon drives him away. You toss feverishly on your couch, your heart contracts, and yet you still clasp your demon to your breast and let him tell you all the things Graecina might yet squander and destroy. No anxiety and grief can restore what is lost, and it is only your demon's fiendish malignity that induces him thus to spoil your present with your past, and at the same time make your future useless."

"Perhaps you are not altogether wrong," replied Phlegon; "but surely it is no evil spirit, that tells me I must provide for my children's future."

"How many children have you?" asked Hermas.

"Eight," sighed Phlegon.

"And how much income could the villa yield annually?"

"In the condition to which Graecina has reduced it, scarcely sixteen sesterces."

"And so you are fretting till you turn gray and yellow, because thirty years hence, after your death and Ennia's, your children will each receive two sesterces less when they are legatees, procurators, prefects, or the wives of these personages, each one of whom will perhaps have ten sesterces from his office. Don't you see how your demon is tormenting you? Phew! I smell the odor of brimstone."

"You smell the sulphur of the Albula, old fool," said Phlegon indignantly. "But you mean kindly, my good Hermas," he continued more gently. "I have heard it read from your books, that we must take no thought for the morrow, must seek food like the birds of Heaven, that search amid the mire and dung in the streets for undigested grain — this may be true wisdom for the great world of slaves and beggars, but I haven't toiled forty years, that my children may commence again at the beginning, in order perhaps not to advance half so far. The fact, that one of the great historical estates in the city is in the possession of my family, will make the world forget that my children's grandfather

was a slave.   That is why I want to retain the old
estate of the Pomponians.   A certain income, be it
ever so small, is a rope to save a family from sinking
into the mire."

"I only fear you will not use the estate for the purpose for which God has given us property," replied
Hermas.   "See, yonder elm-tree bears no fruit, but, in
serving for a support to the vine, it too yields sweet
grapes.   Without it there would be fewer grapes, so we
can therefore probably say that it also yields wine.   So
the rich man, who supports believers, can in the same
manner secure the increase of faith, love and prayer,
though he does not himself believe.   Will you remember this?"

Phlegon indignantly waved him away.

"I now see that you don't want your demon driven
out," replied Hermas.   "As you are not in the Lord, I
have no right to release you from him against your will.
But I will help you, with Nereus, Chloe and the others,
who are also possessed by unclean spirits.   They must
perform the penance allotted by the church, and then I
will come and guard your garden.   The trees are also
God's creatures, I don't want them sacrificed in the
Lord's name by hypocrites.   A servant is coming from
the city towards evening to bring me more sheep; he
can watch the whole flock, while I discuss the state of
the church in your house with Pius and the elders; I
want no scandal, I do not want one single soul lost for
the sake of the hypocrite."

Phlegon held out his hand and walked silently
towards Tibur.   Hermas, shaking his head thoughtfully,
gazed after him a long time.   The reed-pipe was mute,
the sheep often scattered a long distance unnoticed by

the shepherd. It was fortunate that a servant came at noon, who brought him food, and to whom he could entrust the flock, for Hermas was no good shepherd when his dreams took possession of him, and more than one of Pius's sheep might have come to harm, while his castle-building was going on.

At a late hour in the evening, several presbyters, heads of the seven principal parishes in the capital, with two travelling preachers, had assembled in the covered solarium, the spacious balcony of the produce dealer Pius, near the Theatre of Marcellus, to discuss the questions the Bishop of Rome submitted to their consideration. The space towards the gallery, enclosed with canvas on account of the night air, was lighted by a torch, fastened to an iron pole, around which the men had drawn several seats and tables. Most of those assembled were already beyond middle age, and the strongly-marked faces of the weather-beaten old plebeians, illumined by the flickering light, afforded a spectacle at once picturesque and well suited to awaken curiosity. Thus the worthy dweller in the suburb, who praised the quiet of the imperial government and the peace of the Romans, imagined a conspiracy. The presiding officer, the stately Pius, one of those figures whose firm bearing instantly inspires confidence, and whom all are willing to obey, because the trust they feel themselves is communicated to others, was just rolling up a MS. and laying it aside. " After all," he said, " I agree with Niger. In this revised condition of the book I have no objection to its being admitted for use in the parishes. The Brothers entrusted with revision have removed the offence of the denial of the Lord's return in person. Clemens has added distinct allusions to the resurrection of the body. The marvellous story of the libation of water has been replaced by that of the adulteress, hitherto overlooked, and I think we shall do well to admit in this form a book that is still everywhere read and ought to be no longer excluded."

"I don't like to oppose," said a thin, elderly man, whose profile revealed Jewish blood. "I have always found that if a person doesn't understand a case within the first quarter of an hour, he won't understand it in the next ten years. A book, that emanated from the school of Valentinus and degraded all the accounts of our Lord's life to comparisons of gnostic wisdom, cannot be rendered a healthful book of instruction to beginners, either by omissions or additions. To-day, as formerly, I must dissuade your church from allowing itself to be ensnared by the alluring words of human wisdom, by which this work is distinguished. To me all this beautiful language is a glittering serpent-skin. The churches of Judea at least will not accept this book."

"So Hegesipp is against its admission," said Pius, with quiet composure; "the presbyters of the Roman Church, however, have recently expressed themselves unanimously in its favor. But I hear that Pescennius afterwards made objections."

"It is as you say, reverend father," replied a younger man. "Your brother Hermas, with whom, on account of his clear judgment, I read the book at your estate on the *via Tiburtina*, thought the apostle, whom our predecessors have declared to be the founder of the Roman Church, Simon Peter, is too harshly treated in this work. Everywhere he is compelled to give place to John, his denial of the Lord is related, but not his bitter repentance, whose tears washed away his guilt. Hermas has therefore, from tales which, as he says, circulated verbally, made up an addition containing Peter's restitution, and I think it would be worth while if the Brothers appointed for this purpose, would subject it to an examination. Clemens himself supports Hermas's proposal."

"There will be no objection to Pescennius's attempt," said Pius. "So, as no one opposes, I authorize you to again submit the book to your co-laborers, to ascertain whether they think it necessary to take into consideration the scruples since suggested. But there is still another matter that also excited Hermas,—the condition of the church in Graecina's house, which has already often claimed our care. Nereus, who to our surprise has been entrusted with the representation of that congregation, is not present, as usual, and unfortunately the church *ad palmam* could not be induced to send a worthier elder. Do the Brothers consider it advisable, notwithstanding this fact, to examine into the complaints against Nereus?"

"As he was invited, and knew the object of the meeting," replied Simeon, "I would request an immediate discussion. I, too, have noticed certain things there, which make interference desirable and, as I set out to-morrow for Illyria and Macedonia, would fain first unburden my heart of the responsibility that rests upon us all."

"Very well," replied Pius, "the matter is this—in spite of our warnings to the Brothers, the luxurious, idle life in Graecina's house has not improved during the last six months. The condition of both house and estate is the very picture of disorder and, as Simeon says, recalls the field of the slothful and the vineyard of the man void of understanding; of which the wise king of the old covenant speaks. Graecina's large fortune is so exhausted, that she is thinking of selling her estate, which cannot be done without causing great scandal. She will become a horrible example to the whole capital, of the fate that befalls those who have anything to do with Christ's disciples. It may cause a fresh persecution of the Brothers and every other danger. Moreover, her daughter's husband is Phlegon, Hadrian's private secretary, who can obtain another edict against us at any moment. After an absence of many years, he returned to the villa *ad pinum* and saw the desolation wrought by Graecina and some of the false Brothers, devoted to pleasure, who live there. He left the house in anger, after making vain efforts to set things in order. I consider it one of the Lord's special providences, that on his way to Tibur he met Hermas. The latter says that, to his surprise, Phlegon suddenly left his comfortable carriage and forced his way through thorns and thickets to the pasture, following like a sleep-walker the notes of the sacred hymn by which Hermas, playing on his reed-pipe, allured him."

A smile ran through the ranks of the presbyters, then Pius continued:

"Be that as it may, he bewailed his troubles to Hermas, who promised that the presbytery would induce Graecina to make a more judicious use of her property, and above all prevent her from offering her ancestral estate for sale."

When Pius had finished, Simeon added from his own experiences a vivid description of the state of affairs at the villa *ad palmam*, declaring it was quite

time to divest Nercus of his dignity, since he was constantly indulging in pleasure more and more, and subject Graecina's almsgiving to close inspection, that she
might not be fostering laziness under the supposition
that she was exercising charity. Others expressed the
same opinion. Hegesipp alone held different views of
this affair also.

"It seems to me," he said, "the fear that Graecina
may draw persecution upon you, has made you unjust
to her real virtue. What does she do except what the
Lord commands: 'Sell that thou hast and give to the
poor.' Since when has it been the elders' task, to warn
the members of their congregation not to divest themselves of their pelf? We preach everywhere, that it is
hard for the rich to enter the kingdom of Heaven. I
have rejoiced, after long searching, to find a Sister who
really fulfils the directions of the gospel, who does what
we preach. If Nereus is a toper, remove him, but don't
persecute Sister Graecina because she does what the
Lord has commanded."

"What the Lord commanded," said Pius firmly,
"concerned the days when the kingdom was to be
established by force. Those who beheld His holy face,
certainly had more important things to do than selling
fish or sitting in the seat of customs. I don't deny that
times of conflict may return, when we must cast aside
all earthly luggage to have our arms free, as in those
days. But when the kingdom was established, his
apostles no longer said people must give up trade and
business, but that all trade must be honestly done, that
each individual must work with his own hands, that he
might not want, and that he who would not labor
should not eat."

"Your lying apostle!" muttered Hegesipp.

His neighbors started angrily from their seats, but Pius, as if he had not heard the interruption, continued:

"I don't expect Phlegon, an unbeliever, to tolerate a management of his children's inheritance, which I should prohibit in my own house. We will interfere, and as Simeon unfortunately leaves us to-morrow, I propose that we entrust to another Brother the investigation of the state of the church in Graecina's house."

"Hermas!" cried several voices.

"Hermas is the accuser," replied Pius.

"Hermas and Niger then!"

A murmur of assent was heard.

"I have no objection," said Pius, "but in that case request Niger to take the lead and conduct the investigation, that—"

The speaker said no more, for at that moment a heavy stone was hurled from the street through the opening in the curtain, and fell rattling on the stone floor; others struck the canvas.

"Put out the lights!" Pius hastily shouted.

A jeering cry rang from the street, and a shower of stones flew against the wall of the house, breaking the plaster, or dashed rattling upon the shutters and the wooden gallery of the balcony. Then they heard the assailants run rapidly away, in order to escape falling into the hands of the watchmen.

"When will this mischief on the part of the populace cease?" said Pius, shaking his head, after lighting a lamp in the tablinum.

"It seemed to me as if I heard Nereus's unctuous voice among the whisperers, before the stones were thrown," said Pescennius, who had sat nearest the street.

"We were just talking about him, so the delusion was natural."

"Why should he commit such an act of treachery?" said another.

"When will you begin your disagreeable business?" Pius asked old Niger.

"If it is possible for Hermas, to-morrow," replied the old man. "We must twist the devil's neck, without looking at him long."

"Ought you not to remain here for a time, until the rabble has dispersed?" Pius asked the departing company.

"There were not more than three or four men, and we number nine."

"Then may the Lord keep you. I thank you for the peace you have given my house," said Pius, holding out his right hand to Hegesipp, who shook it warmly. Then the cautious merchant himself fastened the door behind his guests with two strong iron bars, and retired to his sleeping-room next the atrium, where the lamp beside his pillow was not extinguished until after midnight.

CHAPTER IX.

WHEN Phlegon had reached the bridge over the Anio, from which the road to the villa diverged to the right, and rested under the lofty evergreen oaks and olive-trees that shaded the tomb of the Plautian family,

he noticed the remarkable amount of work the army of
slaves, masons, and gardeners had accomplished during
the short space of time he had been permitted to spend
with his family in Rome.

When he had left Hadrian two or three weeks
before, pyramids of bricks towered into the air, the forest
rang with the shouts of the workmen toiling in twenty
different places, the foundations of the buildings were
only a man's height above the ground.   Now a solemn
stillness brooded over the blooming hill-side, the piles
of red brick were removed, the lime-pits filled with
earth, the ground levelled, and the turf sown.   Marble
figures, gleaming from amid the dark old trees, appeared
on the right and left.   The front of the Greek theatre
stood forth in glittering relief against the foliage behind.
From the Palaestra, hidden among the laurel bushes,
Phlegon heard the full rich tones of his favorite Antinous, directing the boys' games.   Passing the Nymphaeum, the plashing of the water in the echoing hall
delighted him.   A broad avenue of cypress trees, bordered on the right and left with the most superb statues
carried away from the Greek islands, led past the library
to Hadrian's residence.

" Hail, beloved pair of Centaurs!" said Phlegon to
the works carved in red marble of the master of Aphrodisias, that adorned the flight of steps.   The group on
the right represented an old Centaur, on whose back
rode a Cupid that was binding his arms behind him,
while the young one on the left trotted merrily along,
the sport of the Love.   On the terrace overlooking the
Hippodrome, the Academy, and the Egyptian Canopus,
Phlegon found his master.   The emperor had already
left the breezy height of the temple of Heracles in the

city, and though here and there a skilful architect moved noiselessly to and fro with a few workmen, the Caesar's villa was already as thoroughly fitted out as if he had occupied it for years. The body-guards had also moved into their quarters. Work was still going on in the other buildings, scattered over an extent of seven miles, and the architects of Elysium, Tartarus, Canopus and the numerous temples spent weary days, for Hadrian constantly found something to be improved. He frequently desired architectural changes, in accordance with the latest information he received about the oldest forms of worship—changes difficult to make, although the emperor himself, with practical skill, drew the plans on the wooden tablets.

While Phlegon gazed at this new world and went into the pleasure-grounds, amid whose shrubbery appeared the distant roofs of the capital, the charm of producing seized upon him also, and he took a mental vow that he would some day adorn the villa *ad pinum* with fresh magnificence, by the help of the experience gathered from this superb creation. He would write to Ennia that very evening to retain the magnificently-situated estate at any cost, to enable him at some future day to plant a spot like this amid the dust and noise of the capital.

Hadrian received him more graciously than ever, for he was thoroughly weary of the garrulous Suetonius, who had taken Phlegon's place. The gift of the Triton was accepted with cordial delight, and Phlegon was invited to choose the spot where his bronze friend should be placed. Besides, Hadrian said he needed help at every nook and corner. The villa was to be a remembrance of everything grand and beautiful he had witnessed during his long, wandering life. As the Roman patrician ordered pictures of favorite spots to be painted on the walls of his house, or placed in his dwelling silver models of the temples and citadels he had seen, so Hadrian intended to make the heights of Tibur a huge album of travels, whose sketches of nature imitated the originals; and when the latter were transportable, they were by no means safe from being incorporated within the album. Temples, theatres and statues were removed and set up again beside copies of the great architectural works of Greece and Egypt, which Hadrian had had most carefully prepared.

"Where are we?" the Caesar asked his faithful companion, when they had entered the porch.

"Why, in the Stoa Poicile!" replied Phlegon smiling. "We have the halls, only Zeno* is lacking."

From here Hadrian went up a woodland path, leaning from time to time on his shorter companion, to allow an asthmatic oppression of breathing to pass away. Two stelae, one bearing a head of Homer, and the other one of Achilles, marked a narrow footway, leading between thick laurel-bushes to an outlook. On the opposite side of the valley a group of lofty oaks stood on the bare mountain ridge.

"Dodona**!" exclaimed Phlegon in amazement.

* Zeno. At its close, and after he had developed his peculiar philosophical system, to which he must already have gained over some disciples, he opened his school in the porch adorned with the paintings of Polygnotus (Stoa Poicile), which, at an earlier time, had been a place in which poets met (Eratosthenes in Diog. Laërt. vii. 5). From it his disciples were called *Stoics*, a name which had before been applied to the above-mentioned poets, and by which also the grammarians who assembled there probably at a later time were known.— *Smith's Dicty. of Greek and Roman Biog.*

** Dodona (Δωδώνη; sometimes Δωδών, Soph. *Trach.* 172: *Eth.* Δωδωναῖος), a town in Epeirus, celebrated for its oracle of Zeus, the

"Let us go across," replied Hadrian, delighted that his companion had recognized the scene. "Those who question the oracle will climb the steep path yonder, we will remain here, where the soft west wind fans us. See how distinctly the roofs of Rome can be seen to-day. I think I can distinguish the temple of Venus and Roma. Do you hear the caldrons of Dodona ?"

Following the sound, the two companions soon reached the grey holm-oaks, that shaded a wide, bare spot. No temple was visible, but several dark figures lay stretched under the trees. Wrapped in earth-colored cloaks, they remained motionless on the ground, as if listening to what the inhabitants of the nether world resolved.

"The selli,"[*] said Hadrian, in an undertone.

most ancient in Hellas. It was one of the seats of the Pelasgians, and the Dodonaean Zeus was a Pelasgic divinity. The oracle at Dodona enjoyed most celebrity in the earlier times. It was stated by a writer of the name of Demon that the temple was surrounded with tripods bearing caldrons, and that these were placed so closely together, that when one was struck the noise vibrated through all. (Steph. B. *s. v. Aωδώνη;* Schol. *ad Hom. Il.* xvi. 233). It appears that the greater part of these had been contributed by the Boeotians, who were accustomed to send presents of tripods every year. (Strab. x. p. 402.) Among the remarkable objects at Dodona were two pillars, on one of which was a brazen caldron, and on the other a statue of a boy holding in his hand a brazen whip, dedicated by the Corcyraeans: when the wind blew, the whip struck the caldron, and produced a loud noise. As Dodona was in an exposed situation, this constantly happened, and hence arose the proverb of the Dodonaean caldron and the Corcyraean whip. Respecting the way in which the oracles were given, there are different accounts; and they probably differed at different times. The most ancient mode was by means of sounds from the trees, of which we have already spoken. Servius relates that at the foot of the sacred oak there gushed forth a fountain, the noise of whose waters was prophetic and was interpreted by the priestesses (*ad Virg. Aen.* iii. 466). On some occasions the will of the god appears to have been ascertained by means of lots. (Cic. *de Div.* i. 34).— *Smith's Dicty. of Greek and Roman Geog.*

[*] The Selli, whom Homer describes as the Interpreters of Zeus, "men of unwashed feet, who slept on the ground," appear to have been a tribe.—*Smith's Dicty. of Greek and Roman Geog.*

"It is still very doubtful," thought Phlegon, "whether Homer meant priests by selli," but knowing that Hadrian pardoned no one who raised objections to his learning, contented himself with quoting the verse:

> "Dodonian Jove, Pelasgian, sovereign King,
> Whose dwelling is afar, and who dost rule
> Dodona, winter-bound, where dwell thy priests,
> The Selli, with unwashen feet, who sleep
> Upon the ground! Thou once hast heard my prayer."*

As a stronger breeze rose, strange sounds became audible in the branches of the oaks. On every tree hung a brazen basin, beside which was fastened a whip that supported three iron chains, holding silver balls, which sometimes striking clearly against each other, anon when a more powerful gust of wind swept by, clashing against the more resonant basin, lent the tree a continuous voice. Leaning on the oak, as if she had grown a part of it, and staring into an oddly-shaped urn, covered with strange pictures, which contained the sacred lots, was a weather-beaten old woman, whose white hair hung in tangled strands over her wrinkled face. Phlegon would willingly have asked what the divinities were preparing, but Hadrian seemed like a child afraid of its own toy. He turned in his thumbs, to ward off the old Thessalian witch's evil eye, and walked rapidly down to Tempe.*

* Tempe (τὰ Τέμπη, contr. of Τέμπεα), a celebrated valley in the NE. of Thessaly, is a gorge between Mounts Olympus and Ossa, through which the waters of the Peneius force their way into the sea. The beauties of Tempe were a favorite subject with the ancient poets, and have been described at great length in a well-known passage of Aelian, and more briefly by Pliny; but none of these writers appear to have drawn their pictures from actual observation; and the scenery is distinguished rather by savage grandeur than by the sylvan beauty which Aelian and others attribute to it. (Catull. lxiv. 285; Ov. *Met.* i. 568; Virg. *Georg.* ii. 469; Aelian, *V. H.* iii. 1; Plin. iv. 8. s. 15.)—
Smith's Dicty. of Greek and Roman Geog.

* Translation by W. C. Bryant.

On the way they saw a pale young girl, sitting beside a dark well that extended far back into the mountain. A bundle of torches lay in her lap.

" The Zeus well," said Hadrian, and Phlegon gazed into the black water, on which floated a few bubbles. Hadrian lighted a torch, passed it over the bubbles till they burst, extinguished it in the waves, then held the other end close above the surface and slowly lighted it afresh at the burning gas.

" See, we have brought all the mysteries of Dodona to the mountains of Tibur.   Have you drunk the water to-day, pale prophetess ?"

The slender figure beside the fountain nodded mournfully.

" What say the Chthonian gods ?"

" They say what they tell me every day," replied the girl — "that I must go home to Epirus, or I shall soon be with them."

" Patience, child," replied the Caesar consolingly. " You know the old woman can't do without you.   I dare not vex her, lest she should rouse against me the inhabitants of the nether world.   Perhaps I can find an opportunity to conciliate her.   Then, with good-natured inconsistency, the credulous ruler added :

" Drink no more of the marshy water, Pythia; it causes fever.   Else your oracle might be fulfilled only too soon."

The girl buried her pale face in her long thin hands, while Hadrian hastily pursued the downward path.

" See, Tempe !" exclaimed Phlegon in delight. " How successfully the temple of Zeus is imitated, and you have given the brook all the windings of the Peneus."

The emperor gazed with a look of satisfaction down

the valley, with its artificial rocks and freshly-sown turf, saying: " If the firs only grow well, the resemblance will be complete."

Through Tempe the way led to Elysium. A solemn avenue of cypress-trees extended past the deities who lowered the torch, and the contemplative statue of Hermes, the guide of the dead, to a gate, adorned on one side with a bas-relief of Hercules and Hebe, and on the other with Cupid and Psyche. This gate afforded admittance to a gloomy tufa-cave, which at the next turn gave a view of a smiling lake and pleasant meadows ; again the way grew darker, to reveal an artistically-framed view of the fragrant plains and the blue Sabine Hills.

So the walk continued amid charming new scenes until the blue sky, more alluring than ever, appeared beyond the cave. Through blossoming bushes and fragrant roses the two companions emerged upon a beautiful carpet of turf, where the lake again sparkled before them, reflecting a domed temple and countless palms and statues. Boats lay on the shore, white and dark swans glided over the silver surface, and the warbling choruses of birds reminded Phlegon that it was no dream-vision outspread before him.

" This is the fairest sight I ever beheld, Caesar," he said with a simplicity that best showed how deeply he was moved. A white deer emerged from the dark shrubbery and walked slowly up to the emperor, to whom it nestled caressingly.

" Only wait till we celebrate our first festival here, Phlegon," said Hadrian, " when boats and flags and unveiled beauty animate this shore, when Syrian dancers and female flute-players perform their juggling feats and move in changing circles. What the author of the Elysium dreamed, we will have displayed here before the eyes."

With these words he sat down. "True, the best thing is lacking, the potion of youth, which no Hebe gives us. What avails all earthly nectar to the old man with feeble stomach, what is ambrosia to the sick man's furred tongue—and young people are no longer like us. Antinous dreams the years of his vigor away in dull melancholy, and Verus wanted to enjoy life ere he was mature, so he now has all an old man's aches at twenty. Come," he added, rising, "we can create no Elysium here without the gods, but we shall fare better in Tartarus. Our capacity for pleasure is limited, pain alone is infinite. Go on, I fear the cold down yonder. We will meet again under the blooming tamarind trees, but draw your toga closely around you, it is cool in Orcus."

Without any special desire to do so, Phlegon approached a gate, at whose entrance a Cerberus with iron jaws announced through which door the traveller should pass. After walking a few paces, Phlegon stumbled and nearly fell down a flight of steps that were almost indistinguishable in the darkness. In recovering himself he struck his forehead against the stalactite formations hanging from the roof, and greatly incensed, waited for a time until his eyes were more accustomed to the gloom, then walked towards the light of a little lamp glimmering in the distance, while the noise of water reached his ears. At the lamp there was a bend in the path, and Phlegon gained a sheet of water, illumined by a ghostly light from above, while strange shadows and misty forms glided to and fro over the dark, rocky walls. Turning round, he started, for close beside him in a boat stood Charon, holding out a motionless hand, in which lay several copper coins. For a moment Phlegon had thought this Charon a living man. Now he discovered that this guide also was only a statue. He entered the boat to row himself to the other shore, but had scarcely sat down when the skiff, drawn by a rope beneath, began to move. An offensive smoke, like the vapors of sulphur, whirled in strange forms over the dark lake. " A vein of the Albula must have been conducted here," said Phlegon. Niches, lighted from above, showed, apparently moved by the floating mist, scenes in Orcus. As soon as the boat passed a cave the figures began to move. Here Sisyphus rolled his stone, which monotonously fell back again, here Tantalus was tormented with longing for his fruit, here the Danaids filled their sieve, here Ixion's wheel turned, here a vulture, flapping its wings, devoured Prometheus' sliver. The stalactites hung lower and lower from the roof, so that Phlegon was at last compelled to lie flat in the boat like a corpse, and thus extended reached the other shore. The grimacing Charon still held out his hand with the coins.

"I'll bring Hadrian his obolus, in token that even the terrors of the nether-world have not affrighted the pupil of the Stoa." He seized the coin firmly, but the statue shut its hand, its head was hideously lighted from within and a malicious fire glowed in its green eyes. Then the monster's hand opened again, and Phlegon hastily withdrew his pinched fingers. Indignant at the trick, the Greek looked around him for means to reach the shore, but only a narrow, slippery path led upward. A handle in the cliff showed how it might be reached, but as he grasped it the whole mass of rock turned, and through a narrow cleft Phlegon forced his way into a dark cave, while the rock again revolved, imprisoning him in a gloomy cell. Waterfalls, worked by machinery, were heard close by him, and human cries and groans united to make all the tortures of Tartarus assail the Greek's excited nerves. He stamped angrily at the thought that the emperor had lured him into this snare, but the cell in which he stood instantly rose and Phlegon floated upward, raised slowly in the dark shaft by iron rods, which he now perceived for the first time. A bright ray of light streamed from a side gallery, and Phlegon looked up at a waterfall crushing human limbs beneath it ; a fiery red glow now fell upon his face, and he beheld a flaming fire where tortured forms writhed and sighed. Then through a grating he saw ragged figures lying in a dungeon. But what was that ? A human voice rose from a cavern.

"Save me, Antinous! Forgive me, Antinous ! Antinous, you who are so kind, plead with Caesar."

Phlegon had already passed on, his conveyance stopped and he found himself in a dark, lofty vault, but from below still rang the piteous cries! "Antinous! Antinous!" Filled with horror, Phlegon again groped for the handle. The rock turned as before, and a flood of dazzling light fell upon his eyes. He could not recognize the figure that stood before him.

"Welcome to the upper world!" he heard Hadrian's voice say.

"A sorry jest, Caesar," replied Phlegon indignantly.

"That is what the dead in Tartarus say."

"All who dwell below did not seem to me to be dead," replied Phlegon disapprovingly. "I think I recognize the voice that calls so piteously upon Antinous. Isn't it the temple-servant, who as Suetonious told me, sought to murder the lad ?"

"The same," said Hadrian; "but see that his cries do not reach Antinous, or Nemesis might be robbed of the victim that is her due."

"Who knows," replied Phlegon, "whether it does not cloud his mind with melancholy, to have a tortured human being calling his name day and night?"

Hadrian did not hear the rebuke, but grasped the Greek's hand, which the latter, wincing, withdrew. "Just see these Athenians," he said jeeringly, "they can't stop stealing even on the Styx, the very obulus in Charon's hand is not safe."

"This time it was the stoic who burned his fingers, when trying to show his fearlessness," replied Phlegon laughing; but Hadrian's mood had already changed again.

"I'll send that obstinate Gorgias to Tartarus, to help the spectres howl. He has planted the olive-trees on the southern side, so the whole view of the Academy is unrecognizable. I told the fool how to place them to make the little copy faithful, and at the same time omit the smaller details. Aristeas too is worthless; the entire model of the Academy from here is mere botch-work, whoever notices the resemblance will laugh at it, and whoever does not, will think the whole scene absurd. If I didn't dread the confusion, I would have the building torn down. Away with Aristeas, let him build fortifications against the Getae on the Danube, I have no farther use for the bungler."

The scene with which the walk ended did not occur for the first time. The Caesar had often returned home in anger, after inspecting his Prytaneum, his Odeum; and the Stoa Poicile. Hadrian himself sometimes felt the pettiness of his imitations. Then he upbraided his architects and sought to throw the blame on their shoulders, because his paltry imitations did not prove more magnificent. The Canopus, towards which Hadrian, turning into a long avenue of sphinxes, now bent his steps, had proved the most unsuccessful of all. The hastily-modelled colossi, as Phlegon perceived at the first glance, could not compare with the originals, which had been carved and polished by generations. Their attitudes were stiff and pedantic. The Nile, formed of greyish-black marble, looked ridiculously modern, the green basalt lions wore a sentimental expression, the gods did not possess the rigid angularity well-suited to the representation of a blind power of nature, but the stiffness of a recruit, who does not know how to use his limbs in their unusual accoutrements.

The ironical smile, that curved the Greek's lips, did not escape the emperor's notice.

"I too," he said, "am by no means satisfied with these blocks, but the genuine statues and relics sent from Heliopolis arrived yesterday morning. The priest, who has them in charge, looks as if all the malice and the mysteries of the Pyramids were concealed behind his yellow face. At the reception this morning, he behaved like some nocturnal beast that has been shut into a light room. He crouched on the cushions in the farthest corner, so that Antinous was obliged to point out the spot where he was cowering."

In fact, the day before, twelve wagons had brought a whole ship's load of mummies, bronzes, vases, scarabei and coffins from the ruin of some temples in Heliopolis, and the far-famed Amenophis, a learned priest of Isis, had come to arrange the relics. The old man, a wise but mysterious personage, with a closely-shaven head, deep-set, gloomy eyes, and a crafty, malicious expression, had curtly told Hadrian that his Canopus contradicted all the rules of sacred architecture. At the very first interview, he detected the priest from the temple of Isis in Massilia, a Gaul who called himself Menephta, together with his companions, to be impostors, and perceived by their blunders, that not one of the Roman-Gallic servants of Isis, whom Hadrian had summoned from Rome and Massilia, was capable of reading the hieroglyphics they mechanically painted on the walls. Hadrian had ordered him to unpack the articles, saying that he would come himself towards evening to inspect the arrangement. As Hadrian and the companion who respectfully attended him, wearied and exhausted by walking and gazing, reached the Canopus, a fierce, passionate quarrel was raging. The material for the adornment of the temple, ordered by Hadrian from Egypt, had arrived in large covered wagons. Nubian slaves stood by the horses, but the leader of the caravan, a dark-skinned Egyptian, was disputing violently with the Gaul, who had barred his way. The great theologians, Amenophis the new-comer and Menephta from Gaul, stood opposite each other with clenched fists. At Hadrian's arrival, the Massilians and their leader paused, while Amenophis defiantly, and by no means respectfully, sat down on the pedestal of a sphinx beside the entrance. Hadrian, with an angry glance, asked the cause of the dispute.

"My Lord," replied Amenophis, "let me return to the Nile with my sacred vessels. I will not place the venerable relics of the city of the sun in the gaudy booth these sons of Typhon have built and painted."

"What fault do you find with my Canopus?" asked

Hadrian in surprise. "Haven't I had everything arranged according to the designs of these priests of your goddess?"

"They may be priests of Pandemus, but they don't know the mysteries of the great goddess. Try whether they can interpret even one of the sacred characters." ·

"I have interpreted all the characters to my sovereign lord," replied Menephta. "He knows you are lying."

"Well," said Hadrian, drawing his seal ring from his finger, "read these hieroglyphics, Menephta, and you, Amenophis, see if he is correct."

Menephta, greatly embarrassed, gazed at the crooked characters in the dark talisman. "These are the goddess's doves—I will consult the sacred manuscripts."

Amenophis laughed scornfully. "Let the sacred manuscripts alone, if you have any! Every temple-boy at Philae could tell you that this is the sign of King Sotis."

"And who is this, holding his finger on his lips, whom you have planted here at the entrance?" continued the old man fiercely to the blushing Gaul.

"Harpocrates, the god of silence," replied Menephta in a tremulous voice.

"A pity your Harpocrates didn't teach you to keep silence yourself!" retorted Menephta grimly. Then, turning to Hadrian, he said:

"That is Horus, Isis's nursling, whom the goddess hushed with her rosy finger, and who in remembrance of the fact is sucking his own. He belonged in the inner sanctuary, unless placed as he desires to be, as door-keeper in the atrium, like your deus Silentii."

Menephta shrank back, pale with fear, for he had

met a glance from Hadrian, that predicted his bullet-head would not long be safe on his square shoulders. "Then here," continued Amenophis inexorably, "this son of a dog has given the venerable god Anubis Greek garments and a slender form like a grey-hound, because he saw Hermeias or Hermes, as you say, carved in this way at Elis. Then look at these hieroglyphics, not one of which is correctly painted. He can't read a word. Here, Menephta, or Menelaus, or Mengetorix, or whatever your name is, read this decree of Ptah."

The priest from Massilia hung his head and made no reply. Hadrian fixed an evil glance upon him, and a harsh sentence seemed hovering on his lips, when he met Phlegon's mild, beseeching eyes. The Caesar slowly passed his thin, narrow hand across his brow, and said haughtily, as he addressed the senate:

"I might order you sent to my Tartarus, where you would find a worthy colleague. But mercy shall temper justice, that"—he added in Greek, glancing at Phlegon—"the Roman nobles may not laugh at the deception I have allowed to be practised upon me. Instead," he continued, flashing a wrathful glance at Menephta, "I will make you and all your companions here, for the space of one year, hierodulae of Amenophis. Under the discipline of the whip he wears in his girdle, you may learn what you asserted you already knew." With these words he coldly turned his back upon the temple. "Begin your work, Amenophis," he said in departing. "I will inspect your treasures to-morrow."

Amenophis gazed after him with a gloomy look, then grasping the handle of his whip, with an imperious gesture, turned to Menephta:

"You know the Caesar's will. He can do everything, except make a Gaul a priest of the great goddess. One must be born to that. So you will attend to the business I assign you. The study of the sacred manuscripts is denied you. Here, the first wagon contains the vessels, which we must store for a time in the chambers of your temple, that the carts may return to bring the second load from Ostia. Be industrious, and it shall do you no harm. If you don't know the gods of Egypt, I know little of Italy. So you see we may be of service to each other. Servants who hate me, serve me ill, so you need not fear the camel-whip. I am no Roman. A priest of Osiris treats camels like camels, and men like men, unless they show themselves to be animals."

The Gaul's features brightened very little, though his heart grew much lighter. " Command," said he, " I will obey until my brothers release me."

Amenophis gave his directions, and one after another the wagons were unloaded. The next morning the emperor again appeared, and ordered the first chest to be opened. Amenophis reluctantly obeyed and brought forth a number of lamps, small altars, palm-branches, serpent staves, metal hands, urns with handles formed of snakes, mystic boxes, tiny ships, etc. Another chest displayed an Anubis with a dog's head, half black and half gold, a gold cow standing erect, bull and hawk-headed gods, crowned with the sun's disk. Compared with these genuine relics, Hadrian could no longer bear to look at the imitations prepared for him by Roman stone-cutters, and step by step the Egyptian convicted the theologians of the capital, who had supplied the work, of the most absurd blunders, indignantly declaring these caricatures insults to the divinity, and succeeded in having them conveyed to the darkest cellar. To make amends, he had already prepared a list of the objects still necessary, whose hieroglyphic characters he wrote for Hadrian and curtly declared that one of his companions must procure the things in Heliopolis himself, through whom, by whom, when, where, sacred custom forbade his informing the uninitiated. For the expenses he asked a sesterce, which sum he brushed into a box with a broom, and went away as if carrying out sweepings. Hadrian looked after him with a grim smile, yet it pleased him to be treated in this way. If the things were genuine, he did not care what they cost or what they were worth.

If the affairs of the Canopus were now delivered up to Amenophis, the Greek temple caused Phlegon all the greater trouble. Here Hadrian himself was the authority in matters of worship, and men like Plutarch of Chaeronea might have learned from him. He was all the more difficult to satisfy, and the secretary had scarcely arrived when he was obliged to rush to the Greek library to seek out passages, copy quotations, or examine verses to choose inscriptions, so that he was hunted to and fro from morning till night, and if the emperor had not frequently sent for him to consult for hours about changes in the buildings, he would have seen little of the beautiful spring that was strewing the slopes of Tibur with blue periwinkles, red violets, and the blossoms of the white narcissus. He rarely met Antinous. The youth was downcast and silent, looked pale, troubled, and absent-minded, and preferred to keep out of his old friend's way.

" His freshness is gone," said Phlegon. " His master's experiments have saddened him ; now Hadrian will doubtless try to cure him as hastily as he strove to disturb the mental harmony that was the good youth's greatest charm."

One day, when the Greek was seeking protection from the scorching rays of the spring sun in the cool ravine with the waterfalls, he suddenly saw Antinous, lying on the turf, gazing dully at the rushing waves. The roar of the Anio had prevented him from hearing his friend's footsteps. Now, starting up, he tried to retire, but Phlegon passed his arm through the lad's and drew him towards a secluded woodland nook, where they sat down under a statue of Hermes. Antinous was sad and silent, but Phlegon, stroking his waving curls as usual, asked what had come between them in his absence.

" Nothing," said the boy.

" Yet this nothing makes you pale and silent, rude to your old friends."

" 'That *is* the nothing—I have no friends. Hadrian still has eyes and ears only for that crocodile, that hideous Egyptian, with his smooth head, who is always gliding around him like an ichneumon trying to find eggs to suck. Hermas is gone in search of his god. You stay in the library. What is Antinous to you? I no longer suit the other lads. If I want to wrestle with them, they touch me as if they were afraid of breaking me and vexing the emperor by injuring his favorite statue. If I want to throw the discus with them, they are so embarrassed that they can't see the mark. I've noticed lately how merry they were without me. So I went away again. I wont be a spoil-sport. For the pleasure of which Hadrian deprives me, he keeps me sitting for hours in Décrianus's studio, where to the vexation of the consumptive Verus, I am more frequently modelled than the young Caesar himself, as if there were not enough marble and bronze statues of me already. I wish I could lodge in the barracks instead of Hadrian's sleeping-room, where one sinks knee-deep in carpets. I am tired of luxuries."

After these hurried words, Antinous again relapsed into his melancholy reverie. Phlegon, who had watched the youth more closely than the latter knew, laid his hand on his shoulder, asking:

" Is this all your grief?"

Antinous gazed defiantly at him and answered: " No."

Phlegon quietly waited for a farther confession, and after a time the youth, with tears in his eyes, continued:

" He has already disgusted me with human beings, now he robs me of the gods too."

After the sluices of his secret sorrow were once opened, a series of melancholy confessions followed, affording Phlegon a deep insight into this darkened young soul, and filling him with sincere sympathy. The derision of the popular faith, which had become customary in cultivated Grecian society, had passed over Antinous without leaving any trace behind. These scoffers seemed to him neither specially estimable, nor specially happy, and would have been the last persons he desired to follow. Scarcely awakened from the happy unconsciousness of boyhood to thoughts of religion, he really only listened to what touched some inner chord of feeling, the rest passed him by as if his ears were actually stopped. How could he have desired to deprive himself of the pleasure of seeking a divinity in the whispering breeze, the waves of the clear flood, raising his hands to some deity in the bright, delicious morning,

while repeating a pious sentence, anointing with oil a
stone erected on some lofty height, decking with a wreath
of red and blue flowers some god of the fields, whose
merry face gazed over the waving grain, joining some
pretty unspoiled shepherdess in performing these pleasant tasks while exchanging innocent experiences in harmless conversation.   He loved the gods, and only knew
that they had done him many a kindness.   Therefore
derisive speeches about the Olympians were repulsive,
and he had no more idea of examining into their truth
than a good son would investigate a slander about his
parents.

But since Hadrian had daily ordered temples to be
erected and altered at his villa, altars built and pulled
down, statues of the gods dragged from the plains to
the heights and back again to the plains, or tried, like
an aesthetic connoisseur, whether a Minerva would look
better in front of a hedge of firs, or under a group of
elms, his simple childlike relation to the familiar friends
of his childhood was destroyed.   Up at the ancient
temple of Heracles, some impulse had urged him to
greet the god every time he passed, he knew the divinity himself lived there.   How should he now think of
the will of the god, when he daily saw the emperor, from
mere caprice, order statues to be carried hither and
thither, and could divine exactly the motives that
induced him to build a new cella.   In this secret desolation he had gone up to the waterfalls to pray in the
old sanctuary.   But, while gazing into the rainbow,
whose radiant lustre framed the falling water, he learned
that nature was deprived of her divinity.   Even here he
no longer had the consciousness of the presence of the
gods as before.   Who would assure him a god had

willed, that this exquisite circular temple should stand overlooking this beautiful prospect? Perhaps its erection had happened in an equally profane way, and after frivolous hesitation it was placed here by unbelieving beautifiers of the world, because it would look best in this spot. While, absorbed in this mood, he gazed mournfully into vacancy, words that Hermas had read aloud from one of his sacred books suddenly recurred to his mind—how artists formed statues of the gods, making with the same wood a table and a deity, warming the soup, and finishing the rest of the statue. At that time Antinous repelled him, exclaiming:

"I won't hear such things, it is absurd to ask what became of the splinters of the marble block from which Phidias carved his Zeus."

But what should he now answer, if Hermas repeated those words to him. Was he not right?

Phlegon, notwithstanding his sympathy, could give little counsel to relieve this pain.

"It is Hadrian's way," he said, "to jest with serious things and take jests in earnest. He has seen and experienced too much to be devout. Keep to your faith, lad," he added, "and beware of the Christians. They are destroyers of the world, and if they conquer, all the splendor and power on earth will be over."

The friends parted in silence; Phlegon, dissatisfied with himself for having given so little consolation, Antinous full of regret that he had opened his heart so far to another.

In these troubles the youth's disturbed spirit, often made sore by daily-repeated irritations, found a sort of comfort in the ancient, solemn-looking statues of gods and animals the strange Egyptian was unpacking in the

Canopus. These at least were not carved by Hadrian's order. Here he need not hear, that the artist ought to have made the arm higher and the thigh thicker. The solemn seriousness of these figures proved, that the dead, unknown sculptors of these works had believed in their gods and repeated a sacred type without any additions of their own. So he often lay for hours among the gloomy basalts or gazed into the stony face of a sphinx and dreamed of a meaning in these statues. To the priest, who moved to and fro in this sanctuary, he felt the instinctive aversion of a pure nature towards one that is impure, yet it pleased him to hear how rudely and abruptly the gloomy priest often dismissed the Caesar's ideas and proposals.

"Whoever he may be," the youth said to himself, "he is in earnest in his temple, where the others carry on their jests." Since he had become accustomed to the dismal aspect of this sanctuary, the bright, cheerful forms of Olympus no longer charmed him as before.

"They are gods for the happy," said Antinous; "but whoever is oppressed by heavy sorrow, turns to Isis and Osiris, on whose calm features a similar burden seems to rest." At first Amenophis had not appeared to notice the increasing frequency and longer duration of the youth's visits, nay they seemed to disturb rather than please him. Soon, however, he began to utter an explanatory remark if he saw Antinous gazing at some symbol. Gradually he initiated him into the melancholy myth of Osiris and Isis, and the god's sufferings, the goddess's lamentations, the happy resurrection of the murdered husband seemed to the youth like a consoling revelation amid his own sorrows.

"Even the gods must suffer in this world," said

Amenophis, "and thus enter into new glory, and human beings must also endure grief in order to be enthroned with Osiris in the other world," The Egyptian showed him how in nature this suffering of the god was everywhere represented, how the earth glowed in the sunlight, how the frost murdered the children of the spring, how tempests destroyed rocks and oaks, how a malicious Typhon now stifled the languishing earth with scorching winds from the desert, now lashed her defenceless back with snow and hail, but the mild and beneficent goddess always regained the mastery, poured her soft, soothing light as goddess of the moon over the world wearied by the glare of day, smoothed the raging floods, and as guide of the dead, led those tortured by disease and murder into the silent halls of her Osiris.

The Egyptian priest, repeating his myth in a monotonous recitative, seemed less hideous to Antinous, and he already felt a sort of confidence in his temple, when Hadrian destroyed this illusion also. Antinous had always regarded with special reverence the statue of Serapis with his half-parted lips, when one day, while Amenophis was occupied in another part of the sanctuary, the emperor appeared with his train to inspect the light outer temple and darkened cella. Accustomed to amuse himself with his sanctuaries, he profited by the services of Menephta, who pressed forward officiously, to search Amenophis's secrets. Guided by him, while Antinous followed half reluctantly, he went down, accompanied by Phlegon and Suetonius, into the vaults below the temple, .where the statues were illumined with red and blue light. A potter's wheel was seen, which according to its position at any given moment, threw a sudden shaft of light upon the god's lips. In-

quisitive Suetonius could not refrain from creeping into
the little room built behind the god's statue, that the
oracle might sound from thence, in order to try whether
it would be large enough to receive a grown man. His
insipid prattle, more than aught else, deprived the
statues in Antinous's mind, of the charm which had
hitherto surrounded them. Then the party again
ascended into the upper temple, while Menephta
repeated pious sentences through the speaking-trumpet,
which led to the god's lips. The crafty Gaul seemed
especially repulsive to the youth when he pointed out a
long tube, which concealed behind a beam, led to the
entrance of the outer temple, and through which the
god could be made to speak, even when there was no
one in the room behind the picture. "One is often
unable to watch carefully there," explained the Gaul,
"or to be instructed at the right time. So there are
cases where words can be better placed in the god's
mouth at the temple-door, and the very indistinctness
of utterance, with which the tones seem to come from a
distance, is particularly appropriate for an oracle, and
sounds all the more mysterious."

Hadrian had examined this machinery with visible
satisfaction. He was evidently glad to know his collec-
tion of gods thoroughly on this side also, and again led
his companions into the lower rooms, where they
intended to scrutinize Amenophis's treasures in his
absence. The false Egyptian shamelessly revealed the
secret passages, which for the most part remained as
they had been built before Amenophis's arrival. He
looked on maliciously while Hadrian searched Amenophis's secret stores, opened the chests brought from
Egypt, and tossed over the priestly robes.

"How handsome you would look in such a dress, my boy," said the Caesar with a smile to Antinous, as he loosened the clasps of the latter's tunic, fastened the Egyptian apron around his hips, and put on a diadem with broad bands hanging over the ears. Menephta completed the costume by placing the gold serpent round the youth's neck.

"Magnificent! magnificent!" cried Suetonious and Phlegon, as the youth's superb figure, thrown out in strong relief against the dark background by the light falling from above, stood before them in this scanty attire. Suddenly a harsh voice rang out from the shadow of a pillar:

"The god accepts you as a victim. You wear the fillet of Osiris, come not to his river. He will claim you." With these words, Amenophis emerged from a dusky corridor, darting furious glances from his crafty green eyes at the emperor's startled companions. Antinous hastily snatched off the fillet and hurled it from him. A shudder ran through his naked body in the cold air of the temple-chamber, and shaken by a sudden chill he was forced to sit down.

The attack had been so unexpected, and the Egyptian's undisguised rage had so startled Hadrian himself, that superstition gained the mastery over the whole group. The emperor, with an imperious wave of the hand, closed the Egyptian's lips, and then hastily withdrew, followed by his attendants, to the upper rooms in the temple. Resounding blows and piteous cries of pain, heard through the speaking-tube in the god's lips, announced that Menephta was making the acquaintance of the camel-goad to which Hadrian had delivered him, and the emperor, whose love of mockery had already gained the upperhand, was on the point of laughing at the absurdity of these shrieks of anguish ringing through the temple from the god's lips, as if Serapis himself were uttering the wails. But one glance at the shivering youth restored his seriousness, and he sent Suetonius down to rescue the Gaul from the Egyptian's wrath, while Phlegon supported Antinous to the emperor's rooms. For the first time in his life the lad was really ill, and though under Phlegon's faithful nursing and Hadrian's friendly consolation the attack quickly passed away, it left him with traces of visible weakness, and a peevish, irritable temper. The Greek, under the burden of business that pressed upon him, had again lost sight of Antinous, but remembering the conversation in the garden, said to himself that it would do the youth good to speak freely to the emperor, and when, after a long interval, they were once more strolling with the Caesar through the halls of the Academy, where the plain, gilded by the setting sun, lay before them, and the seven hills and the outlines of the palaces of Rome appeared so distinctly on the glimmering horizon, that Phlegon fancied he could recognize his home on the Esquiline, the latter availed himself of the opportunity by saying:

"Our invalid, oh! Caesar, fears that of late we have meddled too much with the temples and the statues of the gods, and especially disapproves of our directing the oracles at Tibur."

"Oracles," replied Hadrian in an instructive tone, " are necessary. The populace will never understand the truth from their own minds. They must confront it as a plainly-given fact. Reasons are nothing to the people, but they revere the oracle."

" Yes," muttered Antinous, " fine truth that creeping Nile-worm, Menephta, or the wicked Amenophis will devise."

" We will tell them the oracles Serapis mûst give."

" May the gods mercifully avert that," said the youth indignantly — "if there really are gods!" he added sighing.

" If there is grain," said Hadrian, " there is also Ceres, if there is fruit there is Pomona, if there is a universe there is Zeus. Or have you fallen into the hands of the Christians, who illogically enough deny the plurality of the gods, though they have before their eyes the plurality of their own revelation."

" I believe in the gods when I feel them, they don't reveal themselves to me by the language of the schools. But what am I to think of these new altars and shining statues, when my ears still ring with the shouts of your architects, ordering one god to be placed here, another there, only the next day to disturb and re-arrange the whole company of Olympus ? I was just learning to believe in Serapis, but when I heard him howling like a beaten hound, this faith vanished also."

The youth, supporting his face between his hands, gazed dully into vacancy.

" Patience, Antinous !" replied Phlegon. " In the course of time beautiful and sacred memories will be associated with these temples also, so that you will forget how they were built. Even Dodona did not become a sanctuary in a single year."

Similar conversations were now of daily occurrence between the three friends, as they strolled along the colonnades of the Academy, but the more religion was discussed, the more Antinous was forced to allow his inmost feelings to be searched, his most sacred emotions handled, the deeper he sunk into melancholy. There was a wound in his heart, he had lost the sweet, self-forgetful harmony of soul, by whose means he had exerted so soothing an influence over Hadrian, who was constantly irritating his mind with dialectics, and without a definite task and purpose in life his agitated spirit sank into inert melancholy. To the Caesar himself, his favorite seemed like a different person; but even this expression of aimless longing and melancholy suited the youth, and when the latter stood before him with bowed head and downcast eyes, quietly accepting his admonitions, the old tender love for the beautiful boy again surged up in Hadrian's heart, and he thought far more frequently of what could be done to restore his friend to happiness, than was customary in his selfish preoccupation with his own cares.

CHAPTER X.

"LET your sons, Natalis and Vitalis, come to Tibur!" said Hadrian one day to Phlegon. "Antinous insists upon doing regular service in the camp of the body-guard and preparing to enter the army. The youths can occupy the same room and have their special evocatus. For many reasons I cannot allow their enrolment in the maniple.

As Phlegon maintained an angry silence, Hadrian continued:

"You can arrange all the details yourself. I don't intend to interfere with your paternal authority, but do me this friendly service for Antinous's sake."

Phlegon bowed and answered: "I will summon them."

He gazed wrathfully at the Caesar, who after accomplishing his purpose, went to the apartments of Aelius Verus, and leaning on him strolled through the sunny laurel avenues of the villa. "The Romans will say that Phlegon's sons are added to Hadrian's company of boys —place them on the same footing with the Bithynian; Ennia will grieve, Graecina write edifying letters. Accursed service, that only elevates to secretly degrade." Refusal, however, was impossible, so Phlegon wrote a short message to Bassus, and a long letter to Ennia. After sending both, he went to the body-guard's camp to make such arrangements with a young centurion, with whom he was on friendly terms, as would show that his sons were serving in the army, not acting as attendants in the emperor's rooms. Yet he remained in a downcast mood, and his greatest anxiety was to learn how the boys themselves would receive the demand that they should become companions of the imperial favorite. Their Roman pride, as well as their Christian belief, could not fail to rebel against it, and Phlegon himself would have been displeased, if they had felt otherwise. He realized the painful position in which he stood towards his sons all the more keenly, because he could not expect them to correctly estimate the restraint under which he was placed.

Thus, after the lapse of several days, during which matters at the villa pursued their usual course, two weary, dust-covered youths from Rome reached the bridge over the Anio, and sat down beside the tomb of the Plautians.

"Let us rest here, Vitalis, and then take a bath,"

said the elder, " so that we can appear before our father and the Caesar refreshed and calm."

The two youths laid aside their bundles. " We have led an unsettled life since father's return, Natalis," replied the younger. " I had just begun to feel some taste for legal studies, and now we must suddenly exchange Scaevola's books for the helmet and sword. What makes me most uneasy, is the doubt whether military service is not contrary to the precepts of the gospel. The Lord commanded Peter to put up his sword, commanded blows to be answered with meekness, is it not therefore contrary to His holy word for us to bear arms ?"

" No, brother," replied Natalis. " Doesn't the holy Scripture relate a series of the most beautiful and noble wars ? Has it not praised the great heroes of Israel and glorified their memory ? It cannot be contrary to God's command, to defend the frontiers of the empire against the Getae and Alemanni. Remember the blooming fields of Aquae, in whose fragrant pine forests we spent the happiest days of childhood. Shall the savage Germans be permitted to destroy unpunished all that Roman industry has created there ? See what happened to the parts of Dacia which Hadrian abandoned. To stake life against life for such purposes, seems to me as lawful as Samson's battle with the Philistines."

Vitalis was silent, but as he took off his tunic and unbound the sandals from his feet to plunge into the clear waves of the Anio, he remarked :

" Yet I cannot imagine the Lord with a helmet and shield."

" But," replied Natalis, " according to Revelations, he will come on a white steed and fight a decisive battle with Gog and Magog. We will think of that, when they are training us to fight. Perhaps some day it will be said of us, as it was of the two beasts of the Gospel : the Lord hath need of ye."

So saying, Natalis followed his brother's example, and the grave conversation was silenced by the splashing of the waves; youthful delight in the fresh element took possession of both boyish ascetics, and the two slender lads, spattering and teasing each other, afforded a pleasant spectacle, which did not remain unseen. A girl's head was thrust out of the bushes, and from beneath a shock of tangled hair two fiery black eyes rested on the youths. For a time the sight appeared to engross the watcher's whole attention, then her glance wandered to the garments the brothers had laid aside, and gliding softly up to them she searched their folds. In the pocket of one she found several denares, which she slipped into her own, in that of the other a little book, which she contemptuously tossed aside.

" Here, here !" shouted Natalis from the water. " Let our property alone, you thievish magpie !"

When little Lydia, for it was she, found herself discovered, she hastily seized the bundle lying beside the clothes and fled up the hill-side. Natalis wanted to follow her, but shame restrained him. He was obliged to stop to throw on his robe; in the meantime Lydia gained a long start, and when the youth, bare-footed, strove to climb the height, he stepped on a thorn and was compelled to give up the chase. Vitalis, warned by his brother's fate, tied on his sandals, but meantime Lydia had reached the end of the bare slope and was only a few paces from the woods, where she would have been concealed. Suddenly, with a loud cry, she turned

and ran back again, but on the edge of the woods appeared a youth, preparing to pursue the girl.

"Stop thief!" shouted Natalis.

"Stop thief!" called the youth from above.

But Lydia, though gasping for breath under her
stolen burden, did not yet give up the struggle. Avoid-
ing Vitalis, who was rushing towards her, she passed
close by the limping Natalis, now totally unfit for the
contest; Vitalis, exerting all his strength, bounded down
the hill-side after her, but caught his foot in a root and
fell on the ground. Lydia uttered a scornful shout and
had already reached the bridge, when the unknown pur-
suer gained the road and bounded after her like a racer
at Olympia. The fugitive vainly dropped her bundle,
the stranger seized her with a firm grasp, and she
shrieked aloud. Then the brothers saw a knife flash in
her hand. The stranger staggered, but instantly grasped
the girl's arm with his other hand, forcing her to drop
the weapon, then carried her back to the bundle, where
he met the two lads. The latter saw a youth of athletic
frame and marvellous beauty, whom they would have
instantly recognized as Antinous, whose statue was sufficiently well known in Rome, had not his face been
covered with blood, that streamed from a wound over
his eye.

"A finger's breadth deeper, and the little witch
would have destroyed your eye," said Natalis. "We
thank you doubly for your aid."

"You've made us plenty of trouble, you black
fiend," said Antinous. "This stranger has bruised his
forehead, the other one is limping, my cheek is covered
with blood, and I saw very plainly, you mad creature,
that you aimed at my eye. What shall we do with you

now ?   Shall I give you to Calpurnius's servants ?"   The girl remained obstinately silent, but at the mention of this name every drop of blood left her cheeks.

"Look at your bundle and see if you find everything," said Antinous to Natalis.

"She had no time to open it," he replied.

"And where is my purse, Lydia ?" continued the favorite.

"I haven't it."

"Let us see," he said, feeling in the pocket of the struggling girl.

"Here are five denares."

"Oh! the money for our travelling expenses," said Vitalis.   "Yes, she has emptied my pocket too."

"Here is the purse, you obstinate liar," said Antinous angrily.   "Now Calpurnius must attend to it."

"And my little book," said Vitalis, "where have you put that ?"

"It's lying on the grass yonder," said Lydia in a hoarse, frightened tone.

As the others remained silent, uncertain what to do, Vitalis, who meantime had found his book again, was the first to speak.

"It was a good volume that you threw into the grass.   I'll tell you some words in it, which you should heed all your life.   It says : ' Let him that stole steal no more, but rather let him labor, working with his hands the thing which is good !'   As for me, I forgive you."

"And I too will forgive you," said Natalis, "but think daily of the fear you suffered when on the point of being seized by this noble lord. That's the way you'll some day be pursued by the demons after death, if you don't improve.   Remember it."

" As for me," said Antinous, " I believe you to be a poor deluded girl, whom I don't wish to call to account for having almost put out my eye. I can't give you back the money, for you would apply it to a bad use, but if you'll go to Albinus, the gardener, who is a worthy man and has a sensible wife, I'll deposit the sum with him for you and add twice as much at the end of the year, if he says you have behaved well." Lydia stared fixedly at Antinous, but did not utter a word in reply.

" Well, that you may see we have forgiven you," added Antinous, " go where the wooden pail lies yonder and draw some fresh water, that we may wash the wounds you, little demon, have inflicted." The girl again stared long and earnestly at him, then slowly fetched the desired water. Antinous washed his face and pressed a dampened end of his tunic on the still bleeding wound, Natalis sat beside him drawing out the thorn, while Vitalis bathed his head, like Antinous. At this spectacle, all three began to laugh, and Natalis asked :

" Who are you, who have treated the little sinner so nobly ?"

" I belong to the emperor's household," replied Antinous evasively, lowering his eyes.

" And your name ?" asked Natalis frankly.

" Antinous."

The brothers looked at each other in astonishment. Reared under their mother's eyes in the provinces and the seclusion of the villa *ad pinum*, they had yet heard enough of the Roman world from their intercourse with other boys, to shrink from a name they had heard mentioned by their school-mates only with derision, and their mother had forbidden them to utter. Antinous seemed to them to belong to the same class with the famous dancers, mimics, gladiators, who ministered to the pleasure of the rich, but with whom no free Roman associated, and they were too unskilled in the world's ways to conceal their feelings. Yet, when Antinous's brow darkened and his lip curled defiantly, Natalis hastily replied:

"You have acted nobly, and we may learn from you. Let us help in the good work you wish to do for this unhappy girl. We are the sons of Phlegon, whom you know."

"I thought so," said Antinous. "I had gone to meet you, I am to learn the soldier's trade in your company."

"Oh, that is delightful," replied Natalis cordially, "but to judge from your running just now, we shall be the losers if we contend with you."

"I shall learn from you other things of far greater importance," said Antinous. "Let us be friends! Your father is my friend too."

"We are the friends of all good people, and you are good," replied Natalis; "but ere we clasp your hand, we must tell you that we are Christians."

"Christians!" exclaimed Antinous. "What, don't you believe that the gods rule in all the beautiful elements which surround us?"

"We believe in *one* God, who has made the heavens and the earth, who is enthroned in Heaven."

"In Heaven?" cried Antinous, "and is this beautiful earth inhabited only by men? Are the mountains to have no oreads, the fountains no nymphs, is no god to direct the shining sun, no dryad whisper in the trees, no Leucothea rule the waves of the sea? Do you wish to deny them all, make the earth dust and dirt, where only men and beasts crawl about?   Oh, how poor and wretched you are! I will not follow you into this godless world."

" To us the one invisible God is everywhere present in His works."

"What care I for the work, if it is empty?   And how am I to imagine the one omnipotent Being?   I see the nature of Apollo and Diana by their rays, the good Jupiter's when I gaze upward to his eternal sky; that of Ceres, when I behold her grain fields.   The nature of every naiad, every dryad is taught me by the house she occupies; I can talk to her, can offer her a fitting sacrifice.   I anoint their sacred stones, throw flowers into their springs, hang garlands on their trees. But what am I to think of your invisible deity?   How can you love a god you do not see?"

" He speaks to me by His word."

"Oh!" replied Antinous, " the gods have earnest words too.   Does not Apollo say to me at Delphi: 'Thou art!' or 'Learn to know thyself!' Does he not say at Tanagra: 'Enter a good man, but depart a better one.'   Or when I go to the temple of Heracles, do not the mighty works I there see represented, tell me more than long sentences?"

Vitalis seized the roll of MS. that still lay beside him, replying: "Hear whether the God's revelation sounds like the wisdom of your priests," and in the conviction that the Lord Himself would show him the best words, began to read where his eye first chanced to rest: "Come unto me, all ye who labor and are heavyladen, and I will give you rest."

Antinous listened attentively, while Natalis sat by

with clasped hands.   The lad's simple reading sounded musical, yet melancholy, the evening breeze rustled through the pines, the water of the Anio plashed and eddied, the cicadas began their evening song, and still Vitalis read on.   He had already reached the history of the Passion.   Antinous listened, now with contradictory emotion, now deeply moved and absorbed.   Two men emerged from the woods and approached, but Vitalis did not pause, on the contrary he raised his voice. The good seed must be scattered for acquaintances and strangers.

"You are certainly in haste to initiate your new comrade into your superstition," said a harsh voice, and as the three youths looked up, the brothers saw Hadrian before them, while their father stood behind gazing at them with an expression of anxiety and grief, which caused them heartfelt pain, spite of their conviction that they were in the right.

"Have you been breaking each other's skulls first," continued Hadrian, "and are you now trying to heal the wounds with magic words? By Esculapius, that is a cut, my boy! Which of the two fellows aimed at your eye? I will have the truth, Antinous."

"Neither, my lord," replied Antinous. "We were all wounded by the same foe."

"And that was—?" asked the Caesar angrily.

"We have forgiven him," answered Antinous, "so it is not seemly to denounce him afterwards."

Meantime the two brothers looked for little Lydia, but she had silently disappeared.

"You cannot deceive me by such excuses," replied Hadrian, scanning Phlegon's sons suspiciously. "Did you get worsted and draw a dagger?" he added.

"No, my lord," replied Natalis quietly.

"Then name the criminal."

"We cannot."

"You cannot?" exclaimed Hadrian angrily. "My Tartarus shall teach you."

"I will answer for the truth of their statements," said Phlegon coming forward; "but you see, my lord, that the enterprise promises to have as little success as I predicted. Give up what has commenced under such unfavorable auspices. Let my sons go back to Rome, they are out of place here."

Hadrian shook his head. "They shall go down to their quarters, but Antinous must return with me to my apartments till his wound is healed. I think he will change his mind by to-morrow, and tell me what has happened here. But take this conjuror's book with you, Phlegon. If your sons should create a Jewish insurrection in the body-guard's camp, even I could not save them from severe punishment."

Vitalis quietly thrust the book into his pocket.

"Give it to me," said Phlegon.

"I cannot deliver up the sacred MSS.," replied the lad.

"You will obey," answered Phlegon.

"I dare not."

"Ennia has trained your boys admirably," said Hadrian derisively. "Tartarus must come to your assistance."

Phlegon quietly approached Vitalis and said a few words in a low tone. The lad hesitated a moment, then handed his father the book. Hadrian watched the transaction indignantly, then turned away, commanding Antinous to accompany him, while Phlegon said to his sons:

"You have not been at Tibur an hour, yet you have already made an enemy of the man on whom our whole destiny depends. Could you do nothing more sensible, than to read aloud on the public highway books whose possession you knew brought punishment?"

"This punishment should fall on me, father," replied Vitalis, "so give me back the book, as you promised."

Phlegon, sighing, handed it to him. He knew how little could be done with the Christians by force, and his first object was to gain the confidence of his sons, in whose education he had committed such great blunders. The three walked silently towards the barracks on the northern end of the forest. The 'hundred rooms,' as the remains of the Praetorians' barracks are now called, and one of which the two lads entered, met at an angle looking out upon a triangular parade-ground, closed by intrenchments. One room was separated from another to prevent communication between the soldiers, but a wooden gallery ran along the chambers outside. By this Phlegon's sons, passing the quarters of the soldiers, who gazed curiously after them, reached their own lodgings. The third bed in the little room, which was to have been occupied by Antinous, was assigned to an evocatus, who was to initiate Phlegon's sons into the duties of the military service.

"Strange how we fare here," said Vitalis, when Phlegon and the soldier had retired. "I am always wondering what sin we have committed, that we have been so rudely tossed to and fro of late."

"Then think of the apostle's words, my brother," replied Natalis. "We know that tribulation worketh patience, and patience experience, and experience hope. And hope maketh not ashamed!"

CHAPTER XI.

ANTINOUS's hope of being permitted to enter the Praetorian body-guard was now baffled, yet without a murmur he again performed his usual services, for he saw in Hadrian, not only the emperor and his benefactor, but also the invalid, who must be indulged. Still, it vexed him that the Caesar obstinately refused to believe his assurance, that he did not owe his wound to Phlegon's sons, and even before knowing them, reproached his favorite's new friends with hypocrisy and zeal for proselyting. Besides, the words of the sacred book Vitalis read aloud to him had not passed through his mind without leaving any trace. Had all these things really happened ? he asked himself, or was it only a myth, invented by clever priests, as Hadrian daily invented oracles. The explanations of the god's sacrificial death, with which Natalis had occasionally interrupted his brother's reading, reminded him of Amenophis's tales of the sufferings of Osiris, or those of the bleeding wounds of Adonis, which he heard annually at the great festival of the god in Bithynia, but there the celebration related to a symbol of the life of nature, with which no one was unfamiliar. The brothers' story, on the contrary, claimed to be real history. Not three generations had passed since this god walked upon the earth and exclaimed: "Come unto me, all ye who are weary and heavy laden."

"Who would not do so?" the Caesar's favorite sighed mournfully, and as words from the gospel which he had formerly heard from Hermas, words spoken by the Egyptian, and pious memories of his own youth blended confusedly in his mind, he dreamed that the symbol of the Christian's god that he had engraved on the emperor's sword, was burning deeply into his own heart, then again felt Osiris's fillet around his temples, and fancied Amenophis was snatching it furiously from his head and thrusting him into the waterfall, until a deep, dreamless slumber released his soul from this conflict of the gods.

When Hadrian awoke the next morning, Antinous had already stolen away. This, however, was nothing unusual on the part of the Caesar's spoiled favorite. Hadrian dressed himself and went out into the portico, but on hearing the Bithynian's voice echoing from the stadium, blended with the admiring shouts of Phlegon's sons, his anger rose. He instantly felt convinced, that the new-comers had instigated the youth to this failure in the consideration due his master. Passing through an avenue of laurels he approached the stadium, where with a sensation of pleasure he gazed at the three youthful figures, watching with delight Antinous's instructions to the young Romans in the mode of throwing the Greek discus. His disks darted like lightning across the arena, always striking the mark. "You must turn the hand farther inward, hold the disk so, and swing the arm back two or three times, till it has the right motion and you see the mark distinctly. There—that's better already."

Hadrian watched the game for half an hour, then continued his walk. On his return he no longer heard the Bithynian's directions, but a vehement dispute seemed to be going on between the lads. The voices of the two brothers impetuously interrupted Antinous's. Hadrian could only catch single words. At last he heard Vitalis exclaim:

"It is not seemly for one who can hurl the discus like you, to render effeminate services to Caesar." The rest of the sentence was inaudible to Hadrian, but he struck his staff angrily on the ground, muttering:

"Wait, viper!"

He walked rapidly to the stadium, but the bitter words seemed to have caused a separation. As he entered, Antinous, with a defiant bearing, was just leaving the place, while Phlegon's sons were picking up the disks with which they had been playing. At sight of the emperor they greeted him with a respectful: "Salve, Caesar!"

"Has the centurion given you leave of absence?" asked Hadrian sternly.

"At Antinous's request, Caesar," replied Vitalis.

"Then tell him from Hadrian, that no new-comer is to be allowed to quit the barracks during the first thirty days; this order applies to you as well as the others."

The boys bowed, and as Hadrian silently passed them, said:

"Ave, Caesar."

"It will be just as agreeable to me, if we are not allowed to play here," said Vitalis, when the emperor had gone. "Only I feel sorry for Antinous, I'm afraid we treated him too harshly."

When Hadrian returned to his apartments, where Antinous usually poured out his morning draught, he found the boy leaning against the parapet of the terrace, gazing mournfully into vacancy. The reproving words on the emperor's lips remained unuttered. The youth's melancholy oppressed him. Taking from the table the wreath of roses that lay on the silver waiter, encircling the jar containing the morning draught, he was about to place it on Antinous's head, as he had often done. In the act, he gazed at him enquiringly.

" Well, my Ganymede ?"

" I don't want to be adorned like a woman !" exclaimed Antinous indignantly, hurling the flowers away. " I hate this love, which humiliates me in my own eyes."

" Very well, my son," replied Hadrian indifferently. " I am too old for a languishing lover; remember that I am your master."

" And I am too old for a plaything. You promised I should go to the barracks," replied the boy, tears springing to his eyes.

" You shall have your way, as soon as the Christians are gone," replied Hadrian. " I don't wish them to teach you to despise the gods and repay my love with ingratitude." Antinous remained obstinately silent. " Do you want friends, who pass the statues of the gods without a greeting, who never anoint a stone with oil, nor fasten a pious offering to a sacred tree ?" continued the emperor.

" They pray too," said Antinous, " and fear their god more than others."

" Stop !" replied Hadrian with an angry light in his dim eyes. " Say no more. I will overlook the Christians, so long as they keep quiet. But if they try to make mischief here, endeavour to secure neophytes, or bring their mystic customs into my house to turn your head, the stone quarry shall have them, sorry as I should be for Phlegon. Now go ! You have spoiled my morning."

Antinous went out to face one of the purposeless, lost days, that were always his lot when Hadrian was angry. He had spoken the evening before to Albinus, the gardener, and recommended Lydia, so he determined to see her again, but learned that the young girl had not made her appearance. As he had nothing else to do, he went to the forest to search for the little witch, of whom the cut on his forehead still reminded him. He felt a sort of obligation to do so, for he had brought misfortune to all whom he met on the unhappy morning when he wore the disguise of a shepherd. His deception, according to Hermas's expression, had delivered them over to the Father of Lies. So far as it depended upon him, this girl at least should not be lost. He searched the woods where Lydia usually wandered, climbed to the spring where she had once sold flowers, looked through the lemon garden on the hill-side, the olive-grove above Elysium, and on emerging into an open glade found himself on the ridge, at the end of which resounded the ever-green oaks of Dodona. He hesitated. He had been there only once with Hadrian, but the selli had inspired him with horror and repugnance. "Can those stony figures, wallowing in the dirt, really know more of the immortal gods than we?" he had asked Hadrian.

"The gods of the nether-world also dwell in mire and dust," the emperor replied, but Antinous at that moment mentally vowed never to disturb them. He would have turned back now, but not having found Lydia elsewhere, it seemed wrong not to search here also. So he approached the ancient oaks, from which a strong breeze was drawing loud notes and sounds. A hundred voices appeared to be greeting the youthful wanderer. The grey-haired prophetess, as usual, sat stiffly beside her oak, of which she seemed a part. Her eyes were fixed intently upon Antinous, who felt as if they exerted some mysterious spell upon him. To shake off his own fear, he asked :

" Prophetess, canst thou, who knowest what the gods of the nether-world decree, tell me where I can find the little flower-girl, Lydia ?"

" Seek her not, she will not miss thee a second time. With one eye, thou wilt no longer be the handsome Antinous !" and a harsh, repulsive laugh rang from the witch's lips.

" If you know from whom I received this wound, you doubtless know more about her."

" Ask for thyself, favorite of Caesar, hear how the Immortals greet thee; hark to what they say ! Basileus, Basileus, he will rule, rule happily, endowed by Caesar, endowed with crowns by Caesar, Basileus, Basileus !" These words harmonized so perfectly with the clang of the metal basins, that Antinous himself now heard them distinctly in the tones. He gazed at the witch with superstitious horror.

" Hark how the inhabitants of the nether-world rap !" said the sorceress. " Listen to what they say !" Antinous, following her gaze, now first perceived the selli, who lying extended on the ground, pressed their ears to the earth. " He will wear crowns, crowns, so long as he honors the gods."

" Basileus, Basileus !" again clanked from the oak.

" Crowns, crowns ! Avoid women, flee the Chaldeans, slay the Christians !" continued the selli. " Basileus ! Basileus !" clanked the basins. Then the youth distinctly heard a voice from the distance say : " Use the

present, Hadrian is mortal, Aelius loves not Antinous.
Use the present. Basileus, Basileus!"

"Dost thou hear the voices in the air? Favored
of Zeus, lend thine ear! Thou shalt hear the voices from
the nether-world," said the woman. Antinous obeyed
her sign. Placing his ear to the ground he heard a dull
roar, like the sound from a shell laid over the ear.
Then he distinguished cries, lamentations. "Hadrian!
Hadrian! down with Hadrian! Become king, Antinous!
Pray, pray, ere it is too late."

"Horrible spectre!" cried Antinous, rising. "These
are not gods, who give such base counsel."

The priestess made no reply, only stared fixedly at
him, without the slightest change in her wooden features.

"Will Hadrian really die?" asked Antinous mournfully. But it seemed as if he was speaking to a wooden
statue. She remained motionless, and the selli lay on
the ground like the trunks of fallen oaks. Antinous
turned shuddering away, but from the oak behind him
echoed the words: "Basileus, Basileus!"

The youth darted on as if pursued by the furies.
What would Hadrian think, if he heard he had questioned the selli about the length of his life. And he
knew that the Caesar had his spies everywhere.

Reaching the descent to Tempe, he paused beside
the dark fount of the invalid Pythia. The Zeus well
seemed deserted. Antinous wearily sat down on the sun-
scorched turf and gazed at the fragrant, gleaming plain.
The work of nature went on around him, the perfume
of heather and thyme rose dreamily, the spicy odors
of the pine-boughs swept across the warm carpet of
broom, the oaks and pines rustled, and he fell asleep.
It seemed in his dream as if mysterious tones rose from

the well of Zeus.   He heard the humming noise of a top, the monotonous sing-song of an unvarying voice :

"Spin, oh! top, and draw the youth into my house. Hail, Hecate!   Thou terrible one, come and help me with him.   Meal must first be consumed in the flames. I scatter it, saying it is Antinous's ashes. Spin, oh! top, and draw the youth into my house at once!   That Antinous may love me, I burn his laurel.   As the twigs kindle with a loud crackle, suddenly blaze up and are consumed without even leaving ashes behind, so must my heart burn with love for Antinous. Spin, oh! top, and draw the youth to my house.   May the handsome Bithynian instantly melt with love, as by the aid of the divinity I melt this waxen image.   As the bronze girdle turns by Aphrodite, turn Antinous towards our door. Spin, oh! top, and draw the youth to my house." Half-asleep, Antinous drowsily raised his eyes towards the cave, and saw a bluish cloud hovering over the entrance. He still heard the humming of the top, then all was still. Rising indignantly, he approached the cave.   A figure stirred within.

"Pythia!" he cried.

"What is it?" a hoarse voice answered.

"Where are the torches? I want to question the dwellers in the nether-world."

"They will not speak to-day."

"They spoke up yonder, and will not be mute here."

The voice was silent.

"Can you tell me whom I seek?"

All was still.

"If you are really a prophetess, tell me, where does little Lydia, the flower-girl, live?"   It seemed as if a

sigh echoed from the corner. Antinous was groping his
way forward hap-hazard, when he felt a burning breath
fan him. Glowing lips covered his face with kisses,
and long thin arms clasped his neck. It seemed as if
the scorching breath was seeking the eye wounded the
day before. Was it a woman or a child who thus clung
to him? As she drew him down, he saw in a niche a
glimmer of light that touched the well-known bundle of
torches. Holding the little stranger firmly with his right
hand, he pushed back with his foot the door of the niche,
and a flood of light streamed full upon the face of the
supposed Pythia. Antinous started back, exclaiming:

" Lydia, you here?"

" I am not Lydia, I am Pythia," replied the young
girl.

"You—Pythia?" laughed Antinous, then added
gravely:

" Where is your predecessor, the pale maiden from
Epirus?"

" Dead," answered Lydia carelessly, "of homesickness, of the poisonous water, of the blows of the old
Thessalian witch."

" But Hadrian knows nothing about it."

" Because I've already prophesied from the darkness
for three weeks. If they ask for a torch, I pull my hair
over my face so, light it, and thrust the blaze directly
towards their eyes, so that they snatch it hastily away,
and I glide back into the gloom."

" But are you not afraid of perishing, like the poor
Pythia?"

" Oh! I shan't die of homesickness; I'm at home
here, and my mother comes to see me, and I don't
drink the water. I lift it to my lips and throw it away.

I can talk just as stupid nonsense as that crazy Pythia without it."

" Don't anger the gods, girl !" said Antinous in terror.

"The gods ?" laughed Lydia. "How foolish you are, you big boy !" she giggled.

" Do you know how they make the voices ?" asked Antinous, remembering the secrets of the Canopus. Lydia laughed, then embraced him.

" Kiss me, and I'll show you all Hades." Antinous reluctantly endured her caresses. At last she said: "Come," took the lamp from the niche and threw the light behind a rock, where a secret opening appeared. Gliding after the nimble little cat, the youth found himself in a corridor, cut through the soft rock and ending in a natural cave, with several openings above, through which fell a glimmering light, while the breeze sweeping through, produced a strange roaring, ringing and rustling. See this pipe, which passes through the cave like a bow. The cunning Zarobal calls in at one end what comes out at the other like a voice from below the earth. Mother Hunnik too can speak beautifully from a distance. When the voices sound from the air, you must notice how she bends her body, and look carefully at her throat to see how she swallows and gasps, though she understands concealing it very skilfully. It cost Caesar lots of money before he found so clever a ventriloquist. But she's a witch, or she couldn't have taught me how to catch you," and again she threw her arms around the youth. Antinous trembled with anger.

" What have you here ?" he asked, pointing to all sorts of bags and boxes.

" Why, your two companions' bundle would have

gone into these chests, if you hadn't run so fast yesterday." She opened one of the bags, from which gleamed
bronzes, plates, buckles, gold and silver articles, that had
undoubtedly been stolen from all the countries in the
world.

" Free yourself from these wicked people, Lydia,"
cried the youth. " Become an honest girl, and don't
live by theft and fraud. Won't you go to Albinus, the
gardener ?"

Lydia shook her head. " I don't like to work. It
tires one so, and it's so stupid."

" But you'll go to ruin here," said Antinous.

" I won't stay here always, only until I'm larger. But
make haste, somebody might come to the fountain, and
if I were absent, there would be a great ado. Pray
don't betray what I showed you." Again she clung
tenderly to the youth, and Antinous was obliged to
endure her advances till they once more reached the
fountain.

When he had at last shaken off the girl and her repulsive secrets, it seemed as if he ought himself to be
ashamed to face the light of day. " So these are your
gods, Hadrian !" he said to himself. " Does he know
his selli as thoroughly as his Egyptians ? Let him
continue his pastime, but who can restore the faith, with
which on the mountain summit I gazed upward to the
eye of Zeus, and felt Poseidon's breath in the roaring
surges that broke upon the strand ? If Lydia is permitted to play Pythia unpunished, there are no avenging
Chthonian* gods. But if there are no divinities of the

* Chthonia (Χθονία), may mean the subterraneous, or the goddess
of the earth. that is, the protectress of the fields, whence it is used as a
surname of infernal divinities, such as Hecate (Apollon. Rhod. iv. 149;
Orph. *Hymn*. 35. 9). Nyx (Orph. *Hymn*. 2. 8.) and Melinoë (Orph,

nether-world, who will guarantee their existence in the world above ? I wish we had never come here. When we fought with the Germans by the Danube, and were tossed to and fro by the tempest on the Tyrrhenian sea, the Caesar seemed more devout than I. But if I study and imitate the different religions with him much longer, I shall become an enemy of the gods, like Hermas. I will not allow myself to be robbed of faith in the gods as well as in men !" he exclaimed with flashing eyes. " I will escape from this maze ! Yonder, where no human breath floats on the air, I will inhale the breath of the great Jupiter, and wherever a divinity is revealed to me, erect, with loyal hands, an altar."

He did as he had said, and henceforth reclined every day on the heights of the Sabine mountains, without taking the slightest interest in the new creations at the villa. Wherever, on the summits crowned with brown sweet broom and lonely groups of pine-trees, he found a secluded nook, where the divinity appealed to his susceptible soul, he erected an altar of unhewn stone, anointed a smooth rock with oil, or hung flowers on it as an offering. His favorite spot was a grotto of the nymphs which, situated far above the waterfalls, was only accessible by a narrow path from above. Two rocks, towering opposite to each other, rose high above the dimly-lighted space, where beside a still, clear spring, stood the ancient sculpture of the nymphs; rude, clumsy figures with an austere smile on their grave faces, they were totally unlike Hadrian's smoothly-polished statues of the gods. The desolation of the grotto, overgrown

Hymn. 70. 1), but especially of Demeter. (Herod. II. 123; Orph. *Hymn.* 39. 12; Artemid. ii. 35; Apollon. Rhod. Iv. 987.)—*Smith's Dict. of Greek and Roman Biog. and Myth.*

with evergreen-oaks, juniper and box, gave him a feeling
of melancholy. He wished to serve this forgotten
divinity. So he daily climbed to the spot, laid flowers
before the entrance to the sanctuary, eat his bread there
after throwing a crumb into the sacred spring, and
dreamed of a more active existence as soon as the
Caesar restored his freedom. He took no part in
the life at the villa, except so far as his duties towards
the emperor required. Phlegon's sons he entirely
avoided. They had offended him, slandered his gods.
Whatever their gospel might say, gratitude to Hadrian
and the Immortals was too strong for him to escape its
bonds. Yet, precisely because there was a sore spot in
his relations to both, he avoided the friends who had
touched it with a rude hand. He meant to shake off
his effeminate life at the palace, but recognized no one's
right to upbraid him for the past.

CHAPTER XII.

AGAIN life at the villa glided idly and slowly away,
while Hadrian's misanthropy brooded with paralyzing
weight, like a sultry atmosphere, on all the inhabitants
of Tibur. At last a morning came when everything
suddenly seemed disturbed, so that the people swarmed
about like ants. A courier had arrived from the city
with a letter-bag, that had brought all this excitement
into the quiet rooms. The emperor had received a message which caused him to instantly summon the Egyptian
Amenophis, while at the same time messengers dashed
to Rome and various country estates to call a council of

state to meet at Tibur.   But the servants, while making
preparations for the reception of so many gentlemen
and their attendants, sometimes put their heads together
and whispered that extremely dangerous disturbances
had broken out in Egypt.

Phlegon had received a letter from his wife, Ennia,
after reading which he paced up and down the garden,
talking excitedly to himself, sometimes pausing, absorbed
in his soliloquy, sometimes wildly gesticulating.

A letter, addressed to Vitalis and Natalis, had also
arrived from Graecina, which led the two boys to request Antinous to visit them in the barracks.

It was not without an emotion of surprise, that
Amenophis obeyed Caesar's summons, but, while secretly
pondering over the matter, which might threaten him
with an investigation, he outwardly assumed a still
colder and more sullen expression, that seemed to say
life, death, mankind, and events of every sort were
equally beneath his consideration.   So he entered the
peristyle of the palace, where he found Hadrian, full of
restless anxiety, sitting before some Egyptian maps.
The information the Caesar communicated, after inviting
him to be seated, inspired greater interest in Amenophis's
mind than anything that had occurred since his arrival
at Tibur.

After a long period of divine anger, an Apis which
bore all the signs of a genuine god, had been found in
the district of Memphis. Glittering black in hue, he had
on his forehead a white triangle, on his back a white
spot in the form of an eagle, on the right side a figure
in the shape of the crescent moon, and under his tongue
a knot in the form of a scarabæus.   The longer this
popular incarnation of the deity had been absent, the

greater was the joy and exultation throughout Egypt. The sacred animal was taken to Pi-Ha-pi (the abode of the Apis) a luxuriant meadow on the right bank of the Nile near Heliopolis. All Egypt flocked to greet the sacred guest, who concealed beneath this form the soul of Osiris, and looked on with delight to see the god graze, chew the cud, and caress the cows, that had been given him for companions.

After the expiration of forty days, the animal was placed on board the golden boat to be conveyed to Memphis, when it was seized by the priests of the Thebais and dragged by force up the river towards Thebes. The procurator thought such a breach of the peace should not be permitted, and, ere the robber priests could reach the Thebais with their sacred prize, took possession of the golden boat, but did not venture to instantly decide the question concerning the possession of the sacred animal, and therefore conveyed the bull to Besa, an oracle on the borders of the disputing districts. The priests of the temple of Osiris, located there, joyfully availed themselves of the opportunity to increase the renown of their sanctuary. A green pasture was enclosed as at Pi-Ha-pi, companions for the sacred bull were sought, a costly double fence was put up, and a stable, the god's palace, erected according to the legal proportions. The province was congratulated on its good fortune, and the priests from Memphis vainly demanded their rights. When, at an attempt made by the latter to steal the bull from his pasture, the animal, rendered furious by the glare of the torches, wounded the temple-servants, the whole district rebelled, the boat with the golden chapel was destroyed, three priests were slain, several wounded, and the Roman procurator now decided that the bull must remain where he was. But the inhabitants of Memphis now took up arms, demanding the restoration of the god, that had been born on their territory, while the Thebans fought on the side of the natives of Besa, their neighbors. The procurator, aware of the fanaticism of the mob, attempted to bargain with them, and at last declared he must await Hadrian's commands. Meantime the spirit of lawlessness and anarchy increased; not only did little skirmishes constantly occur in the two provinces, but in many places the Roman garrisons were besieged in their citadels. The character of the hot-blooded population was so incalculable, that a single false step might lead to a general insurrection.

Amenophis read this report without moving a muscle, but Hadrian saw his eyes flash with pleasure. "This news seems to please you?" the emperor asked suspiciously.

"Every son of the black land rejoices, when Osiris is given to her again."

"And to whom, in your opinion, should the sacred bull be conducted?"

Amenophis bent his head, and said hesitatingly: "In general the claim of Memphis is not to be disputed; but if an ancient custom is to be neglected, the precedence should be given neither to Besa nor Thebes, but to Heliopolis, because the priesthood of the latter is now the most important. Perhaps Memphis will be satisfied, if the privilege of having the Apis graves is confirmed and the right to the sacred mummy secured in this case also. But these are matters, which can be dealt with only by an Egyptian."

Hadrian looked at him suspiciously, but made no reply. While reflecting on the subject, he determined to go to Egypt himself, accompanied by Amenophis, and soothe the unruly populace. A procurator might cause a war to increase his own importance, and Egyptian wars, from the days of Caesar and Pompey, had been disastrous. Besides, Hadrian's interest in religious questions found fresh food in this incident, and he already saw his name carved in the Egyptian hieroglyphic characters in all the temples, as the Roman Pharoah who had made peace between Memphis and Thebes. So he dismissed Amenophis, commanding him to be ready to sail with him for Alexandria. In the evening he jestingly told Antinous that they would probably both be sculptured in the Apis tombs, clad in Egyptian costume, their chests represented by a front view, their heads in profile, with almond-shaped eyes, their hands raised beseechingly, advancing to receive a blessing from the horned god. But Antinous answered repellently :

"Amenophis has taught me, that as the deity here dwells in sacred trees, so beside the Nile the gods become incarnate in the sacred animals. Before the river rises by the god's command, the sacred heron always appears to direct the people to make their preparations. The sacred bull, born of a chosen cow and a ray of sunlight, is wonderfully marked in a manner seen in no other land. The nature of the gods, which we adore in symbols, there finds expression in the conduct of animals, and therefore it is just that the productive power of Osiris should be worshipped in Apis, as the destructive might of Typhon is adored in the crocodile. The deity himself has assumed bodily form in them, made himself manifest in their nature; Amenophis adores the god, not the animal as such."

"I am glad to see you thus, my favorite!" said Hadrian. "I perceive you have shaken off the Christians' superstition. You shall accompany me to Egypt and we will crown you with lotus flowers, as we did the last time."

"Give me a bow and arrows again instead. You know I killed my first lion in Egypt. The chase will dispel my gloomy thoughts."

"Very well, my son, we will hunt too, and since you don't like our new temples, I hope you will find some on the Nile old enough to please you."

Antinous expressed his thanks, and secretly congratulated himself on being removed from the sky of Tibur, which weighed so heavily upon him.

"Phlegon, too, must go with me to Rome and Egypt. Call him, I wish to consult him about to-morrow's council of state."

The news which had so greatly agitated Phlegon was a short communication from Ennia, which far surpassed even his worst forebodings concerning the villa *ad pinum*. Ennia wrote, that the Roman bishop's interference and Hermas's impetuous reproof had driven Graecina entirely into the hands of the hypocritical Nereus and his allies. She had declared that she would allow no one to force her into servitude again. Thereupon the Roman church had severed all connection with the congregation in Graecina's house, but since she had called herself the mother of a church of her own, the latter's folly had reached its height, and her Brothers daily told her that the true doctrine could only be found with her. Nereus, Ennia continued, was now trying

to persuade Graecina to make over her estate to him, on
the pretext that this was the only way the house could
be preserved to the parish, in case of her death. The
old lady was also told, that the act would not change
her own position in any respect. The first step had already been taken, by Graecina's making Nereus a freedman, so that he was now authorized to hold landed
property. How far the actual sale had progressed, Ennia could not say, but since his emancipation Nereus
had acted the part of the rich man, who would be able
to pay cash for the whole villa. If Phlegon wished to
make an attempt to save the property for his children,
he must come himself. Ennia had lost all power over
her mother, who was now more completely in the hands
of her slaves than ever.

Such were the tidings that rendered Phlegon unable
to eat, drink, or sleep, till he gazed feverishly, with
weary eyes, at the world around him. He had just determined to ask the Caesar for leave of absence, when
he was summoned by Hadrian, in order, as Antinous
whispered, to receive orders for the departure to Rome
and Egypt. Hadrian gazed at his secretary in surprise,
and with the humanity that never wholly deserted him,
even in the days of his gloom, clasped the Greek's hand,
saying:

"What is the matter, Phlegon? You are ill, your
hands are burning!"

"Would my sovereign permit me to begin by speaking of myself?" asked the Greek humbly. "I should
be better able to attend to business, if I might first unburden my heart."

"You know I am your friend," replied the emperor.
"Speak freely."

Phlegon then described the condition in which he had found his household on his last visit, Graecina's increasing weakness of mind, the hypocritical fleecing practised upon her by her slaves, the shameless extortions of the sycophants, and repeated Ennia's last message. Hadrian listened attentively, showing his sympathy by occasional exclamations of anger. When Phlegon had ended, he replied:

"We must do something against the Christians. Their insolence and boldness daily increase. I will direct the praetor to display the full severity of the law, instead of the indulgence that has hitherto prevailed."

"My petition was, that the settlement of Graecina's affairs should be entrusted to me. I wished to ask your permission, Caesar, to go to Rome. I hear you will soon depart yourself to the long-deserted Palatium. Then I might arrange these matters. It would cause me pain, if through my complaints the cruel trials were renewed. You know alas, that Graecina has led my sons and daughters astray. Grant me time to win them back to the gods. If Natalis and Vitalis were permitted to go to Upper Germany with the eighth legion, it would be the best way of securing them from Graecina's influence."

"I will grant your request all the more willingly," said Hadrian, "because if the trials are once commenced, I can make no exceptions, and your sons seem to me very hot-blooded sectarians, not to be gained by a handful of incense. Write an order for their transfer and I will sign it; we set out to-morrow, and they can be on their way to the Alps next week." Phlegon bowed his thanks, and then read aloud the letters that had arrived.

While Phlegon was holding this conversation with the emperor, his two sons, depressed and wearied by their military service, sat in their narrow room, into which the setting sun was casting its last golden rays. Before them lay Graecina's letter, an epistle little calculated to cheer their drooping spirits. Their grandmother wrote that she had separated from Pius's church, as it had become a house of hypocrites. Pius had wished to forbid her making friends with the mammon of unrighteousness and placed her under the charge of an almoner, appointed by himself. But she clung to the apostle's words, that no man can serve two masters, and had released herself from the bishop's tyranny. Yet, in order to give an example and be perfectly just to the gospel, she had determined to preserve the villa *ad palmam* to the church by having it registered in the name of Nereus, who on his part would recognize Chloe as joint owner. In all these transactions, she had found no one but Hermas show a right spirit, though he too had vehemently opposed her. Therefore, that he might understand her better, she had requested him to take her letters to her grandsons at Tibur, through whom she had had the word of truth proclaimed in the emperor's household. The zealous man had now forced her to aid him in a plan from which he expected great results. If he came, she entreated the brothers to help him, for though he had said a great many foolish things to her about her house-keeping, during which time, instead of listening, she had secretly counted how many Brothers now belonged to her parish when they were all present, he was nevertheless a true disciple, and if he succeeded in converting the emperor, it would be a great piece of good fortune, for many Brothers said the

Senate was earnestly requesting Hadrian to commence a fresh persecution of the Christians. The letter was diffuse and vague, pervaded according to Graecina's way, with all sorts of complacent remarks, but what the boys gathered from it was ill-suited to rouse them from the sorrowful mood that had come over them in the solitude of the barracks. The *ad palmam* parish separated from the Roman church and under the direction of Nereus, while the worthy lady allowed it to be distinctly seen that it was really she who attended to everything, was news over which the elder lad, Natalis, in particular, shook his head. Besides, the congregation had not pleased them so well of late. The number of those who only sought gifts and bread had constantly increased, and if the travelling preachers had not brought with them a fresher atmosphere, little blessing would have rested upon the meeting. Spite of their grandmother's angry contradiction, both lads were firmly convinced that Nereus was a hypocrite, for they had seen him intoxicated more than once. It seemed to them a disgrace, that he should now be the uncontrolled director of the parish and both agreed that this state of affairs ought not to continue.

But the transfer of the villa to Nereus made the boys still more anxious. How would their father receive the news? What would become of their mother after Graecina's death? Of course they had often been told what a misfortune it would be to the church if, after Graecina's death, Phlegon should expel the congregation from the villa. Once Natalis had answered angrily, that the words of the gospel: 'Take no thought for the morrow,' applied to the church as well as individuals. Was it not very strange that Graecina's property had been disposed of without her knowledge? Moreover it was very doubtful whether Nereus would not abuse the authority the reckless old woman had placed in his hands. What torture to be chained here, while such important decisions were being made in the city, whose columns of smoke they saw mounting into the evening sky. Graecina, according to her sly nature, had veiled the most important part of her letter in such mysterious vagueness, that the reader could not possibly obtain a clear idea of the matter. Neither could they understand in what way Hermas expected to bring about Hadrian's conversion. "To rekindle that burnt-out ember would be a task for an angel, not for a man," sighed Vitalis, but meantime he remembered the promise they had both given their father never again, without some urgent necessity, to cross the path of the emperor, whose angry glance they had once met.

While thus pondering over this unexpected news, a cheerful voice rang through the grated window of their room: "Why, you're hanging your heads like willow shoots, that miss the water of life. Cheer up, Brothers, rejoice always, and again I say, rejoice!"

"Hermas!" cried the lads.

"Yes, I come with the spirit of power and consolation and testimony, and if the Lord grants His favor, we will trample on the great dragon's mouth and wrench out his teeth."

The boys smiled sadly. "Can you explain this strange letter?" said Vitalis, pushing Graecina's roll of MS. towards him?

"So I'm to read one of Sister Graecina's inspired epistles," said Hermas, and glancing sarcastically over the long roll, added: "It's a pity you were not separated from your grandmother sooner; if she had composed such a volume every day, there would have been less time for her other follies, and the church of the saints would not have fallen into the mouths of the blasphemers. I have learned one thing from Graecina. I formerly supposed begging proceeded from aversion to work, but she has taught me, that there is a benevolence founded upon distaste for serious occupation. She believes the Lord has said: 'It is more amusing to give than to work!'"

"Please read it and explain the contents," said Vitalis, interrupting the loquacious speaker. So Hermas was obliged to glance over Sister Graecina's long letter. He did it with the practised haste with which one preacher reads another's sermon, as if he perceived from the beginning of each paragraph what the end would be. During this occupation, a superior smile distinctly expressed his contempt for his feminine colleague's prophetic spirit. But the appreciative remarks concerning himself, at the end of the letter, softened his mood, and dropping the sheet he said compassionately: "Poor woman, she certainly means to take the best course, but has not the gift of distinguishing the possible from the impossible, and of examining souls."

At Vitalis's request for a more detailed account the prophet, who was reluctant to enter upon worldly matters, replied:

"It is as she writes. Pius informed her that she must submit the alms-giving to the poor of the parish in her house, to the oversight of a neighboring deacon, who, she said, was too partial. To another proposition she made no reply, but the next day announced that she no longer belonged to Pius's church, since every servant must stand or fall according to his own master. So she really excommunicated us, not we her, but as we don't wish to be responsible for what the hypocrite Nereus may yet undertake with the foolish old woman, we have renounced all connection with the church *ad palmam*, until she shall have satisfied the bishop's command. But Nereus is expressly forbidden to share the body and blood of Christ, he must have his part with Dathan and Abiram, no Brother is permitted to greet him, and he is to us like a heathen and a publican."

" And the sale of the villa ?" asked Natalis.

" 'This is the first time I have heard of it," said Hermas. " I fear Graecina is being greatly deceived by Nereus. But enough of the works of darkness! We are here that the light may be revealed, and you must open the doors for it. Hadrian is being urged to persecute the church like Nero and Trajan, of horrible memory. On the calends of June the venomous Fronto made a speech in the Senate, in which he again brought forward all the old nursery tales—that at the Lord's Supper we eat a Hellene's flesh and drink his blood, that we have a book commending the burning of Rome by Nero, that at our meetings we light only *one* torch, which is fastened to a dog's tail. If the time for giving rein to our wild orgies is too long delayed to please the youths, one kicks the dog, the torch is hurled to the ground, and in the gloom the works of darkness begin. They have heard this nonsense for the hundredth time, yet for the hundredth time have believed it, because this they can understand, while for the word of truth they have no comprehension. ' People don't expose themselves to the rack, just for the purpose of hearing a book read aloud and singing songs about sheep and lions,' that conceited Suetonius said to me with a simper, when I met him to-day at the baths of Albula. Let him grin. But you shall know I intend to hold a meeting at this very villa, so that he can see for himself whether the gospel we preach leads to such customs as an empty head like Suetonius says."

The boys shook their heads mournfully.

"What? Do you hesitate?" cried Hermas. "Hadrian is collecting all the gods here. He wishes to fathom every mystery. Surely it cannot be difficult to induce him to attend our worship once. Only tell him—"

"He hates us," replied Natalis. "You must apply to Antinous."

"He hates you? And Graecina is revelling in the thought that you are his favorites, and have already half-converted him."

The boys smiled at their kind old grandmother's fancy, and then related the story of their unfortunate meetings. Their military duties confined them to the barracks, and the promise given their father would also prevent them from aiding the enterprise. All Hermas could persuade them to do, was to send by a soldier on duty for Antinous, who instantly appeared. His manner was not wholly free from embarrassment, as he entered the brothers' room for the first time after so long a separation, feeling ashamed of the neglect with which he had treated both, while the latter were also somewhat confused by the memory of their last quarrel. But Hermas, in his eagerness to urge his request upon the Bithynian, would allow no expression of their emotions.

"I have long desired to witness your mysteries from beginning to end, that I might form an opinion how far

your customs harmonized with the beautiful book Vitalis
once read aloud to me," replied Antinous. "But just
at this time Hadrian's mood towards you is such, that I
don't believe he will grant your request."

"Ask him."

"It would be useless."

"Then leave the doors leading from the peristyle into
the gallery open. We will come at sunrise and compel
him to hear the word of truth, even against his will."

"That I dare not do, without first asking him."

"Very well, let him entrench himself as he chooses,
God's mercy will find him yet. If locked out from the
peristyle, we will steal into the gallery and read the gospel under his windows till the soldiers drive us away
with the sword. What the Spirit has prompted, no
coward shall dissuade me from doing. Oh, ye of little
faith, if you only had faith like unto a grain of mustard
seed."

Antinous smiled.

"I will gladly listen to your religion. That it will be
more honest than that of the selli, I believe from your
kind face and the service you rendered me at the lime-
pit, but there are so many strange new gods now, that
one cannot leave the doors open for all the priests. I
should fear, ere you could sing your hymns, the Pythia
of the Jupiter of Dodona would have robbed the whole
peristyle. But, for the sake of old friendship, I'll
carry your request to Hadrian."

So they parted. That evening, while Antinous was
unbuckling the Caesar's sword-belt, he said:

"I paid my first visit to Phlegon's sons to-day."

"So I was told. What have you to do with the
Christians ?"

"They have a design upon you, Caesar," said Antinous, smiling, but the latter cast a gloomy glance at him.

"Their request is not unreasonable," continued the youth loyally. "They think you might listen to one of their meetings before casting them to the lions, and I confess I would rather become thoroughly acquainted with their mysteries than those of the selli or of Serapis, of which I already know more than is agreeable to me."

Hadrian maintained an angry silence.

"They have made it very convenient for you too, they will perform all their religious ceremonies in your peristyle at sunrise to-morrow."

"In my house?" cried Hadrian. "Are you mad, boy? An assembly of the Galileans here? That would be just the opportunity for Servianus's friends to make an outcry against favoring Eastern superstitions, and show the Senate how I trampled under foot the edicts of the idolized Trajan. Did your friends Natalis and Vitalis suggest this boyish trick?"

"It is Hermas's idea," replied Antinous. "Why do you hate Phlegon's sons, when it was you yourself who summoned them here?"

"Phlegon disgusted me with them, by acting as if they were too good for you. Besides, there is an expression on their faces, which irritates me. They are devotees. When I first saw them, I knew they were trying to make you faithless to me. I know these Christian tricks. When I perceived the blows you had given each other, I was sure at once what you were quarreling about."

"But"—Antinous tried to interrupt.

"No, no," continued Hadrian. "I heard with my

own ears that slender Vitalis call out, that it did not beseem you to render effeminate services to Caesar."

Antinous turned pale. " Were they so far wrong ?" he asked after a pause, in a troubled voice. " Let me be your friend, not your favorite. Set me free. I will serve you with redoubled loyalty."

" That is the Christians' nonsense," replied Hadrian. " As if a youth could be so beautiful as you, without winning the love of a friend so much his senior. Years will make a man of you, and when you once bristle with an ugly beard, no one will stroke these smooth cheeks."

Antinous silently bowed his head. After a pause, while in the act of removing the lamp, he asked:

" So I must not admit the Galileans ?"

" Let them do as they choose," said Hadrian harshly; " the consequences be on their own heads." Then he turned his face towards the wall, as if he wished to sleep.

Antinous put the lamp in the niche. The doors of the peristyle still stood open. Antinous shut them, but without pushing the bolt. Then he himself sought his couch. It was a long, sleepless night to him, as well as to the Caesar. When the first dawn of light in the East announced the approaching day, low, murmuring songs, which in some portions rose into exultant melodies, echoed from the corridor that surrounded the viridarium.* The emperor, still half-asleep, listened quietly. The hymns died away, and a prayer began, which seemed to the Caesar like an Orphic or Pythagorean

* An ornamental garden was also called *viridarium* (Dig. 35. tit. 7. s. 8), and the gardener *topiarius* or *viridarius.—Smith's Dicty of Greek and Roman Antiq.

passage. "Oh Lord, Thou hast searched me and known me," he heard: "Thou knowest my downsitting and mine uprising, Thou understandest my thought afar off. Thou compassest my path and my lying down, and art acquainted with all my ways. For there is not a word in my tongue, but lo, O Lord, Thou knowest it altogether."

Hadrian listened approvingly, thinking: "This may be a way of introducing the lessons of Pythagoras and Plato among the common people. So long as nothing worse comes, we will let it pass." But this approval suddenly gave place to an expression of fierce hatred, he started from his cushions as if an adder had stung him, and listened intently to the sounds from the peristyle. "Can the insolent fellows have left the barracks?" he muttered, grinding his teeth. A musical boyish voice echoed clearly and distinctly, saying: "There went out a decree from Caesar Augustus, that all the world should be taxed. (And this taxing was first made when Cyrenius was governor of Syria.)"

"Wait, fellow," cried Hadrian furiously, "I'll show you who is emperor now!" Hastily throwing his cloak around him, he crossed the atrium to the peristyle, and drawing aside the curtain, saw the reader of the gospel directly opposite to him, illumined by a slanting ray of sunlight. It was not Vitalis, as he had supposed, but a young slave, whose industrious quiet labor in the garden had often pleased the Caesar, and who was numbered among his special favorites. His wrath subsided, especially as he did not discover Phlegon's sons among the congregation.

"The old fool!" he muttered, perceiving Hermas, who was gazing at him with the most eager attention.

Then he heard the body-guard march under the gallery. The tribune, attracted by the unusual sound of singing, advanced with four Praetorians. Hadrian went out and beckoned to him. "Find the leaders of this meeting, and deliver them to the praetor. Leave the others unmolested, they are among my best servants. The strangers must be punished for their intrusion into my apartments, but I will pardon the folly of the rest."

The tribune saluted, and the emperor retired. The sonorous reading of the gospel suddenly ceased, and a malicious smile flitted over Hadrian's face. Antinous rushed in.

"Caesar," he cried in anguish, "they are arresting Hermas."

"They are doing their duty, boy," replied Hadrian coldly.

"So you have lured him into a snare," cried Antinous. "That is unworthy of you."

"I told you he would act at his own peril. I did not summon the guard, the soldiers came of their own accord. But I cannot suffer it to be said, that I myself hold Christian meetings in my peristyle. Who told you to play with fire?"

"Caesar, one word from you and he is free."

"I cannot, boy."

"No one will know it."

"Folly! At this moment it is known in the villa, in an hour Tibur, and in a day all Rome will hear the tidings."

"I owe my life to Hermas, he saved me!" Antinous sobbed despairingly.

Hadrian passed his hand over the youth's waving locks, saying kindly:

"Thank the gods, boy, that your friends, Natalis and Vitalis had sufficient military discipline to remain in their barracks, and that you may see I don't indulge my hatred, run across to Phlegon, who already has my signature in his hands, tell him to have his sons' baggage packed at once and take them away in his own carriage before the formal investigation begins." Antinous wiped away his tears and obeyed the command. Hadrian gazed after him long and earnestly. "Let matters remain as they are. In Germany they will no longer trouble him with their scruples."

CHAPTER XIII.

On the morning the court moved to the imperial palace on the Palatine, there was a great bustle before Graecina's house on the *via lata*. Groups of ragged beggars and poverty-stricken citizens were standing outside of the gate or within the area, greeting companions who came out of the door of the mansion with exclamations of inquiry, while others pressed in to also receive the noble Graecina's farewell gifts.

"What did you get?" cried the fruit-seller Tryphaena to her son Titius. The boy held out a silver candlestick, which the mother weighed with an expert hand. "Now wait a while, till she has forgotten I've already been in twice, and I'll try again. What luck, Justus?" she continued, turning to a ragged, half-drunken vagabond, who came staggering out of the doorway.

"Enough for another jug," replied the tippler, chinking some coins.

"Accursed fool!" scolded a neatly-dressed woman behind him. "I thought I should get so much, and she handed me this basket of roses she had gathered, and when I told her my children couldn't eat roses, added a loaf of bread. It was worth while to come from the Janiculus for that."

"Why did you dress so well?" said another, who was hiding her booty in an old basket. "If you had put on clothes like mine, you'd have fared better."

"What luck! What luck!" shouted voices from the crowd, as one of Spartianus's slaves, bearing a bronze candlestick the height of a man, appeared behind the scolding woman. "By Hercules, that was a gift!"

"It will be sold to Jacobus the Jew, to buy freedom for my old age!" At these words a fresh group pressed eagerly towards the door. "Don't let Tryphaena in again," cried several: "she has already been twice, and her Titius too."

"What's that to you?" replied the woman, releasing herself from the speaker's grasp.

"Stop! The comites and assessors of the court," was suddenly heard. "Make way for the practor's assessor!" The common people drew back, and a foppishly-dressed young magistrate, followed by two secretaries, passed through the throng of beggars and entered the house, before which the apparitores stopped, preventing farther intrusion by their presence.

"This will be rare sport," the young man said to his companions. "The estate of the Pomponians snatched from under the nose of the upstart Phlegon, who is beginning to play the patrician, and sold to an ex-slave—by Jupiter, the whole amphitheatre will be talking about it this evening."

A strange spectacle presented itself, as he entered the atrium. Graecina's tall figure towered like the mast of a ship above a group of beggars, kneeling around her, while she rummaged in a chest or with her long arms snatched from the niches in the walls, vessels, clothes, valuables, sealed packets, packages of money and fruits, handing them to the different individuals with a happy smile, while repeating to each some sentence that referred to herself and not to the recipient: "Sell that thou hast and give to the poor!" "To give is more blessed than to receive!" "Make to yourselves friends with the Mammon of unrighteousness!" Behind her the corpulent Nereus moved to and fro with evident agitation and impatience, his face flushed with joy at the coming of the day when the most superb estate in Rome would fall into his hands, and yet enraged with the spongers, as he now called his companions, who were rapidly emptying the house before it passed into his possession. At last he could no longer control his anger and exclaimed: "Tryphaena has already received gifts twice."

"Hold up your dress, Tryphaena," said Graecina, taking as many of the packages as her long arms could clasp, and while pouring them into Tryphaena's lap, added: "Haven't I the power to do what I choose with my own?"

The young magistrate had hitherto watched the strange scene with evident amusement, but now came forward, saying:

"The law can wait no longer, noble Graecina; I have prepared the deed of sale. Where are the purchaser and the witnesses, that the business may be concluded?"

"The purchaser is here," replied Graecina, "as we are assembled in his name, and here are the witnesses."

"The witnesses must be free-born citizens."

Graecina gazed helplessly around her, while Nereus came forward, saying:

"Will not freed-men suffice?"

"No, not for the sale of a family estate."

"Then I will instantly send messengers to the neighbors."

"You should have thought of that before, lucky buyer. But for the noble Graecina's sake, I'll give you an hour's time, and meanwhile will finish the papers."

Yt this moment a piteous cry from Tryphaena was heard at the door.

"They're taking away all my gifts! Graecina, Nereus, help me!"

"Shut the door and drive out the rabble," said the assessor to the apparitores. The doors of the atrium were closed, while the noise outside continued and finally degenerated into a general fight:

"You sell the villa *ad pinum*, with all its appurtenances, rights and privileges—to whom?" the young magistrate now asked Graecina.

"The villa *ad palmam*," murmured Graecina.

"In the deed the villa is called *ad pinum*, and your house has never been known in the city by any other name."

"It is the same," said Nereus; "write *ad pinum*, noble lord." Graecina stared into vacancy.

"What is the buyer's name?"

The latter answered for himself. "The freedman Nereus."

"The seller must reply!" said the magistrate sharply.

"I have offered it to the Lord," answered Graecina.

"To what lord?" said the magistrate impatiently.

The freedman answered in her place: " Nereus."

" Christus !" sighed Graecina.

" Now I have two purchasers, what is the name of the right one ?"

" I bear the surname of Christus also," replied Nereus.

" He lies," cried the slave Tertius from a corner; " he was never named Christus."

A convulsive tremor ran through Graecina's limbs, and she murmured :

" Mammon has obtained dominion over him."

" Shall I write Nereus ?" said the magistrate.

" Nereus," faltered Graecina.

" And you sell him the villa as his absolute, independent property ?"

" As his independent property, but on condition that everything remains as before, and I am not disturbed in my habits."

" That is no independent property," replied the assessor. "So you retain the free use of it during your life ?"

Nereus here interposed. " What was arranged between the noble Graecina and myself, has nothing to do with the deed of sale. Merely write: 'as independent property.'"

" As soon as Graecina requests it," replied the official. " Speak Graecina l"

Graecina stared fixedly into vacancy. " I wanted to sell the villa *ad palmam*, not the villa *ad pinum*, and to Christus, not to you, Nereus. It seems to me, that you have wandered from the true path, it will be better for us both to examine our hearts again."

" But consider, Graecina," said Nereus humbly, " how

long we have already examined our hearts, now this
noble gentleman is here, and the Brothers are sent out
to bring witnesses. The law will not be at hand immediately a second time."

" What the law will do, you can leave to me, fellow,"
replied the magistrate arrogantly. Graecina rose, while
Nereus held her beseechingly by her robe. His whole
plan seemed baffled, and the old tippler's face grew livid
with emotion as a knock at the door frightened Graecina,
who had already turned to go, back to her seat. " Open!"
cried a voice outside, familiar to all.

" It is Phlegon!" stammered Graecina, sinking back
upon her pillows.

The Greek entered, followed by old Eumaeus, who
had slipped over to the palace at the beginning of the
legal business. Graecina tried to make her escape, but
he already stood before her, and scanning the table
heaped with papers, the magistrate, and Nereus, asked
angrily :

"What is going on here ?"

" We are arranging a sale," replied the young official
carelessly ; " the noble Graecina is selling the villa *ad
pinum* to the freedman Nereus."

"That cannot be done," replied Phlegon resolutely.
" Graecina is incapable of undertaking transactions of
this kind. You see yourself she is feeble-minded," he
added, pointing to the old woman, who was lying in
convulsions, with her eyes rolled up till the pupils were
scarcely visible, while the whites glared horribly.

" Has she been placed under guardianship?"

" No."

" Has a suit to place her under guardianship been
commenced ?"

" I shall enter one to-day, in the name of her daughter and grandchildren."

" That should have been done before, and I cannot interrupt the legal business begun after the three weeks delay required by law, unless Graecina herself draws back."

Phlegon glanced towards the old lady, and saw Nereus behind her. The freedman was whispering:

" See how he plays the master."

" Graecina, is it your wish that the business should be concluded ?" asked the magistrate.

" Yes, my lord," replied Graecina, fixing her eyes on the wall.

" In the name of Ennia, in the name of your grandchildren," cried Phlegon, fairly beside himself, "defer this matter, or you will repent it."

" I wish to remain mistress of my house," exclaimed Graecina. " I sell it to obtain protection from this man."

" Where are the witnesses ?"

" Here," replied two plainly but neatly-attired citizens.

" Nereus !" shouted Phlegon, "one step more, and I will demand from the praetor your punishment for taking part in forbidden assemblies."

Nereus smiled coldly.

" I am not jesting."

" I suppose you will let your sons enter the amphitheatre and your daughters be given up to the gladiators, like Danae and Dirce ?" sneered the fat freedman.

" Hadrian will know how to protect them from it," replied Phlegon proudly.

" Do what you choose," replied Nereus.

" Proceed, proceed !" said the magistrate impatiently.
" Your private bargains have no place here. I command silence. The deed runs as follows."

While the assessor began to read the long document
aloud, Phlegon, pale and trembling with fury, approached
the secretary's desk, tore off a piece of parchment and
wrote a notice to the praetor, worded : " The freedman
Nereus holds Christian meetings at the villa *ad pinum*
and profiting by Graecina's shameful superstition, has
gained possession of the ancient estate of the Pomponians, wherefore your interference is requested in the
name of the legal heirs." Nereus looked on indifferently, but listened all the more attentively to the reading of the deed of sale. " The price is not yet inserted,"
said the magistrate.

" Five hundred thousand sesterces," replied Nereus.

" Where did Graecina's slave obtain such sums ?"
cried Phlegon.

" That is his business," answered the judge. But
Chloe approached Nereus, saying in an undertone :

" Don't push matters any farther, Phlegon will denounce us."

" Nonsense !" replied Nereus.

" I'll take back my savings," whispered Chloe. " See
who'll give you the eighty thousand. I don't want to
be thrown to the lions."

" Don't be foolish, if Phlegon accuses us, we'll deny
it on oath. The villa *ad pinum* is worth a handful of
incense."

" Yes, if it could be done," replied Chloe timidly.

" Be calm, I know the laws."

" I have entered the sum," said the magistrate.

Deadly pale, but with glowing eyes, Phlegon approached his mother-in-law, and held out the roll of MS. he had just stamped with his signet.

" Here is the notice to the praetor. Will you draw back or not ?"

Graecina began to tremble. The young magistrate stepped between them. " I can allow no threats and intimidation here. Graecina has a right to do and leave undone what she chooses. Will you sign or not, noble lady ?"

" I will," said Graecina, stretching her long thin arm towards the reed.

" Eumaeus," said Phlegon hoarsely, " take this letter to the praetor."

" I will fly, my lord," said the old man, vanishing through the doorway.

" All the misfortune that will now burst upon this house I cast upon your head, old fool!" exclaimed Phlegon in furious wrath, raising his arm as if he wished to crush Graecina's skull. But he controlled himself, and casting at the young assessor a glance to which he could not remain wholly indifferent, left the atrium. Graecina, guided by Nereus, was just taking the quill to sign the bill of sale, when the assessor, who wanted to gain time, withdrew it, harshly remarking that the duplicate must first be prepared. This task would occupy an hour, which the young noble wished to use in considering whether the admiration he would reap from his companions for such a trick on Phlegon, would be worth the hatred of the imperial favorite. Besides, he was curious to know what message the Greek had sent the praetor. If the latter, in blind fury, ran himself on the spit, so much the better, then he would have his hands out of the affair, which was be-

ginning to grow rather hot. So, much as Nereus panted
and begged that he might at least be permitted to sign
the document itself, as the copy could be legally certified, the young official was not to be persuaded. So the
fat sinner, though greatly excited and constantly listening for the result of Phlegon's message, sat in his former
place, while Graecina gazed through the open roof of
the atrium at the blue sky, twirling her thumbs incessantly, while unintelligible words sometimes fell from her
drooping underlip.

Phlegon had ascended the stairs on the left, leading
to the apartments of his wife, who received him with
eyes reddened by tears, sobbing:

" Phlegon, believe me, I have done all in my power
to deter my mother from committing this folly."

Phlegon turned angrily away. " I too have done
what I could, the rest is the praetor's affair."

" By all the gods of Rome!" exclaimed Ennia in
horror. " You have summoned the praetor ?"

" I am not obliged to give up my children's heritage
to the Galileans."

" Phlegon, is it thus you keep your oath, thus you
spare my mother, your children ? Miserable man, will
you plunge us all into ruin, to save this patch of earth,
this heap of stones ? I implore you on my knees, recall
your accusations! Phlegon, keep your promise!" The
beautiful woman knelt weeping before her husband, her
whole frame trembling with grief and terror.

" It is too late," said Phlegon ; " they are here."
The footsteps of several persons were audible on the
staircase. Phlegon drew back the curtain to greet them,
but instead of the lictor and his attendants, his own
sons stood before him.

"What do *you* seek here?" said the terrified Greek. "If your lives are dear to you, back to the camp of the body-guard, to which you are assigned. One fresh folly, and you are lost!"

"He that loseth his life shall save it, father," replied Natalis. "Chloe sent us word that Graecina was suffering for the Lord's sake; we will not desert our old grandmother."

"Away to the barracks, remember your oath of military service."

"We are off duty till sunset." At this moment the blows of the lictors sounded on the door.

"It is too late," said Phlegon in a hollow tone. "Restrain yourselves now, I beseech you. Graecina shall not be sacrificed. I only wished to prevent her from reducing you to beggary. Her evident feebleness of intellect will shield her from every danger."

As if this consolation was to be instantly destroyed, the aged mistress of the house appeared at the same moment, the very image of despair, leaning on her blooming granddaughters, Paula and Cornelia. Her head nodded to and fro, her feet shuffled. "Save me, Ennia, save me! The lictors, the soldiers, oh, I am dying!" and her head sank on her breast. Ennia sprang forward, laid the terrified woman's head on some pillows, and was beginning to rub her feet and hands, when the shrill voices of Nereus and Chloe echoed from below. A few loud blows silenced them, and only piteous moans of pain were heard. Phlegon was going down to interpose, but the centurion already stood before him.

"We have orders to bring Graecina and all the Christians in this house before the praetor." ·

Graecina rolled up her eyes, and went into convulsions.

"Graecina Pomponia is ill," said Phlegon. "I will answer for her appearance. Cannot the trial be deferred?"

"My orders are absolute," replied the soldier, and turning towards the stairs, shouted:

"Quadratus, order the closed litters to be brought."

Graecina started up, shaking as if with a feverish chill, and stared at the centurion as if he were a demon.

"Follow me, noble lady," said the soldier, "or I shall be compelled to carry you."

"Go, go!" shrieked the old woman. "Leave me, I am the daughter of Pomponius, the widow of Plautius, this is my son-in-law, the emperor's friend."

"It is he who made the accusation against you," answered the soldier, shrugging his shoulders. "Quadratus," he called, "do your duty!" Two soldiers appeared in the doorway. Graecina bent forward, then pressed her hand on her heart, and fell lifeless into Ennia's arms.

"She is dead!" wailed the children. "Father, you have killed her."

Phlegon gazed unmoved at the departure of this hated, useless life. His sole thought was—how much she would have spared me, if she had only died a few years sooner. The centurion approached and quietly examined the corpse.

"My orders don't concern the dead; tell the magistrate below he must testify to the death of Graecina Pomponia, which makes their execution impossible. Are the slaves locked up?"

"As many as we found; most have fled. Chloe

and Nereus, Eumaeus says, are the instigators. They
are among the prisoners."

"That is fortunate," said the centurion, and turning
to Phlegon, continued: "My commission is not yet
finished."

Phlegon turned pale.

"Who among those present has attended the meetings of the Galileans held here?"

"I!" cried Natalis and Vitalis at the same instant.

"We too!" exclaimed Paula and Cornelia.

"Are you all Christians?"

"We are!" cried Phlegon's children in one breath.

"Then you will come with me, instead of Graecina.
Here, lictor!"

"They are free citizens," said Phlegon beseechingly,
"descendants of Pomponius. Accept bail."

"I must execute my orders," replied the soldier.
"Offer bail to the praetor."

Ennia had gazed at her children with dilating eyes,
extending her hands as if to protect them. As the lictor
forced them towards the door, she stepped forward, saying: "I will not be separated from my children, I too
am a Christian."

"Ennia! Mother!" exclaimed father and children in
the same breath.

"Then come, noble lady," said the centurion compassionately.

"She speaks falsely," exclaimed Phlegon. "She offered sacrifices to the gods this very day."

"That is not for me to investigate," replied the centurion. "She too will follow me to the praetor."

"Might I not take the four little ones with me?"
said Ennia gently. "There is no one here who loves

them. Without me they will be frightened, weep, perhaps die."

" Ennia—what do you leave *me* ?"

" The villa *ad pinum*," said Ennia coldly.

" I have no orders to take the children, noble lady, but the praetor will surely allow them to share your imprisonment. Quadratus," he called down the stairway, " another litter !"

" But listen to reason, Centurion," Phlegon again began. " It is known throughout the whole city, that Ennia has always been seen in the temples among the Roman matrons, the praetor certainly did not summon girls and children, and the boys are ordered · to the body-guard's camp this very day. Be satisfied with the criminals below. My accusation was solely against them."

The centurion raised his head scornfully. " You must have known that being tried for holding the Christian faith is no jest. You reap what you sowed."

" Farewell, father !" cried the two boys.

" Farewell, Phlegon," said Ennia, " farewell forever !" The curtain at the door fell. The Greek stood alone beside Graccina's corpse. Covering his eyes with his hand, he leaned against the wall as if utterly crushed. The room was whirling around him, the Cupids painted on the walls laughed scornfully, and he perpetually saw in the centre of the apartment the lifeless body. At last the wretched man so far regained his self-control, as to determine to hasten at once to Celsus and beseech him to defer the trial. Yet how could he expect any mercy from the malicious scoundrel, whom he had so deeply insulted ? Then he resolved to go to the prison. But no one was admitted before the preliminary examination, and he had just experienced what degree of kindness he might expect from the magistrates. Better still, he would go instantly to Hadrian. But the emperor was sleeping after his journey, and no audience could be thought of until the next morning. What might not happen ere that time! His blooming wife, his lovely daughters in that man's power! What was it Nereus had exclaimed? "Like Danae and Dirce!" A thrill of horror shook his frame, and drops of cold perspiration started on his brow. He could not think of the misery he had brought on all whom he loved. Even if everything resulted as favorably as possible, his sons were under military rule. They could not be saved. He saw the sword glittering above their heads, saw them impaled, crucified. "Nero's nature appears more and more in Hadrian, who knows what new tricks the crazy invalid may devise?" Again his glance fell on the corpse, a feeling of inexpressible bitterness stole over him. How had she, who wrought all this woe, borne the consequences, when they became serious? Crept whining like a beaten cur under Ennia's robe, and when the fate she had conjured up stretched its hand towards her, done the most comfortable thing she could, breathed out her life, blown away like a vapor. His sense of justice rebelled against this escape, and angrily approaching the corpse, which lay before him cold and waxen, like a cast-off garment, his brain began to burn, his eyes rolled in their sockets.

"Holloa, Graecina," he exclaimed hoarsely, with mad fury, "wake, rise! You want to remain mistress of your house, now answer for what you have done! You rejoice that you have punished me so, don't you? Answer, Graecina, or.....; you won't, silly goat? Wait, I'll teach you to speak!" He seized the dead woman by the arm and shook her. "You shake your head, it wasn't you? Was it I? You still nod? What?" He again shook the lifeless woman furiously. "So, you can still laugh? How handsomely the big goat's mouth opens. Wait, I'll make you howl. Down with your lip! Down with the whole husk."

He kicked the dead woman in the chest. The corpse rolled from the cushions, and the arm was thrust stiffly into the air. It seemed as if Graecina were trying to seize him. Filled with horror, he fled to his own room, where he fell senseless.

When, long after night had closed in, Phlegon was roused by the chill breeze sweeping through door and windows, he pressed his hand upon his brow. It seemed as if the dead woman had stood beside him all the time, clutching his throat with her cold fingers. He felt a sharp pain in his heart, and it was difficult for him to rise. The wind was playing with the curtain at the door, the window-shutters creaked. A broad band of light from the full moon rested on the staircase leading to the dead woman's chamber. Here and there the wainscoting creaked, making Phlegon start in terror. His hair fairly bristled. "She is rising, she is coming here," he muttered, closing his eyes, but at every sound fancied he could distinguish the old woman's creaking, shuffling step. Then he again heard Ennia's sobbing voice: "Phlegon, you struck my mother, my dead mother!" He saw the corpse, as it lay with upturned face on the cold stone floor, one clenched hand thrust into the air. The hand grew longer and longer, and again clutched his throat, stopping his breath. No matter how often he turned towards the wall and drew the coverlet over his head, he could not shake off the vision. He felt that never, during his whole life, should he be able to forgive himself, unless he atoned for what he had done in the madness of his rage. He walked mechanically towards the room, the moonlight showing him a thousand phantoms. He shut his eyes, that he might not see the Lemures and spectres gliding amid the columns of the peristyle, and thus groping his way onward, reached the room where Graecina lay. The full moon, shining through the window, poured a flood of light into the chamber. Phlegon forced himself forward, seized the corpse and laid it on some cushions, then gently pushed a pillow under the little head and folded the arms peacefully across the bosom. A mild, gentle look now rested on Graecina's countenance. The expression of timid weakness and complacent inquisitiveness had given place to the repose of death, and nothing remained save the great kindness of heart which had been the predominant trait in a character so little governed by intelligence and wisdom. As this look dawned upon him in the moonlight, bitter remorse overpowered the impulsive man. In the presence of this peaceful corpse, he could no longer think of Graecina's failings, but pressing his hand on his aching heart, asked himself:

"Did you really exhaust all expedients in trying to strike a balance between the different objects of your lives? Did you appeal to the motive she understood, instead of constantly harping upon those you knew had no existence for her? Did you not always reproach her for her childishness, and yet judge her as if she were capable of sound reasoning?" He had no answer to these questions. The consciousness of his guilt pierced his soul like a sword. Sobbing convulsively, he fell upon his knees, and pressing his face to the garments of the dead, wept bitterly. After an hour spent in unavailing remorse, he rose, murmuring:

"Let us save what is left!"

"After lighting lamps beside the corpse, to banish the evil spirits, he went to his room with the intention of going to Hadrian early in the morning and endeavoring to stop the trial. "I will ask the liberation of my family as a reward for my long and faithful service. If Hadrian is a man, he cannot refuse this request from one he calls his friend."

Somewhat soothed by this hope, he again lay down and fell into an uneasy slumber. Towards morning a buzzing and murmuring, like the sound of prayers, blended with his dreams. Then strange melodies, such as he had heard at his last visit, fell upon his ear; but the chorus was not so loud as at that time, the singers' ranks must have been greatly thinned. The listener too had changed. The weary, broken-spirited man no longer heard the tones with displeasure, they no longer sounded alien and mysterious. It seemed as if the deeper meaning of these melodies had been revealed, since this heavy burden was laid upon him. They told him something that had long slumbered in the depths of his own soul. He could not distinguish the words, but the music spoke of suffering, submission, resignation. They said that the substance of life was bitter, but whoever trusted himself to the mercy of God would rise to a higher world, to taste its sweetness. Long after the notes had died away and the footsteps of the congregation had crossed the area, Phlegon lay on his couch, lulled by a dreamy feeling of submission and peace, unknown the day before. "Whether my gods or yours help us," he said at last, "they must be saved."

Rising, he arranged his dress and resolved to go at once to the palace. When he went up to Graecina's death-chamber to look at the corpse once more, it had disappeared. He could easily understand the connection, but was not angry.

"Let her rest in the vaults of the Nazarenes, instead of the proud tomb of the Pomponians or Plautians, to whom she never really belonged," he murmured.

Besides, it was a relief to be spared the embarrassment of the funeral, the sarcastic condolences of the relatives. On the threshold of the gate he met Eumaeus and Tertius, who said that Antinous had been there the day before enquiring for him, but they supposed he was at the praetor's. Ordering them to lock the house and admit no one, he went down the steps to the *via sacra*.

CHAPTER XIV.

It had cost Phlegon much trouble to obtain an audience with the emperor, who preferred to refuse admittance to those whose requests he intended to deny. But after a beseeching petition handed him by Antinous, the Caesar could no longer refuse his faithful servant a hearing. The Greek found him buried in rolls of papyrus covered with hieroglyphic characters, while Amenophis stood by his side, earnestly explaining the deep importance of the conflict now going on in Egypt. Hadrian greeted his old companion curtly, like a stranger. Phlegon explained that Ennia had never been a Christian, that his sons' folly would be forgotten during their absence with the army in Germany, and urged that his daughters had become the victims of a foolish grandmother.

Hadrian briefly answered, that Phlegon knew he never interfered in trials until the judge had pronounced his sentence, least of all could he depart from this rule for a servant of the palace, without exposing himself to just censure. When Phlegon fervently, passionately besought him not to send him away so, to consider the anguish of a father's heart, Hadrian angrily threw down the roll of papyrus he had been twisting restlessly to and fro, exclaiming imperiously:

"Was it I, who gave the praetor information against your family? Did I, out of base avarice, seek to deliver Graecina, your nearest relative, to the lions? You were the man of honor that applied to the malicious Celsus, whose disposition you knew. Now that the axe falls differently from what you expected, and threatens to hurl others into the gulf you opened, I am to use the imperial power to set aside the law. It cannot be. Hadrian exercises the right of pardon only after sentence has been pronounced. Beware that you don't utterly disgust me with using it. You must eat the dish you have prepared."

With these words the emperor turned back to his rolls and Phlegon, deeply agitated, left the friend who in a moment of such distress, could speak in this tone.

"It would be best to kill myself at once, that I may not experience what is to come," he muttered. "But we will try the praetor."

Again he went down to the *via sacra*, and dragged himself wearily up the steps to the *via lata*. Several times he was forced to sit down, but at last reached the villa *ad pinum*. When he saw Celsus's house before him, and remembered under what circumstances he had last entered it, his heart stood still. What could the humiliation to which he was about to expose himself, avail? But perhaps the avaricious man could be bought? Why, save to extort money, had he arrested the boys, the young girls, who had never offended him. His whole past life proved it. Sorely disheartened, Phlegon said to himself:

"Now I must give up the heritage for which I sacrificed my family, give it up to buy them back. If I had turned my back with them yesterday upon this house, on which rests the curse of the gods, how happy I should be now. What should I have cared whether Nereus or Celsus owned it—my conscience would be clear and my family happy. Oh, Jupiter, what bandage hast thou placed over my eyes! I pray thee to accept this sacrifice."

He grasped the knocker at Celsus's gate. One blow, and a richly-dressed slave opened it and asked what he desired. After a time he conducted the Greek into the area and requested him to wait with several other clients. All were admitted before him, then he too was permitted to pass the fasces of the lictors and enter the atrium, where Celsus received him with distant courtesy. Phlegon gave the praetor the same explanations made to Hadrian, declared Ennia's imprisonment illegal, asked that his sons might be sent to the camp, pleaded for his daughters. Celsus coldly replied that he had entered upon the matter very reluctantly, the course he had pursued for years in overlooking what was going on before his eyes in the neighboring villa, proved the forbearance shown an aged woman and a patrician race. Then, receiving one day a reprimand from Caesar for his indulgence, and the next an indictment from Phlegon, he could not help supposing that the emperor desired the utmost strictness. Now that the trial had been officially commenced, it would not do to let it drop, which would naturally create great excitement in the city.

"For of course people are amazed, that Phlegon himself appears as the accuser of his own family," he added with a malicious smile.

The Greek now offered bail for the release of his wife and children. As Celsus shrugged his shoulders, he added with downcast eyes, that in case of liberation he should never ask payment of the sums deposited. "The villa *ad pinum* itself would not be too high a price for me."

"And what security do you offer for the fulfilment of this promise?" asked Celsus craftily.

Phlegon uttered a sigh of relief. So the man could be bought.

"I'll give you a bond in any form that may be arranged between us."

Celsus seemed to reflect, then handed the Greek a wax tablet. "Write: 'In case of the liberation of my family, I declare myself ready to sell the villa *ad pinum* to the praetor Celsus, at a price fixed by him.'"

Phlegon wrote the words, and with a heavy sigh signed his name. Celsus then added a few lines, tied both tablets together, and struck the metal basin.

"Bid the lictor and the runner Celer enter."

Phlegon supposed one was to be sent to the prison, the other to the judge, but Celsus folded his arms, wrapped his toga closely around him, and drawing his short figure up to its full height, stood before the Greek with the mien of a Cato. As the officers entered, he said coldly:

"The culpable attempt at bribery you have made, Phlegon, would justify me in having the lictor conduct you at once to the praetorium. I will content myself, however, with forbidding you to leave your villa, which you can enjoy in peace until the emperor has decided upon the matter. Lictor, you will see that this man does not quit his house." Then, turning to the courier, he added: "Take this letter to the palace and offer the Caesar my greetings."

Making a sign to the lictor he left the atrium and withdrew to the viridarium. Whoever had watched him as he stood before the flower-beds, apparently gazing at them, would have perceived an expression of intense satisfaction resting on his yellow face, and doubtless wondered whether Flora's innocent children had ever before been watched with so malicious a smile.

Phlegon, utterly overwhelmed, followed the lictor, who walked before him. All was lost, he would hang himself at once to Graecina's stunted palm-tree, fit symbol of this desecrated home, rather than survive all the horrors that threatened his family, his sons' death, his daughters' shame, Ennia's madness or suicide. Like hounds released from the leash, these ideas, repressed for a few hours, again assailed the soul of the pitiable man. The lictor took his station at the gate until two guards from the neighboring barracks at the Palatine relieved him. Phlegon dragged himself to the upper rooms of the house and measured the depth to the area, to ascertain whether it would be enough to kill him should he throw himself down. But ere he could do so, he fell senseless, in which condition Eumaeus and Tertius found him and carried him to his room. While lying on his couch next day, enduring the same agony,

Antinous again appeared at the villa and asked for him. The slaves led him softly in, and when Phlegon opened his eyes the youth sat before him, affectionately enquiring about his health.

"What does the emperor intend?" asked the Greek in reply, starting from his cushions in terror. He then sank back, pressing his feeble hand upon his heart, which throbbed almost to bursting.

"Be calm, be calm, my friend," said Antinous gently. "I bring news, which at least gives hope that all is not lost."

"All?" murmured Phlegon. "To Ennia *one* child is all. Whether he kills eight or one—Niobe will still be Niobe."

"I hope he will slay none," replied Antinous. "I know he honors Ennia, and Hadrian is incapable of condemning children and young girls to severe punishment, irritable as his mood is now. The fact that he has given orders for them to be imprisoned in a separate house and treated with respect, does not seem like harsh designs."

"The gods be thanked—and you!" exclaimed Phlegon, pressing the youth's hand.

"I only fear for Natalis and Vitalis," continued Antinous, "and give up Hermas as lost."

"Yes, I know Hermas is imprisoned too. I had entirely forgotten it in my own sorrow. I dragged him also to destruction, by complaining of the Galileans to Hadrian."

Antinous shook his head. "Hadrian was so enraged by his sleepless night, that I believe the storm would have burst even without your information. He has been unfriendly to your sons ever since that unlucky meeting by the bridge. Yet I don't resign hope, for I am here to settle your affair with Celsus, which might have turned out far worse, if Hadrian were really angry with you. Here is your unfortunate letter to Celsus, and this is the praetor's report. Hadrian says, that to show you he is not the monster you believe him, he will pardon this attempt at bribery on account of your excitement. The best part of the affair was, that he distrusts Celsus. For the rest, the Caesar persists in his declaration that he cannot prevent the trial. You must avoid the palace and keep quiet in your villa. This is the smallest punishment he could impose, after Celsus's report. It is really none at all, for he thereby restores the estate you promised Celsus."

"Always the villa, the villa," groaned Phlegon. " I thank you," he added feebly. " I will wait now and pray the gods—I have had no good fortune in this matter. Do you plead the cause of my family with Hadrian. Your intercession will be of more avail. There is nothing left me save the last consolation of the stoic, and I do not shrink from that."

" Rather appease the anger of the gods by prayers and vows," said Antinous gently. "Since I have known the insults offered to the Immortals in this house, I understand the misery into which it has fallen. You now see that the arrows of Apollo and Artemis hit their mark."

" If they strike the guilty, they must surely spare me, since I sought to prevent the blasphemy. Everything is dark above and below. I no longer know against which gods I have sinned, ours or the Christians'. When I heard the Christians' lamentation for Graecina this morning, I seemed myself to be the criminal, because I had betrayed her, and when I listen to you, I am rebuked because I did not restrain her impiety sooner. So I am like a floating log, tossed from billow to billow, yet know not how I could have avoided them."

"I too had grown wavering," replied Antinous; "the Christians' songs, which so exasperated Hadrian, moved me deeply. I slipped into the guard-house to see Hermas, and his confidence shook mine. 'As Hadrian' he said, 'invented temples, gods, oracles and mysteries, so all the others had arisen.' After what I experienced with Menephta, the selli, and your oracular verses, I could not contradict him. On the journey to Rome, spite of Hadrian's frowning brow, I sat in the chariot with Natalis and Vitalis, and though the latter had not the book, he repeated from memory all the sayings of their god, what things he praised as blessed, and over what he exclaimed 'woe!' Many words seemed strange, especially the command to throw away our property, not to swear by the gods, and to allow ourselves to be robbed and ill-treated without retaliating. But then came beautiful sayings about charity, peace, and many other things that touched me. I did not yet clearly understand, when that garrulous Suetonius came running up and told me I must ride in Hadrian's chariot. I found Hadrian in the mood I don't like to see. He asked with apparent indifference about the purport of our conversation, but I felt that his eyes rested suspiciously upon me. I told him your sons had been speaking of their god. He answered harshly: 'this god will give me no peace, till I have again sent a few hundred Christians to the stone quarries.' When we arrived, the council of state met, and I could go where I pleased. I wanted to inform

Pius, Hermas's brother, that the latter was in prison, as
I had promised the poor fellow. At last I found the
house by the fish-market, but no one ventured to call
down the episcopus, as they name him. It was an assembly of the elders in the Solarium.* If I had a message concerning Hermas, I might go up and deliver it
myself. So I climbed to the upper room, but when
about to draw aside the curtain, heard such a quarrel
that I thought I must wait for a quieter moment before
summoning Pius. Through a gap I saw fifteen elderly
men sitting together, disputing violently. The point in
question seemed to be a book, which some desired to
have in their assemblies, while others loaded it with the
most scornful names. Well, I thought, I shall get to the
bottom of your secrets. I should like to know whether
matters go on in the same way among you, as among
the selli and Menephta. Pius, Hermas's brother, suggested that certain passages in the book could be omitted.
The majority opposed this, but the principal disputant
thumped on the table, exclaiming that if this book were
read aloud at the meetings, he would separate from
Pius's church. The others shouted vehemently, some
exclaiming that he ought to go, some that they would
not force the book upon him. The little choleric man,
with furious black eyes and Arab nose, talked more and
more vehemently—Pius's church had become a refuge
for all heretics ; Graecina had been wronged. Then they
cried out again about the book, and Pius came forward

* Solaria, properly places for basking in the sun, were terraces on
the tops of houses. (Plaut. *Mil.* ii, 3, 69. ii. 4, 25; Suet. *Ner.* 16.) In
the time of Seneca the Romans formed artificial gardens on the tops
of their houses, which contained even fruit-trees and fish-ponds. (Sen.
Ep. 122, *Contr. Exc.* v. 5; Suet. *Claud.* 10.)—*Smith's Dict. of Greek
and Roman Antiq.*

anew with his proposals about what should be erased and added to the so-called sacred book. This was enough. 'Well,' I said to myself, 'your passages shall trouble me no longer.' I now knew, that their sacred books were made just like the oracles prepared by you and Hadrian at Tibur. I went quietly down and told the porter to inform Pius, that Hermas was a prisoner in the body-guard's camp, and wanted to see him. I walked through the noisy streets as if in a dream, until I had reached the Carinae, thinking how strange it was such holy words should be invented in so unholy a manner. When I arrived in the *via lata*, I saw before your house a great crowd of people, carrying bundles and all sorts of articles. Some were trying to snatch them, others running away as if they had stolen them. One woman was screaming and scolding because she had been robbed. I thought I ought to know the voice and approached, when she suddenly shrieked, darted around the corner and dashed down the steps towards the *via sacra* as if pursued by hounds. It now first occurred to me that it was Tryphaena, the fruit-dealer from Tibur, who had tried to throw me into the lime-pit, and just as I turned towards your door her Titius came out, carrying under his arms all sorts of packages and bundles. I stopped him and asked if his leg was well. At first he was timid and wanted to escape, but soon grew confidential and told me Graecina, a strange lady, who made it a rule that everything must be given to the poor, lived in the house. To-day she had distributed most of her property and he had received all this, but as the others tried to take it away from him, he hid himself till they had all gone. Just then two old slaves came out of the door, addressed him with all sorts of abusive words, and would have snatched away his gifts, had I not interfered.

"The slaves now told me Graecina was a Christian and believed people must give their property to the poor, eschew everything beautiful as wicked pleasure, eat nothing nice, and tolerate no statues of the gods. Then they showed me how her villa was formerly arranged, pointed out the pedestals where marble statues had stood, the stumps of the sacred trees Graecina had hewn down, the empty marshy grottos, in whose mire still remained fragments of the marble limbs of the nymphs and naiads your mother-in-law had ordered to be shattered. When I found in a corner a head of Hermes, whose nose was broken off and whose beautifully-formed lips still seemed to be complaining of the insolent Nazarene fist, that had abused the god, I was seized with indignation that I should have listened so long to the tales of these abominable men, and could not understand how noble souls, like Vitalis and Natalis, could take pleasure in these horrors."

"Do you comprehend now," replied Phlegon in a trembling voice, "how I could have allowed my feelings to carry me so far, as to imperil those dearest to me by my reckless accusation ?"

"I at least understand how you could let matters go so far," replied Antinous evasively. "At any rate, I am cured forever. When, in your justification, I told Hadrian what I had seen, he answered: 'For that very reason, this sect must be rooted out. All the splendor, all the magnificence of the world, all that makes life desirable to us would be destroyed, if these people conquered. The empire I have filled with glory would soon look like the villa *ad pinum*, hordes of beggars would people the earth, idleness and superstition would increase. I will help Phlegon so far as I can, but no mercy to these destroyers of the world!' After thus interesting himself in your grief, his mood grew milder; he told me about Celsus's report, and I coaxed both documents away from him. They will cause you no farther annoyances. Then I wrote an order that Ennia, with her daughters and little children, should be treated in *custodia libera*, as beseemed patricians, and Hadrian smilingly signed it with his seal-ring. It seemed to relieve him, to be free from this reproach. The only thing I fear is that your sons will be sent into exile; but be consoled, we'll find an hour when we can persuade the Caesar to grant a pardon."

The sick man gazed at the beautiful youth with deep emotion. "May the gods reward you, Antinous!" he said gently.

"The gods, Phlegon, yes, I wanted to speak to you of them. We will appease their wrath. Let us rebuild this ruined house! The shining forms of the Olympians must again look down upon the *via lata*, the sacred springs again bathe the feet of the naiads in the silent grottos, the sacred trees be replanted. You have learned how the Immortals avenge themselves; we will now beseech them to pardon, and they will forgive."

Phlegon shook his head. "How can I promise what will seem to my children the greatest abomination! You are all happy, each in his own belief. I am weary and cold, my child. If your prayers obtain my dear ones for me, I will go far, far away from here to Aquae, where we were so happy for ten years, and no one asks what god we honor. Ennia will pray to the gods, I will read the philosophers, my children will serve the crucified

Christ, and we will all bear with each other, because we have experienced whither passion leads."

" I expected a different answer," said Antinous indignantly. " My firmest trust vanishes, when I see you so coldly pass over the wrong, which here calls down upon you the wrath of the gods. But you are ill, I will argue no longer. I'll come back to-morrow, and when you are once more yourself and can see how the Immortals have been trifled with, you will allow us to atone together for the sins committed by your family."

With these words Antinous left Phlegon and went down to the temple of Roma and Venus, pausing before the latter to take breath. "Since I have known how Hadrian builds his sanctuaries, I no longer like these superb structures," he said to himself. "Whenever I wish to pray to the goddess, I always think of Apollodorus's foolish witticism, 'that if she should rise from her chair, her head would knock a hole in the roof.'" He passed on without the customary salutation, then asked himself how this conduct agreed with the reproof he had just given Phlegon.

An idle throng filled the *via sacra*, and as he walked on he everywhere heard remarks concerning the Christian trials, Graecina, and Phlegon.

" Now the lions in the amphitheatre will get some food," cried the loud voice of a fop.

" I want to see the fair-haired Ennia and her slender daughters," said another.

" What will they probably be ordered to perform ?"

" Lucretia, or the Rape of the Sabine women, or Danae with the golden hair. It will be a beautiful spectacle at any rate."

A shiver ran through the Bithynian's limbs, as he saw

the satyr-like smile that followed the young noble's
words.   Disheartened, weary of gods and men, he
ascended the Palatine, and after hearing from the porter
that the council was not yet over, glided out among the
laurel-hedges of the emperor's garden, where outspread
below him lay the noisy, restless city, with its swarming
crowds, smoking chimneys and gleaming domes and
towers.   Separated from all his friends amid this noisy
wilderness of Rome, a feeling of infinite desolation,
abandonment, hopelessness overpowered him.   Faithful
Hermas imprisoned awaiting the lions, which were already gnashing their teeth for him, Phlegon's lovely
children, of whom the Greek had so often spoken, exposed to the tortures of martyrdom, while below in the
city beasts in human form were racking their brains to
determine what horrors they would most enjoy seeing
inflicted upon them.   And Phlegon, the cause of all this
misery—how base, how cowardly he had been.   Hadrian
was perfectly right, the Greek had brought this misfortune upon his family out of avarice, after having quietly
endured the insult offered to the gods.   His wife and
daughters had been led to disgrace before his eyes, and
he had survived it.   The youth shook his head.

" I pity him, but my respect is gone."

Hadrian too he could no longer recognize.   To
allow all this cruelty out of paltry fear of the Senate,
the council of state, Servianus !   Everything seemed
black and cheerless.   He could find support neither in
men nor gods.   As he gazed down upon the people
standing in groups about the forum, and saw individuals
running busily to and fro, while his ears still rang with
the conversation he had·heard in passing, he clenched
his fist.

" How the beasts rejoice in human flesh and blood !
Yes, yes, Hadrian is right, they are insufferable, both as
individuals and as a whole.   One noble horse is worth
more than hundreds of these blood-thirsty, malicious
apes."

When the confused murmur of voices rose from below, it seemed as if he heard the names: " Hermas,
Vitalis, Natalis, Ennia !"

" Why don't you call Antinous too ?" he murmured.
" The handsome Antinous, ha, ha, ha ! Who knows
whether Hadrian may not some day wish to enjoy the
spectacle of seeing the beautiful Bithynian torn asunder
by magnificent panthers, or mangled by a wild-boar,
like Adonis !"

The youth hid his face in his hands and bowed his
aching head.   He was lonely, abandoned alike by gods
and men. He had remained in this attitude a long time,
when a white robe gleamed amid the laurel-bushes, and
eyes that had already watched him for several days
appeared. The branches parted, and Amenophis stood
before Antinous, intently noting the boy's attitude of
despair. Solitary in the palace, shunned by the Romans,
in constant peril of being destroyed for practising some
forbidden superstition, the Egyptian, after his quarrel
with Menephta, knew no human being in this strange
court in whom he could find support, save Antinous.
But as the Bithynian had not entered the Canopus for
some time, Amenophis had found no opportunity to approach. As the presence of a human being, even though
unseen and unheard, often reveals itself to the mind,
Antinous's thoughts had just wandered towards the
priest. The insult to the gods, beheld at the villa *ad
pinum*, forever separated him from Natalis and Vitalis.

Hadrian's trifling with religion was as repulsive to him as Phlegon's weak indecision. Who still believed in the gods so firmly, that he could rely upon him, that his heart could once more become firm and steadfast? Then he remembered Amenophis, who clung rigidly and sternly to the customs of his ancestors, and had never thought of treating sacred matters otherwise than as sacred tradition required. Just as the recollection of the Egyptian was passing through his mind, he opened his eyes and suddenly beheld his tall figure, bathed in the fiery glow of the setting sun.

"Amenophis!" faltered the startled youth.

"I was at the other end of the garden," said the Egyptian, when it seemed as if some one here was calling for help to save him from drowning, and following the voice, I saw you, boy. Did you call?"

"Probably in spirit, Amenophis. But I implore you, by Serapis and all the inferior deities, do not deceive me. I have been so much deluded of late by gods and men, priests and slaves. Be truthful, Amenophis, for water already reaches my throat; you speak the truth, I was drowning."

"I will gladly help you, boy, if I can," replied the Egyptian in a more gentle tone than usual. "I never deceive anyone. If the sacred rite transmitted by the ancients is a delusion, upon them be the responsibility. I have neither added anything nor taken anything away, nothing is required of a priest except that he shall faithfully serve the altar and guard the mysteries."

"Ah, if your gods love you, pray them to release Hermas and Phlegon's children."

"My son," replied the Egyptian, "I might falsely tell you that the gods had revealed the contrary, but I am neither magician nor deceiver. Not from the gods, but from Celsus, who has just made his report to the emperor, did I learn that the sentence is pronounced. Hermas, Natalis, and Vitalis are condemned to fight with wild beasts. Ennia and her daughters were to have been sent to the stone-quarries, but Hadrian has changed the sentence to exile, and assigned Ennia for a residence his imperial estate at Aquae, where he made her acquaintance. The two worthless slaves, Nereus and Chloe, who caused all the mischief in the *via lata*, to the astonishment of everyone, escape unpunished. The old wine-bibber and the worthless wench denied the accusation on oath, sacrificed to the gods, and declared that their mistress compelled them, as slaves, to pretend to be Christians. The destruction of the statues of the gods they ascribed to Natalis and Vitalis, who showed themselves far too magnanimous in their contempt for the wretches. Hadrian was furious, but Celsus appealed to Trajan's edict, according to which no Galilean is allowed to be punished, if he offers sacrifices to the gods and curses Christ. At the utmost Chloe, as a slave, could have been delivered to the punishment of Ennia, her mistress. But the latter was guilty herself. Therefore no legal objection could be made to Celsus's sentence, though the emperor suspects Celsus was compelled to purchase by this mildness Nereus's silence concerning certain money transactions, that took place between the praetor and the weak-minded Graecina. The wretches are already free, and will know how to conceal themselves. Ennia and her children will remain in *custodia libera* until their departure. Would that the horrible day of the games in the amphitheatre were over!"

"The gods he thanked, Amenophis, and you also, that such are your feelings. Oh! have you no means of saving my three friends?"

"We all have one and the same means — to pray to the gods. Whether they will grant the petition, I know as little as you."

"But you have a way of making the gods favorable, I know," said Antinous beseechingly. "See, you are silent. You can, if you choose. Be humane, Amenophis, I beseech you."

"No man, no conjuration, no talisman can constrain the gods," said the Egyptian gravely. "But there are expedients which move them, because they prove the petitioner's sincerity. If you wish to undertake these exercises, there is something in your pleading eyes, your earnest entreaty, which makes me hope the great goddess may incline her will to yours. If the attempt fails, seek the cause in your own lack of earnestness, not in me; I told you that we could accomplish nothing with the gods save by sincere prayer."

"And what must I do?" asked Antinous.

"You must fast until the day of the games, according to the rules of Serapis, which you know; before sunrise and sunset you must thrice repeat to this statue (he handed him a small image of the god carved from green basalt) the prayer engraved here below in your language, and on the god's back in the sacred characters." Antinous read the words on the base of the tiny figure. They ran as follows: "Apis — Osiris, great god, who sits in Amenti, ever-living Lord, everlasting Ruler, save, preserve, for thou art the living Osiris, thou art Tum, all thy feathers are on thee, thou dost grant everlasting life."

Amenophis continued: "As long as the games last,

you must stretch out your arm and hold the statue straight before you. Let not your arm fall, but remember that your friends' fate sinks with it, that the thread of life spins on while you hold firm. Through yonder row of windows in the palace you can watch the games. So long as the fighting lasts, hold firm and repeat the formula. May Serapis be gracious to you! I will arrange the gods on the most favorable conjuncture, and address them with all the formulas I know." While speaking, he drew from his pocket a string on which numerous tiny figures of the gods, carved from blue stone, were arranged as if on a rosary, and showed them to Antinous, who gazed at the strange forms with a shudder.

"If our prayers are not heard, be sure, my son, the Christians' sins were so heavy that they could only be expiated by blood."

"I will do as you have commanded!" replied the youth. "If your gods are gracious to me, I will devote myself to their service all my life, and the venerable temples of the black land shall have seen no more grateful worshipper than the Bithynian Antinous."

Amenophis laid his hand on the boy's head in benediction, then made three signs incomprehensible to the latter on his brow and cheeks, and turning towards the setting sun, said :

"Let us pray."

Antinous obediently repeated with him the prayer to Apis—Osiris, who sits in Amenti, and both returned in silence to the palace.

CHAPTER XV.

A FRESH morning breeze swept clouds of dust along the *via sacra* towards the capitol. The sun had not risen, only a faint glimmer of light in the eastern horizon announced his coming, yet groups of the common people already surrounded the doors of the Flavian Amphitheatre, and as soon as they were opened rushed to the upper galleries, which were assigned to the plebeians. The same centurion, who had arrested Phlegon's family, commanded the guard at the main entrance and made the rounds of the sentinels stationed at the side doors of the colossal circular building. He was in a peevish, sullen mood, for as chance had allotted to him the duty of watching the execution of the sentence imposed on those whom he had arrested, he seemed to himself an executioner, rather than a soldier.

"Back, cursed rabble!" he thundered more than once to the thronging crowds, for their blood-thirsty talk, their eagerness to see the games, disgusted the brave officer, whose mind was still deeply impressed by the scene attending Ennia's arrest. To escape the repulsive spectacle, he went in and walked down the inner corridor, which was dimly lighted by lamps. "What did the Egyptian want with you yesterday evening, that you took him into the larder?" he asked the Nubian slaves, who watched the lions.

"He wanted to see the lions."

"But I saw him dropping something from a bottle on the pieces of meat."

"It's the meat intended to lure the animals back, and he gave us an essence that excites pleasure and curbs their fierceness."

"What is that to him?"

"He belongs to the emperor's household, and speaks our language. A wise man, who had the animals of the god Tum under his charge at Heliopolis, and taught us many clever rules."

"I hope you haven't fed the beasts?"

"Certainly not, my lord, they are keen. Hark, how they roar!"

The centurion passed on. As he emerged into the open air through the next doorway, Suetonius greeted him. "My dear friend, might I stand in the lowest row, among the soldiers who defend the parapet? I must be able to get out at any moment, for the court is going to Ancona to-day, yet I shouldn't like to lose the spectacle."

"If you have the courage, I've no objection."

"The courage of a lion," replied Suetonius, and the centurion pursued his way. Suetonius beckoned to several female friends and court officials, offering to provide them with the best seats, if they had the courage to look straight into the beasts' yellow eyes.

"We won't sit among the plebeians, Chloe, now we're rich people," squeaked the voice of a little waddling man, whose saffron-yellow toga gleamed for a long distance. "Let us crowd in among the nobles, we shall be least likely to be recognized there."

"Oh! Nereus, I'd rather turn back," said Chloe, who had transformed herself into a well-clad Roman matron.

"Noble lord," said Nereus, accosting Suetonius,

" don't you know of a good seat for a stranger from the provinces ? We would gladly offer you our provisions." He pointed to a basket carried by his companion, in which appeared a round flask of Falernian wine, superb grapes and melons.

"That will come in very opportunely," thought Suetonius, glancing covetously at the bottle. Then he said patronizingly :

" Come with me, worthy guests. The centurion has permitted me to sit in the first row among the soldiers. I'll guide you. See, the doors are just opened. By Jupiter, what a crowd ! If only two or three hundred are not stifled and crushed again. There, here to the left, now we're safe."

" Well, well, friend Nereus, have you grown so fine, that you no longer know your old friends," suddenly exclaimed a little fat woman, in whom Chloe, to her terror, recognized the fruit-dealer, Tryphaena.

" Tryphaena !" cried the startled Nereus. " Don't betray us," he added in a whisper; " we said we came from the provinces."

" Well, may a body be allowed to join you ?"

" Come with me," said Suetonius, and descending two steps, the magister epistolarum's* clients reached the row of seats directly over the podium,** where they were nearest to the games, but also to the danger. They seated themselves comfortably on their cushions, while

* Magister Epistolarum answered letters on behalf of the emperor. (Orelli, *Inscr.* 2352.)—*Smith's Dict. of Greek and Roman Antiq.*

** Podium, in architecture, is a continued pedestal, for supporting a row of columns, or serving for a parapet, or forming a sort of terrace, as the *podium* in the theatre and amphitheatre. (Vitruv. III. 3, v. 7, vii. 4; Amphitheatrum.)—*Smith's Dict. of Greek and Roman Antiq.*

outside the noise, pushing and crowding continued. When the first rush was over, the more aristocratic spectators arrived. Here and there appeared a white toga, with a purple stripe, taking its way towards the boxes of the patricians and senators. The praetor Celsus was among the earliest arrivals, and Salvianus had attached himself to him.

"We are not to blame, most noble Celsus; we warned them sufficiently, as faithful neighbors," said the fat man unctuously, "and if I could still save the good boys, I'd give up the whole spectacle."

Leather-hued Celsus smiled ironically, and took his seat beside the consuls.

In the imperial box preparations were being made, which indicated that Hadrian would attend the games in person. A servant was straightening the cushions and drawing the heavy curtains farther to the right and left. Every moment the gaps in the audience filled, and the vast amphitheatre, thronged with people, was a majestic spectacle. At last the shrill music of the Phrygian pipes began in the lowest circle, drowning the roars of the hungry wild beasts, the buzz of conversation, and the deafening tramp of feet still passing through the narrow corridors towards the upper gallery. While the greatest bustle everywhere prevailed, the hawkers began to pursue their trade of selling refreshments, flowers, and trifling gifts for pretty maidens. The small provision-dealers were most largely represented, but they preferred to ply their calling in the lowest rows of seats.

"Buy some food, my noble gentlemen!" cried a boyish voice. "The games will last eight hours. Sausages, roast meat, all neatly wrapped in leaves. Sausages, good sausages!"

" Begone with your sausages ! Bring fruit, figs !" shouted one of the persons seated in the first row, in whom we can easily recognize the garrulous Suetonius from Tibur. " Who wants sausages in this heat ?"

" You'll think differently two hours hence, Suetonius," said his neighbor. " You don't know what an appetite for meat the excitement of the games produces—" and he bought a large rib.

Another purchased sausages. The example had an effect. The rest called for fruit or water, and the boy went to the other rows of seats. The cry: " Roast meat, sausages !" was heard elsewhere, and as eighty-seven thousand people are hard to satisfy, the despised baskets of meat finally became as empty as the much-praised baskets of fruit, and as curiosity diminished and the commencement of the games was delayed, here and there young girls began to suck their figs, reserving the meat for the time when hunger might assert itself.

While the time was already growing wearisome to the waiting multitude, the prisoners were all under the influence of that feverish mood, which knows not whether the moments are rushing by or lengthening themselves out to eternities. One thought drove every other from their minds, yet in their excitement no one was aware of it. The same mood took possession of the snub-nosed barbarians, the weather-beaten gladiators, the brutalized criminals, who were all to meet a like fate with the Christians. The roar of the throng, the rush of footsteps along the corridors, the diabolically-shrill tones of the Phrygian flutes and pipes, the furious howls and yells of the starving animals, echoed with a ghostly sound through the vaults, where the prisoners were assembled to be led out in turn for the games.

As the Christians were condemned to special performances, a separate cell was allotted to the two brothers and Hermas. The latter, on entering the circus, had asked for the shepherd's costume, with scrip and pouch, which had been taken from him. The boys wore a military tunic, from which all badges of honor had been removed, with neither helmet nor armor, but the usual short sword was promised them on entering the arena. Even at this moment, they were filled with gratitude to. God, who had imposed such suffering upon them, for being permitted to be alone with Hermas. Their young minds seemed lost in a dream. Was return to life really shut out by that iron-bound door? Should they never again gaze into their mother's faithful eyes and hear the merry childish mirth of their brothers and sisters? The world, which stretched in glittering splendor below the villa *ad pinum*, was walled away from them, and when the opposite door opened.they would look into the jaws of blood-thirsty brutes, and the faces of many thousands of their fellow-men, who would rejoice in their tortures.

"What harm have we done you," the boys asked themselves, "that you should gloat over our suffering?"

"If it were not for my mother and the children," said Vitalis, "I would gladly leave a world, whose malignity is so great. What have we seen since that terrible last evening at home? Our father's harshness, the baseness of Nereus and Chloe, the cowardice of the others, the blood-thirstiness and cruelty of the judges, executioners, and those whom we call our fellow-citizens! Oh! Lord, take us from this world of the devil. Let us bear palms and sing Thy praises. The battles for Thee, of which we dreamed, have come to naught. Thy warriors have fallen."

" Let us not be unjust, brother," replied Natalis. " Might we not have been effeminate and irresolute, but for the military discipline received from Bassus and at the emperor's villa ?   Who knows how the hour of danger would have found us, had it not been for this steeling of the sense of honor, this school of defiance, the habit of looking pain in the face ?"

" Possibly, Natalis," replied the younger lad, " though I don't believe I should have been weaker than my sisters."

With these words he threw his arm around his brother's neck, saying: " Since I can no longer see Paula, I watch you like a lover, because you resemble her so much in the shape of the eyes and temples, and hold your head in exactly the same way."

While the boys caressed each other, Hermas sat quietly on a chest in one corner of the room, sometimes murmuring indistinctly in his symbolical biblical language: " Yes, yes, we shall be like dreamers ... it is so written.   Daniel in the lions' den, Hermas in the lions' den.   Art thou not a prophet ?   Thou didst desire to be one."   Then he cleaned his flute and blew a few notes, making the lads look up in surprise. " What has the prophet said ?" the old man murmured on ... " ' many will pass through, and wisdom will increase' ... ay, colleague of the lions' den, thou hast passed through, I too will pass through," and he played the Song of the Lamb so clearly and with so much feeling, that the two youths, in their agitation, burst into tears.

" Cease, my good Hermas," exclaimed Vitalis ; "you

are making us soft-hearted, and we must be firm and hard." At that moment the lock rattled and the key was heard to turn. The boys grew pale, and Vitalis, half-fainting, clung to his brother's neck. But the man who entered was not the magister of beasts.

" Phlegon!" cried Hermas. " Father!" exclaimed the Greek's sons.

"Alas, hope for nothing," said Phlegon in a hoarse voice, choked with anguish. "I have been unable to avert your fate. Yet I wanted to see you, implore you to forgive the woe I have brought upon us all. How willingly would I suffer myself to be torn in pieces with red-hot pincers, or meet all the wild-beasts in the theatre, if I could save you."

" Do not weep, father," said Vitalis; " what happens is God's will. He has punished you, because you were too much attached to earthly things, and us because we did not love you as we ought."

" How shall we thank you for coming to us in this hour?" added Natalis. " How pale and ill you look, my poor father! You have suffered sorely on our account."

"Ah, my son, I have endured all the tortures of the nether-world in feverish days and sleepless nights. What formerly seemed important and valuable, has shown itself to me what you termed it, dust and tinsel. To-day Hadrian might offer me in vain all the villas in the world. I shall go into the wilderness, to ask God for a pure heart and a new conscience."

" Oh! Father, God has heard our prayers!" exclaimed the youths, throwing themselves at Phlegon's feet.

" Do not talk any more of me," said Phlegon. " I

come to you also, that I may be able to tell your poor mother of your last hours. How is it with you, my dear boy, during this awful time?"

"Why," said Natalis, with a gentle smile, "it is childish, but last night, when contrary to habit, I was awake, I remembered the time when we lived in the camp of the *colonia Agrippina* and I was to have a tooth extracted, which had caused me a great deal of suffering. You promised me, if I were good, a goat-carriage like one owned by the Legate Publius's son. I still recollect how I dreaded the pain of having the tooth drawn, and yet rejoiced in anticipation of the coming pleasure. The memory that the pain was not so great as I expected, gives me courage to-day. My own tooth comforts me for the teeth of the lions and tigers. I think it will be over directly. I won't hurt or irritate the animals, but throw away the sword, shut my eyes, and let them eat me. The Lord made them to eat flesh, let it be as He has willed."

While Phlegon, in voiceless anguish, gazed at the beautiful boy, whose pale face was flushed with pleasure at this meeting with his father, some one knocked at the door.

"I am coming!" cried Phlegon.

"Forgive me, my friend, for interrupting a father's parting with his sons, but I have a petition to make."

"My good Hermas," said Phlegon, grasping the old man's sinewy hands, "if Phlegon's petitions could still win the Caesar's ear, would these boys be here?"

"It is nothing great, they won't refuse you," replied Hermas. "Only manage to let me have a word with Brother Lion or Brother Tiger before your sons, and Natalis and Vitalis shall receive no injury."

"Are you mad?" replied Phlegon angrily. "If you did not speak so seriously, I should think you were joking, and this is no time for jests. Miracles no longer happen, my poor Hermas."

"Oh! man of little faith," replied the old prophet, "when will you at last learn to understand the voice of truth? I told you on the pasture near the albula, that I could smell the devil's brimstone, but you said it was the albula, the sulphur baths. Had you believed, you might now be sitting, a happy man, with Ennia and your children. Believe me now. Arrange to have my turn come first, and all may yet be well."

"The order of the games is settled and the magister will not change it at the last moment," replied Phlegon; "but I don't think the boys will be called into the arena before you. Either you will all appear together, or you, Hermas, will come first alone, and then the two brothers. The other plan would weaken the effect, and these men of blood certainly have excellent taste."

"We shall not be summoned together, for these lads wish to fight with swords and I with the flute."

"We wanted to salute the emperor," said Natalis, "that he may see our loyalty then we will lay the swords aside."

"Then Hermas will probably come first," said Phlegon. "But if it should be otherwise, and God desires to work miracles, He can perform them on my sons."

"God can do all things," said Hermas, "but He has given us an inner light, that we too may bring about marvels sensibly. My angel gave me good counsel last night, and by a wax tablet thrown into my cell, I see the Brothers intend to come to my assistance. So He was with them as well as with me, and I now fear the wild-

beasts no more than your sheep-dogs at Tibur, which
you ought to tie up better, that they may not bite little
girls, like good Pyrrha's poor little Decimilla; tell the
Caesar so, it is my last request to his godship."

Phlegon gazed enquiringly at the old man, who
seemed so sure of his cause, and a sort of superstitious
horror thrilled him.

" Expect no stately apparitions," answered Hermas;
"it is the Lord's will to turn their fears into laughter,
though he might terrify them by ten thousand angels."

At this moment the door was torn open, and the
jailer cried angrily:

" Away, Phlegon, away ! What did you promise me?
Am I to lose my place ?"

One hasty embrace, kisses from lips burning feverishly, and Phlegon felt himself roughly seized by a
rude hand and dragged outside. The jailer shut the
door, put the key in his pocket, and left Phlegon lying in
dull misery on the threshold, until the resounding brazen
plate gave the signal for the commencement of the
games. It echoed like the trump of the Last Judgment,
of which Graecina had so often dreamed. The Greek
raised himself and staggered out, that he might not be
compelled to see his children led forth to death. As he
stood before one of the doors of the vast edifice, where
everything was now silent and empty, he felt like a condemned criminal.

" It was your own will," he murmured. " Now
plant the villa *ad pinum* with ornamental trees and erect
statues to your Dioscuri, whom you have delivered to
the clutches of the tiger," and in a wild outburst of anguish, he tottered on through the arch of Titus to the
palace garden, to hide his shame under the dense

laurels, or end his life with a rope—if he found courage.
A loud shout from a thousand throats rang from the
Flavian Theatre. " Hail, hail to the Caesar!"

" Hail to the Caesar," said Phlegon in a choking
voice, " the Caesar I have served all my life, and who
has thus rewarded me!" and throwing himself down
upon the turf of the imperial garden, he wept bitterly.

CHAPTER XVI.

SHORTLY after Phlegon's departure, the guard appeared and summoned Hermas, who without troubling
himself farther about the outside world, was playing on
his flute, while the boys, agitated by the last interview
with their father, clung to each other in one corner,
weeping. This deep sorrow pierced their innocent souls.
" How happy we might have been, if we had earlier understood how to win his affection by love and obedience."

" Farewell, Hermas !" cried the boys, embracing the
old man. " May the Lord repay you with His comfort
in His kingdom, for the consolation you have given us."

" Be calm, children, be calm, farewell till we meet
in freedom, here or there."

" He still believes in liberation," said Vitalis; " I no
longer hope, and it only disturbs me and destroys my
composure, when he speaks of it. How could I live
after enduring these horrors ?"

" We should be like the youth of Nain," said
Natalis.

. " May God not punish my sin," replied the younger

brother. "The last time I was obliged to read aloud the story of this youth, the evil spirit tormented me with the doubt, whether the awakened youth could be satisfied, after tasting the sweet slumber of those awaiting the judgment, to be roused again to the bustle of the world. Now he was compelled to torture himself, struggle, fall ill, and endure the death agony once more. I felt that I should not thank the Lord for it, then a cold shiver ran through me for having such bold thoughts about what He had done."

"Let us submit ourselves to Him," said Natalis, sinking back wearily against the wall. "He will do what is right."

Meantime Hermas, constantly playing on his flute, was conducted to his last cell. "A horrible odor," he said, laying the instrument aside. "Demons dwell in the stench."

"It is the perfume of your host," replied the warder, and Hermas now heard the restless pacing to and fro of the lion, only separated from him by a narrow chamber, where lay pieces of meat, water-pails, brooms and other articles used in the service of the animals.

"The door is really only ajar, not locked," Hermas said to himself, and now for the first time his heart began to throb faster. The beasts had had nothing to eat all day, yet the meat was kept there to lure the lions back, in case the emperor was disposed to pardon, or the animals were to be driven from the corpse for some other reason — it did not always suit the august population of the city, to wait until the tigers or lions had eaten their fill.

"Do you persist in fighting only with your flute?" asked the magister.

" I want an ordinary kitchen knife, such as the cook
uses to cut meat," replied Hermas.

" You ought to have said so yesterday, but as I won't
refuse a man in your situation, I'll fetch a dagger," said
the magister, hurriedly withdrawing, in order not to be
surprised by the signal for producing the prisoner.

" I want no dagger, only a butcher's knife," said
Hermas harshly, as the magister retired. " There is what
I need," and he went into the next cell unimpeded by
the warders, who knew that its sole means of egress was
into the lion's cage.

The old man, who had requested permission to
appear as a shepherd, opened his pouch, pushed several
juicy pieces of meat into it, wrapped another in a blue
apron that lay on the shambles, and took a knife.

" Thanks, unknown counsellor," he said, " you have
kept your promise," and returned to the cell, which the
warder entered at the same moment, just as the signal
for opening the door was given.

" Hand me the knife," exclaimed the keeper angrily.
" Here is the dagger."

" But I want a knife."

" You ought not to enter the arena with such a
ridiculous weapon ; away with it."

Hermas reluctantly allowed the knife to be snatched
from him.

" What bundle have you here ? "

" I'm going to stop the lion's jaws with it."

" That won't do.   Take a net for aught I care."

" No, I want to choke him."

" Quick, quick ! " cried the slaves ; " they are opening the door of the lion's cage.   He'll come in here ! "

" Away with the bundle ! "

But Hermas released himself, and rushed out into the arena. The slaves hastily closed the doors. "We want no visits from lions. Why shouldn't the man fight with a blue apron? Myrrhon was allowed to wrap the lion in a carpet, and the four Cappadocians tossed the tiger in a large coverlet; we must let people be eaten according to their taste. Hark! the grating of the lion's cage is just going down."

The lion, "Agamemnon," a noble son of the Libyan wilderness, had been pacing unweariedly up and down for hours, like an evil spirit, giving vent to his rage and hunger by growling and gnashing his teeth. His keen scent detected the odor of fresh meat, the smell of blood roused his appetite to fury, but the keepers must have forgotten him. He lashed his tail fiercely against the walls of his cage, and roared until a pleasant thrill of horror ran through the audience in the theatre. This was the prelude to the beautiful spectacle promised them. As roaring did not avail, the huge yellow cat pressed itself close to the side from which the smell of blood proceeded. Never yet had the scent of meat been so alluring to the sovereign Agamemnon; the beast stretched its paws through the grating, and began to fawn and play. Then, growing furious again, it dashed its claws against the bars and sprang fiercely on them, but only to recoil, howling with pain, and resume its restless pacing to and fro.

"A superb lion," said the spectators, who could watch the scene from the opposite seats. "He'll tear in pieces. See what leaps!" The lion, weak and exhausted by rage and hunger, had lain down again, and now looked out through the bars at the crowd. There were a great many people, and the sight disturbed him;

but he would have attacked them to fill his stomach. Just at that moment a man, who was drawing wonderful sounds from a flute, appeared in the centre of the space before him, and the arena instantly became perfectly still. It seemed as if this devotion moved even the son of the wilderness, he rose and gazed at the man before him, while his tail swept the ground less fiercely. Could he be a keeper? The blue cloth he held in his hand was the keeper's well-known apron, and the animal's keen scent detected the familiar odor of meat emanating from it. "At last," thought the king of the desert, "feeding time has come." But instead of the side door, the grating suddenly fell before him, and as if touched by a spring the lion instantly found himself outside in the freedom of which he had so long been deprived, saw sand beneath and the blue sky above him, as in the days of his youth, and a joyous roar gave expression to a mood worthy of a king. But the ignoble part of man and beast, the stomach, instantly asserted itself again. Sweeping the ground with his tail till the dust whirled upward in clouds, he approached the nearest tribune and turning his back on Hermas, steadily scanned the rows of spectators, till the blood receded to their hearts and from the lowest seats, where several women had forced themselves among the court officials, a shriek of terror was heard. A fat woman fell fainting under the bench, or did she only want to conceal herself? The stir at that point attracted Agamemnon's eyes, and the yellow toga beside the screaming woman roused his anger. The wall of the podium did not seem too high for his strength, and not far below the edge ran a round rail which he thought he could surely reach. Then he would have a rich harvest among the shrieking women. So he crouched and risked the leap, reaching the rail amid the applause of some and the terrified screams of others. Alas, the faithless rail to which he meant to cling, turned. It was put there to deceive the animals. The king of beasts fell heavily back on the sand, and though he instantly sprang up again, uttering a furious roar, his confidence was sorely shaken, and he ran grimly around the amphitheatre, pressing his head against the wall. The fat face of the fruit-dealer from Tibur, suffused with a crimson glow, again appeared. Haggard Chloe, who now looked as yellow as a quince, slowly followed, but the stout man in the saffron-yellow toga was no longer visible. The women stooped over him, and the soldiers drew nearer.

"By Hercules! he is dead," said Suetonius.

"Carry him out," called Hadrian's secretary; "the fright has killed him." The soldiers seized the heavy corpse and bore it out, while the weeping Chloe vanished behind it.

"Poor man!" said Suetonius; "he came from the country to have a little pleasure. Hand me yonder basket, woman, he invited me to share his refreshments."

"Here, noble Suetonius," said Tryphaena. "But don't you know who the dead man was? Nereus, who talked Graecina out of her villa, and then abjured his god before the praetor."

"The Christian! That's certainly a visible sign from the gods, a *prodigium*, I must tell Hadrian of it this very day. But where is the lion? What a cowardly beast! I once saw at the theatre in Carthage" ... but nobody learned what Suetonius had seen in Carthage, for a hasty gesture towards the arena made by a young girl who sat beside him, stopped his loquacity. Following the direction of her hand, he beheld a strange spectacle. The lion was approaching the Christian, who steadily played the same tune, a melody Suetonius remembered having heard once before at Tibur, very early in the morning, in the street where the Nazarenes held their assemblies. " It is their Song of the Lamb," he whispered to his neighbor. " Look, look!"

The lion had advanced within springing distance of Hermas, who still playing his flute, gazed fixedly at him with his bright, sparkling eyes. Then he paused, and was just crouching for the leap, when Hermas stopped, took the blue apron he had hung on his wrist, that it might not interfere with his playing, and flung it to the wild beast, exclaiming:

" In the name of the Lord, Who has created you and all other animals, eat."

The lion hesitated, but the fiery eyes of the man, who now held in his right hand a glittering blade, intimidated him. Again the well-known odor of meat saluted his nostrils. Creeping slowly towards the apron, he tore it open with his paws, and unheeding the laughter and shouts of the throng, quietly began to eat, as he was accustomed to do in his cage.

" A fine champion," screamed a woman's voice.

" Eat the Nazarene!"

" He likes veal best," said another.

" No wonder, I wouldn't want the lean Christian either. He's nothing but skin and bones."

" Hark, now he's playing again. A queer tune. Didelumdum, didelumdum! There must really be some spell in it."

The magister of the games paced up and down his box, scolding angrily.

"Those accursed dogs of slaves have helped him, or he couldn't have played me this trick. I'll drench you for it. There, now he's pulling another piece of meat out of his pouch, there goes a second."

"Haven't you something for him to drink too, Hermas?" he heard Tryphaena's shrill voice scream.

"I'll put a stop to this," muttered the magister—"Loose the tiger, the tiger!" he called down to the slaves, through the square opening in his box.

After Hermas had dispensed the contents of his pouch, with the exception of a few pieces of meat reserved for unexpected emergencies, he thrust the dagger back into his belt, took up his flute, and played quietly on, though without averting his eyes a moment from the lion.

A shout from the blood-thirsty crowd first called his attention to the new danger. The grating of a cage on his right had been raised, and with stealthy tread and pliant limbs a magnificently-striped royal tiger, which did not seem to doubt for an instant what prey was destined for him, steadily approached. The next moment Hermas would surely have lain mangled under the beast, had not the throng, delighted at the dramatic turn of affairs, burst into a shout such as could only proceed from eighty-seven thousand Italian throats. The animal, perplexed by the din, paused and cast a suspicious glance over the throng. The lion also stopped, angrily lashing his tail, as if to ask who dared to disturb him? Thus Hermas, still playing his flute, and without averting his eyes from the new enemy, gained time to reach a position behind the lion, so that the latter, with his pieces of meat, separated him from the fresh foe. The manœuvre had been instantly noticed by the throng of people, who now fairly held their breath. The amphitheatre had grown so still, that the clear melody of the flute was distinctly audible over the whole vast space. As soon as the disturbance ceased, the king of beasts, apparently untroubled by the new visitor, returned to his food. But the cowardice, peculiar to nocturnal beasts in the daylight, awoke in the tiger. He beheld in the shrieking multitude friends of the flute-player, and seeing the lion eating, seized the nearest piece of meat. But with a single bound the lion sprang forward, roaring loudly, to defend his property. The tiger's claws clutched the lion's, and a fierce struggle began. The lion aimed terrible blows at his antagonist, which the tiger avoided with marvellous skill; the tiger's teeth seized the lion's mane, but at the same instant the latter tore off with his claws from the upper part of the tiger's head half the skin, from which an ear and an eye hung horribly. With hasty bounds, leaving a broad trail of blood upon the sand, the tiger returned to his cage, where he howled piteously. The grating was raised, and soon only a faint whining was audible. Either the animal was dying, or the keepers had stupefied him to be able to cure him. The lion stood fiercely over his prey, which no one now disputed. But the furious conflict seemed to have destroyed his appetite; he sought a fresh foe, and his eyes again rested on Hermas.

" Nothing will save him now!" crowed Tryphaena. The fiery triangular pupils of the beast and the glittering eyes of the man, sparkling with superior intelligence, again met. These eyes had already subjugated the lion once, and lowering his head he returned to his food. Hermas instinctively felt that he must approach nearer the wall of the arena, partly to cow the animal by the sight of the multitude above, partly to render assistance possible in case it should be at hand. He was not mistaken. As he put down the flute to take breath, he heard a voice saying:

"Stand here to the left, we will help you."

Looking up he beheld his brother Pius, and nodding pleasantly again took his flute and resumed his playing. The contest had now lasted half an hour, but owing to its numerous variations, seemed to the spectators twice as long.

"Something else!" shouted several voices. "Mercy for Hermas!"

The magister glanced towards the emperor, who had watched the strange battle of his old acquaintance with intense interest, but now again sat apathetically in his corner, lost in thought, evidently hearing the cries for mercy without the slightest sympathy. The magister had keen eyes. As the herald did not move, he shouted: "The panthers!"

"I must keep the leopards for the two brothers," he said to himself, but without any feeling of annoyance at the unsuccessful commencement of the combat, which had made the spectators indulgently disposed, instead of irritating them. Three cages were now opened at the same time, and the panthers, with agile bounds, leaped into the middle of the arena. But the fiery eyes of the lion, which had lain down about twenty paces from Hermas, subdued their courage. Unwarned by their predecessor's fate. one of the cats began to gnaw a bone. The satiated lion allowed it. and two of them were

soon fighting over the remnants of the meal.   The third
alone had not lost sight of Hermas, and was creeping
towards him along the wall, where it was concealed
from the crowd, and escaped the lion's threatening gaze.
Neither the man's eye nor his flute-playing disturbed it.
As Hermas seized his dagger, the blade glittering in the
sun stopped the panther, but its companions were now
beginning to share the chase. Again a breathless silence
pervaded the amphitheatre. Suddenly, from one of
the nearest galleries, a piece of roast meat fell directly in front of the panther, which had already
crouched to make its spring. The cat instantly leaped
upon it, and after carrying its booty away from Hermas,
pressed close to the wall and began to eat. The next
instant another piece of meat fell from above, and the
other two panthers bounded towards it to snatch it
while in the air. Either from preconcerted arrangement,
or pleasure in this beautiful spectacle, the shower, despite the herald's signs and the scolding of the guard,
could not be stopped. Sausages, pieces of roast meat
and ribs flew over the soldiers' heads, and the bounds of
the agile panthers so delighted the spectators, that the
whole amphitheatre was soon covered with rolls and
meat. The herald had looked at the Caesar to learn
whether he should put a stop to this nonsense, but it
either suited the emperor's blunted sense of enjoyment
that a tragedy should end in a jest, or he desired to save
Hermas, for he watched the conduct of the sovereign
people with an ironical smile, and motioned to the
herald to let the sport continue. The lion had again
risen, and walking with royal dignity from scrap to
scrap, reserved a large portion of the amphitheatre
for a feeding-ground, on which the panthers took care

not to trespass. Meantime Hermas had gone to the obelisk erected as *meta** for a recent chariot race, and seated himself on the pedestal, where he continued to play his flute, as a conqueror, while the lion and panthers fed at his feet, as the prophet had predicted. Once more an incident attracted the attention of the throng, who had been occupied in watching the animals. The satiated lion merely snuffed at the pieces of meat, then suddenly turned and walked straight towards the obelisk.

" Now this absurd tooting will be stopped," said the spiteful Celsus. The monster came directly up to Hermas, who did not turn his eyes from him. Every 'one expected that a blow from the lion's paw would destroy the poor musician, and all held their breath in suspense. But the animal lay down directly in front of the old man, who with the mixture of cunning and simplicity peculiar to him, stretched out his foot as if to set it on the lion's neck, though he avoided touching him, and blew with redoubled energy. The Christians in the circus could no longer be restrained : Their voices rose, accompanying the melody :

> " We praise Thee, Lamb of God,
> Thy sacred wounds we praise !"

The crowd kept time to the rhythmic chant, or sang without understanding the words :

> " All the earth doth worship Thee,
> Cherubim and Seraphim,
> Join in the exultant hymn.
> Angels cry unceasingly,
> Unto Thee, with one accord
> Holy, holy, holy Lord !"

" It's time to put an end to this nonsense," said Hadrian. " The beloved Quirites, in their ecstasy, do

* *Metae*—the goals.—*Smith's Dict. of Greek and Roman Antiq.*

not know what they are doing," and he signed to the herald. As the hymn ended, Hermas let the flute fall, raised his hand to Heaven, and triumphantly drew back his foot. A loud blare of trumpets announced an imperial command and produced silence.

"The Caesar," proclaimed the herald, "is of the opinion that the condemned man has undergone the combat, and can be released. Is the populace of the same opinion?"

"Surely! Yes! Hail! Ay!" and other loud shouts of assent drowned a slight degree of opposition from the senators' benches.

"As Hermas was the instigator of the three Nazarenes, the Caesar has determined to make the other two slaves of the exchequer, especially as after the sport just witnessed some other game would doubtless be more amusing to the Quirites."

"Right! Excellent! Hail! Pardon! Jupiter increase thy years from ours! Hail to the Caesar!" rang from the lips of the multitude. Although the assent this time was less full than before, the proposal was accepted.

"The aedile," continued the herald, "declared that after the new aqueduct was completed, the arena could be flooded in a half an hour without any previous preparation, and a naval battle take place. Instead of the fight with animals, the Caesar orders a naval battle."

The aedile hurriedly withdrew, a general buzz and murmur of voices arose from the benches, which however instantly yielded to the interest of watching to see how Hermas would be removed from the circle of wildbeasts A door opened and the guards entered with lowered spears, but Hermas motioned them to keep back,

and passing the cats with steady gaze, walked with
solemn dignity through the gate, accompanied by the
exultant shouts and applause of the multitude. The
soldiers muttered angrily:

" Juggler, sorcerer! How shall we get the satiated
beasts in again ?"

One of the guards cautiously extended a piece of
meat to the lion on the end of a long fork, but the
animal shook his mane angrily, and at the second trial
uttered a spiteful growl. Another, relying on his friendship with the panthers, attempted to pull the nearest one
in, but the creature struck its claws deep into the man's
arm, who covered with blood, was released from the
growling beasts by the soldiers' pikes.

" Well, was what we have just seen a miracle or
not?" Pius asked a scoffing neighbor. The soldiers
were already ordered to form a phalanx, and with lowered spears drive the beasts back to their cages, when
the Caesar commanded the aqueduct to be opened instead. As the pipes poured jets of water the thickness
of a man's arm in every direction, and the cold moisture
began to wet the ground under the animals feet, the
dainty panthers instantly bounded back to their dens,
and the grating was lowered behind them, but the lion
calmly lay down on the pedestal of the meta and quietly
watched the rising flood. When it overflowed the steps
he rose, roaring; then the water touched his paws, and
the stately beast resolutely flung himself into the cold
waves and swam proudly across to his cage, whose grating instantly fell.

The distant sounds of the events occurring outside had reached the cell occupied by the two brothers; not one had escaped the sharpened senses of the martyrs, but they knew not how to interpret them. The roaring of the lion, who had stationed himself just in front of their door, startled them from their dreamy stupor. Then followed a strange silence, during which they waited anxiously for Hermas's death-shriek—but it did not come. Instead they heard the notes of his flute, whose joyous melody harmonized ill with the terror and grief of their throbbing hearts, yet to which they listened with every nerve, as if it were a message of their friend's fate. If the music ceased, they looked anxiously at each other, and when it was drowned by the uproar that hailed the tiger's appearance, Vitalis pressed Natalis's hand, murmuring:

"He is happy, it is over."

But the flute was heard again, mingled with the horrible howls and roars of the wild-beasts. Was Hermas's angel really standing by his side, chastising the animals with a fiery sword? They heard the whining of the wounded tiger, as it dragged itself into the cage beside them. Then followed the hoarse growling of the panthers, the laughter and shouts of the spectators—if they had not heard the notes of the flute blending with the rude uproar, they would have again numbered Hermas among the dead. But what was this? The crowd was joining in the Song of the Lamb. The hymn rang forth with a rushing sound.

> "We praise Thee, Lamb of God,
> Thy sacred wounds we praise!"

"The Lord has come, Maranatha! The Pagan

world is paying homage to the Son of Man. Oh! Lord, send Thy angel, that he may burst these bolts, and we not remain prisoned here on the day of Thy glorious appearance!" cried Natalis fervently.

"Wait, I'll climb up to the window, or do you get up on my shoulders, I can hold you."

Natalis brought the box on which Hermas had sat, lifted it upon the blocks they had used for their own seats, and rested them firmly against the wall; Vitalis then climbed up, while his brother held him from below.

"What do you see?"

"Only the crowd, singing and shouting, but they are not devout."

"Don't you see Hermas?"

"I must get a little higher," said Vitalis, clinging to the iron bars of the window.

"A miracle, brother!" he exclaimed. "Hermas is sitting by the obelisk with his foot on the lion's neck. The panthers are devouring food, which must have fallen from Heaven. Hark, the trump is sounding. Maranatha!" He sprang down and fell on his knees.

"My child," said Natalis, stroking the younger lad's hair, "that is no angel's voice, it is the herald!"

Vitalis nodded. "What torture this uncertainty is!"

Again a long pause ensued, then the brothers once more heard the roaring of the wild-beasts, and a man's shriek of pain fell upon their ears. Could it be Hermas, his flute had long been silent?

"Does the torture last so long, so horribly long?"

Again they sank into a dull stupor.

"Doesn't it seem as if the deluge were coming? I hear the rush of many waters, Natalis. Are they cleansing the earth from the blood of Hermas, or what is it ? Feel the dampness entering through the window."

While the brothers were gazing upward, steps approached, the chains rattled, the bolts were pushed back.

. "Lord, we are ready," said Natalis, clasping his hands.

Hermas entered, followed by the aedile and jailer.

"You are saved !" cried the former to the two lads, who silently fell into his arms.

"The emperor grants you a pardon," said the aedile ; "you are to go to Aquae as prisoners of the exchequer. May time restore your liberty." The two brothers, deeply agitated, clasped each other in a close embrace, while a beneficent flood of tears relieved the terrible tension of mind and body, that had so long oppressed them. A friendly evocatus, whom they had known at Tibur, was to conduct them in *custodia libera*, as soon as the games were over, to the house where Ennia lived with their younger brothers and sisters. Meantime Hermas joyously sat down on his chest and related his experiences, which sounded strangely enough from his lips, as he declared that he distinctly felt the presence of the angel of the Lord, who terrified the wild-beasts and aided him in the conflict.

CHAPTER XVII.

ANTINOUS stood at the narrow window of an unoccupied cell, in the round corner-tower of the palace, opposite to the Flavian Theatre, feverishly excited by the

thought that the next blast of the tuba might announce
the death of the man who had saved his life, and the
playfellows to whom he had promised friendship. Much
as their characters had secretly estranged him, he could
not understand the apathetic indifference with which
Hadrian left to their fate a former member of his household and the sons of his most faithful servant, and felt
that if this blood should really flow, it would form a
deep red stream, which must forever separate him from
Hadrian.

" For his sake also, help me, Osiris-Apis !" murmured
the youth, clasping the little green image of the god
closer in his hand.

Just at that moment the blast of the tuba, announc-
ing the commencement of the games, echoed on the
air.

The young athlete instantly stretched his arm straight
before him, fixed his gaze intently on the tiny seated
figure of the god carved from dark-green stone, and devoutly repeated the words engraved on the pedestal :
" Apis-Osiris, great god who sits in Amenti, ever-living
Lord, everlasting Ruler, save, preserve, for thou art the
living Osiris, thou art 'Tum, all thy feathers are on thee,
thou dost grant everlasting life !"

With inexpressible fervor he repeated the prayer in
his deep, melancholy voice, especially the words : " Save,
preserve !"   But when reciting the formula for about the
two hundredth time, he began to grow weary, and
through his burning brain darted the terrible thought :

" Suppose your lukewarmness, your absent-minded
praying, should endanger the poor prisoners' lives," and
he began again with fresh ardor.

He beheld in imagination the dark god seated

amid the gloom of the nether-world, nodding to him, and whispered imploringly : " Save, preserve !"

But what was the meaning of the words : " All thy feathers are on thee?" They confused him, whenever he uttered them. Already his arm was beginning to be paralyzed. Accustomed to athletic sports, he had thought it an easy matter to hold his hand outstretched a few hours, now it began to shake, his muscles and veins swelled, it seemed as if a hundred-pound weight were trying to drag his arm down.

Then a sudden terror seized him. While extending the arm with redoubled energy, he had altered the words of his prayer. The sentence was still ringing in his ears : "Thou who dost sit on thy feathers, all thy amenti are on thee." Weeping bitterly, he continued his petition. A loud uproar sometimes resounded from the theatre opposite. The combat must have reached its fiercest point, but he dared not avert his eyes a moment from the tyrannical little god he held in his hand. Again he eagerly, steadily repeated the prayer, gazing fixedly at the image. But what was this? It had changed its color —a convulsive tremor shook his arm; the green god had suddenly turned blue. Terror overpowered Antinous, who dropped the idol. It fell from the tower, and rebounding from roof to roof vanished, shattered into a thousand pieces, in the giddy depths below. Antinous tottered, his strength failed, and leaning with dim eyes against the window-frame, he gazed mournfully at the theatre, where a great commotion prevailed. Blasts of the tuba and the herald's shout announced that a part of the games was over. A Nubian slave, in the dress of the keepers of the wild-beasts, was just leaving the theatre and hastily crossing the open space towards the palace. Antinous mutely leaned back. The omen by which the god had spoken, portended death. After the lapse of some time spent in gazing into vacancy, in a state of cheerless apathy, he suddenly saw beside him the Egyptian priest, who with a joyousness of manner infinitely encouraging to the Bithynian, said:

"My omens are favorable. I think the god has heard our prayers. Where is the image?"

" It changed color, and I was frightened and let it fall." Antinous answered sighing. " It lies shattered below."

"What color did the god assume?" hastily asked the Egyptian.

" He turned perfectly blue."

" Then they are saved. Had the god denied your prayer, he would have appeared red. Yet the accident is an evil omen. I fear we shall have some unpleasant consequence. But I will send across, and ask how matters stand; look, they are arranging a mock sea-fight, two boats are already floating yonder."

Antinous looked after him with a divided heart.

" They are saved, but through my fault some fata. event will follow. Alas! oracles have trifled with us since the days of Croesus."

At this moment, the Egyptian returned. " Suetonius is here, and says Hermas escaped uninjured, the animals acted as if chained by some higher spell. Your prayers have saved them. The gods have also worked a second miracle. The freedman Nereus, who deluded Graecina and caused all the trouble, was seized and killed by the lion's spring, while sitting among the spectators. Natalis and Vitalis were not obliged to fight at all. They will go as slaves of the public treasury to Aquae, whither Ennia is also exiled."

" I thank thee, great god, who sits in Amenti," said Antinous, devoutly raising both arms towards Heaven.

" Direct the omen, Isis, goddess of the universe !" added the Egyptian solemnly.

" Let us go across before your friends are taken away," he then said cheerfully. " As soon as they are assigned for transportation, you will hardly be able to speak with them, especially as we set out for Ancona this very day.   Perhaps the Christians' madness will subside, when they learn to whom they owe their deliverance."

Antinous, his large brown eyes sparkling with gratitude, held out his hand to the Egyptian.

" Forgive me, Amenophis, for having destroyed so effective a talisman."

" The god will live," replied the priest, " even if all his idols should be shattered. He is present in each one of his images, if it is clasped with a believing heart."

He again drew from his bosom the cord on which the images of the gods were arranged, loosed from the chain a small dark-green statue of Serapis, and gave it to Antinous.

" You believe; the god will be with you.   Pray to him daily, and if you ask as you have done to-day, he will answer as faithfully as you have asked. The gods lie only to hypocrites.   You know the sign that indicates the god's favor, and that which announces his wrath. It is not seemly to utter sacred things a second time."

Antinous raised the hem of the priest's robe to his lips, and concealed the amulet.   He did not see the expression of shrewd satisfaction that smoothed Amenophis's harsh features at this moment.   Silently, as if in a dream, the Bithynian followed the Egyptian, who on reaching the theatre, stopped before a small side-door, and after mentioning to the guard his own name and Antinous's, passed into a corridor unhindered, walked to a door at the end, and uttered a few words in a foreign tongue, through a grating. The Nubian slave's face instantly appeared at the window, the door opened, and the new arrivals found themselves before the cages of the wild beasts. The walls that admitted the animals into the theatre were now firmly closed, and the space where Amenophis and Antinous stood admitted light and air into the cages between strong, but not too closely-arranged iron bars.

"Don't go too near," said Amenophis; "they can reach quite far out."

After the youth's eyes had become accustomed to the dim light, he saw the lion's majestic head and fiery eyes directly opposite him. In the adjoining cage lay the tiger, rolled up in a ball.

"Did the remedy act?" asked Amenophis.

"The animal instantly fell asleep," replied the Nubian. "We managed to sew up the skin on its head, and I hope the creature will live."

"Are the prisoners still in their cells?"

The Nubian nodded.

"Tell them Antinous would like to bid them farewell."

The Nubian opened a door leading into a connecting room, and through the opposite one Antinous looked into a little cell. Hermas, still clad in shepherd's garb, sat in the middle, while beside him reclined the two brothers, clasping each other in an affectionate embrace, as they eagerly listened to the tales of the happy prophet.

"Hermas!" cried Antinous mournfully, and over-come by emotion his arms fell by his side. But Hermas had already started up, and in speechless agitation the two friends embraced each other, while the brothers greeted the new-comer with a cordial pressure of the hand. After the first outburst of joy was over, Hermas drew himself up to his full height, saying solemnly:

"Do you now believe in the power of the Naza-rene?"

Antinous was silent a moment, then answered gently:

"I believe a good god saved you."

At this moment the Egyptian's stately figure emerged from the shadow, exclaiming in a stern, re-proachful tone:

"Antinous, will you deny Osiris, who has just heard your prayer?"

"No, Amenophis," replied Antinous, and hastily turning to the three prisoners, said:

"It is to this holy man's god, that you owe your deliverance. I called fervently on Osiris-Apis, who gave me a sign and at the same moment saved you."

"Are you raving, boy?" cried Hermas indignantly. "The deity of this lying prophet, an image of wood or stone, which cannot stir, cannot speak, save us, us, the Christians, to whom all demons are hostile?"

"You will not escape your doom!" exclaimed the Egyptian with flashing eyes. "Not to save you from a just punishment, but to give this pious youth a sign, does the god who sits in Amenti grant you a reprieve."

"Do not believe the priest, Antinous," cried Vitalis beseechingly; "why should his god work miracles for us?"

"With this flute," exclaimed Hermas, "I played the Song of the Lamb. With it I lured Phlegon from his carriage at the Albula, till obeying the father's call to the son, he came to me. With this same song to-day I have tamed the lion, sent him to battle with the tiger, and made the panthers so merry that they jumped for joy."

"But without the meat, over which I made the sign of Tum, they would have sprung at your throat—ask this Nubian. How is it, Hadad?"

"This holy man made the sign of his god over the meat, and thus tamed them," replied the Nubian. "We know the animals thoroughly, you can believe it. He is a great philosopher and has power."

"And the message the angel brought me yesterday—I suppose that too was from your god Tum?" While speaking Hermas drew from his pouch the torn fragment of a wax tablet.

"It too came from me," replied the Egyptian, scornfully drawing the other part of the tablet from the folds of his robe. "See, the edges fit."

"Avaunt from me, Satanas!" exclaimed Hermas in furious wrath. "The devil is seeking to draw the works of the Son of Man into his mire of lies. Christus did it."

"But Hermas!" cried Antinous indignantly, "if I swear to you that in the hour of your deliverance the god gave me a distinct sign, surely you will believe me."

"What kind of a sign?" asked Hermas fiercely.

"His image changed color."

"Lying arts of the priests of Baal!" shouted Hermas. "What is this sign compared to the miracle witnessed by the people of Rome through me an hour ago ?"

"Well," said the Egyptian with icy contempt, "here is your pipe, and here is the lion. Go up to him and ask him in the name of your god, to shake hands with you."

"You shall see, prophet of lies!" said Hermas fairly frantic.

"Don't do it!" cried the three youths in the same breath, but Hermas had already entered the cage.

"In the name of the Lord, Brother Lion—" but he went no farther. His companions saw a quick stroke of the lion's paw, heard a horrible cracking of bones, a stifled cry—Hermas was no more.

"Back, Agamemnon!" shouted the Nubian, thrusting an iron pole at the beast. The lion immediately released his prey, and the prophet's lifeless body fell on the floor. The Nubian cautiously drew it out of the animal's reach and laid it in a side room, closing the doors between on the beasts. Natalis and Vitalis knelt beside their dead friend in speechless grief.

"His neck is broken, there is no help," said the Egyptian with cold composure.

"Woe betide you, terrible priest, you urged him to tempt the Lord!" exclaimed Natalis, rising indignantly.

"Antinous," pleaded Vitalis, "release yourself from this servant of darkness."

Antinous sorrowfully shook his head. "Your blindness is incurable. Have you not yet seen whose god is the true one? An hour ago this priest of the great god, who sits in Amenti, predicted what has now happened. When his god gave me the sign, I was so startled that the image fell from my hand and was shattered. Then

Amenophis said: 'Your friends will be saved, but a bloody event will follow their deliverance.' This is the man whom you call a lying prophet."

"A fine god, that breaks into pieces!" said Vitalis.

"Not the god," replied Antinous indignantly, "only his image."

"A pretty god, who saves to destroy the next hour!" retorted Vitalis.

"You are speaking of your own," replied Antinous bitterly. "If he saved before, why not now? Look at poor Hermas, it is thus your god gives life."

"Do not blaspheme!" cried Vitalis angrily.

"You are blaspheming yourself," replied Antinous.

"My friend," said Amenophis with dignity, "you see they do not believe, because they will not. Even should Osiris permit this poor dead fool to rise, they would say that their god alone was the resurrection and the life, and ascribe all honor to him. So let them commend this corpse to him. But do you come away. Companionship with sacrilege brings misfortune."

"Go, murderer!" cried Vitalis. "You lured our faithful Hermas into the snare. He did not consider, that the Lord does not work His miracles for the unbelieving."

Antinous had already reached the door, towards which the Egyptian drew him.

"Farewell!" he cried, but the brothers made no reply. Then the door closed. They were parted forever.

"So our tears of joy are again transformed to mourning," said Natalis. "Fatal visitor! But for him our companion, our faithful Hermas, would still be living."

While the sea-fight was going on in the theatre, the Egyptian appeared in Hadrian's box, followed by Antinous, who looked sad and agitated. Amenophis, in an undertone, told the emperor that Hermas, relying on the name of his god, had again offered his head to the lion, and had his neck broken by a blow from the animal's paw. The rude laughter, with which Hadrian received the tidings, cut Antinous to the soul. Lost in grief, he leaned back in the corner of the box, without vouchsafing the spectacle a single glance. If he had not dropped the image of the god, the misfortune would not have happened. If he had not gone to the prisoner's cell, the whole wretched quarrel would not have occurred. Was there not some truth in the brothers' reproach, that the Egyptian had lured poor, excitable, foolhardy Hermas into a snare? He felt a horror of this man. It was not that he doubted his alliance with the gods, but the miracle did not seem so pure since he had learned that Amenophis had given written counsel to the prisoners, and undertaken special manipulations with the meat. The Egyptian had not spoken of that. Who knows whether the latter's expedient might not have had precisely the same result, without his earnest prayers in the tower?

The poor youth gazed mournfully into vacancy. He had lost a faithful friend, that was certain — whether he had found a true god in Amenti he dared not doubt, but drew neither courage nor cheerfulness from the nature of this revelation. Suetonius's entrance roused him from these dreams.

"Caesar," said the secretary, "the body of Hermas, according to the centurion's orders, was to be dragged by hooks to the common death-cart and at the close of

the games conveyed with the others to the Gemoniae,
where they are thrown down the steps into the Tiber,
like all the bodies from the amphitheatre. But when the
servants opened the doors, hundreds of Christians appeared, who had come to accompany the victorious
martyr to the house of their bishop, Pius. When they
learned the misfortune that had happened, they burst
into loud lamentations. They believe Hermas has been
murdered, in order as they say, to remove a witness of
the truth, and resolutely demand his body to be interred
in their burial place. As you declared Hermas free before his death, the centurion is doubtful whether he must
not obey their will."

"The law wages no war against the dead," said
Hadrian, yielding to a beseeching glance from Antinous.
" Order the centurion to deliver up the body. Let them
bury Hermas or restore him to life. He has fulfilled the
praetor's sentence."

Suetonius withdrew. A short time after, Antinous
heard the well-known monotonous chant rising from the
street, and approached the open bow-window in the corridor behind the imperial box. A long procession of
mourning Christians was following Hermas's bier, which
was borne along the road leading to the catacombs outside the Porta Praenestina. The youth gazed after
them a long time, equally alone between the devout
Christians without, and the Pagan throng within, now ex-
ulting with blood-thirsty joy over the hewing down of
the gladiators on a ship just boarded.

CHAPTER XVIII.

The Nile, swollen on its course to the sea by the melting snows of the summer months, spread its waters with majestic breadth over the land of Egypt. A moist heat brooded over the waves, and the white mist of the atmosphere dazzled every eye. Surrounded by numerous boats used by the river police, Hadrian's trireme was working its way upward against the moderately strong current of the middle Nile. Beneath a dark-blue canopy on the stern deck lay Hadrian, ill, emaciated, worn by the fatigue of the journey, and looking actually corpse-like in the blueish dusk of his awning. Transported from the fresh breezes of Tibur and the invigorating sea-air to this sultry climate, the asthmatic invalid suffered severely from shortness of breath, and his deep-set, mournful eyes looked more misanthropic than ever. Beside him reclined Antinous, paralyzed by the emperor's gloomy mood, by the leaden weight of the atmosphere, the memory of the past. Before the invalid and his favorite sat Amenophis, pointing out the sacred monuments appearing on the right and left behind their protecting dams, above the surface of the flood, and mentioning the names and sizes of the cities and villages. The surface of the water stretched before their eyes in a monotonous, wearisome expanse, from whose dull level here and there rose the tops of slender palm-trees and the gnarled branches of flooded sycamores. Now and then a crane, standing on one leg on the shore overlooking the water, or a pelican with its head hidden under its wing, formed the stifl accessories to this monotonous picture. The whole scene had a somewhat soothing influence, an impression increased by the beat of the oars. Antinous only half listened to the conversation between his two companions. He could not understand how Hadrian could bury himself all day long in discussions with the Egyptian concerning how far the animal's sure, quiet instinct and unvarying nature would represent the eternal unity of the gods more faithfully than the character of men, tossed to and fro by thought and self-will—and how the self-same man, after such an apology for the worship of animals, could curse himself in ·hours of sleeplessness for not having had the Apis poisoned, to rid the world of the cause of strife, instead of taking such a journey on account of an ox and finally falling a victim to this bull-fight. The youth, whose mind was not sufficiently elastic to follow such bounds, occupied himself in the old way, shut his ears to external things, and thus instead of the priest's words, heard the beat of the oars, whose monotonous rhythm drowned the uniform plash of the waves. While thus dreaming on the ancient, sacred river, the olive and pine woods of his native land rose before his memory; instead of the broad charmless expanse of the Nile, he heard the ripple of the clear mountain streams of Bithynia. The vision of his father's house, so long repressed, rose before the youth in clear, distinct outlines—a dwelling surrounded by vines and fig-trees, a plain residence at Claudiopolis, shaded by a tree of enormous size. His parents' faces appeared before him as if in a dream, the merry laughter of his round-cheeked sister Pauline echoed in his ears. He recalled the day the emperor took up his abode in the city, how the splendor and magnificence of the court allured him, how he was bought from his father, and, he scarcely knew whether as the Caesar's slave or friend, placed the sea between himself and his home. A strange word, "home," to him, who for years had wandered restlessly around the world, not by his own choice, but like a whirling leaf, and the beat of the oars said distinctly: "You have lost it, you have lost it, you have lost it ..." How brilliant and joyous the court was then. Old Servianus, with his merry tales of the camp, who in those days was still Hadrian's right-hand man, understood so well how to be the intercessor for clever people. Then the emperor's hatred interfered, Antinous himself knew not why. Where was the whole joyous circle the old tippler had gathered around him? The oars still beat the cadence: "Lost, lost, lost ..." Then he had formed a friendship with the clever Phlegon; how kindly the Greek had instructed him, introduced him to the poets and philosophers of his country. The youth had hoped to go to Egypt with him. But temptations with which he was unable to cope, assailed the feeble man. He had degraded him-self, he was no longer Phlegon. "Lost, lost, lost!" said the Nile. Phlegon's sons, scarcely won as friends, ere they were lost again. And faithful Hermas, at whom he had so often laughed heartily, yet loved so well because he made every one's grief and joy his own, who had saved his life:—"Lost—lost!" And the gods: "Lost—lost!" So said the oars distinctly—these were the words heard amid the plashing of the waves. Should he not let himself slip softly down into the deep, still water, ere any one noticed him? It was so cool below the surface, there was peace, there was deliver-

ance, there lay the gates to Amenti. Just at that moment a gull's shrill scream close beside his ears so
startled him, that he sprang up in bewilderment, gazing
confusedly at the emperor. He now perceived that the
Egyptian had gone away. Hadrian, stroking his hair
caressingly, said :

" We are alone in this watery wilderness, alone in the
world."

" Yes indeed, alone !" thought Antinous. " Whom
have I still and whither shall I go, if this feeble invalid
succumbs to his next attack ?" But ashamed of the
selfish thought, he took the emperor's burning hand and
pressed his forehead on it. He had devoted himself to
this man, and was he not the most important person in
the whole world ? Were not thousands benefited, if he
succeeded in restoring this disjointed soul for days to its
old harmony, dispelling suspicion, driving away distrust,
and soothing angry words ? Was it not a life-purpose ?
He would live on for the task. With the emperor's
death he would have nothing more to seek here. And he
dreamed mournfully of offering himself as a sacrifice for
him who had raised him from obscurity, that his fidelity
might bloom with eternal renown, here and in Hades.

" What are you thinking about, boy ?" asked the
Caesar.

" I am consecrating myself to be a sacrifice on your
funeral-pyre."

" You won't have long to wait, and when the time
comes will quickly dry your eyes, and let black-eyed
Lydia console you in the cave of the selli."

" Hideous !" exclaimed Antinous. " Have you spied
that out too ?"

" I know a great deal, boy."

" Then you might see that your selli steal less, instead of believing I find any pleasure with that sooty Pythia," and he relapsed into an offended silence. Was it worth while to die for a man, who thus repelled his ardent love ? Yet was it not still harder to live for him ? Sorely out of humor, he sat gazing into the flood.

What did Hadrian mean by his hint about the little girl at the Zeus well ? Did this man understand how to read his soul ? Did he suspect, that ever since that morning the youth had been haunted by pangs formerly unknown ? He often dreamed of the burning lips, the eager arms that had embraced him at Tibur. Even when he had shaken off the disagreeable memories, he often became absorbed in thoughts of strange faces. He could not help imagining Phlegon's daughters, whom he had never seen. Even now they stood distinctly before him, resembling their tall brothers, and his dreams passed on into the future. He saw the pine-woods of the Abnoba mountains, he would seek the exiles there, settle in Aquae, till the fields as a farmer, and some day come before Phlegon .... just at that instant the anchor splashed into the stream, the trireme stopped. Opposite was the sacred meadow where the Apis grazed, and whither Hadrian had ordered the disputing priests of Memphis and Thebes. A wide ferry-boat, adorned with pennons, put off from the shore; the little boats with gay sails, which had preceded the imperial galley, took up positions on the right and left. Roman soldiers formed a line on both sides of the landing-steps, which were covered with a purple carpet. The procurator of Egypt and several high officials came forward to meet the Caesar, and supported by Suetonius and Antinous, the imperial invalid tottered down the steep ship's-ladder to the ferry-boat. The shore behind the soldiers was thronged with countless Egyptians, fellahs, who had only an apron fastened around their hips, veiled women, priests in ample robes, crowds of naked children. Hundreds of voices greeted the emperor with a unanimous hail.

A master of the world, who could no longer rule his own limbs, a god grazing in the green field in happy apathy, without a suspicion that these thousands of people, including the sovereign of the earth, had assembled here on his account—such was the meaning of the moment, whose irony only Hadrian understood. He missed Phlegon, to whom he liked to whisper such remarks, which Antinous did not yet comprehend.

The Caesar, still leaning on Antinous, first received the procurator's report, and then addressed a few pleasant words to the chief priests about the blessing the god promised to bring this year upon the meadows, as a reward for the faithful service he had received in the temples.

"May my mistress Neith, the great goddess of Sais, bless your words," replied a dignified old man, whose white beard was arranged in countless curls, while his bald head was entirely destitute of ornament.

"Let us go at once to the god, who has brought us here," said Hadrian.

From the downs of the sandy shore, a road bordered by ancient white poplars led to a hill crowned by the wall of a temple and two mighty pylons. Hadrian, walking slowly, ever and anon pausing to take breath, passed through a sacred grove into a paved fore-court, where the sun sent down scorching rays. Beyond this began a long avenue of sphinxes, which the emperor entered, supported by Antinous, the procurator and

Amenophis following. Only the priests accompanied the Caesar, most of them wrapped in white robes, others clad merely in aprons, panther-skins, and fillets. The rest of the attendants remained behind. A sensation of being abandoned in this strange world, overpowered the emperor himself, who beckoned to Amenophis to remain by his side.   Behind the pylons to which the avenue of sphinxes led, opened a second court-yard, above whose entrance glittered the golden disk of the sun. Opposite to this gate-way stood the temple, supported by round pillars, whose capitals represented a lotus-flower. Passing this, the priests now entered a path leading to a group of trees, and emerging from the shadow of the huge sycamores the new-comers saw a smiling meadow extending to the mountains, which situated above the region inundated by the Nile, afforded a superb view of the vast watery mirror, now animated by countless boats, flags, and sails, while beyond it gleamed the red sand-stone rocks of the Libyan mountains. This was the rich green pasture the inhabitants of Besa had allotted to the sacred bull, and whose juicy herbage seemed to please him better than the thin grass of the city of Ra in Lower Egypt, or the bundles of dried herbs in the temple at Memphis. In the temple of Osiris, which Hadrian had just passed, the bull was daily bathed, perfumed, and surrounded by the most costly incense, while his head and horns were decked with the most superb ornaments. He was now walking with a herd of stately cows in the wide enclosure, which lest unsuitable food should be given to the god, was separated by a low fence from the gilded palisades, behind which thronged the people. The High Priest of Besa verbosely explained to Hadrian, that this meadow lying on the borders of Heptanomis and Thebes, was best calculated to reconcile the opposing interests of the inhabitants of Thebes and Memphis.

The emperor and his train soon found themselves confronting the bull, alone with the herd of animals, but outside stood the crowd of Egyptians, watching to see whether the god would be gracious to the Caesar.

"What means do you use to secure the animal's eating from a man's hand?" Hadrian asked Amenophis.

"We are forbidden to tell."

"Don't affect reserve," hissed Hadrian angrily: "I'll pay you for it."

The Egyptian shrugged his shoulders.

"I don't wish the beast to disown me; the people hate the Caesar from whose hand the Apis will not eat. Remember Cambyses."

"Don't feed him," rudely answered the priest of Isis, "then he won't deny you."

"I will make you remember that," said Hadrian. "If your god doesn't eat from my hand, I'll eat him myself, and you shall sit at my table and swallow the juiciest morsel, though it choke you, faithless priest."

"I must be faithful to the gods, not to men," replied Amenophis quietly. "To-morrow you would repent having tried to deceive the divinities, and what would you think of the priest, who had-aided you in doing so?"

Antinous glanced at the Egyptian with a look of assent. It was long since he had heard so many words from the gloomy, silent man, and never one that pleased him better. Meantime they had reached the palisade, and the priests conducted the Caesar between the barrier that excluded the populace, and the fence surrounding the Apis's pasture. The animal came towards them at a lively trot. Hadrian noticed that the herd had eaten the red clover as far as they could reach it over the fence, while near the outer enclosure it still grew high. Not without a quickened pulsation of the heart, he broke off with both hands a large clump and offered it to the bull, that putting his head on one side eat the aromatic food with evident pleasure.

" He has accepted him," shouted the fellahs outside.

" The god has fed from his hand!" cried the women and children, while universal exclamations of joy filled the air. The animal, excited by the sudden noise, raised his head and bellowed loudly.

" Apis greets Hadrian, he recognizes him as a god. Hail to the Caesar, the son of the great Neith, the goddess of Sais!" shouted the priests.

"He has acknowledged me as a brother," said Hadrian to Antinous with a faint smile. " Let us get away before our lofty brother changes his mind," and cheered by the throngs, the emperor, leaning on Antinous's arms, dragged himself back to the temple. The discussions concerning the rival claims of Memphis and Thebes to the sacred animal were to be held there, and the priests forbade the youth's entrance. He was obliged to await Hadrian's return on a flight of steps between the colossal stone rams. It was with difficulty that the Caesar had succeeded in obtaining permission for the procurator and Amenophis to accompany him.

Antinous remained behind with very contradictory feelings. He had come to this strange land for the second time, and at the new visit his recollections of the past lost much of their magic. All the annoyances

of the journey, the discomfort of the climate, the disagreeable character of the people, which had been over-
shadowed in memory by greater impressions, now pain-
fully asserted themselves, yet he had just witnessed the
grand spectacles again. Besides, the half animal world of
gods around him seemed less worthy of reverence
when close at hand, than it had appeared in imagination after Amenophis's descriptions. These temples,
with the gloom of their subterranean crypts and the
colossal statues of the gods, were undoubtedly majestic,
but after the first thrill of awe Antinous felt that he was
still a Greek, and surrounded by the dog and sparrow-
hawk-headed figures of this Barbarian land, remembered
the last Greek temple where he had prayed, the sanctuary
of the joyous Aphrodite of Ancona, and how he had
stood enraptured on the sun-steeped rocks, seen the blue
sea almost encircling him, and before his eyes the
slender Corinthian columns, while in the niche appeared
the perfection of physical beauty in the blooming
Cypris. Suddenly, amid the half-animal forms of
syenite and the sacred bull, such a longing seized upon
the youth for the gods of whom Hadrian had robbed
him, that he would fain have wept.

"However profound may be the ideas the priests
embody in these symbols," he said to himself, "they are
not the gods of my childhood, and I can only pray as I
did then."

He gazed without interest at the gay hieroglyphics
that covered the walls. The silver stars on a blue
ground, glittering from the vaulted roof, seemed puerile
when compared to the clear sky that had sparkled over
his home, the odor of kyphi oppressed him, made him
gasp for breath. From the meadow he heard the bel-

lowing of the Apis, and the lowing of the herd of cows. The theory that the unvarying nature of the gods revealed itself more clearly in the calm instinct of animals, than in the restless human soul, had seemed excellent when Amenophis explained it at Tibur, but the Apis's pasture at Besa looked like any other meadow. He could not conceal from himself the feeling of disappointment that stole over him. He saw the priests bustling about in the .temple court; shining bald heads appeared and vanished, censers of incense were swung to and fro, and water was poured from gold and silver vessels into the chalices on the altar. Dense clouds of kyphi smoke poured through the sanctuary till his head swam. It had all been far more beautiful in imagination, than it was in reality.

"How will Hadrian endure this smoke?" was the only thought the sacred ceremony awakened in his mind. Suddenly the procurator rushed out.

"Quick, Antinous, the Caesar is ill!"

At the same moment the emperor appeared, supported by two priests. His eyes were starting from their sockets, his face looked livid.

"Water, water!" cried Antinous. "Lay him here in the shade. Away with the unhealthy incense! Get a draught of air."

Pushing the priests aside, he dipped his linen robe in the water on the altar, and laid it on the invalid's brow, then seized one of the sacred vessels and slowly sprinkled Hadrian's head. The emperor began to breathe more easily.

"A litter!" said Antinous imperiously. The procurator hurried off to get one, and Antinous ordered the sovereign to be conveyed on it to the sacred grove above the bank of the river, where fanned by the cooler breezes rising from the water, the Caesar gradually recovered consciousness.

"It is said to be a sign of good fortune, if our brother Apis eats from the hand," were his first words. "I see no welfare the omen has brought me." Then he relapsed into a fevered, delirious condition.

The officials consulted with Antinous and Suetonius concerning what should be done. Suetonius wished to have the priests' rooms converted into a sick-chamber, but Antinous opposed the plan. The unusual surroundings, the strange objects, would excite the invalid, the warm air of the building would torture him.

"We'll pitch his tent here and put his camp-bed in it," he added. "Then he will dream of Dacia and the Parthian campaign, the days of his renown and happiness."

The Caesar's physician had now been brought from the trireme, and agreed with Antinous. The precincts of the temple were quiet and secure from intrusion, the grove was dry and fanned by healthful breezes. The servants quickly laid down a firm floor and spread soft carpets over it. In an hour a tent was pitched, several smaller ones for Antinous and the attendants being placed beside it. The procurator sent a report to Aelius Verus, who was in Alexandria and soon reached Besa, accompanied by the oldest and most trustworthy members of the Council of State and the prefect of the body-guard. The illness had commenced with an asthmatic attack, and threatened to speedily end in a violent fever. Since he was placed on his camp-bed, Hadrian had fought over all Trajan's battles, and called to Servianus, but in the tone of former friendship. At times the bloody shades of Lucius Quintus, Palma, and Nigrinus appeared. Antinous never left the sick man's couch night or day, and the physician, who knew his patient's temperament, kept all strangers from his bedside. The young heir, usually averse to labor, eagerly seized upon all the business of the government.

Aelius Verus Caesar was the son-in-law of Nigrinus, who had conspired against Hadrian. As a handsome youth, he had once been on most affectionate terms with the emperor, but one of the Caesar's strangest acts was taking as co-ruler this consumptive fop, whose state of health promised a much shorter duration of life than his own. If he had followed the plan of interesting Rome in his own existence, by making her tremble at the idea of a future under the rule of Aelius Verus, he had attained his purpose. Every one preferred the present to such a future. Hadrian's design in appointing such an heir remained an enigma to the Romans. Phlegon, in his biography, asserted that the Caesar knew Verus's horoscope, and was aware that he would die ere he obtained the empire. The city believed that by this adoption the emperor had fulfilled a promise. Often, when strolling through the wide laurel avenues at Tibur and the fragile young Caesar went away coughing, Hadrian quoted Virgil's lines:

> "This youth (the blissful vision of a day)
> Shall just be shown on earth, then snatched away."*

According to Spartianus's testimony, the foppish young man pleased Hadrian more by good looks than by good morals; he was a wit, agreeable in society, the inventor of peculiar dainties, and possessed a special liking for

* Dryden's translation.

cushioned swings and hammocks. Spartianus relates that
he invented a kind of couch with four cushions, stuffed
with rose-leaves, whose coverlids were scented with lily-
leaves and Persian perfumes. Here, covered by a net
that kept off the flies, he dallied with his fair friends.
He named his four couriers East Wind, South Wind,
North Wind and Zephyr, and pitilessly sent them forth
according to the quarter of the world to which his errands were directed. The companions of the rose-
stuffed cushions he called the four roseate clouds, and
when his wife reproached him for loving all his sweet-
hearts better than herself, he told her the name of wife
should only be rated as an official dignity.

Since the man, whom Roman writers describe in such
unpleasing colors, had reached the temple of Osiris, the
courtiers' eyes roved restlessly between the rising and
setting sun. Aelius Verus feigned deep anxiety, but
could not help sending for his four winds, rose-clouds
and wonderful hammocks. He ordered a second camp
to be pitched on the opposite side of the temple, from
whence only too frequently gay laughter, and exclamations in women's voices, betrayed the real feelings of the
heir to the throne. He too had visited the Apis and
tried to feed him, but the perfume on his hands and
clothing was probably disagreeable to the animal, for he
turned angrily away, and as the Caesar followed the
herd, one of the cows whisked her tail so close to his
mouth, that the elegant young man, livid and shuddering with disgust, left the pasture. Streams of rose-water
were required to restore him to a condition worthy of
his dignity. The Egyptian priests, on the contrary,
could scarcely conceal their delight at the conduct of
their Apis, so in harmony with the dignity of a god, and

regarded Verus as having committed a crime, because, in his horror, he had first washed himself in the sacred river.

Antinous foresaw a gloomy future for the empire, if Hadrian died without repairing the greatest error of his reign—the appointment of such an heir. His own position too was very solitary. It was known that Aelius Verus pursued him with jealous hatred. Antinous felt that people shrank from him, and his contempt for mankind increased. What a future lay before him, if Hadrian really descended into Hades.

Meantime the emperor's health improved, and with it the wind of public opinion again shifted. At the conference between the priests, which cost Hadrian so dear, an agreement was made, commemorated by the striking of a coin that bore Hadrian's image, offering his hand to Osiris and conducting him to the Apis-bull. As the invalid expressed great pleasure at the gift, envoys soon came to present similar votive coins, from all the temples Hadrian had visited. One displayed his figure gazing into the mirror of Isis, while the sparrow-hawk-headed god Ra's hand rested familiarly on his shoulder; others represented him in the guise of Horus battling with Typhon, as the dog-headed Anubis, or standing holding a sistrum before the ibis as a friend of the good god, striking clappers to drive the evil ones away—in short, the intimacy between him and the monstrous divinities of the Egyptian temples was displayed by all kinds of works of art heaped around him, till the Roman officials found it difficult to win the invalid, who plunged more and more eagerly into mythological studies, to take the requisite degree of interest in affairs of state, which he preferred to leave to Aelius Verus.

He sighed over the trifles with which he was troubled, and secretly wished for the ill-treated Phlegon, who always as if by intuition translated every wink and frown into an imperial decree, and invariably hit upon Hadrian's opinion, without annoying him with questions, like Suetonius.

Thus time passed quietly with Antinous. He sat all night long by the sick man's couch, which sleep almost deserted, and again enjoyed the delightful versatility of the gifted ruler, who now that he was thrown on a sick-bed, and deprived of the attractions of the outside world, recalled all the memories of his changeful life and all the faculties of his rich intellect. The invalid persisted that his life was drawing to a close, and in a softened mood, composed the well-known lines:

> "Ah! fleeting spirit! wandering fire,
> That long hast warmed my tender breast,
> Must thou no more this frame inspire?
> No more a pleasing, cheerful guest?
> Whither, oh whither, art thou flying?
> To what dark, undiscovered shore?
> Thou seem'st all trembling, shivering, dying,
> And wit and humor are no more!" *

Once, when he spoke of his speedy death, Antinous summoned up his courage and urged him to recall the appointment of Aelius Verus or at least give him an able co-ruler. "Restore Servianus and his grandchildren to their rights," pleaded the boy.

"Never!" replied Hadrian.

"Then take Antoninus, Aurelian, or any one else, but do not leave the empire to this weakling."

"What have you against Verus?" asked the Caesar angrily. Antinous spoke of the arrangements in the

* Pope's translation.

other camp, tales of which had been brought to him,
described Verus's effeminate character, and gave free expression to the aversion he felt for the weak, marrowless
dandy.   The Bithynian had spoken in loud, eager, passionate tones, yet it seemed as if Hadrian's mysterious
face gleamed with secret satisfaction.   The emperor
evidentally mentally assented to Antinous's description,
but the prospect of leaving the empire to such hands appeared to afford him pleasure rather than pain.

"Caesar!" exclaimed Antinous passionately, "do not
let me believe what they say, that you have intentionally
given yourself an unworthy successor, to make people
wish you back after your death."

Hadrian frowned, then answered:

"The idolized Titus lived precisely the same existence as Verus, the idolized Trajan had far worse vices,
yet Rome deified them. People have hated me because
I was harsh to myself, strict in service, tireless in labor.
So we must give them another Titus.   Like flock, like
shepherd!"

"Then give them two shepherds, that the good ones
may not go uncared for—adopt Aurelian!"

"Hush—I see a shadow outside the tent, boy—
who shrieks such things aloud?   You are a child, and
always will be. What would Rome say to a Caesar you
had recommended?"

Antinous turned pale. True, he too was a weakling!
What availed his good intentions, the emperor's favorite
remained unhonored.   He kept silence.

"It seems as if the perfume of violets and roses, of
which you were speaking, floated through the curtain at
the doorway.   I am certain Aelius Verus has been listening to us."

But Antinous, without moving, gazed mournfully into vacancy. What cared he whether Verus had heard or not! His misery could not be greater than it was.

CHAPTER XIX.

" Verus is insufferable," said Eos to Aurora; " I can do nothing to please him. Come, we'll find Boreas, since he has sent all the other winds away, and play ball with Hesperus. If he gets bored, he'll be more amiable." The pretty rose-cloud threw her white arm around her friend's waist, and glided with her into the temple-court to play ball among the venerable monoliths and gloomy sphinxes, laughing merrily when the toy rebounded from the cheek or forehead of a solemn-looking deity, and bringing the gaily-painted plaything back from between the lion's paws of the stone statues.

Rosy-fingered Eos was right. Verus was insufferable—and Hadrian was also right; Verus had been listening. Nay, it was because he had listened, that he was insufferable. He did not recline at ease in his hammock, but sat impatiently at a little candle-wood table, drumming restlessly on it with his slender hands.

" Hadrian must go, ere he alters his arrangements, and then the crocodiles of the sacred river shall eat the insolent Bithynian. In Hadrian's present condition, his death would surprise no one, but how to manage it? Antinous watches him like a body-guard, and his own suspicion has Argus-eyes. His attendants would all die for him ... All? All? The Egyptian might perhaps be bought. But will he consent?"

The pale young Caesar paced restlessly up and down his tent.

"We need not begin with Hadrian," he said to himself at last. The real danger is the Bithynian, who will not cease to rouse his master's anger against me. If Amenophis aids me to get rid of the youth, I shall be sure of him. He must assist me to take the second step too."

He struck the metal basin near him. A fantastically-dressed courier entered; spite of the heat he wore around his hips a shaggy skin, and had wings fastened on his shoulders.

"Boreas," said Verus, "blow over to Amenophis, the Egyptian, and take him on your wings. Bring him hither, but secretly, that no one may see him. Do you hear, very secretly, or I'll have you crucified."

"I will blow softly," replied the runner, and instantly vanished.

When he had gone, Verus would gladly have recalled him.

"One false step," he muttered, "and I am lost." Sighing heavily, he threw himself on his purple cushions. "Why do I give myself all this agitation? If I reach the goal, I shall have a dog's life. Florus is perfectly right: *Ego nolo Caesar esse, ambulare per Britannos, Scythicas pati pruinas.* I'll take a warm bath till Amenophis comes, and meantime consider how I can best suggest my wish to this crafty Egyptian." He left the room, humming:

> "'Tis baths and love and wine that destroy us;
> Yet life is—baths and love, and wine!"

When at the end of half an hour the young Caesar

returned, he heard the Egyptian's harsh voice threatening and scolding, mingled with the sobs and shrieks of his page Hesperus. Hastily tearing aside the curtain, he saw Amenophis shaking the boy violently, amid words of vehement upbraiding.

"How dare you take such liberties in a stranger's house?" cried Verus harshly, releasing his white-robed page, "Evening-star," from the priest's hands. The weeping lad smoothed the silver star embroidered on his breast, straightened his rumpled tunic, and sobbed :

"He beat me, because I climbed on the dog-headed god's shoulders."

"I will return your question, Caesar," replied the Egyptian sullenly. "How dare you take such liberties in a stranger's house, the house of my gods? Your frail fair ones play ball in the temple of Osiris, and this young fop torments the sacred animals, and defiles the sanctuaries of my native land. Do you wish to be murdered by the Egyptians, when Hadrian's death-hour arrives, that you thus provoke the people?"

"I knew nothing about it," said Verus, giving the whining lad a box on the ear and pushing him out of the door. "Do you think Hadrian's death-hour so near?" he added eagerly.

Amenophis looked watchfully at him, then nodded gravely.

"Very well," said Verus haughtily. "Then you will possess the friendship of the future emperor, if you serve him."

"You sent for me," replied Amenophis indifferently.

"Choose between my friendship and the Bithynian's.

They say you are his ally. You can be mine, if you will remove Antinous. Hadrian must be delivered from this fellow."

Amenophis's face remained as stony as before, but he thought: " I was mistaken in supposing I could rely upon this inactive, melancholy dreamer."

" Ask any price you wish, but he must go."

" I am no assassin," said Amenophis quietly.

" Nor I," replied Verus, " but I am a statesman; you are a priest, and Antinous is an obstacle, so see that it is removed. I know every bargain has its price, what do you demand ?"

" It might please the goddess to call the Bithynian to herself," said Amenophis after a pause, " if you should offer her services in return."

As Verus nodded, he continued:

" Promise that all the temples of Isis in Italy, Gaul and Spain shall be subjected to my direction and un-limited authority, and I will bear your proposal to the great goddess."

" But everything that could attract attention must be avoided," whispered Verus.

" I have already told you I am no assassin. The goddess will summon him, not I."

" What value shall I place on so vague a promise ?" replied Verus angrily.

" The same that you put on your own," and the Egyptian drew from a fold of his under robe a small round piece of parchment, which he handed to Verus. The young Roman saw, drawn around the edge, pictures of the principal deities of the Egyptian nether-world. A few words in hieroglyphics were beneath each, and the centre of the space was left free.

"Write your name here, if you feel disposed to enter into the compact."

"I am to make you the head of all the Egyptian temples in the West, if you fulfil your promise?" asked Verus.

The Egyptian nodded. "I would rather have you take money," said the Roman suspiciously.

"I tell you, for the third time, I am no assassin."

"And what will you do with this parchment, in case I put my name here?"

"Devote you to the gods of the nether-world, if you should break your word."

"If that's all," said Verus derisively, as he dipped his calamus in the black writing-fluid, "here is my full name: Aelius Ceionius Commodus Verus. Now devote me to whom you choose, if I deceive you, but keep your promise."

"You shall see by Antinous, whether we have power to draw men to the nether-world or not." He thrust the little sheet back among the folds of his robe, adding: "If you appeal to our gods for aid, respect them. These girls must no longer enter the temple-court, or I will drive them forth myself with blows."

"Very well, Egyptian jackal!" said Verus angrily. "I'll settle that; the rose-clouds can play ball on the bank yonder, and take the air in Hadrian's garden, though I doubt whether your priests' bald heads are more pleasing to the gods, than the tiny little feet of my Eœa. Farewell."

The Egyptian bowed and withdrew.

"Now I shall be anxious to see what kernel will appear from this mystical cloud," murmured Verus. "If they pray him to death, I can't help it. But the old crocodile's green eyes don't look as if he were jesting."

———

Meantime Hadrian lay on his couch in a very jovial mood. The side of the tent had been turned back, and over beds of bright-hued flowers and tall ornamental plants, conjured up by his gardeners during the days of his convalescence, the Caesar gazed through groups of slender palm-trees at the sluggish Nile.

"Amenophis requests permission to enter," said Antinous.

"Spite of his horoscope," replied Hadrian, "I believe the improvement in my health will prove but temporary; but let us see what tidings the priest brings."

The youth admitted the Egyptian and retired. He did not like to meddle with astronomical mysteries. He prayed to the stars, but to watch their conjunctures seemed to him insolent temerity.

"Your stars are right, Egyptian," said Hadrian; "I feel stronger every day. But has your science no means of hastening my recovery?"

"My gods have aid for every earthly ill, but you know that, as an individual, I have no right to reve. the secrets of the temple."

"Well, and how can we earth-worms penetrate your mysteries?" said Hadrian derisively.

"You are in the sacred abode of the Osiris of Besa, who has given oracles from the most ancient times. Ask the god for counsel."

"I received one good omen from your god in the Apis meadow," said Hadrian scornfully, "and was stricken down. I fear a second proof of favor might kill me.   The gods of the black land are too ardent in their caresses."

The Egyptian drew himself up proudly.   "It seems you deride these gods, Caesar.   Look at the images hanging on yonder columns, count the waxen limbs that attest cures made by the divine pair, the pictures of the chase, of battles, of ships, which show a prediction fulfilled, the thousands of offerings, each indicating some granted prayer.   Who are you, man, that seek to jeer at Isis and Osiris?   Did not even your Tibullus exclaim: 'Help, Isis! all the tablets hanging in thy temples prove that thou canst!'"

Hadrian's only answer was a contemptuous shrug of the shoulders.

"As you choose," said Amenophis, "but the people would rejoice to see a proof, that their ruler really believes in the goddess.   If Alexander questioned the oracle of Jupiter Ammon, Hadrian need not be ashamed."

"Well," said Hadrian, raising himself, "you have not addressed so many words to me for a long time, you closed pyramid of Heliopolis.   Doubtless your brother-priests are very anxious the Caesar should set a good example, but I won't make the matter quite so easy for you as you expect.   I hear that oracles are given in Greek to the Alexandrian sailors in the temple of the cat-headed goddess Bast, daughter of Ra, at Bubastis. Are her oracles acceptable to you?"

"The temples of the Delta belong to the league of Heliopolis.   Why should not their decrees be acceptable to me?" said Amenophis.

"Very well.   My secretary Suetonius can go down to Bubastis, when he brings the new report of the Senate from Alexandria.   I'll give him a sealed question to the goddess. Six court officials can accompany him with presents to the daughter of Ra, that the people may see we reverence their goddess."

Amenophis bowed, and a blow on the cymbal summoned Antinous.

"Write a question clothed in rhyme," Hadrian whispered into the youth's ear, "but seal the roll at both ends. The goddess has cat eyes, she will be able to read in the dark."

Amenophis waited, his face wearing its usual stony expression.

"There, Egyptian," said Hadrian at last, "give this to Suetonius, and tell him how and where he is to question the goddess. But beware of trifling with me. You know I am myself something of an expert in this department."

Amenophis took the roll.

"You are aware, Caesar, that it is not I, who play with sacred things."

Antinous gazed at the impenetrable priest with a trustful glance. He had given aid in Rome in a most desperate situation, surely his power would not fail now. Seating himself beside Hadrian, the youth clasped the sick man's hand in his own, repeating in an undertone the words the Caesar had told him to write:

"Some potion that in failing limbs youth's vigor will implant,
Oh! goddess, name, or unto me a swifter course to Orcus grant."

Then he pressed the emperor's thin right hand, as if to say the remedy would be found.

The breeze from the garden grew warmer, and Hadrian fell asleep, while Antinous still sat beside him in the half-conscious condition between sleeping and waking, occasioned by dreaming over a question already considered a hundred times. Outside the bees buzzed, and the sultry air fanned the flower-beds. The peace of a sick-room, from which danger has passed away, exerted its beneficent influence upon the youth, who was doing his duty faithfully and earnestly, and after the excitement of the last few days a pleasant fatigue subdued the anguish of his troubled mind.

After a time, as the invalid still slept, Antinous drew from a fold in his belt the little image of Serapis Amenophis had given him, and holding it rigidly before him, asked with fervent prayer, if Hadrian would recover. There was a long pause, then it seemed as if the image showed a bluish glimmer, and with a feeling of relief he rose to leave the tent. But his foot did not cross the threshold, for on looking out into the garden he beheld a charming scene. Behind the bushes at the end of the pleasure-grounds his keen eye discovered a fair girlish head, whose owner, bending eagerly, sometimes vanished behind the green foliage, sometimes reappeared, her face flushed with pleasure. Long lashes shaded merry, sparkling eyes; the pretty child with the figure of Hebe possessed the proud head of Diana, yet while arranging in a basket the flowers she had gathered, seemed to represent Flora in person. She now emerged into the sunlight, and Antinous's heart throbbed stormily as the wondrous apparition came directly towards him. The breeze played with her light robe, revealing the rounded girlish figure in all its symmetry.

"So must Aphrodite have looked, when she ensnared the Phrygian shepherd!" thought the eager youth. The girl turned into a side-path; Antinous saw the light figure glimmering through the bushes for a time, then it disappeared, and for the first time he summoned courage to follow the goddess. But the faint traces of a woman's foot in the Nile sand were all the tokens left by the supernatural vision. The sound of the metal basin in Hadrian's tent recalled him to his place beside the sick-bed. Deeply flushed, as if caught in some evil deed, he seated himself beside Hadrian, who told him of the temple at Bubastis, and praised the ancient traditions, according to which the worship of the sanctuary was conducted. Antinous dreamily performed his duties. The lovely vision of the young girl gathering violets constantly hovered before him. She was doubtless the daughter of one of the worthy men Hadrian had gathered in the little city, to attend to the management of the public business. For the first time the arrow of Eros had grazed the heart of the youth of eighteen. Thus he had imagined Phlegon's daughters, whose brothers talked so enthusiastically about them. Yet he sighed. How was Hadrian's attendant to approach the daughter of a Roman senator? A feeling of bitter resentment against his lot darted through his young heart. Here also Hadrian had poisoned his life. He moved sorrowfully about his tasks, and at an early hour sought his couch. But even in sleep Eros pursued his sport. The dreamer imagined himself in the cave of the selli, groping timidly about in the darkness, and then feeling little Lydia's arms embrace him. But it was not Lydia. He clasped the form of the lovely flower-gatherer, a thrill of delight ran through his frame, and he awoke.

On going out into the garden the next morning, he fairly trembled and hastily retreated into the emperor's tent, for close before him, though with her back turned, stood the fair-haired girl he had seen the day before.

When, ashamed of his timidity, he again ventured forth, she had vanished, but he heard merry, girlish voices from the sandy bank. They were neither Egyptians nor Greeks, he could distinguish that from the distance, though unable to understand their words. The day passed like the former one, only Antinous was in a still more restless, feverish state. The following morning he did not venture out until he had glanced through a crack in the tent. At first all was still, then he heard footsteps approaching from the left, a direction in which he could not look, and the lovely figure appeared a few paces from him. She was gathering roses, and a smile flitted over the fresh, charming face. What were her thoughts? Then she turned into a side-path and vanished. Antinous smiled as he mixed the emperor's morning draught, and as he opened the letters which had arrived and handed them to the Caesar. With a beaming face he adjusted the cushions for the evening meal, and lay down to rest—even in his dreams he smiled. On the fourth morning he at last resolved to speak to the beautiful Flora. He had smiled himself into courage, for cheerfulness inspires bravery, while melancholy begets cowardice. After watching vainly a long time behind his curtain, he heard voices. Two girls had come to gather flowers that day. They jested and laughed together, which gave Antinous redoubled confidence. Going out before the door of the tent, whose curtain fell behind him, he felt as if he had stepped out of a musty bath-house on the cool shore, before essaying the leap into the treacherous element. Both young girls smilingly turned their faces towards him and walked on, gathering flowers, stopping from time to time to arrange them in a little basket. At last they went down to the river, and Antinous saw a large ball fly to and fro. Approaching the edge of the garden, he gazed with delight at the two charming figures tossing the toy — now bending backward if the ball was passing over them, now stretching forward after the flying plaything, the two girls presented a picture that would have charmed the eye of a Phidias. Suddenly the ball turned aside and fell directly before Antinous.

" Eros sent it," cried the youth, and springing over the hedge at a single bound, knelt and offered the toy to the Hebe of the day before. She accepted it, but as somewhat embarrassed she bent towards the lad, it again slipped from her little hands. For the second time both grasped at the smooth sphere, their arms, their cheeks touched, the ball rolled on, both hurrying after, for the plaything seemed on the point of falling into the river. Suddenly Antinous seized the ball with one hand, clasping his Hebe's slender waist with the other arm. She did not seem to object very strongly.

" What reward shall I receive, fair goddess ?" asked the youth, amazed at his own courage.

" Why, a rose, my handsome hero." Her sister smilingly approached. " Here, choose."

" Are you Romans ?" asked Antinous.

" Of course, and you are a Greek ?"

" Yes."

" What is your name ?"

" That I can only trust secretly to your little lily ears."

" Well, I am curious," said the flower-gatherer, gracefully bending her little head towards him. Antinous approached and pressed an ardent kiss upon her dazzling neck.

"See the faithless Greek! There is neither faith
nor truth among these sons of Ulysses! Now tell
your name aloud. I won't enter the snare a second
time."

"My name, fair goddess, is Antinous."

The Hebe started back, but her sister laughed
loudly.

"So this is the young Roman you vanquished, Hadrian's handsome peacock, ha! ha! ha! I congratulate
you on your conquest, I must tell Verus at once, poor
Eos."

"Be quiet, Aurora," cried the other, "or I'll scratch
your eyes out. Farewell, handsome Adonis! As you
are the Caesar's favorite, I have no need of your
kisses."

Once more she turned, exclaiming:

"Just wait a while, my handsome flamingo, till your
emperor is dead. Verus will pluck your shining feathers,
so that you can never deceive any one again."

"Farewell, dainty bird, farewell, golden pheasant!"
called Aurora with a mocking courtesy, and both vanished around the corner.

Antinous, utterly crushed, stood still. Indignation
that words so base should be uttered by lips so lovely,
anger against himself that he should have believed
Verus's fair friends beings of a higher order, merely on
account of their beauty, and fierce bitter anguish at
being an object of aversion to even the rose-clouds, suc-
cessively assailed him, as the strokes of the wheel fall upon
the tortured criminal, destroying with their dull blows the
last remnant of self-respect he still retained. It was
evident that he was nothing without Hadrian. As soon
as the emperor died, he would be an outlaw. The ground

was cut from under his feet. Never before had he so
clearly beheld the abyss over which he hovered. Again
he heard Natalis's exclamation at Tibur, and seating
himself on the shore of the sacred river, gazed into the
turbid waves.

CHAPTER XX.

HADRIAN had been well aware of what he was doing, when he chose Suetonius Tranquillus to' bring the
oracle's decree from Bubastis. The fact that the Caesar
offered this homage to the goddess was to be made
known throughout Egypt, and Suetonius provided for
this of his own accord. Accompanied by six attendants,
who bore Hadrian's gifts with the utmost possible display, Suetonius entered his superb ship, decked with
fluttering pennons and adorned with the cat-head of the
goddess. Wherever it was possible, he disembarked and
proclaimed his high embassy.

" Friend, can't you get me a jug of clear water? I'm
taking Caesar's gifts to Bubastis, where I am to obtain
the goddess's counsel." "What do you think of the
weather, old man? I'm bearing Hadrian's gifts and a
most important charge to the sanctuary of the goddess
Bast, so it would be fortunate if we continued to have
this wind."

Thus Suetonius, in the consciousness of his own importance, had announced his mission from station to
station, far too much engrossed with himself and the
speech by which he intended to awe the priests at

Bubastis, to have time to consider that Amenophis did not deliver the Caesar's roll of MS. to him for several hours after it had been received, and that a small boat in which sat a young oarsman and a priest, had been overtaken on the first day by his trireme, but came up with him again, and during the time occupied by his frequent disembarkations even gained on him, so that he saw it fastened to the bank when he at last reached the canal of Bubastis. His companions thought the incident strange, and spoke of it to Suetonius, who attached very little importance to the matter. The goddess's temple, which even in Herodotus's time was the pleasantest in all Egypt, stood in the heart of the city. A paved road forty feet wide, shaded on both sides by tall trees, extended across the market-place to the sanctuary. The enclosure of the temple, a furlong square, was surrounded by a ditch a hundred feet in width, filled with water from the Nile canal, and also shaded by trees. The porch was ten fathoms high, and adorned with colossal statues. Gaily-painted mythological scenes glittered on the surrounding walls of the enclosure. The temple itself, which contained the statue of the cat-headed goddess, was pleasantly shaded by tall palm-trees. All day long processions of pilgrims from the Nile wended their way hither, led by flute-players, who vied with the women using the sacred clappers, to make a deafening din. While some pressed into the sanctuary to offer their sacrifices, others who had already presented their gifts, lay outside, fed the sacred cats, drank the sacrificial wine, and performed frantic dances. Suetonius joined this throng of pilgrims, exclaiming incessantly:

"Make way for the Caesar's gifts! Make way for

the emperor's offerings!   Room for the mission of
Sebastos!   Thus he found his way into the fore-court of
the temple, where the high-priest of the goddess Bast
received the gifts with dignity, and graciously assured
the envoy that the daughter of Ra would be mindful of
the illustrious invalid.   Without even looking closely at
Suetonius's MS., he laid it in the lap of the cat-headed
goddess, before the eyes of the ambassador and his
companions.   After a time the Romans heard low,
mournful songs rising from a subterranean chamber.
The odor of kyphi pervaded the temple, the chants
grew fainter and died away, then the high-priest again
stood before Suetonius and mutely handed him a roll
of parchment.

"May I take the Caesar's inquiry back with me?"
asked Suetonius, "that he may see the goddess did not
find it necessary to break the seal, in order to learn his
wish?"

The high-priest silently gave him the roll.   Suetonius bowed low, the priest took a brush and sprinkled
the strangers with water from the lowest vessel on the
altar, and the envoy withdrew, only half satisfied, for he
had found little opportunity to display his eloquence.
The crimson parchment he held in his hand tortured his
curiosity.   It was sealed at the top and bottom, like the
one he had brought from the emperor, but the seal
represented a cat, whose right fore-paw rested on a
serpent's head, while the left held a broad knife, with
which the animal was cutting the snake's neck.

"It is the good goddess's victory over the hydra of
pestilence," said Suetonius to his companions, but his
longing to know what the oracle contained hastened
his journey.   After a courier had brought the letter-bag

from Alexandria, the slaves were all obliged to take their places at the oars and urge the trireme up the river, till it again reached Besa. The sacred act seemed to have already exerted its power upon the Caesar, for the new arrivals found him pacing up and down the flower-gar-dens, leaning on Antinous, who gazed mournfully into vacancy, and listening to the transactions Aelius Verus was conducting in his stead with the prefect and pro-curator, while Amenophis, who daily gained ground in Hadrian's favor, mutely followed the conversation.

The entrance of Suetonius, reverently holding aloft the roll of MS., interrupted this business.

"See, the message from the goddess!" exclaimed Hadrian. "I hope you have not trodden on the tail of any sacred cat, worthy Tranquillus, lest we should suffer for it."

Suetonius delivered his report with great verbosity and detail, while Hadrian, with a subtle smile, scanned the seals on his own roll of MS. as well as those of the goddess's. Suetonius emphatically declared, that he distinctly saw the priest lay the roll at once on the god-dess's lap, and there it remained until he delivered the answer to the inquiry into his hands.

"I was standing no farther off than I am now from you, sublime Augustus, and I'll answer for it with my head, that no one opened it. These men too could watch every movement of the priest. He couldn't de-ceive fourteen eyes."

"Well," replied Hadrian, "the priests scarcely need to take that trouble, to know what I would ask them to-day. Open our roll and read the question, An-tinous."

Antinous took the parchment on which he had written six days before, cut the seal, unrolled it, and a cry of terror escaped his lips.

"The characters have gone!" he faltered.

"What!" cried Hadrian furiously, "have they sent me back an empty sheet, as they formerly did to Alexander?" He hastily tore off the seal on the goddess's roll. "No, here are some lines." And he read the words formed in large, shapeless characters :

"The years a friend will sacrifice, to thee the goddess gives,
But only voluntary death, Osiris, Neith, receives."

"Ha! ha! ha!" laughed Hadrian, "a cheap present! The gracious Bast bestows upon me the years a friend will voluntarily sacrifice. Well, my good friends, who will contribute? Eh! Suetonius, have you no inclination to jump into the Nile for my sake?"

"How could I presume to call myself the Caesar's friend, my lord?" replied Suetonius.

"And you, Verus?"

"You would gain little by my years," said Aelius Verus, coughing violently and pressing his hand upon his heart with a gesture of pain. Antinous bent his head lower. "With mine," he thought, "Hadrian would outlive this man, and the world be spared the reign of the rose-clouds."

"Well, all of you," said Hadrian, scornfully addressing the rest of the group, "how often you have exclaimed: 'May Jupiter increase your years from mine!' You hear, the goddess is ready to take you at your word."

The courtiers forced a smile, Antinous alone gazed steadily into vacancy. He wished to warn Hadrian to carry the jest no farther, but when he raised his eyes, he saw the Egyptian's burning glance fixed intently upon him.

"If I sacrifice myself, what is it to you?" thought the youth, angrily returning the Egyptian's gaze.

"Here, Antinous," said Hadrian carelessly, "we will keep this cat's oracle. Perhaps later it may please the goddess to reveal the meaning of her words. For myself I feel that I have a cat's life, and the shears of the Fates will find the thread of my existence full of notches. But lead me in, Antinous, the evening breeze is chilly. So, Aelius Verus, we will do without the loan of your years. Besides, I did not ask Bast for the prolongation of life, but for strength or speedy death."

With these words Suetonius was dismissed, greatly disappointed, and the emperor continued his business with the Roman officials, while Antinous, seated outside the tent, gazed aimlessly into vacancy.

"Go to rest, lad," the emperor's voice called kindly from within after a short interval. "You have a great deal of sleep to make up, and we shall not finish our business for a long time."

"Farewell, Caesar!" replied the youth in a hollow tone.

"I wish you a long, sound sleep, dear boy," Hadrian called in answer.

"Long and sound!" murmured Antinous, turning towards his own tent.

As he raised the curtain that hung over the entrance, a white object lying on his bed shimmered through the dusk. He seized it, and held in his hand the fillet of Osiris, which Hadrian had formerly pressed upon his head at Tibur. Again he heard the Egyptian's voice exclaim: "Beware of coming to the sacred river, the god will demand his victim." Could Amenophis have a hand in this game? Yet, since the revelation of the oracle, he had not left Hadrian's side. A thrill of superstitious horror shook Antinous's limbs.

"*Numen et omen!*" he murmured. "Art thou still angry, great god, who sits in Amenti, dost thou still demand atonement, that the curse the Caesar and I have called down upon ourselves may depart?"

The youth went out into the evening dusk, already faintly irradiated by the pallid light of the first moonbeams. Drawing from a secret fold of his garments his green image of Serapis, he pressed it closely in his burning hand and repeated the sacred formula. He had not uttered the words for the third time, when emotion paralyzed his voice. The little statue had turned blood-red, and slipping from his hands, fell into the cool, damp sand. When, after a short time he again seized it, the old hue had returned, but Antinous knew he had not been deceived. "All the omens point downward, and what have I still to seek in the upper world, if my death will be more useful to Hadrian than my life?" He sat silently for some time, absorbed in thought. The moonlight fell on the beautiful head, bowed in sorrow, and hovered caressingly around the symmetrical outlines of the young limbs. A low voice whispered: "The oracle is false, they all deceive, Amenophis made it like the rest." But another inner voice replied: "Yet, if you neglect this opportunity of going, when will you perish? Suppose the oracle should be true? Suppose Hadrian dies, while you might save him? Go, go, ere it is too late. Be thankful that you are permitted to end your days." He again remembered the young girls in the garden, Vitalis's words, and rose. Softly, as if he feared he might be prevented, he took a small tablet from the tent and wrote :

"Antinous bids the Caesar farewell. To serve him was the purpose of his life, and is the object of his death. May the years he adds to the Caesar's existence bring prosperity to the empire. Antinous will prove to the dwellers in the nether-world, that Hadrian is good. Again farewell!"

A tear fell on the waxen tablet the youth laid on his untouched bed. When he again left the tent, the Osiris fillet was lying on the ground before him. He crowned himself with it, like a victim for sacrifice, and then walked softly across the stone dyke, the cool sand, and the sharp potsherds, down to the reedy margin of the river. A flock of coots, startled by the unusual interruption, whirred upward, flying to the left, but he did not notice them. There was a broad, flat, marshy region to be crossed, ere he reached the pier that ran out into the deeper part of the stream. Wide circles of light shimmered around him like a halo, on the moon-illumined water he passed. He climbed the high dyke with great difficulty. The sharp stones cut his feet, the rushes and thorns tore his limbs, but he did not feel the pain. At last he stood on the top. The moon cast a broad stream of light on the dark surface of the water, and the youth's shadow appeared in gigantic outlines on the stagnant pool behind him. The evening breeze fanned him gently, and his walk through the cool element had calmed and cleared his mind. Thus he stood at the end of the pier where the low gurgle of the sluggish current reached his ears. Again he deliberately considered his resolution. The sweet love of life stirred once more, luring him coaxingly back to the land, which lay beyond the inundated region, but he resisted the temptation.

"It is the will of the gods. It is for Hadrian's welfare and your own," he murmured, and raising his beautiful, earnest face to the moon, devoutly extended his clasped hands towards her disk, saying:

"I thank thee, gentle goddess, for thy farewell. I thank ye also, ye other gods, whom I no longer know how to name. Whoever ye may be, I thank ye for all the kindness ye have shown the poor Bithynian youth. I thank ye, my native mountains, ye dark woods and clear springs, that made my childhood so happy. I thank thee, sunlight, that shone so brightly on my boyhood. Ye too, I thank, masters of harmony, who lulled my soul with music, and ye whose marble statues delighted my enraptured gaze, who made me feel what beauty was. Thanks, infinite ether, whose radiance illumines me. Thanks, mother earth! Thee too, I thank, omnipotent Zeus!"

Bowing his head, he went forward to the water, but feeling that the yearning for life would be stronger than the firmest resolve as soon as he sank into the river, he took the fillet from his head and skilfully made two slipnooses into which he thrust his hands, so that any pulling would only draw them tighter. For a time he stood still with fettered hands, then the fishermen who were sitting just beyond the inundated lowlands heard a fall, and a figure appeared above the water struggling with the waves. His sob sounded like a suppressed cry for help, and all was still again. Ever widening circles in the water, which glittered in the moonlight, were the last signs of life given by the beautiful boy. Then the mighty river flowed on as before..

Thrice had Hadrian struck his metal basin the following morning, but Antinous did not appear. At last the Caesar sent a slave to look for him, but the trembling servant returned, saying:

" My lord, his couch was untouched, and this tablet lay on it."

Hadrian sprang from his bed with a loud cry, like a wounded tiger. Terror and grief made him shake off every trace of weakness.

"Go and ask if any one has seen the youth!" he commanded. " Let Quartus search the shore, Titius the dyke, while Suetonius asks from hut to hut, from boat to boat, if any one knows anything of him. Whoever brings the boy back alive, I will make a rich man. Great gods, ye cannot wish to punish me thus for having blasphemously trifled with you!"

The old man trembled so violently, that he was obliged to sit down; an image of woe! For the first time he beheld himself utterly crushed and miserable. Verus, who now appeared with tender words and empty consolations, thought: " We shall surely destroy Hadrian at once through Antinous. Amenophis is really a great man, he shall be chief of all the priests of Isis throughout the whole West. The expedient was so simple, and yet so effective. Who will hold us responsible, if the young fool voluntarily goes to his death, and the old one perishes of grief for him."

" I wish to be alone," said Hadrian, and Verus gladly returned to his own camp, where the rose-clouds, the four winds, and little Hesperus found him far more cheerful than he had been for a long time. Eos alone was troubled. She felt as if she were concerned in the misfortune that had befallen the beautiful boy, whom she had only mocked to escape being jeered at herself. .

Twilight was already approaching, yet no trace of Antinous had been discovered. No one had heard of him, no one had seen him.

"Perhaps he repented of his design, and is now hiding somewhere out of shame," said the prefect. "It is not so easy to die at eighteen, we shall find him yet."

Hadrian shook his head.

"You don't know him."

Just at that moment Suetonius brought three boatmen to the imperial tent. . .

"My lord, these people alone seem to me worthy of your examination. Some sailors thought they had seen the fugitive on a boat, but the messengers sent after it brought back a simple fisher-lad. A slave said he had seen Antinous on the border road leading to the mountains, but when I questioned him more closely, became confused in his statements. I ordered him to be lashed, and he confessed that he had lied . . . "

"And what do you know ?" said Hadrian, interrupting the loquacious secretary.

"My lord," replied the oldest of the three fishermen, "last evening, when the moon was about two hours high, we were standing on the shore opposite the Ibis-dyke, disputing whether the water would rise higher, or had already begun to sink. While thus engaged, we heard a noise in the distance, as if some beast or human being was forcing a path through the rushes. Birds flew upward, and here and there a frog splashed into the river. As we talked on a youthful figure, clearly visible in the moonlight, appeared at the end of the 'dyke. 'Why does he stand there so quietly ?' I asked. 'He is probably fishing,' replied my neighbor, and we went back to our former discussion. Suddenly we heard a fall into the water, and when we looked across the figure had vanished. There was another splash, and a sob reached our ears like a low cry for help. But all was over instantly. What could we do? We had no boats, and before we could have reached the spot, rescue was impossible."

Hadrian buried his face in his hands, and a sorrowful silence pervaded the tent. The men had seen aright, that was evident to all.

"Can you raise the body?" asked the emperor.

"We will not take advantage of your grief, my lord," replied the old man. "We might accept the task, but it would be a fraud. If the youth you seek plunged into the water from the Ibis-dyke, he will undoubtedly come to land on the second or third day, at the first flood-gate of the Apis canal. The current sets that way."

"Then post sentinels there, till you have found him."

The fishermen were about to retire.

"One thing more," asked Hadrian; "will not the crocodiles devour the youth?"

"At this season of the year the animal sacred to Typhon lives farther up the river, where the water is shallower. But it will do no harm for us to lash the river, and drive the beasts away with Isis clappers."

"Very well," said Hadrian, "do so."

Ere long, the beating of oars on the water was heard from the stream; the sistrum rattled, the Nile-clappers resounded. Boats constantly arrived, every one wanted to please the Caesar. The rattling of the sacred instru-

ments reminded the fishermen of the festival of Osiris,
and several women commenced the usual songs. Were
they not seeking the sacred corpse of a beautiful youth,
whom Typhon retained ? The wailing on the river soon
corresponded with the rites within the temple. The
priests, eager to win the emperor's favor, sent forth towards heaven the melancholy chants, usually sung at
the time of the lamentation for Osiris, when the Nile
disappeared. The mourning ceremonies were performed;
the symbol of the goddess, the golden cow, draped with
a black veil, was borne seven times around the temple.
Messengers went up and down to the Isis canal, bewail-
ing that the sacred body was not yet found. One alone
sat in silence, gazing with a harsh, scornful look at the
servile conduct of his brother-priests—Amenophis, who
in a corner of the temple-court brooded over what had
occurred, and secretly pondered how soon Verus would
probably be in a situation to pay him his reward for the
removal of his rival. The day passed without finding
the body. Again the priests at dawn performed the
sacred rites—the wood was cut for Osiris's coffin, the
linen torn for bandaging the corpse, the serpent, the animal sacred to Typhon, killed in effigy. Amid these
noisy lamentations the second day also passed. On the
third morning, attracted by the tumult and the strange
tidings of the imperial favorite's death, the Egyptians
flocked to the spot from a distance of many miles. Boats
with black sails passed up and down the river. Everywhere the lament for Osiris was heard, and the high-
priest of the Apis temple went to inform Hadrian, that
the people had placed Antinous among the gods.

" He who, at the command of the goddess, sacrificed
his life for the beloved and august Caesar, is worthy to

be placed among the Immortals!" said the priest solemnly.

Hadrian's eyes sparkled with a feverish light. " I will build him a temple," he said feebly, " I will pray to him, who gave himself for me. I will remember, Priest, that you were the first who announced his divinity."

This promise produced its effect. That very evening another priest appeared, with tidings that on the night of Antinous's death, when the moon was two hours high, a new star never before seen by the astronomers, had been discovered from the sacred observatory at Memphis.

" We have named the whole cluster of stars the constellation of Antinous, because we are sure it is the divine boy, whose star rose there in his death-hour. If the Caesar will come out of doors, the star of Antinous can be seen shining brightly between Berenice's hair and the constellation of the Eagle."

Hadrian rose, and vainly seeking the beloved youth who usually supported him, was overwhelmed by his grief.

" My love has brought a curse on every one. My own person was my god, and now I am left alone with myself. Beloved boy, if you have really gone into another world, you are in truth a star there, as you were the star of my life."

Leaning on a slave, he went out in a softened mood under the clear sky, and the priest pointed out the new speck of light near the milky way. " Let it be called as you wish: the star of Antinous, and henceforth bear this name in all the observatories of the empire."

When Hadrian awoke on the fifth day, Suetonius informed him that the body had really come ashore that morning at the flood-gate of the Apis canal, as the fishermen had predicted; it was only slightly disfigured, and if the emperor felt strong enough to see the beautiful boy again, everything was ready.

"We have made an Adonis couch and laid the sacred body on it. The boy looks beautiful and peaceful on the purple mantle strewn with flowers, for the priests understood how to remove the water from the corpse by clever expedients and strange instruments used in embalming. It will touch you to see how quietly he lies there."

Hadrian hesitated a moment, then said:

"Call Aelius Verus, he shall support me! Verus makes himself very invisible during these days," he murmured.

When Verus appeared, the Caesar took his arm and walked silently along the shore, until Verus proposed using a litter, as he too felt ill. So they reached the canal, which bordering one side of the Apis pasture, emptied its waters half a league below the temple into the Nile. Skilfully availing themselves of the tall columns that supported the pulleys of the floodgate, the priests had erected a platform, which removed the body so far from the eyes of the crowd, that it was impossible to distinguish any traces of the progress of corruption. The priests had also painted the corpse, so that death was robbed of its horrors. People really believed that they saw the sacred corpse of Adonis, as it was annually exposed in Alexandria. In consequence of this the Greeks and Phoenicians, who had come up from Alexandria, pressed eagerly around the bier, and a maiden, who was in the habit of repeating the lament for Adonis in the great theatre at Alexandria,

stepped forward and recited in touching tones the usual
lines:

Lo! purple tapestry, arranged on high,
Charms the spectators with the Tyrian dye;
The Samian and Milesian swains, who keep
Large flocks, acknowledge 'tis more soft than sleep.
Of this Adonis claims a downy bed,
And lo! another for fair Venus spread!
Her bridegroom scarce attains to nineteen years,
Rosy his lips, and no rough beard appears.
Let raptured Venus now enjoy her mate,
While we, descending to the city gate,
Arrayed in decent robes that sweep the ground,
With naked bosoms, and with hair unbound,
Bring forth Adonis, slain in youthful years,
Ere Phoebus drinks the morning's early tears.
And while to yonder flood we march along,
With tuneful voices raise the funeral song:

Adonis, you alone of demi-gods,
Now visit earth, and now hell's dire abodes·
Not famed Atrides could this favor boast
Nor furious Ajax, though himself a host;
Nor Hector, long his mother's grace and joy
Of twenty sons, not Pyrrhus safe from Troy,
Not brave Patroclus, of immortal fame,
Nor the fierce Lapithae, a deathless name;
Nor sons of Pelops, nor Deucalion's race,
Nor stout Pelasgians, Argos' honored grace
As now, divine Adonis, you appear
Kind to our prayers, O, bless the future year!
As now propitious to our vows you prove,
Return with meek benevolence and love!*

A feeling of deep compassion for the fate of the
beautiful dead pervaded the whole throng, and the
spectacle intended to do homage to the Caesar, produced a profound and genuine outburst of religious
enthusiasm in the excitable population. The call for
Adonis was passionately repeated, men threw themselves on the ground and writhed in convulsions, women
tore their bosoms, and with dishevelled locks ran up and

* Translated by Francis Fawkes.

down the shore of the stream, while the frantic cry echoed far over the surface of the Nile, startling the sacred animals in the Apis pasture, till they bellowed loudly in unison with the lament for Adonis.

While the guard forced the noisy throng nearer to the river, the Caesar approached the bier, and the prefect, who had himself made the arrangements, showed the emperor the place where the body had appeared.

"The boy had bound his hands, probably to prevent himself from swimming, for there is not the slightest trace of violence to be found on the body. The unfortunate oracle of the goddess Bast was discovered in a fold of his tunic. Strangely enough, he tied his wrists with a priest's head ornament, called a fillet of Osiris. The priests I questioned said they did not use such linen in their temple, the fillet probably came from the sanctuary of Heliopolis."

"Did not the relics you sent me by Amenophis come from Heliopolis?" Hadrian asked the procurator, who stood by his side.

"Certainly, Caesar! We thought at once, that Antinous must have brought the sacred ornament with him from Tibur."

"Give me the fillet," replied Hadrian, "and call Amenophis. Verus, if you are not well, go into your tent." The last words were accompanied with a strange glance at his heir, who pale as a corpse, was leaning against one of the pillars of the flood-gate.

"It is over," gasped Verus.

The fillet was brought, and Hadrian carefully examined it.

"It is the same one he wore in my Canopus at

Tibur," he murmured, and then paced restlessly to and fro, till the guard returned with Amenophis.

"Was this fillet your property, Egyptian?" said Hadrian imperiously.

Amenophis looked quietly at the linen, then answered:

"It is possible."

"Does any one know how this fillet came into Antinous's hands?" cried Hadrian.

"My lord," replied Suetonius, "all these days I have suspected, that the Egyptian has had something to do with this melancholy affair. During the session of the last council of state, I met a boy creeping out at the back of Antinous's tent. At first I thought he had stolen something and stopped him, but he protested he had been ordered by Amenophis to take something to Antinous, and as in his half-naked condition, he really could have concealed nothing, I let him go. Directly after, I found on the ground a small bottle, which exhaled a strange odor. The contents had all run out, and the stones where the liquid had flowed were dyed red. It now seemed to me that I had seen the lad before, and I soon remembered that while on our journey to Bubastis, a boat containing a boy and a priest followed us day and night, and at last overtook us. I did not see the priest again, but the boy was sitting in his skiff at the goddess's stairs in Bubastis, when we arrived, and it was the same one who glided at dusk into Antinous's tent. At that time of course I gave no thought to the matter, but when affairs took this turn, I sent men to search for him, but he has disappeared."

"The prefect will investigate these statements," said Hadrian. "If they are correct, crucify the Egyptian!"

Amenophis attempted to reply, but at the same moment Verus fell senseless beside the wooden column, and the attendants sprang forward to raise him.

"Carry him away," said Hadrian; "he was ill just now. . . . We have leaned on a crumbling wall," he added, turning to the Roman official, "and the donation for the elevation of a Caesar may soon be repeated. It was Antinous's last wish that I should make Antoninus Pius a co-regent. What do you think?"

"The advice was good, whether it proceeded from god or man," replied the gray-haired procurator.

"Only one question, Caesar," Amenophis exclaimed. "If I confess I tempted Antinous to suicide, will you still sully the black land with the temple of a boy who killed himself?"

Hadrian seized his sword.

"So you confess your intrigues?"

"I confess them, that you may see your favorite was no god. Do not sully the sacred river with your abominations."

"Typhon outwitted Osiris also," replied Hadrian coldly, "and the wild-boar of Mars slew Adonis, yet both were gods, for there is one thing stronger than Zeus, and that is Fate. But you were the beast of Typhon, who destroyed the good god."

"Very well, then I too was a part of Fate, so worship me!"

"I am not an Egyptian, who adores the beasts of Typhon," replied Hadrian, "but a Persian, who is commanded to extirpate the creatures of Ahriman. Prefect, he has confessed, crucify him! Let his death propitiate the soil on which will stand the temple of Antinous he so much dreads. We will bind his demon here, that he may work miracles in the service of our friend's spirit. Place the god's body in nitre, and then bring from the temple of Heliopolis the largest sarcophagus and inter within it the body of my favorite and god. What are you doing with your thumbs, Egyptian?"

" I am devoting your soul to Typhon."

"The star of Antinous will rule over me, I do not fear your gods."

With these words the emperor returned to his tent, whither the principal architects were instantly summoned to discuss the plan of the temple. Hadrian wished to build a city called Antinoupolis on the site of ancient Besa, and an oracle of Antinous was to be established. An Egyptian sculptor was ordered to carve a statue of the new god in red syenite as Osiris; the best artists in Hellas were to represent him as Hermes, Adonis, Bacchus, Dionysus, and the god of Spring with flowers in his hands and hair. Fire was kindled on an altar, that the smoke might rise to the star of Antinous, so long as it remained in the sky. A form of worship was arranged, combining the touching lament for Osiris with the yearning Attis-cry and the ecstatic tumult of the Dionysian, Bacchic, and Attis festivals. As a flower was named from the blood of Adonis, there was soon a flower of Antinous also. Hadrian transferred his residence to Alexandria, for the time that his favorite's temple was being built. One day the poet Pancrates was announced, and brought him the marvel of a pink lotus, which had sprung up on the spot where Antinous had once killed a lion. Hadrian eagerly accepted the offering. Lotus-wreaths were henceforth the attribute of the beautiful youth, and the blossom itself was called the flower of Antinous. The originator of this happy idea, Pancrates, received as a reward a position in the Academy at Alexandria. To the poet Mesomedes of Crete, who, when Hadrian arrived in Greece on his return from Egypt, presented him with a hymn to the divine boy, the emperor assigned so large a yearly pension as a reward, that his successor thought it his duty to diminish it. Verus, who, seriously ill, set sail for Italy from Alexandria, zealously ordered statues and temples to Antinous to be erected everywhere, especially in Rome and Tibur. Whether he desired by these means to atone for his own guilt or only to win Hadrian's favor, nobody knew, perhaps even he himself was not sure. The worship of the beautiful youth spread with unprecedented celerity as a new faith. Not only in Alexandria and Rome, but in Achaia and Asia Minor the Greek artists seized upon the sympathetic task here offered them, and the world became full of the statues and sanctuaries of the Bithynian god.

It would be preposterous to attribute this phenomenon solely to the servile spirit of the age, which might surely have found hundreds of other opportunities to display itself. The fate of the beautiful youth touched sympathetic souls, and the task of representing the beauty of a melancholy boy, under an ideal form, was alluring to artists. After the masters of Aphrodisias had fixed the type, this innocent, sorrowful figure made a strong impression upon the imagination, and to create a real Antinous head was for a time the highest problem of art. In Italy the youth was reverenced as Bacchus. We still have a colossal statue sixteen feet high, representing the Bithynian as this deity, with a garland of ivy twined amid his long, floating locks. He bears on his head the pine-cones of the god, the ample upper robe is fastened on the left shoulder, revealing the rounded left arm, arched chest and delicate hips. In his upraised left hand he holds the thyrsus, also ornamented with a pine-cone, on which he leans, while his gaze seeks the earth, and he ponders over the affairs of the nether-world. Other colossal statues, with ivy or lotus-wreaths, must have stood in the adytum of a temple. A bas-relief placed by Hadrian in his villa at Tibur was a memorial of the festival of the consecration. Standing in a chariot, adorned with the lotus-wreath, extending his left hand filled with flowers, the youthful hero makes his entry among the Olympians as the risen god of Spring. A head of Antinous, three times the size of life, must also have been the remains of some huge temple statue. The thick masses of hair, daintily raised and twined with a garland, float over the shoulders in two long tresses. The outlines of the superb oval face are feminine in their delicacy. It is the most beautiful head of the later period of the empire. But the Canopus at Tibur contained a different representation of the divine boy. Adorned with the fillet of Osiris and clad in the scanty attire of the Egyptian priest, Antinous stands between the Sphinxes in the rigid attitude of the deities of Thebes and Memphis, his brow shadowed by the gloomy melancholy of the judge of the dead. In the temple of Isis at Rome also was found the inscription: "To Antinous, co-ruler with the gods of Egypt, this stone is consecrated by his prophet Ulpius Apollonius."

There was scarcely a city in the empire, which did not have a medal struck, to send the Caesar in memory of the beautiful youth. He is sometimes represented as Iacchus, sometimes associated with the Egyptian Harpocrates as the guardian of life, sometimes he appears as the divine youths Apollo and Mercury. A griffin, a ram or a bull marks him as this or that god. The panther, the animal sacred to Bacchus, and the thyrsus staff are most frequently seen, or the moon and stars symbolize Isis and his own star. The principal temple, erected in honor of Antinous-Dionysus-Bacchus, was consecrated by Hadrian, when he returned from Greece to Mantineia; but the real sanctuary of Antinous was the temple at Besa, on the borders of Thebais, where the youth's body had been rescued from the water. Built according to the rigid rules of Egyptian art, provided with a secret niche for an oracle, conducted by a richly-endowed priesthood, this new temple was to indicate the reconciliation of the Egyptian gods with Rome, as the Ptolemies had established the Greek worship of Serapis, in order to be represented among the gods of Egypt by a divinity of their own race. Not until Hadrian had consecrated the new city and temple, and announced the first oracle, composed by himself, did he return to Rome by way of Athens and Corinth.

CHAPTER XXI.

The winter Hadrian spent in Egypt and Greece had passed very quietly at the villa *ad pinum*. Phlegon was forgotten by the world and apparently by the Caesar, who had added no farther orders to the command that Phlegon should remain in his house on the Esquiline. The Greek's desire to again urge his little skiff into the whirlpool of life in the great capital was very slight, his

thoughts wandered yearningly only across the Alps to
Aquae, but he dared not, on his own authority, leave the
residence assigned him, and it seemed perilous to remind
Hadrian of his existence. So he lived on in gloomy
apathy, searching the books his boys had left behind,
among which the new writings of Epictetus, and the
ancient volumes of the Jews and Christians soon riveted
his attention.

The servants at the villa had dispersed, with the exception of the two old men, Tertius and Eumaeus, who
performed the duties of the household. There was also
a good-natured old Christian woman, Decimilla, who
more faithful than the rest, wished to accompany Ennia
on her journey to Germany, but had been ordered by
the latter to remain at the villa. The slaves had at first
suggested plans for gradually restoring the estate to its
former condition. The aqueduct was to be repaired,
the walls mended, the garden planted, but Phlegon only
shook his head mournfully, saying:

"Leave it as it is, I shall not stay here."

True, the old men had used the autumn in clearing
up the ground as far as their strength would permit, but
the estate was too large for two old people, so the hemlock and other weeds shot up still higher than before in
the garden-paths. The snails ravaged the Land of Benjamin, Reuben's thorns outgrew the tender vines of
Ephraim, and kind-hearted Graecina's whole sacred
realm looked like a field where weeds have choked the
good seed. The house itself was even worse. Eumaeus
and Tertius could not prevent the decay of the roof and
walls, or the increasing marshiness of the area, and when
winter brought rain and snow, and the frost and dew
began to work upon the loosened joints, the villa pre-

sented a sorrier spectacle than ever, without Phlegon's having any eyes for it.

"He's bewitched by the Christians' sacred book," the old men whispered to each other, and it really seemed so. The Greek pored over the sacred writings night and day. Pius probably heard of it from Decimilla, for one day the stroke of the iron knocker resounded on the deserted door, making Phlegon start up in affright. Had Hadrian remembered him, had a letter come from Ennia, or did the praetor Celsus wish to wreak his rage upon him? He hurried into the area himself, and opened the loop-hole in the door to ask who was there.

"The tradesman Pius, Hermas's brother, craves permission from the master of the house to visit him and Decimilla."

Phlegon opened the door and saw the pleasant, but firm countenance of a stately citizen, who looked as if he were appointed to rule, and owed his mastery over others to his own self-control and confidence.

"I greet you, my lord," said the visitor.

"And I return your greeting," replied Phlegon cordially. After all these months of loneliness and abandonment, it was pleasant to have some human being remember him. "You are the brother of my poor friend, Hermas?"

"The same Hermas," replied Pius with a faint sigh, "who conquered the wild beasts by his brave, trusting spirit, and then did not consider that God will not aid us, if we recklessly tempt Him."

"That is the way I also regard my poor friend's death," said Phlegon. "I owe him much," he added. "He opened my eyes to what is important and what trivial in life. True, I was forced to undergo bitter experiences, ere the truth of his words revealed itself to me. The first time I really understood him, was when I learned in my own person whither one is led if, to use the words of your sacred book, he makes Mammon his god."

" I rejoice that a portion of the Saviour's teachings, at which the majority take umbrage, has revealed itself to you."

Phlegon now told the bishop, that his experiences in Graecina's house had made the Christian religion seem to him a Saturnalian jest for the slaves, and did not conceal, that even now the injunctions to give one's property to the poor and neither provide for nor think of the morrow, appeared to be opposed to any system in life.

" The Lord cannot have meant the words in that sense," replied Pius. " He did not intend to regulate the daily life, but rather to name a method of battling for the establishment of the kingdom of God. The apostles, who were to seize upon it by force, make the first breach in the world's walls and storm them, were compelled to cast aside all superfluous baggage. Graecina had no summons to do this. Besides, do you really believe she would have wasted her property less, if she had not been a Christian ?"

Phlegon's eyes sought the ground, and after a pause he answered: " No."

" I thank you for this acknowledgment," said the bishop, " thank you for no longer desiring to ascribe to the Christians, sins committed by a feeble old woman in her weakness and want of judgment. She injured the parish more than it harmed her."

This exchange of opinion had removed the bitterness from Phlegon's heart. The two men talked of Hermas a long time, then Pius looked for Decimilla, to whom he wished to give some errands if her master would permit. Phlegon assented and urged Pius to come again; as he was not allowed to leave the villa, he did not wish to afford the praetor an opportunity to commence proceedings against him. From this time Pius became a regular visitor at the villa *ad pinum*. If Phlegon's heart was deeply moved by the simple, sublime sentences of the Sermon on the Mount, while his philosophical interest found abundant nourishment in the Epistles of Paul, this inclination soon changed to a keener feeling, a more passionate sympathy, when Aelius Verus, on his return from Egypt, according to the emperor's orders, commanded divine honors to be everywhere paid to Antinous.

Phlegon received the news of his young friend's voluntary death with compassion all the more sincere, because he had witnessed how systematically Hadrian had poisoned the poor boy's healthful impulses, taken away the ground on which he stood, inspired him with distrust of every prop to which he clung.

"After shaking his faith in his gods, disgusting him with suffering and striving as a man among men, driving him to suicide, it now suits his caprice to raise him to the rank of a god," he said to Pius, who had listened to Phlegon's story with sympathizing interest. The Greek's indignation against Hadrian was all the greater, because rumor asserted that the Caesar himself had forced Antinous to make the sacrifice. Not to borrow his years—Hadrian's weariness of life and the longing for death that had haunted the invalid for years were well-known—had Antinous been sacrificed, but rumor

stated the Egyptian priests had said, that one of their in-
cantations could only succeed, in case a youth would
voluntarily devote himself as a victim, for only a soul
that had voluntarily descended into Hades could obey
the summons they desired to give. So Antinous had
been sacrificed to Hadrian's curiosity concerning the
things of the other world. But these dark tales did not
prevent the people of the capital from enthusiastically
embracing the fashionable worship. Statues, busts, and
bas-reliefs of Antinous appeared in every direction. The
new hymns and antiphonies were sung in the streets,
which echoed with the Adonis and Iacchus cry, chapels
were dedicated to him in the villas, and even tavern-
keepers put up large gaily-painted placards at the street-
corners, inviting their customers and friends to the consecration of a sanctuary to the divine friend, who gave
his life for the Caesar.

Phlegon fairly glowed with indignation. How often
he had heard Antinous tearfully lament that Hadrian
did not believe in existing deities, but made gods as he
chose. Now, even in death, the boy fell a victim to the
Caesar's love of manufacturing divinities, and the
oracles he had so hated were issued in his name.

"It will disturb his Manes, his ghost will walk
abroad," said Phlegon. "Even in the nether-world Hadrian gives him no rest. Poor Antinous!"

While thus expressing to Pius his wrath at this last
excess of superstition, the latter silently unrolled the
Epistle of Paul to the Romans, and pointed to a passage which Phlegon read. It said that there was a
spiritual god, whom every one could perceive in the
works of creation, but because men were not satisfied
with that and thought they must add something from

their wit and imagination, they had gone from one god
to many.   "Professing themselves to be wise, they became fools.

"And changed the glory of the incorruptible
God into an image made like to corruptible man,
and to birds, and four-footed beasts and creeping
things."

"Therefore," Pius added, "the apostle continues:
'God gave them up to the sins, whose leaden weight oppressed the poor new god and dragged him down into
the waters of the Nile, because he did not take pleasure
in the Son of God, and yet knew not why.' You are
right: poor Antinous!"

"It was not that alone," said Phlegon, "we all sinned against him, in not assigning him any definite purpose in existence.   Man is here to labor, and it is no
life-task to be beautiful, least of all for a youth.   From
this void his melancholy arose, and he could not escape
the death of which he perished."

Pius nodded assent and held out his right hand to
Phlegon.   Again the two men had advanced a step
nearer each other.

"The most valuable thing to me in your sacred
book," said Phlegon, as Pius took his departure, "is the
fact that it records the experiences of thousands of years,
for I am of the opinion that the deity revealed himself
more fully and richly to so many generations, than to
one alone.   Doubtless the Greek and Roman gods are
also old, but the tradition is lost. They cannot act as in
former days, for what I now see and hear in the temples
dates from yesterday, and new ideas are constantly
added. When I read your gospel, it seems like the
revelation of primeval ages, and the laws your teacher

gives can never grow old, because men will never attain to them."

" Search the Scriptures farther," said Pius; " you are in the right way. We shall surely meet yet."

The simple-hearted man had seen aright. A morning came, on which Phlegon formed his resolution. " He who uttered the words of the Sermon on the Mount, can be no deceiver," he said to himself. " I have confessed the old faith," he continued, " and been miserable. I have dwelt alone in vacancy, and been doubly wretched. I cannot go back to the old gods. Shall I sing hymns to Antinous, and to-morrow perhaps to Aelius Verus and Hadrian? No! I will enter this church, allow its powers to work upon me; if they do not lead me to firm ground, I shall merely hover between heaven and earth as before. Things cannot be worse. I should like to have the same religion as my children—my wife," he added softly.

" Take me among your catechumens!" said Phlegon the next time Pius visited him.

" You have long been my catechumen, but how shall I bring you into the congregation?"

" The congregation can come here again, the peristyle is just as Graecina left it."

" And the praetor?"

" Has gone to Athens to meet Hadrian," replied Phlegon.

" Then the villa *ad pinum* would be as safe as any other place, especially as our ranks have thinned since the persecution, but there is still an obstacle in the way."

" Well," replied Phlegon, " and that is—?"

" The condition of your house will be a reproach to us. Look at this dilapidated roof, which admits the rain, these broken shutters, these falling walls. Ere the Lord enters, order must be restored here in the sight of God and man."

"I will attend to having everything repaired this very day," said Phlegon, greatly ashamed.

"No, my Brother," replied the bishop. "Those who called themselves by our name, have destroyed this house, those who belong to us, must restore it. You shall see that Christians work, even though they may feel no anxiety about their daily bread."

With these words the worthy man departed. But the next morning, while Phlegon was still asleep, the noise of hammering began to resound about his house, he heard footsteps on the roof, horses dragged carts into the garden, and when he went out he saw a crowd of cheerful workmen, cutting and setting stones, removing bricks, repairing and putting to rights. They greeted him as courteously as if he paid them to work for him. Thus the labor went on steadily and silently from morning till night, one day precisely like another. There was little conversation, and if Phlegon heard any one singing the Song of the Lamb or some other hymn while engaged at his task, he no longer felt angry, but joined in an undertone. Thus, in the course of a few weeks the walls were rebuilt, the house was freshly plastered and whitewashed, the roof glittered with new tiles, the paths with gravel, and the soft Spring sunlight rested warmly on the well-arranged beds, and neatly-clipped shrubs and trees. Everything began to bud, shoot and grow, as if to cover with fresh green foliage the horrors and rubbish of the past, and it seemed as if the Lord Himself cried from heaven: "Old things are passed away; behold all things are become new !"

Pius refused to accept any payment.

"You would wound the Brothers," he said; "others will come, who must be helped, then we will ask your aid." Phlegon, who had inveighed so bitterly against begging, hailed this as joyful news: it dawned upon him that it is more blessed to give than to receive.

The workmen withdrew, and quiet was restored to the villa, which looked as charming as before, though in the places where the statues of the gods had formerly glittered, its sole ornament was young blossoming trees.

One evening, when the master of this pleasant abode sat silently poring by lamplight over his sacred books, Decimilla entered, saying:

"Master, an old man, who refused to give his name, but entered the atrium with me, requested admittance. He looks very strange, but like a nobleman. You will find him in the peristyle."

Phlegon went down-stairs and gazed at the stranger in amazement. At last he exclaimed:

"Caesar, you in Phlegon's house?"

"Yes, it is I," said Hadrian. "You can scarcely recognize me. Ay, I have grown white with grief and care, but the gods have not deceived me. Aelius Verus lies dying, while I am spending the years of Antinous."

"Peace be with him!" said Phlegon gently.

"And honor throughout the world."

Phlegon was silent.

"It was Antinous's wish that I should aid you," said Hadrian, seating himself, "and I came in person, that the envy of go-betweens and your own awkwardness may not complicate matters again. I was compelled to act as I did, unless I desired to give the Christians, now the most venomous enemies of my deified favorite, express permission to practise their preposterous rites. Now the state of affairs is different. The Christians keep quiet, and are forgotten. Nothing is talked of except Antinous. I have deprived the praetor Celsus of his office; his measure was full. I cannot pardon your sons now. That would require a decree, which would be discussed and cause the Christians to press forward again, so I have chosen another method of fulfilling Antinous's wish. You will purchase of me the estate of Hasalicus on Mt. Mercurius at Aquae, which with its slaves belongs to the exchequer. Your sons are among the number. As master, you can free them as soon as you choose. Ennia will remain in exile, which will not trouble her, if you share it. Here are two copies of the bill of sale, the names of the quaestor and procurator are already signed. Here is the receipt for the purchase-money, which I paid for you; I owed some compensation for your long service. I did not realize your value till you were absent."

Phlegon had stood motionless during all these joyful tidings. Now he bent his knee, seized Hadrian's toga, and pressed burning kisses on its hem. He could not speak.

"Rise, Phlegon," said Hadrian. "Do not make me give way to emotion. We have both suffered and erred, but by the divinity of Antinous, I have done for you all that lay in my power."

"I know it, my emperor."

"Well," said Hadrian jestingly, to give the conversation a lighter turn, "the villa *ad pinum* looks very neat since the Christians were driven out."

"Pardon me, my lord, it was the Christians of

Rome, who rebuilt this house as an atonement for Graccina's sins."

"Why, then you must be in their favor, spite of the wrong you did them. How did you manage it?"

"I am not yet a Christian, Caesar, but—do not be angry—am on the point of becoming one. Since I have seen how gods are made, I long for the one God, who existed before Adonis, Mithras, and Antinous."

"I too revere the one *numen* in the divinity of the boy, who died for me."

"In a certain sense we still agree," replied Phlegon. "I have faith in the same deity as before, and believe that Pindar, Sophocles and Plato were true prophets for their times. Those times, however, are past. You would not invent and introduce new forms of worship, if the rites transmitted from our ancestors sufficed. Yet the deity has not ceased to speak from the old forms, because they have fallen somewhat behind the age, but because he wishes to reveal himself in a different way. The lesson taught us by Osiris's dying for the welfare of the world, and sitting in the dark chambers below until he rises to restore prosperity and fruitfulness to his country, what we praise in the worship of Adonis, the wounds of the god who dies and returns with the buds of Spring, were symbols of the life of the universe. That God dies for our sins and rises again for our salvation I am taught by every glance at nature, by Osiris, Adonis, Proserpina, Mithras. Their worshippers testify that these gods really lived, really endured their sufferings. Well, we have received tidings that God was born as a man in the reign of Augustus, suffered and was slain under Tiberius. When I heard it, I laughed at the tale. But I saw those, who believed and lived according to the laws of this God, happy, cheerful, and at peace with themselves, in spite of all human weaknesses. I found Hermas always gentle and joyous amid the sorest trouble, I saw my sons, betrayed by their own father, in the presence of the most horrible death, reconciled to themselves and to me. Then I said to myself: 'It would be fortunate if you were so too.' 'How have you accomplished this?' I asked Hermas, Natalis, Pius. They replied: 'We have acknowledged and believed that God was in Christ, and made atonement for the sins of the world, and have given ourselves entirely to Him.' Then I thought: 'Wherever there is strength, a source of strength exists.' The contempt for all earthly things which the Stoics praise, while they scrape money together like Seneca, I here had before my eyes, without any theory as the result of belonging to Christ. I was told; 'If you wish to find the peace we possess, do as we do, seek it!' And I mean to seek it, Caesar!"

Hadrian rose.

"You will act on your own responsibility. The edicts of Trajan still exist, and you best know that I cannot abolish them. I am not angry with you, I know you desire, like myself, to exchange the dreariness of this godless age for new mysteries. But I fear, my friend, we have both made too many experiments; the delusion won't last long."

"My lord," replied Phlegon eagerly, "these are no delusions. During this long, sad winter I have read the books of the Jewish prophets, and they are no deceivers. I was in the amphitheatre with Hermas and my children; people do not defy the lion's paws unless they are sure of being in the right. Among all the forms of religion I see, this alone has vital energy, this alone possesses a future. Besides, a man cannot have a religion solely for himself. We must pray together, to escape the feeling that we are not simply talking to ourselves. My children hold this faith; my wife has been converted to it, I too wish to possess it. I will not languish alone in this wilderness."

" But when all are now flocking to our friend's temples, why don't you come with us ?"

" My lord, you know yourself that Antinous sought God, and did not find Him."

Hadrian, to conceal his embarrassment, bent over a flower in the viridarium. A roll of MS. fell from the folds of his toga. He picked it up, saying:

" In one respect at least your god has an advantage over Antinous; he left no sister. See this letter I have just received from his sister Paulina, requesting aid."

He handed Phlegon an awkwardly-written petition, in which an uneducated girl, in affected sentences, begged the emperor to give her a dowry, as otherwise she would find it difficult to obtain a husband. In return she would tell the Caesar about all the games her brother had played with her in his childhood, and how much he had suffered from their cruel pedagogue.

Phlegon smilingly returned the letter, saying:

" You are mistaken, Caesar. Our God had brothers and sisters, who did not believe in Him. But He appeared to them after His death, and then they had faith."

" It would be scarcely worth while to appear to this Paulina," said Hadrian sarcastically.

" That is just what separates us, Caesar; we know through Jesus Christ that every human soul has infinite value, and it would be worth while to save even the most stunted from being lost. We shall heal the sick world, only by caring for individuals."

"He, who like myself has to care for millions of souls, my friend, cannot trouble himself about individuals, and when I see how Antinous's image appeals to the heart, I believe I have now found the right means. In a century Antinous will be a god like Mithras, while no one will ever speak of your crucified Jew. Farewell!"

"Those who come after us will learn!" said Phlegon. "But I thank you, my lord, for all you have done for me, and will daily pray God to reward you as I desire. Farewell!"

So Hadrian went out into the starless night, and Phlegon returned to the pleasant lamplight that shone upon his sacred books.

We have little more to relate. The interview with Hadrian had sealed Phlegon's resolution. While arguing with the emperor, the Greek first realized that he stood on the *same* footing with the Christians, and his breach with the old gods was a definite one. If many things in the new community seemed strange or repelled him, he consoled himself by the thought, that at fifty we do not believe so thoroughly and fervently as at fifteen. The preparations for the removal to the Agri Decumates country, required some time, during which he daily attended the meetings in Pius's house, and became more and more familiar with the new parish. He made the acquaintance of many good and happy people, and felt more and more at ease among those who held as far aloof from the ambitions and the intrigues of public life, as they rigidly attended to the care of souls in their own and their friends' homes.

"Oh! you are right," he said one day to Pius, "in seeking the happiness of the world in the consecration of the home, not in the selfish tumult of the Forum and the Curiae, and in worshipping beauty by the culture of your children, not by laboring at an art that daily grows more and more degenerate."

"We must not look at what makes us better than the world, my Brother," replied Pius, "but at the long distance we still remain behind our goal. A greater man than I has modestly said: 'Not as though I had already attained, either were already perfect; but I follow after.'"

The morning appointed for Phlegon's admission to the church arrived. Again at an early hour before sunrise, the hymns that had formerly roused the Greek from his slumber, echoed from the villa *ad pinum*. He now stood, wrapped in a white baptismal robe, in the impluvium, which had to-day been arranged for the baptism. Pius made an impressive address, in which he alluded to the history of the house, the sins that had caused a persecution of the church, and increased the world's hatred of their people. Here too stood a Saul, to whom the errors of individuals had been the occasion of threats and anger. But in the conflict with the Christians Phlegon had perceived, that he himself was much farther from salvation than those with whom he quarrelled, and God, who aids the sincere, had changed his heart. The candidate for baptism, with deep emotion, made the confession of his sins and faith, and the bishop baptized him by thrice pouring water over him. In the evening the Lord's Supper, at which Phlegon for the first time took part, was held at Pius's house. When the sacred ceremony was over, Pius informed the congregation that Phlegon had left the villa *ad pinum* to them for an indefinite time, entrusting its management to him. Decimilla and the two old slaves, who were to quietly end their days in the house, would keep it in order. The presbytery, to avoid even the appearance of evil, had declined to accept it as a gift from Phlegon.

When the morning of the next day dawned, the Greek took leave of Pius, and a sturdy mule bore him and his baggage through the *porta Salaria* towards the North. From city to city he lodged at the Brothers, and when he at last looked back from the Alps to Italy, he felt himself new born in every respect—a new creature. Thus he went through the gloomy *via mala* to Curia, and from thence to the valley of the Rhine, whose course he followed to Augusta Rauracorum. There, where the broad river turns towards the North, he left his beast and a strong boat bore him towards a spot which lay on the right bank of the Rhine, below Argentoratum. From thence a straight road led to the fortress of Aquae, which dominated the whole valley of the Rhine and Ausonia. Descending to Hadrian's bath, where the vapors of the hot springs floated through the marble-halls, Antinous's well-known features greeted the traveller. The new religion had already penetrated here, but to Phlegon this silent statue was not an object of political or religious aversion. A friend, over whose beautiful image a sad fate had cast a gloomy shadow, looked affectionately down upon him. Phlegon stood before it a long time, then said:

"To me also this sorrowful boy is a reproach. God

grant that my hand may have grown stronger to support those who are sinking."

Thinking of the past he descended the hill, while the noble outlines of forest-clad Mount Mercury towered before him. Opposite, on the heights overlooking the valley, he saw the gleaming white walls of the imperial estate of Hasalicus, which contained all his loved ones. He followed the road up-hill for another hour. Then Ennia was clasped to his heart, Natalis and Vitalis held his hands, his children surrounded him.

" Here I am, children, your father, your master, your Brother in the Lord! Now let us make this beautiful garden of God, on which He has poured forth the full abundance of His gifts, an image of His kingdom, and show the world that the Christian's condition is no empire of folly."

END.